AND THE RIVER DRAGS HER DOWN

AND THE RIVER DRAGS HER DOWN

JIHYUN YUN

ROCK THE BOAT

Content warning: This book contains depictions of body horror, graphic injury, violence, violence against animals, death, drowning and racism.

A Rock the Boat Book

First published in the United Kingdom, Republic of Ireland and Australia
by Rock the Boat, an imprint of Oneworld Publications Ltd, 2025
Reprinted 2025

Text copyright © 2025 by Jihyun Yun
Cover art copyright © 2025 by Yejin Park

The moral right of Jihyun Yun to be identified as the
Author of this work has been asserted by her in accordance
with the Copyright, Designs, and Patents Act 1988

All rights reserved
Copyright under Berne Convention
A CIP record for this title is available from the British Library

ISBN 978-1-83643-052-0
eISBN 978-1-83643-053-7

Printed and bound in Great Britain by Clays Ltd, Elcograf S.p.A

This book is a work of fiction. Names, characters, businesses,
organisations, places and events are either the product of the Author's
imagination or are used fictitiously. Any resemblance to actual persons,
living or dead, events or locales is entirely coincidental.

Quotation from "The Five Stages of Grief" by Linda Pastan. © 1978 by Linda Pastan. Used by
permission of the Estate of Linda Pastan in care of the Jean V. Naggar Literary Agency, Inc.

No part of this publication may be reproduced, stored in a retrieval system, or
transmitted, in any form or by any means, electronic, mechanical, photocopying,
recording of otherwise, or used in any manner for the purpose of training artificial
intelligence technologies or systems, without the prior permission of the publishers.

The authorised representative in the EEA is eucomply OÜ,
Pärnu mnt 139b–14, 11317 Tallinn, Estonia
(email: hello@eucompliancepartner.com / phone: +33757690241)

Oneworld Publications Ltd
10 Bloomsbury Street
London WC1B 3SR
England

Stay up to date with the latest books,
special offers, and exclusive content from
Rock the Boat with our newsletter

Sign up on our website
rocktheboatbooks.com

For daughters and for latchkey kids

> But something is wrong.
> Grief is a circular staircase.
> I have lost you.
>
> —Linda Pastan

> The mansin say that "the hand of the dead is a hand of thorns" (*chugŭn sonŭn kasisonida*); it cannot touch living flesh without inflicting injury.
>
> —Laurel Kendall, *Shamans, Housewives, and Other Restless Spirits: Women in Korean Ritual Life*

PROLOGUE

Sister, of the hours before I died, I remember little. Only the watercolor blur of the aspens made livid with wind. Our small town overcome with Queen Anne's lace and other invasive species so beautiful no one cared to tame. I remember my feet stuttering on the trestle-bridge tracks I'd balanced on countless times before, arms outstretched as if to take flight.

I fell instead.

My breath steamed white before my face. It was only after my head hit the rain-glutted river, after my hands failed to find purchase and I was tugged swiftly under, that I realized I might not survive.

Water killed me before cold could; my lungs, an overfilled vase. Thank you, lord, for letting what couldn't be painless at least be quick. Search teams trawled the river, but I'd been carried away too far. It took days for me to be found, blue and swollen, snagged across a distant bank's rocks. Online, the boy who came across me said he thought my mass of rib-length hair was a tangle of beached seaweed until he saw the rest of my body.

Every so often, a photo of me postmortem crops up across forums to be ogled like the spectacle that all untimely deaths inevitably become. But I was loved. In the Korean way, our family wept at my wake for two nights and three days. You rejected all food and rice wine offered until you weakened and were carried out like a doll.

My funeral was small. Our family took me home in a celadon vase embossed with white-deer filigree. Made a makeshift altar above the fireplace with a photo of me smiling at something beckoning from just beyond the frame.

But this doesn't mean I never woke up again. Sister, I hear you, feel your hands in the dirt, searching.

I will answer your call—I'll return.

PART I

Girl

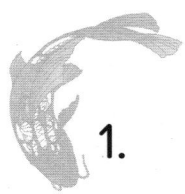

1.

Despite her best efforts, the rat was dead.

Soojin knew it by the way Milkis didn't leap toward the cage door the moment she entered the room. Normally, the sound of her pawing the newspaper shavings or scuttling down the ramps was an omnipresent music. But this evening there was only perfect, unwelcome silence.

She found Milkis in one of the hammocks hanging from the top tier of the cage, body curled like an apostrophe. She had not been dead long. Rigor mortis hadn't set in yet, and her pink nose was still damp to the touch. At least she had died painlessly, unlike last time, when her mammary tumors grew as large as almonds from her underbelly.

Soojin pulled the rat into her palm. Milkis was not a beautiful animal: unusually large for her species, with white fur grown patchy from skin conditions, eyes wet and protruding like pomegranate seeds. But she was cherished, and would be back soon.

After donning latex gloves, Soojin laid the rat on a lined plastic tray and cut the tail off with a dissection scalpel swiped from biology class. It yielded beneath the blade easier than expected. A small, wet snap, not so different from cutting through the spine of a cutlassfish. Then she was transferring the severed length to a ziplock bag. This was what she would use to call Milkis back. The rest of the body must not be returned to the ground.

Though they had not had a chance to get large, the growths were in the rat's belly again, waiting to turn malignant. Burying a sick body revived the ailments. Best to work with a healthy cut or from scratch, which is to say bone. But the tail was immaculate. It would work well.

Soojin swaddled the body in tissue and placed it into a shoebox for the pet cemetery's hearth. The blood where it was severed spread crimson ringlets through the white, and she swallowed hard against the familiar sickness rising in her throat. The crude surgery finished, she held her quivering hands together, digging her nails into the wrist of her scalpel hand, waiting for the sharp pain to steady her.

At only seventeen, Soojin Han was no stranger to death. She had seen Milkis expire and rise countless times, but this would be *her* first time resurrecting anything alone. Her sister, Mirae, though only a year older, had been the bold one who could calmly stomach anything and so had always taken the bloodier tasks upon herself. *Close your eyes,* Mirae would say, and by the time Soojin opened them again, the grim division would be done. The healthiest body part neatly excised from the rest, ready to be fed to earth and fire, respectively.

Last fall, Mirae drowned in Black Pine River, which wended

its way through their small town and beyond it. Soojin still glimpsed her sister everywhere: Mirae at the sink, humming as she rinsed suds off dishes. Mirae in the golden-hour light, brushing her hair by the window, screen popped out, feeding strands to the wind. Mirae, named after the Korean word for *future*, which she would never possess. The intervening ten months between her death and now had mitigated nothing. Soojin still felt picked at by grief's carrion birds.

A tap on the wall startled her. Her father stood by the door, eyeing her warily.

"Knock-knock," he said, aiming for levity and missing. How anyone could make *knock-knock* sound like a grave missive, Soojin would never know. He cleared his throat but did not cross the threshold, opting instead to lean on the doorframe, arms folded across his chest. His awkward body language irritated her.

It hadn't always been this way. Just a year ago, Soojin, Mirae, and their father would lounge in front of the TV, laughing at game shows. They would cajole him into midnight drives to the gas station for shitty taquitos and Coke slushies. Their small family unit had felt tight and impenetrable. But after Mirae's death, everything changed.

"Leaving tonight?" Soojin asked. Her father's face was gaunt, darkened with uneven patches of stubble like dapples on a horsehide.

"Yeah." He nodded. "The house is stocked up. If you need anything, call. I'll be home every weekend."

Their home was in Jade Acre, a tiny resort town afflicted with too much beauty, nestled between miles of woods and towering bluffs, the sea such an uncanny shade of blue it was like diving into the iris of an eye. The summers were long and sultry and asphyxiated with tourists brandishing money like green artillery.

For a few months, all was generous: the fruit-bearing trees, the nesting birds, the shallow bays where tourists paid heftily to dive by day for three endangered red abalones and illegally snuck in by night for more. But in the off months, the town became dreary and isolated, taxed by rain that beat the landscape into mulch. A waterlogged softness grew into everything, and the townsfolk rarely left.

Father was one of the rare leavers. Every year, once the tourist months ended, along with the modest stream of income from the family's bed-and-breakfast, Father packed his bags and drove three hours east to the city of Bragg Hills to work for his cousin's construction company. The long commute too difficult to manage, their father stayed with his cousin during the week and made his way back to Jade Acre on the weekends.

It wasn't ideal. You either made enough during tourist months or spent the rest of the year scraping. When Soojin's mother was alive, she had wanted to leave Jade Acre for that reason. Han's Bed & Breakfast was unsustainable. Every year they put away a little less. But Father had dug in his heels.

How can we sell the house our girls grew up in? Wasn't this our dream?

When Mother died seven years ago in a car wreck, the possibility of leaving died with her. No one wanted to leave the home where the memories of Mother still lived, and now of Mirae, too. Soojin felt them lingering everywhere in the house. Her loves, curled in the window alcove and inside each doorframe like endless questions.

"Will you be okay, Soo?" her father asked. This would be the first time she'd be left completely alone. After Mother passed, when Soojin was ten and Mirae was eleven, the sisters still had each other. They adapted to being latchkey kids—even grew to enjoy it at times. The freedom to sleep when they wanted, eat what they wished, and feign adulthood as they imagined it. But this time Soojin would have no one.

"Dad, I'm not a kid," she said. "I'll be fine. And besides, I won't be alone." She showed him what she held.

"It's that time again already?" he asked, recoiling slightly from the severed tail.

Her father worried his lip, rubbing at his jaw in a way that told Soojin he was debating something in his head. But whatever it was, he quietly dismissed it. Instead he repeated what he'd told his two daughters so many times before.

"Make sure no one sees you."

The magic would become a family heirloom, passed down through the blood of their women. But at the beginning, there was wreckage and a famine-struck village.

It was a cursed season of a cursed year. All winter, hailstorms battered the land and would not go. An unnatural freeze shocked the earth well into summer, singed the finally germinating seeds with frost. Then, when the cold abated at last, a spate of earthquakes rippled through their suffering peninsula, destroying whatever crop the weather had failed to cull.

With no harvest, the villagers slaughtered their livestock down to the last emaciated sow, sparing nothing of them, not even the bones.

Or so they thought.

Under the cover of night, lit by the light of an anemic moon, a girl snuck from her home and ran toward the dried-up well on the outskirts of her village. In time, she would become an ancestor, but for now, she was only a girl made animal by hunger, tipping her ear against the well's mouth until she heard a faint scuffling from within.

When she was certain she was alone, she pulled the rope that dangled into the dark and, instead of a water bucket, withdrew a rusted cage. Inside it was a hen, pecking at the clippings of grass and desiccated insects laid out for it.

Shh, the girl said as she unlatched the cage. She needn't have warned it. The bird had been hatched frail and docile; it never so much as cooed.

She stroked its meager body, the smooth patches of baldness left from the feathers it had torn away to pass time in its solitude. The girl had hidden the hen from the slaughter and secretly kept it alive in hopes it might lay eggs. Anything to reliably feed and sustain her family. It never did.

The girl told it she was sorry, though she wasn't. The killing was swift and the devouring was swifter. The girl and her surviving family tore through the bird's body in ecstatic, guilty secrecy.

The next day, for the first time in months, the girl woke satiated, still sucking on a bone she'd tucked between her cheek and teeth. Fed and hopeful, she went to the fields and buried it in the soil, meaning for its nutritious marrow to feed the fallow. Instead she saw a beak emerge from the earth, stammering for air. The ground remained sterile of crops, but she pulled a live hen from the dirt, where it scratched and pecked at nothing.

She ran screaming into her home for her mother. Too desperate for wonder, they swiftly slaughtered the bird and ate the bird, then sent its breastbone back into the dirt without fanfare. The gift taxed the girl heavily. Her hands trembled with exertion. Blood slid from her nose. She buried the bone while smiling.

Again. And again. Wing bone and spit. Like this her family thrived as the rest of her village hungered, grew gaunt, then sickly, then dead. The villagers whispered of demons in their family. Their secret hen died a hundred deaths.

Autumn's onset was coming early this year, the deciduous trees ever so slowly beginning to fringe themselves gold. Soojin hated fall. It was the season when Mirae had left to attend a house party and never returned. Her body was found a few days later in the next town, snagged on some rocks for a kid from a neighboring high school to find. In the photos the boy snapped before calling the authorities, her sister's features were bloated and anonymous in the way of all drownings left to the water too long; the autumn branches reflected around her head like a thrashed crown.

The turning of seasons would never again be beautiful to her. She tore her eyes from the treetops and planted her gaze firmly on the road.

As Soojin crested the hill, Peaceful Paws Pet Cemetery rose to meet her. In the gloaming, the building's pale paint shimmered as if to vanish. Behind the intake office sprawled a field where small stones marked the resting place of well-loved pets.

Soojin could see the cemetery owner's son, Mark Moon, down on one knee, tending to the pot of geraniums by the office entrance. Sunset caught in his hair, picking up the streaks of auburn in his otherwise black mane. He hummed off-key as he worked, and despite the racket of gravel beneath her feet, he didn't hear her coming. Not even when she stopped right behind him, her long shadow stretching across the wall directly in his line of vision. She knelt.

"Hey," she said. He jerked, and the pruning scissors missed the dead leaf he'd been aiming for and instead took off a cluster of flowers.

"Damn." Mark dropped the shears and picked up the lopped geraniums.

Aside from the flowers she'd startled him into cutting, the geraniums were blooming excellently, even in this unusually cold September. She wasn't surprised. She'd known Mark for as long as she could remember, and not once had she ever seen any living thing fail by his hand. She wondered if growing up surrounded by so much death had taught him to appease it, allowing small concessions to hold it longer at bay.

"I didn't mean to startle you," she said. "Sorry about your flowers."

Mark looked up, only now registering her presence. Though he was built tall and lithe, his face had not yet outrun the puppylike countenance of his childhood: his brown eyes were still a little too wide for his face. He had that brand of boyish charm that disarmed peers and vacationing wine-moms alike, especially when he smiled the way he did now.

"Don't worry about it." He stood, brushing soil off his hands before offering one to Soojin. He pulled her to her feet, and when he withdrew, he left a damp grit on her palms that she wiped without bothering to be discreet.

"So, what's up?" Mark asked, though he likely knew. Every couple of years, Soojin and Mirae would visit him with shoeboxes of dead things. Rats, usually—sometimes birds. Small lives that took no longer than twenty minutes to bring completely to ash. She opened the box, and he reached in, moving the tissue paper to see Milkis lying inside. His expression remained remarkably even. Not that Soojin expected him to balk at a corpse.

Mark had helped his parents with their business since he was fourteen, doing everything from manning the phones to ordering bespoke cat caskets. But most often he helped with cremations. Soojin figured it technically wasn't legal for him to do this work, but the town's adults winked and let it slide the way they winked and let slide many transgressions: kids working or driving before they legally could, teenagers sneaking water bottles of rum into the town's one-screen movie theater or smoking at the pebble beach on nights when the weather was generous.

"Sure, I got you." Mark took the box and opened the door. "My parents aren't in, so it's on the house." If he found it at all strange that she cremated her pet rats rather than just burying them in the garden like most others, he didn't mention it. "Come in."

Inside, Soojin was greeted by the familiar smell of lavender and antiseptic. As usual, the fireplace was cheerily burning away in the corner and the front desk was adorned with fresh-cut herbs. At a glance, no one would assume this quaint room with pale yellow wallpaper was a pet funeral home. But the displayed urns embossed with things like ALL PAWS GO TO HEAVEN and WOOF! in gilded lettering gave it away.

"This looks like the one you brought a couple years ago," Mark said, peering at Milkis again. The red crescents of her half-lidded eyes had gone foggy. "And a couple years before that."

"I like albino rats." Soojin shrugged.

"Let me guess. You named this one Milkis too?"

She took off her jacket and set it by the door, then sat heavily on one of the plush waiting-room chairs. "Just as I'll name the next."

"Is this a genealogy thing? Like, 'Here lies Milkis the Eighth, she lived a full life of teething blocks and fine cheese'?"

"I'm probably on about Milkis the Tenth by now."

"Right . . . ," Mark said. She could see he thought her unreadable. "Well, do you want me to . . . you know . . . bring you the ashes back? It'll be a tiny amount. Not even a fistful, really. But I can put it in a ring box or something."

"No thanks. Feel free to use it as fertilizer."

"Actually, cremains aren't good for plants. Too much calcium and salt, you know? It makes the soil too—" He noticed her gazing past him with thinly veiled disinterest. He stopped talking, his mouth shutting with an audible click. Soojin had this way of halting people, a human em dash.

He cleared his throat. "I'll get this done, then," he said, and turned to leave, then paused. "But you should wait. I'll bring you the ashes, okay? Do whatever with them."

Soojin watched his back disappear through the cremation chamber door, and she knew that was that. She took off her scarf. She hadn't been planning on sticking around, but she supposed she would wait lest Mark Moon come seeking her, brandishing a fistful of rodent ash. He was stubborn in that regard. Mirae and Mark in some ways had been remarkably alike. Soojin wasn't sure how she'd failed to notice it as a child, back when the three of them had been inseparable friends.

Mirae had always insisted on witnessing Milkis's cremation. Their low voices muffled by the clang of the furnace, her small hands pressed against the viewing room's glass.

Why do we have to watch? Soojin would ask. *We'll bring her back tonight anyway.*

It still matters, her sister would reply.

After Mirae's body was found, the funeral director expressed how some families found comfort in viewing their loved one's cremation. Being present during the final physical journey helped some people heal, he'd said. Father had opted for the witness cremation, weeping as Mirae's body headed into the retort in its unassuming box. But Soojin had not. She'd stood outside, looking out over the rolling hills cleaved by sunset, dry-heaving into the grass. Birds of dusk sang in the trees, their bodies bright ornaments. She felt wounded by everything beautiful her sister was not alive to see.

What the funeral director didn't understand was that Soojin didn't want to heal. If she didn't wake each morning ransacked by her sister's absence, it would mean her memory was growing farther away. She would rather hurt than heal.

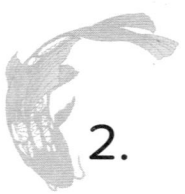

2.

Mark had been in the cremation chamber for no more than a few minutes when the front door burst open. A tiny woman stumbled in, cursing colorfully in Korean as she struggled to balance three boxes stacked so high Soojin could see only her hairline. The topmost box began to slide, and Soojin jumped to her feet just in time to catch it before it fell.

"Shoot. Thank you, my baby," the woman grunted from behind the boxes. "Can you believe all this crap your father ordered? Three dozen tennis balls and who knows how many rawhide bones. He wants to hand out care packages. Care packages! What good is a bunch of pet stuff for a bereaved family? If his stupid ideas give me a herniated disc, so help me god..."

They set the boxes down, and with a sigh of relief, the woman straightened up, pressing her fists against the small of her back. Only then did she notice she was not ranting at her son. "Soojin! I'm sorry—I thought you were Mark. What are you doing here, honey?"

How strange it felt to hear that question from her. Seven years ago, there would not have been any question as to why Soojin was at the Moons' house or even in their funeral home. She had so many memories of playing behind the front desk with Mark and Mirae, making flower arrangements in the urns with dandelions and other weeds torn from the garden.

"I'm . . ." Soojin looked down at the woman who for most of her childhood had been as good as an aunt. Her familiar warm brown eyes and tiny hands. When Soojin's mother was alive, she and Mrs. Moon had been best friends. Soojin remembered how the women would be raucous with laughter long into the night nearly every weekend. She felt sure Mrs. Moon wouldn't mind Mark doing her favors, but business was still business, and his mom didn't have to know.

"I just came to pick something up. I missed class yesterday," Soojin said, fishing through her bag for some random crushed piece of paper to wave around as proof.

"I see." Mrs. Moon's eyes flitted toward the paper, then studied Soojin's face with an uncomfortable tenderness. Soojin looked down at her hands, the obviously blank sheet of binder paper she held. Feeling stupid, she stuffed it back into her bag and stared hard at her feet.

"How are you doing lately?" Mrs. Moon asked. "Have you been keeping up with school? Eating enough?" She asked this last question while pinching Soojin's ribs, as if disapproving of her boniness.

"I've been fine."

"And your father?" Mark's mother pressed. "How is he?

Working a lot?" There was a pointed quality to her questions, such earnest concern in the woman's eyes that it made Soojin nervous. Soojin wasn't particularly chatty about anything, least of all this. The murky legality of leaving a minor alone for days at a time kept her private about her father's weeklong work trips. But of course the Moons knew. They understood well that Soojin's family walked a fraying financial tightrope, and what her dad had to do to keep that rope taut.

Mrs. Moon reached out, took Soojin's cold hands in her warm ones. The motherliness of the gesture was not comforting. It was painful. "If you need anything, you are always welcome to . . ."

Soojin pulled away.

"Thank you," she said, gathering her things. "I'm sorry, I have to go."

Soojin didn't wait to retrieve the ashes. She left the funeral home, feeling Mrs. Moon's unbearable sympathy tracking her until the door closed between them.

By the time Soojin got home, it was dark and beginning to drizzle. She made her way briskly through the woods, a lantern held aloft to light her path. She needed to get the tail buried before the rain turned the ground into mud.

Soojin wouldn't have to go far. Her home, like most others in Jade Acre, was isolated and surrounded by woods. Aside from the two fully furnished cottages her family rented out in the summer, there was nothing nearby to witness her but fog and the trees.

Soojin knelt when she reached the clearing, putting her hands to the dirt and letting it sieve through her fingers. In happier years, their mother used to bring her and Mirae here to coax life back into being. Perhaps that was why the soil was always so loose: the ground never set because so much was demanded of it.

With a small spade pulled from her pocket, Soojin began to work the earth. It yielded easily. A shallow hole would do, but it had to be wide enough to accommodate new growth. When it was dug, she placed the length of tail into the hole and covered it with unpacked dirt, then sank her hands back into the earth, the tail cupped between her palms. All that was left to do was wait.

At first, nothing happened. Insects trilled in the dark. Overhead, an owl watched her, the flat white dish of its face gleaming briefly between the leaves before something perturbed it into flight. It vanished in a burst of feathers; then silence descended like a cloak upon the clearing. A dense and impenetrable silence that made the evening feel suddenly uncanny, like a barrier had dropped between Soojin and the known world.

The first sensation was a distant electric tingling in her fingertips that quickly traveled the length of her arms like a current. The air around her felt crowded, as if a hundred imaginary eyes were turning toward her in the dark. The hairs on the back of her neck rose. Crackles of gold jolted the edges of her vision, casting the world in jagged sepia light. And then it began in earnest.

The whispers reached her. That was what Mirae had always called them. A hushed amalgamation of voices she didn't recognize but knew—the same way a mayfly intuits its own brutally short lifespan—were her ancestors. Soojin could hear them: the women before her who had partaken in this same ritual of bone and soil and never letting go. She bowed her forehead toward the dirt and listened through the first wave of nausea. Occasionally, a voice rose from the tangle like a radio signal making itself heard above static; it was just clear enough for Soojin to make out some words before the voice flexed and yielded to another.

Sometimes she heard the round, new language of a child whose tongue had yet to calcify around consonants. Other times an elderly woman, speech garbled around the heavy stone of a stroke. *When the crops failed, we— And then Mother said—When I wrung its neck, it didn't fight me. We ate and we ate—*

It all meant nothing to her. But then, through the muted menagerie of memories generations past, she heard a familiar voice.

My daughters, her mother's voice said in dialect-lilted Korean, halfway toward laughter, *focus.*

Soojin's concentration rattled. She wanted to seek out the blood of that memory and follow it like a hound. She still remembered it. Summer, a girlhood ago. The exuberant white flowers of tomato plants sagging with bumblebees. An owl pellet in the fresh-turned soil. She could feel her control slipping. Milkis's tail rotting in the earth. *Focus. Here, my daughters. Look.*

Soojin pulled her attention back toward her hands, and like the apparitions they were, the voices receded all at once. She was alone in the woods, and she couldn't, couldn't do it. Her labored breathing fogged against the night.

"Damn it," she breathed. Soojin blinked back tears; the tail lay dormant against her fingers, cool and limp like a worm drowned then discarded by rain. She thought back to all the times she had tried and failed. The snakes she'd pulled from the earth writhing and red because she'd failed to regenerate their scales. The birds that had twitched against her hands but remained dead: synapses firing, firing . . . failing. Hadn't Mother or Mirae always had to finish what she could not? What made Soojin believe that in her solitude she'd grow suddenly capable just because she must?

But no. Something *was* happening. It was almost imperceptible at first, but the plant life that brushed against her knees was dying. Her proximity browned and bowed the grass, as if its vitality were being siphoned to the palms of her hands. An iron bloodiness permeated the damp air, its scent so strong she felt sick with it. The dirt against her fingers abruptly became drenched, as if out of nowhere; the earth relinquished impossible blood, becoming silt, becoming mud.

The air had taken on a viscous quality, a thickness that hurt to breathe and pressed like fingers against her lungs. Above her, the trees had stopped swaying in the wind, the leaves inert as if suspended out of time. It was wrong. Everything felt wrong. A distant keening mounted in her ears, her heartbeat arrhythmic and throttling as the magic mounted.

And, *oh god*, there it was: a compacting between her palms. The viscera came first, slick and pulsing and unincorporated. Spleen, liver, tiny beating heart. They moved in the earth like slugs, finding their proper alignment and arranging themselves just so. Then the soil stitched into scaffolding. Bones: the undulating grooves of a pelvis, a rib cage's fine accordion, sharp enough to lodge in a throat. Moist, red eyes ballooned to fit the new sockets of a freshly melding skull.

Soojin bit her cheek to force down the urge to withdraw her hands. *Don't you dare*, she thought. *Don't.* Bile rose in her throat. God, the revulsion—but still it continued.

Flesh formed, filling in the gaps between skeleton and organs. The unhusked meat shuddered, the muscles of its haunches slapping against her fingers rapidly, the way a dog kicks in the throes of dreaming. *Thunk, thunk, thunk.* Hadn't she learned about this in class once? Something about neurons firing. Something about even dead things moving sometimes.

She sucked slow breaths between her teeth. Distantly, she could hear laughter as her memory unfurled like a split-screen film. On one half was her present self: alone and seventeen, dry-heaving in the clearing. On the other was that day so many years ago when her mother had brought her and Mirae out to this very spot to show them what girls of their blood were capable of.

Mirae had been better, like she was at most things. Sure-footed, less squeamish, she had gotten the hang of it right away. It was Milkis then too, on one of her countless lives returning to them all.

This time, she would return to only Soojin.

A sharp pain stabbed her finger. Teeth. Soojin gasped, withdrawing from the dirt, and in her hands squirmed a rat, pelt dirtied with blood and soil. The animal was vividly alive. Soojin unscrewed a flask of water, gave Milkis a quick rinse. The earlier tears of frustration were gone. Now Soojin was crying for real, sobs interspersed with laughter. She whispered, "Shhh, shhh," by which she meant, *Thank god.* Milkis melted quickly into her familiar touch, nibbling an apology into the pad of Soojin's bleeding finger.

"Welcome back." Soojin kissed the rat's head before tucking her into her pocket.

A wave of lightheadedness came over her then, and even as the rain picked up, she couldn't move. She was spent, and her hands shook—but she'd succeeded, and she felt much less alone for it. *I did it, Mom,* Soojin thought. The memory of her mother's voice still rang in her head, urging her to focus. *Thanks for your guidance.* She tried not to think of how she hadn't heard Mirae—the simultaneous yearning and relief of that. It was foolish, she knew. But hearing her sister's voice among those of her long-dead relatives would have made everything real.

Soojin held a wrist over her eyes as Milkis shifted in her pocket, grooming with a feline fervor. The wind had returned with teeth, weaving violence through the trees, forcing the rain sideways. If she delayed longer, she would get sick.

But then to her left—a metallic slam. Her heart leapt as she swiveled toward the sound. It wasn't just the cymbal of weather slamming against a branch—she'd been seen. There he was: a boy flanked by tall trees. The twin black smudges of his eyes. How long had he been standing there? His face was slack and bloodless. The lid of what he held slammed again. To Soojin, it sounded like a deadbolt driving itself home, the toll of an executioner's bell, but it was neither. It was Mark Moon. In his hands he clutched a pot of soup.

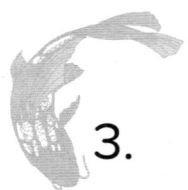

3.

Soojin wasn't sure how long she and Mark stood frozen in that clearing, staring wordlessly at each other. It felt like she'd drifted out of her body and was observing herself from a distal elsewhere. She was aware of the rain, though she could not feel it against her skin. She understood that her knees were pressed in soil that was swiftly becoming mud, but that too was only a dull acknowledgment. She could only truly register Mark and the way the lantern light reflected in his wide eyes.

"Wha—" she breathed, but he beat her to it.

"What is this?" His voice was weak. "Soojin, what did you just do?" His eyes flitted from her hands to the patch of dead grass behind her, then finally to her pocket, where Milkis's tail whipped like a pendulum.

"That rat." He pointed. "You . . ."

She sprang to her feet. He didn't flinch back. Instead he took a step forward to meet her, his eyes urgent with questions.

"You just—"

Soojin was past the point of thinking. She pressed her hand over his mouth and felt a stunned exhale against her skin.

"Please," she said. It was a miracle her voice didn't tremble. Mark was here, he'd seen her, and suddenly even the secluded woods around her house felt treacherous. Her eyes darted for other watchful faces in the dark. *I messed up. I messed up.* In her panic, she could think of nothing else. "Please just be quiet and follow me."

She strode out of the clearing and toward the lighthouse of her home's brightly lit windows. It took a while, but she heard Mark follow her. She didn't let herself glance back. His presence felt overwhelming, the mounting questions between them a physical, battering thing. Soojin was surprised he managed to hold his tongue all the way home. He held it even as she left him in the foyer to lock Milkis in her cage in the bedroom, but as soon as she returned downstairs, his dam broke.

"What was that?" he asked, his eyes bright, straddling an emotion between fear and awe. "I saw you bury that tail, Soojin. But it was severed. I know it was. Your rat. You just—"

She couldn't handle this barrage right now. She needed time.

"Stay for dinner," she commanded. The demand caught Mark off guard, derailing him.

"What?"

Soojin looked at his hands. The pot he held was pearled over with rain. The cold was finally beginning to penetrate her shock, and she realized they were both shivering like dogs.

"You brought soup."

He looked down, blinking as though he'd forgotten he held anything at all. "My mom told me to . . ."

"Bring me enough food for the week. I figured." She took

the stockpot and strode into the kitchen to drop it on the stove. "You should stay. I can't eat all of this by myself."

She shed her sweater and draped it over the radiator, urging Mark to do the same, then rolled up her sleeves and got to work in the kitchen. Bewildered and having been left no room for argument, Mark followed her.

There was a relief in turning all her attention to a task. They worked in complete silence, as if by an unspoken agreement to pretend, however briefly, like the world hadn't opened up beneath them both. As Mark washed rice, Soojin pulled two fillets of mackerel from the fridge, brushed them with cooking wine, and salted them liberally as oil champagned in the pan. When she laid them skin-side down, the alcohol and grease kicked up a flare before dying to a robust sizzle. By the time the dishes were cooked and the table set, the dread had returned full force in Soojin's belly.

They picked up their spoons in taut silence. Soojin ate fretfully, too anxious to actually enjoy anything, and by the time she gave up and set her chopsticks down, her soup had gone cold. Mark too had barely touched his plate.

"Are you ready now?" he asked gently.

No. "Yes."

She must not have sounded very convincing, because he nodded but didn't ask the first question, conceding the tempo of the conversation to her. She chewed her lip before she swallowed and asked quietly: "How much did you see?"

"Everything," he said, and then, in a hurry, began to ramble. "But I swear I didn't mean to. I knocked and no one answered and I didn't want to just leave the food on the porch for the raccoons. My mom would kill me if I didn't make absolute sure you got it. I didn't mean . . ." He seemed to glean her exasperation. He coughed. "Basically, I'm sorry."

Soojin brought the heel of her palm to her brow, striking it softly as if willing herself to wake. This was a nightmare. She knew it was petulant, but she couldn't stop blaming Mrs. Moon. Without her stupid pity, her stupid soup errand, none of this would have happened.

"Mark, nobody knows about this," she said slowly. A headache was sprouting behind her eyes, but whether it was stress or an aftershock of the magic, she couldn't be sure. "Only my immediate family knows." Soojin worded her sentences elusively, but her plea was obvious: *Nobody* can *know*.

"I understand," Mark said, not waiting for her to elaborate. "I won't tell anyone, Soo. I swear."

She pulled her hand away from her brow and looked at him. His expression was adamant. *Soo*, he'd called her. A nickname he hadn't used since they were kids. It sent a strange feeling through her stomach, like she'd lurched through time. But there was comfort, too. This was Mark Moon: still the boy she'd sat behind every Sunday in the repurposed barn that church service was held in, holding their noses against the lingering outhouse smell, passing notes back and forth as hymns swelled toward the rafters.

Even though they were no longer friends, even if the trajectories of their small lives traveled congruently but no longer touched, they were still beholden to each other, in a way. She felt sure he would keep her secret safe. She had no choice but to believe.

"Thank you." She filled the awkward silence following the promise by loudly clearing away the still-full dishes.

"So that rat. It's the one I cremated this morning, right?" Mark asked, getting to his feet to help.

"Yeah," Soojin said. "We bring Milkis back every few years. Sometimes more often, if her health fails quickly. She was our mom's childhood pet. It was our mom who taught us everything."

"I'm guessing you guys coming to me to cremate things all these years has something to do with . . ." He seemed to sift for words. "All of this," he finished, gesticulating vaguely in her direction.

"Yeah. If you bury multiple parts of a body in separate plots, it won't work. Whatever part you aren't going to use, you need to destroy. Have to get rid of the leftovers somehow."

Mark winced at her wording. "I guess so. That reminds me—ah, *shit*." He reached into his pocket and retrieved the ring box of cremains. It was damp from rain. When he opened it, the ash was clinging to the sides of the box like smears of graphite.

"You're joking. Please throw it away."

"In the trash? Seems unethical somehow."

"Does it?" She considered him as he laid their bowls in the sink. "Come with me."

Upstairs, Soojin pushed Mark to one side of Milkis's cage while she stood on the other. "Look," she said. Between them, the rat happily teethed on a wood block, her body both older than them and brand-new. Dead, not dead any longer.

Faced with the living evidence of Soojin's magic, he was

once again pale. Slow waves of disbelief rolled over his expression. "It's just not possible," Mark thought aloud, rubbing his lips. The light played violently across his face, his features partitioned by cage bars.

"And yet." Soojin opened the hatch and Milkis scurried up her arm. "See?" she said, her voice affectless. She reached to scratch the rat's back. "Alive and well. Does this please you, O ethical burner of bodies?"

Mark threw the ring box of ash into her wastebasket, then scooped the rat from Soojin's shoulder, holding Milkis to his face as if trying to smell for rot where there would only be damp newspaper and animal musk.

"Satisfied?" Soojin asked when he finally put Milkis down on the vanity, where she darted around, chaotically licking lotion bottles and gnawing on things she shouldn't.

"I guess so," he said before going uncharacteristically quiet again. The sound of Milkis pawing through Soojin's pen holder was the only sound in the room.

Soojin sighed. "You're freaking out, aren't you?"

That drew an unexpected smile out of him as he deflated into a chair. "I totally am. Is it obvious? I'm sorry, it's just . . ." His fingers fiddled absently with his hoodie drawstrings. "I can't believe, all this time, you and Mirae were capable of this and I never knew. When did you find out?"

She studied him. Much had changed. His hair, once stick-straight like his mother's, had taken on his father's subtle waves. His formerly plump cheeks had hollowed out, though he'd kept the pearlescent scar above his lip from the time they'd all gotten chicken pox and he couldn't resist biting off his oven mitts to scratch.

But his eyes had stayed the same. Wide and bright, and guileless.

"We found out by accident. Mom wanted to keep it all secret from us for as long as possible," Soojin said. "Because kids are irresponsible, you know? She didn't want us going out and doing anything stupid or showing off.

"When I was seven, Mirae and I found an owl pellet and decided to hold a little funeral in the yard. We buried it next to the tomatoes. Next thing you know, all the plants were dead and a half dozen mice were screaming in the ground, trying to claw their way out."

She smiled at the memory of it, the way her sister had shrieked when the first snout pushed its way out of the dirt, followed by no less than five more half-formed rodents. Their parents had come running, brandishing shovels as if to club a kidnapper with them. Instead they found just their daughters, clutching each other, screaming their heads off.

"And then we fainted. It was our first time reviving anything, and it was like six animals at once. We slept for a full twenty-four hours. Our parents almost took us to the emergency room. When we woke up, Mom thought it would be safest to teach us what we could do. How to be responsible and do it right."

Soojin's mind felt unruly with memories. She and her sister kneeling in the garden with their mother, hands turning the dirt to bury the foot of a bird that had struck their window. The crabgrass had sagged with magic as the chickadee took flight in an eruption of down and soil.

Soojin turned her head toward the window to avoid Mark's gaze. She thought of these moments often, but it had been years since she'd attached language to them. Who was there to tell? Her father didn't like to talk about the past. He didn't like to talk much at all.

There was nothing she wouldn't give to relive those first brilliant days of knowing. The magic and newness of it all clung to them like static back then. An immaterial heirloom passed down girl to girl. Mother had said that bringing things back helped her feel close to her own late mother. Soojin hadn't understood then—everyone she'd loved had still been with her—but she did now.

"I can hear them, you know," she said.

"Hear what?"

"I can hear people while I'm resurrecting things. Women in my family who are gone now."

"What, like ghosts?" Mark asked. "You can talk to them?"

"No. Not like that. It's more like . . ." She searched for the words. "Like a collage of memories. I hear girls laughing, talking. I can't control what I hear. It feels like listening in on someone in a nearby room switching through radio stations." She tore at a half-moon of skin curling from her cuticle. "Sometimes I can hear my mom. It's not like listening to a voice recording. It's almost like she's right there, invisible but near enough to touch."

She looked down at her hands, at the spot of blood pearling from where she'd picked at her skin. She wasn't quite sure why she was sharing all of this, but now that she'd begun, it felt impossible to stop. There was something comforting about knowing these memories could now live in another mind. It felt as if Mother and Mirae were still resurrecting small beasts elsewhere, even if only in the garden of someone else's imagination.

"Is your whole family . . . able to do this?"

"My dad can't. It's just women from my mother's side of the family. Just me and—" Her voice hung in the air like a fishhook.

"Yeah," Mark said softly, an affirmation. And there it was: that look of pity she so hated. How useless it must seem, this gift of hers. She was the only one left. A house packed to the brim with miraculous, life-giving girls, and it still could not save them.

An uncomfortable silence settled between them, and as if needing to look at anything but her, Mark began to study her bedroom. Soojin felt momentarily self-conscious. Would it seem childish to him that so little had changed since they were kids? The glowing constellations still stuck to the ceiling, the pasta-sauce jars on the nightstand filled with origami stars. Would he find it grim that almost a year after her sister's death, neither she nor her father had dismantled the second bed?

All of Mirae's things still sat exactly as she'd left them the day she disappeared. Her contact case on the vanity with the dried-out lenses inside. The bottle of saline she'd forgotten to cap. A fine-tooth comb, strung densely with black hair. In a way, Mirae's desk was an altar for an irretrievable past.

"I've missed this place," Mark said, in a way that sounded like, *I've missed you.* He glanced at her and then, as if startled to find that Soojin was looking at him too, turned his gaze hurriedly back to the phosphorescent stars on the ceiling.

Soojin was unused to seeing him in her room again. It was a collision of eras in her life that had been torn in half: the hours before the deaths, the hours after.

"Do you remember that time when Mirae lost a bunch of her baby teeth, so you pulled out one of your own to make her feel better? You were sitting right there, where you are now."

He didn't.

"I still have it. Not yours, of course. Mirae's. She literally thought they'd been picked up by God when they actually just got stuck in the roof gutter—long story. Mom found one after it rained." Soojin got up and pulled out a ziplock bag with a single milk tooth rattling around the bottom. It was the world's oddest litmus test, but if he reacted with revulsion, she suspected she'd kick him out.

He didn't. He took the bag in his hand and studied the tiny tooth through the clouded plastic. "Soo, please don't tell me you saved this to bring . . . to bring Mirae—"

"Don't even joke about that," Soojin cut in, though she would be lying if she said she'd never dreamed of it. Of her mother there'd been nothing left to bury, but of her sister she had this relic. The tooth was intact, gleaming. Healthy enough to sprout new life.

"I wasn't joking," he said quietly.

"Our gift isn't without cost, Mark. My mom made us promise we'd never resurrect anything but small animals, and even those not too often. There were people in my family who did otherwise, and it didn't go so well for them, apparently," Soojin said, her tone more flippant than she meant. She wasn't sure why she felt suddenly aggravated.

"There was this story Mom used to tell us. About a great-aunt whose younger brother got hit by shrapnel during the war. He was her only surviving sibling. No matter what the rest of the family told her, she couldn't let go. She carried his body on her back until it was impossible." Soojin swallowed. She could hear horseflies buzzing around her ear. She was sure she and Mirae had heard this particular great-aunt once, years ago, screaming hysterically as Milkis stuttered back to life in their hands. It had been awful, an unbroken syllable of animal horror. They had stopped resurrecting for at least a year after that.

"Eventually, my great-aunt cut off her brother's finger and burned his body. She tried to bring him back."

Mark no longer fidgeted with the tooth. Rapt, he'd gone utterly still.

"She thought she'd succeeded, for a bit. Her brother returned, perfect. No wounds, chubby cheeks as if he hadn't been going hungry on and off for months. But she couldn't get him to speak. It was like he was there but also wasn't anymore. He'd shovel fistfuls of gravel into his mouth when unsupervised. He vomited mud every night and just sat there, filthy until someone cleaned him."

"He died. Again," Mark breathed.

"Yes. And the effort of the magic killed my great-aunt too, only a few months after the resurrection. By the time she died, her body was covered in bruises and her nose was always bleeding. Or so I was told."

Soojin wasn't sure how much of this was allegory—Mother's way of instilling caution in her daughters. "My dad wouldn't survive another loss, Mark," she said, her voice so quiet, he leaned forward to hear it. "I know he wouldn't. And that's why I can't."

But it wasn't merely the possibility of bodily harm that halted her; it was Mirae's own words. Shortly after Mother passed, there had been a night when the sisters huddled together in this room. Father still hadn't emerged from his room, momentarily stunned out of parenthood. No lamps were on, but the harvest moon bleeding through their curtains lit the interior of their home in diaphanous coral light.

We can make this right, Soojin had said in Korean, the language she fell upon during her most vulnerable hours. She said it while crying, while gripping Mirae's hand. This wasn't persuasion—she was begging her sister. *We can look through the urn. There must be something. We can bring Mom back if we do it together.*

Who would that be for, Soo? Mirae asked.

For all of us. For Daddy.

Mirae shook her head. *You're lying,* she said. *I can't forgive that sort of lie.*

Mirae had left no room for argument. Soojin never brought up resurrection again.

"I hate this," she said now. A tear threatened her lash line, and she blinked it away hard.

Mark's hand hovered up, as if to brush her cheek the way he might have a decade ago. But he thought better of it, letting his hand fall instead to the desk with a heavy thump. "I'm really sorry."

Soojin didn't know what to say. She took the bag with her sister's tooth from his slack grip and tucked it back into her drawer.

4.

The summer that Mirae turned six, she lost five baby teeth in the span of one week. The first fell out in her sleep. She woke up with it next to her on the pillow, sitting beside a small stain of spit-diluted blood. The second and third, loose enough to sway when she whistled, needed a little help. Mother tied a thread around them both, one hand ready at Mirae's side, and the other holding the thread. She said, *One, two, three*—then assailed her daughter with tickles. When Mirae threw her head back in laughter, the teeth tethered to the thread fell painlessly away.

The final two fell out at church while she played with Soojin and Mark. The congregation's only children, they were always let out early from worship to cause chaos in the playground against a backdrop of hymns sung in sonorous, soaring Korean. As Mirae climbed the slide steps, her foot faltered and her face hit the metal ledge, splitting her lip. She spit two bottom teeth out and sobbed, while Soojin sprinted for her mother and Mark dabbed blood from her mouth with the sleeve of his nicely ironed church shirt.

At home that evening, Mirae was inconsolable. Mark's family was over, and she could hear the bustle of the adults downstairs. Even with windows wide open, the house was smoky with searing pork belly.

Mirae wasn't hungry, though, wasn't even sure if she could chew. When she opened her mouth before the mirror, she resembled the coyote in those vintage Sunday cartoons whose teeth fell out like piano keys. She buried her face in her hands.

"Come on, it's not *that* bad," Soojin said, though her small face looked concerned, like she was seeing her future and didn't like it. Soojin and Mark were both a year younger than Mirae, and Soojin still had all her milk teeth.

Mark sat in front of Mirae. "Let me see," he said. He was wearing his mother's purple sequined cardigan while his shirt soaked in vinegar to lift the blood off it. You could fit two Mark Moons in that cardigan; he looked like a tropical lizard with too much skin.

Mirae shook her head.

"You aren't the only one, you know. Wanna see mine?" He opened his own mouth wide, and sure enough, one of his canines was gone, with a small white stub just beginning to show in the depression of the gum. "I can make it whistle." He whistled a bit to prove it.

Mirae looked at the goofy little gap between his teeth before opening up reluctantly so Mark and Soojin could peer inside.

Mark laughed immediately. Soojin tried to shush him with an elbow to his side, but it only made him laugh harder.

"You promised you wouldn't make fun!" Mirae pouted,

though he'd promised no such thing. But Soojin was smiling a little now too, taken by the infectiousness of his cackling. Mirae was not amused.

He straightened up slowly, his face still glowing.

"Sorry. It's really not that bad."

When Mirae made an unconvinced noise, Mark scratched his chin solemnly, then said, "I'll tell you what." He opened his mouth, pushing one of his front baby teeth forward with his tongue. It was already loose, yielding easily outward like a dog door with its hinge pushed to its limits.

"What are you doing?" Soojin asked, and when she realized what he was attempting, she hit him and squealed. "Ew, stop!"

Mark continued pressing forward until the tooth was almost horizontal and the root finally dislodged. The tooth fell into his waiting palm, glistening with spit and just slightly reddened at the root.

He smiled up at them both, triumphant, with two wide gaps in his smile. "See, it's not so bad. Now we match."

The next morning, Mother and Father took Mirae outside, her baby teeth rattling in a bowl. They told her to throw the teeth up, as hard as she could, into the air. If they didn't fall back down, that meant God had caught them and would grant her a wish.

She made her wish and threw them hard, one by one. None fell back to earth. Mirae jumped for joy, wind whistling through the many gaps in her teeth. Her father hoisted her over his shoulder, spun her around and around. He asked what she'd implored God for.

Mirae giggled and reached for the sky and never told him. The teeth, of course, had merely landed on the roof. Ravens would collect some for their ivory luster, and come next rain, the remainder would be washed away. One would fall into the gutter pipe and come clattering back down to earth for Mother to find.

For a long time, Mirae believed her milk teeth had been collected by the heavens, the memory of tossing them shrouded in the enduring magic of a child's memory. Her mother let her believe it for a few years longer, until she one day pulled a ziplock bag containing a single molar out of a drawer. Mother laughed as she shook it into Mirae's hand. She asked her mystified preteen daughter what she'd wished for so many years ago.

The particulars were fuzzy, but Mirae replied—

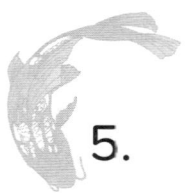

5.

Soojin was doing the dishes when her phone buzzed. Without looking at it, she knew it was Mark. The only other person in the world who texted her was her dad, and he was home for the weekend. She wiped her hands on her apron and peered at her phone. Sure enough, Mark Moon's name loomed on her screen.

A week had passed since the resurrection, and things between them had changed. He still gave her space, but sometimes after class he would linger by the door to catch her on the way out and they would walk together, chatting about nothing in particular. A couple of days ago, while dropping off banchan his mother made, Mark pulled two cans of strawberry Milkis from his backpack and they sat on the stairs of her wraparound porch to drink it.

You like this stuff, right? he'd asked as they sipped the fizzy milk soda, watching the sun sink below the tree line. *I figured you must if your rat is named after it.*

It was a brittle rekindling of a long-dead friendship. She didn't trust it, but she'd be lying if she said it wasn't a little pleasant.

What are you up to? his message read.

My dad's back for the weekend. Please tell your mom I don't need food, she replied.

> It's not that . . . are you free?

Soojin shut off the sink and leaned against the kitchen island. She supposed she was. Though her father returned only on the weekends, they didn't hang out much when he was home. Tired from the labor of his workweek, he usually just said some perfunctory words over dinner. She would regale him with stories of all the fabricated friendships she did not have, and he would retire early to his bedroom with a small nightcap.

Somehow they'd become ghosts to one another, caught mostly in peripheral vision as they retreated to their rooms or out the front door.

> I guess so, why?

His response was immediate: Wanna hang out?

She looked toward her father's door. The lights were off, but she could hear the staccato of news anchors. He was likely tipsy and dozing. It was Saturday, just a few minutes after nine. Years ago, Saturday evenings were game nights. The family would gather in the living room to snack, play Monopoly, and have an excuse to good-naturedly shout at each other. Or at least Father and Soojin would shout, though in the end everyone would be laughing.

It was easy to forget there had ever been a time when Soojin and her dad had that sort of dynamic. Perhaps if they'd known back then that their easy banter was facilitated by the mediating presence of Mirae and Mother, they could have built a better foundation between just the two of them, might have salvaged their relationship from the little it had become.

Sure, she typed.

Cool! I'll pick you up in twenty.

"So, where are we going?" Soojin asked. It was chilly and she'd forgotten her gloves. She warmed her hands between her thighs until Mark noticed and turned up the heater, shifting the vent toward her.

"This is the last clear day in a while. It's going to be wet as hell next week, so I figured we should take advantage of it." He smelled like antiseptic, having come straight from the crematorium. In his fraying gray hoodie, he looked underdressed for the weather.

"What do you propose?" she asked.

"The beach!"

"You've got to be kidding me. It's cold."

"Don't be dramatic—it isn't that bad. Also, I have a plan to keep us both warm, don't you worry." He winked.

What would have sounded lewd from any other boy's mouth sounded innocuous coming out of Mark's. It was the only thing keeping her from smacking his shoulder. That and the fact that he was driving down a very narrow road made visible only by high beams.

"And what is this grand plan?"

"When I was jogging down at the cove this morning, I saw someone had prepared a firepit but didn't use it. Their loss—we're going to have ourselves a bonfire," he said, his eyes bright.

After walking down from the parking lot, he lifted the lantern to point toward the sea. He was right: someone had prepared a bonfire pit and abandoned it. Maybe they had decided it was a little too cold for such clownery. A person of good sense, which Mark had none of.

Still, she couldn't deny there was something strangely nice about revisiting this place on a cool September evening. She'd only ever come to the beach this late at night with her family, and only in summer when the shore was pockmarked with dozens of bonfires, vibrating with the cacophony of several different radios. This was better.

As the dim parking lot glow grew further behind them, nothing illuminated their steps but their camping lantern. The moon and its many cascading reflections streaked down the water's face from horizon to shore. Otherwise, the darkness felt complete, like they were walking alone through a womb: nothing but a black amniotic sky and the sound of cresting waves.

They reached the pit and Mark got to work, opening his full-to-bursting backpack. From it came a book of matches, one of which he lit, holding the flame to the bramble until it caught and devoured the stack.

The heat felt delicious. Soojin only pulled her hands away from its radius when Mark unearthed a bag of marshmallows and two long metal chopsticks.

"I didn't have time to stop by the store for skewers, so . . . ," he said sheepishly, stabbing the marshmallow on the tip of his chopstick.

"Innovative," she said, doing the same and lowering the utensil to the fire.

They toasted their marshmallows in easy silence for a while before Mark's caught flame. He cursed and blew it out, but its surface was already coal black and beginning to slide off the molten core. Mark lifted the burnt bit and it came away in one clean layer, leaving just the gooey center on the chopstick. He held the charred crust to his mouth.

"Don't eat that! It's bad for you," Soojin said, but he dodged her and ate it.

"It's the best part," he said. His eyes crinkled in satisfaction until the overheated mass on his chopstick slid onto his lap like a pile of seagull shit. "Aw, man."

The tragic look on his face coaxed a laugh out of her. She was surprised at the sound of it, how open and clear her voice was. Though Soojin had rejected the company of anyone but her family for so long, she found Mark easy to be around. He disarmed her; after so many years stockpiling her internal armory, Soojin was no longer sure who she was without it. She forced her mouth shut and turned her attention back to the chopstick in her fingers.

"You don't have to do that, you know," Mark said, lowering his chopstick to the fire, bumping hers.

"Do what?"

"Force yourself to stop laughing. Enjoying something is nothing to be ashamed of." He blew smoke off his second marshmallow and, perhaps to not draw her ire, threw the blackest bits back into the fire before eating.

"I don't—" she began before her own ignited and she paused to blow it out. She had no response anyway. Was she ashamed of feeling good? She hadn't had to think about it, since she'd enjoyed nothing since Mirae died. She passed from school to her job at the diner to home like a ghost.

But there had been a time when she'd let herself laugh until her stomach cramped. When exactly did that end? Mirae's death had been the final nail, certainly, but Soojin's distrust of joy predated that.

It must have been when Mother's car crashed, so many years ago. Soojin remembered the day with the impossible clarity of heartbreak. Father had had a fever, so Mom had gone to the liquor store for aspirin—the only place to get medicine so late in their sleepy little town. It had been an unusually rainy night, and she'd lost control of the car, flipped into a gully. Since the back roads were not often traversed in such weather, it was an hour before another car came upon hers and phoned for help. Mom was already gone when the ambulance arrived to cut her loose from the seat belt.

Soojin had been doing homework when her dad got the call. Belly down in their warm house, laughing with her sister. It was the fact that Soojin had been comfortable, happy, while her mother died alone only miles away that she could not forgive herself for.

Mark leaned forward, studying her expression, and Soojin knew she had gone quiet for too long.

"I'm sorry. Did I overstep?" He put the half-eaten bag of marshmallows back into his backpack and handed her a thermos of tea in a vaguely conciliatory manner. "Forget what I said."

They passed the thermos back and forth, steam billowing before their cheeks, which had gone mauve with wind and bonfire heat. Somewhere in the dark waters, a night heron sang.

"I'm not mad," she said finally. A lie. She *was* mad. Not at

Mark, but at the past. The way its idyllic luster dulled her present into negatives, an afterimage of itself. "I was just thinking." She let the sentence drop there, but its continuation hovered, obvious to both of them.

The fire crackled; an ember rose effortlessly in the air before landing on her arm as ash.

"I think of the past a lot too, you know," Mark said, pulling his gaze from the water. He passed the thermos back to her, and she held it in her hand, letting its heat warm her palms. "I keep wondering if there was anything I could have done to save our friendship back then."

A brief image struck her. A young Mark in the back of his mother's car, his hand pressed against the window, refusing to look her way. She shook her head, and the scene dissolved into the crackling flames.

"It wasn't your fault," Soojin said. Her family had wanted nothing to do with anyone while they grieved the loss of Mother, and when they'd emerged from their catatonic spell, there'd been no one left around them. Though Mirae eventually managed to bounce back to her former social life, Soojin and her father had become an archipelago. Even the Moons had slowly drifted away, Soojin's mother having been the bridge that kept the two families together.

But it was the difference Mother's absence made in her own family that had struck Soojin the most. She had always known that their mother was the scaffold of their home. It was obvious in the way her hands could produce miracles, but more so in the space her laughter occupied. The way it could travel through closed doors, unlatch windows, and coax joy from even deeply serious Father, who liked to build things and pray alone at the dinner table in a home of nonbelievers already tucking into their meals. The accident had changed everything. What could one boy's efforts have achieved in the face of such home-shattering loss?

"We were ten. There was nothing you could have done."

"I know, but . . ." Mark kicked sand off his shoe before shaking his head. "Never mind. You're right. I'm glad we're getting a second chance now, I guess is what I'm trying to say. I think our families will be glad," he said, offering a crooked smile, which meant he was about to get ahead of himself. "Maybe you and your dad can come over for dinner like you guys used to. And you should start eating lunch with me and Jay at school instead of alone."

"What if I like being alone?" she asked.

He pulled a Swiss Army knife from his pocket and snipped a ligament off a branch to feed the fire. "Then whatever. But I'm not convinced you do." The twig he'd thrown began to belch dark smoke from the leaves that still clung to it. Mark cussed under his breath and fanned the smoke away with his backpack. She regarded him while his attention was elsewhere and saw his younger face superimposed over his current one.

"Fine," she said. "But you'll have to introduce me to Jay first. I don't think I've ever actually spoken to her."

Mark stopped his battle with the twig. His smile was so infectious, she didn't dare look at it long. "Really? Okay! How about we meet up next weekend at—"

His eyes looked past her, the rest of his invitation forgotten. Soojin looked over her shoulder toward the parking lot they had trekked from. Several cars were snaking down the cliffside road, their high beams cutting through the night.

"Shoot. Well, I guess you might get the chance to hang out with her a lot sooner," Mark said. People were getting out of their cars, the loud racket of voices and music from their open windows carrying even from a distance.

"Did you plan this?" Soojin asked.

"No, but I guess we solved the mystery of the abandoned bonfire pit. Should've known." He pulled her to her feet, brushing a spot of ash from her shoulder. "Do you want to leave?"

Soojin watched the gaggle of seniors spilling onto the sand, cell phone flashlights sweeping the dark like nocturnal eyes. Leaving would be the peaceful option, the comfortable one. But there was a part of her that felt resigned to the night. Besides, the group had seen them already and were walking closer, a few of them waving and calling out to Mark.

"It's fine."

A petite girl with curly auburn hair was the first to reach them. She pulled Mark into a tight hug and, small though she was, lifted him off his feet.

"Hey, you! I thought you weren't coming out!" the girl said before turning her head and locking eyes on Soojin. Jay was lovely in a Disney princess sort of way, with kind hazel eyes and a dusting of freckles across rosy cheeks. She looked taken aback to see Soojin, but recovered quickly and offered a smile.

"Hi! Nice to see you out and about!" Jay said, as though there were years of history between them, which in a way there was. Though they barely spoke, they had shared classes since elementary school. Everything Soojin knew about her was by osmosis. She knew that Mark and Jay were best friends now. She knew Jay had a long-distance girlfriend she'd met through some MMO game, which had launched a month of gossip before the next non-scandal arose and the town turned its collective eyes elsewhere.

Soojin had always resented Jade Acre for this: the way even functional strangers could know everything about one another.

The rest of the entourage caught up, speaking over each other and the blaring old-school radio someone was carrying under their arm like a football. Some eyes snagged on Soojin's unexpected presence, though not for long, as everyone busied themselves with spreading tarps or dragging driftwood to sit on. Someone had brought a cooler and pulled from it two handles of vodka, frosty with condensation, a sleeve of red Solo cups, and several jugs of orange juice. They made swift work of haphazardly throwing together screwdrivers, more vodka than juice, and passing them around.

"Here ya go." Jay tried to press a plastic cup into Soojin's hand. The diluted orange juice sloshed over the rim and onto both their hands. Even from afar, it smelled astringent, like the orange-peel cleaner her father used on the hardwood. "Do you drink?" Jay asked.

Only once. When they were kids, Mirae and Soojin had snuck some raspberry wine from the fridge. What they'd always imagined would taste sweet shocked their tongues with tannins. They replenished the bottle with grape juice, thinking themselves clever, but got caught—of course.

Their father had been scandalized, but Mom had thought it hilarious. She'd promised that when they turned fifteen, she would share some soju with them at the dinner table. It was important that teens drink first with their family to learn their limits before they inevitably began drinking with their peers, Mother claimed. But she didn't live long enough to make good on that promise. While Mirae went on to drink occasionally at parties, those hurried gulps in the white refrigerator light were the last time Soojin had tasted alcohol.

She didn't take the cup from Jay. Behind her, she heard Mark trying to cajole whoever was mixing the drinks into giving him a plain orange juice.

"You don't have to if you don't want to, you know," Jay said breezily. "More for me."

Mark returned to them, triumphant with his unspiked OJ.

"No, I'll try some. Thanks." Soojin took it from Jay's hand, and the three tapped their cups together. The first sip was awful—it made her gag.

"Should've warned you it would be disgusting. It's bottom-shelf stuff, basically nail polish remover." Jay laughed, taking an unbothered sip.

"It wouldn't be so bad if Damien wasn't so adamant that a fifty-fifty ratio of vodka to OJ is the only way to make a screwdriver," Mark said loudly, earning a jovial middle finger from the boy mixing drinks. "Don't feel pressured to finish that—you won't hurt anyone's feelings if you want to pour it in the sand."

It was certainly not tasty, but there was something about the slow burning in her stomach that Soojin found agreeable. She liked how the awful bitterness obliterated the thinking part of her. She took another tentative sip, and now that her tongue knew what to expect, it wasn't so bad.

A couple more cars pulled up, bringing with them a flurry of snacks, mixers, and a case of beer that, upon trying, Soojin decided tasted like carbonated urine. A second bonfire was hurriedly made to accommodate the growing party. It felt like all the upperclassmen had shown up, as well as a few sophomores.

Bentley Porter, Jade Acre's prodigal newcomer, arrived late, already drunk, with a pretentious flask in his pocket. He took one look at Soojin and raised a surprised eyebrow, filling her with a visceral dislike, but he was folded quickly into the crowd that surged and ebbed between them. No one else paid her any mind except to knock their Solo cups against hers and chat idly about school or how drunk they felt. The conversations were impersonal enough to disappear behind, and Soojin realized there was no better place in the world to vanish than a party.

Eventually Mark swung back around to her after his social migration through the crowd. He pointed out a log close to the fire, and they sat, a small smudge of calm in a sea of activity.

"Having fun?" he asked. He'd finished his cup of orange juice a long time ago and held his hands up to the fire. His knuckles were red and chapped. Soojin wondered if it was from all those long hours spent working the cremation furnace, or simply from the cold. She wasn't cold anymore, though. She was on her third drink and radiating heat. Something molten and unpleasant settled in the core of her. She'd even pulled off her coat despite Mark's nagging. It was draped across the emptied cooler now, under a pile of other coats.

"I guess so," Soojin answered. The words felt sticky and elongated leaving her mouth. She took another sip to wet her tongue, but it didn't help.

Mark hesitated for a moment before leaning in close and saying in Korean: "I think you should stop drinking."

It always felt odd to hear Korean from him. When they were kids, it had been their default language, the one used to exchange secrets in the schoolyard. Secrets traveled fast in Jade Acre, and the most surefire way to prevent one from spreading was to keep it the hell away from English. Hearing the vowel-rich language from Mark thrummed a raw, nostalgic nerve in her. She wanted him to stop speaking it.

"I think you should worry about yourself," she replied in English. Who was he to come sauntering back into her life after so many years just to order her around? She took another long swig out of sheer defiance.

"I mean it, Soo; it's Saturday. Your dad's home. He's going to be mad if you come home drunk," he said, taking the half-empty thermos of corn-silk tea from his backpack. He unscrewed the top and handed it to her. "Here, drink this. You have to sober up before I take you home."

Soojin was far past the point of sobering up. She was either going to throw up or sleep, whichever came first. But she took the thermos from him out of courtesy. It was tepid, the rim salty from their lips.

Around them, the party showed no signs of slowing down. Drunk, students shrugged off their inhibitions like exoskeletons. Some danced clumsily, bare feet sunk in the sand, swaying off-beat with red cups held high in the air. A girl she knew from PE snored on a tarp behind them, waiting for her designated driver to take her home. By the second fire's heat, a senior girl was letting a sophomore kiss her, though she looked indifferent about the clumsy exchange. She kept her eyes wide open the entire time, occasionally glancing down at her phone.

Soojin's stomach turned. She didn't want to be here anymore. When she looked out toward the sea, the horizon quivered. She put her head against the heel of her palm. "Why'd you let me drink so much?"

"Me? I tried to—you know what? Never mind." Mark stood. "I'll get you home. Just wait here, okay? I'm going to say bye to Jay."

"I'll go with," she said, but the world was moving faster than her body. She swayed before Mark caught her and eased her back down.

"No, you don't. Stay put, I'll be right back." He found her coat and held it behind her so she could shrug herself in before disappearing into the crowd.

As soon as she lost sight of him, Soojin deflated into herself, swallowing against the tide of sickness rising slowly in her throat. If she ended up throwing up in front of Mark or, god forbid, in his car, she would never speak to him again.

She had just set her forehead against her knee, the world going soft and roaring in her ears, when someone sat heavily beside her, startling her alert.

"You scared me!" she hissed, but it wasn't Mark. It was Bentley Porter, stretching his legs casually toward the bonfire.

"Sorry," he laughed. His pale gray eyes had an unspooled quality about them, softly undone as often happens after a third hour of liquor. "Strange to see you socializing for once. What's the occasion?"

The gel in his hair had failed over the course of the night, weighed down by wind and heat, forcing him to keep pushing his brown waves away from his face. As he did, her eyes caught on the reflective sheen of his designer watch, that physical indicator of how out of place he was here.

Bentley and his father, Christopher Porter, had moved to Jade Acre around eight years ago, but in a town like theirs, where the population was static and people passed through only to vacation, they were considered—even now—newcomers. They'd brought with them a hurricane of redevelopment that had led to the slew of trendy boutique hotels and Airbnbs that had so badly impacted Han's Bed & Breakfast, along with the rest of Jade Acre's room-and-board industry. Misplaced though the feeling might have been, she resented Bentley for it. His very presence felt like a harbinger of shitty things.

"What do you want?" Soojin asked, her voice barely audible over the flames. For his part, he seemed unmoved by her curtness. This was how they'd always been, after all, since the first time they'd met in elementary school.

She didn't remember what had instigated the fight, but she could guess. A barked order, leading to an argument, leading to a scuffle on the school's blacktop that had left them both with skinned knees, sitting in the principal's office, waiting for their fathers to pick them up.

Soojin didn't think she'd ever forget the look on Porter's face as he passed her en route to his son that day. His eyes a brutal gray, they held the exact opposite of regard, the way one might look at a set piece or a mounted taxidermy head. Then he'd passed her, collecting Bentley with a cold *We're leaving.* Bentley had been back at school the following morning, while she was suspended for three days.

In a way, that should have been an indication of the sort of impunity the Porters would have in their town. Whether by local donation or the way their aggressive business ventures pushed your own off a cliff, the Porters became central figures in Jade Acre. Love them or hate them—that's just how it was.

The fire before them popped. Bentley fed in another twig, watched it flare, the bird-talon shape igniting red-hot before disintegrating into ash.

"What do you want, Bentley?" Soojin asked again. The vodka had stripped away the air of cool disregard she tried to maintain in front of him. This boy's family was the reason why her father toiled away all week in a town three hours east. His nearness made her feel mean and raw, like an exposed nerve.

"Wow," he laughed, shaking his head. "Do you think you're Dartmouth or something? Are people not allowed to sit next to you without submitting an application and three letters of recommendation first?"

"*You* can't."

"Well, that's too bad. All the other seats are taken." He gestured vaguely out toward the shore, where each log was occupied. By coats, by people vomiting or kissing or completely passed out. Soojin grimaced as one rolled off and face-planted directly into the cold, damp sand.

Bentley took a sip from his flask, then tipped it toward her in some sort of shitty peace offering. She didn't take it. Rolling his eyes, he took another defiant swig.

"Nice night," he said, looking up. It was. A clear and generous night, overlush with stars, but small talk with Bentley Porter was the last thing Soojin wanted to engage in. She tried to ignore him, but he nudged her and pointed up toward the sky, adamant.

"What?" Soojin barked.

"I'm trying to show you something," he said. His voice held a distance in it, like he could have been talking to anyone. Just how drunk was he? Still, Soojin looked up, following his hand.

"There," he said, dragging his finger first across the heavens, then down. He sounded proud of himself. "That's the constellation Cygnus. The Swan. See it?" His fingers swept across the sky laterally again. "There are the wings." He pulled his hand down. "And that's the body of the bird."

She saw what he was tracing. A bright rib of stars drawn against the darkness. It didn't look much like a swan at all. It looked more like a tiny cross or perhaps a bow with an arrow notched against it. Soojin already knew how to identify Cygnus for the same reason she knew how to identify many constellations: Mirae's lifelong fascination with the stars, which Soojin had never quite been able to share—who cared about the light of long-dead suns when she had so many immediate problems?

Even so, Bentley's drunken stargazing felt like an intrusion on something that belonged only to the sisters. In his expression, which had softened toward the sky, vivid and eager, she felt a sudden, intolerable proximity. For a brief moment, she was not at the beach; she was in her yard, crickets trilling in the near-perfect dark. A towel spread over the damp grass, and the two sisters side by side atop it. *That bright star there is the North Star.* Mirae had pointed before swinging her arm elsewhere. *And that's Cygnus, Soo. See it? The Swan. It symbolizes transformations. Rebirth and—*

"I don't see shit," Soojin said. Her voice was a deadbolt. The memory of her yard dissolved, and she was once again at the beach, the fire dying and her sister nowhere.

The change in Bentley's face was swift. For a suspended moment, his gray eyes looked afflicted; then the fire undulated, and the wounded look in his eyes was gone.

"I suppose you wouldn't," he said. The cautious eagerness had drained from his voice, and he sounded once again like the boy she was used to. Cold, pompous. But there was something else there too that she couldn't quite place.

"I've been meaning to ask you something. . . ." He raised a hand to gesture toward her, but his tipsiness made him overreach. His finger grazed the side of her neck, an accidental touch, but she jerked back as if singed.

The intensity of his gaze sent a bolt of nameless discomfort through her. A sudden and urgent need to leave overtook her and she stood. She was horribly drunk. The fading fire smudged gold over everything. Where was Mark?

"Wait," Bentley said. He stood, grabbing her wrist. "Hold on, I'm trying to talk to you."

"About what?" she snapped. "About what, Bentley? Stars?"

He had the audacity to look stunned, confused. "What? No . . ."

"Don't touch me!" She wrenched herself from his grip.

He threw his hands into the air, exasperated, before speaking again. "Goddamn, Soojin. Why are you always so damn pissed off? I just wanted—"

"I don't care what you want. You already fucking have everything." And he did. Money. His huge house. A father who, with words or a check, got Bentley out of any trouble he got himself into around town. He could say anything, treat others however, and it never mattered. A perfect, unassailable life. She hated him for it.

The tides rushed violently up the shore and receded, leaving a hem of froth on the sand. They stood in a quiet stalemate as the party continued on without them.

Something about her words had halted him. A muscle worked in his jaw, his eyes overbright, and she realized that for whatever reason he was suddenly furious. He leaned close enough for her to smell the whiskey on his breath, and for one frightened, disoriented moment, she thought he would kiss her. Instead he glared at her with a surprising resentment.

"You're fucking exhausting, you know that? Everything is zero or a hundred with you," Bentley spit, running an agitated hand violently through his hair. "No wonder your sister needed breaks from you. I bet she couldn't breathe. I bet you never let her breathe."

It was a low blow, the mention of Mirae. Soojin knew he was zeroing in on the one thing guaranteed to wound, and the effect on her was brutal and immediate. Her throat tightened. She couldn't speak.

When Soojin failed to respond, he continued, his breath hot and venomous in her ear. "I feel bad for your dad. It must be hard for him that the wrong daughter survived."

Her vision tunneled like a constricting aperture. Suddenly she was home again. The day after Mirae's funeral, when she'd woken delirious in a living room bathed oceanic with television light. She'd heard stifled sobbing in the kitchen and crept toward it, but couldn't go in. Instead Soojin had stayed hidden behind the banister, watching like a specter as her father grieved in the ever-expanding gloom. He might as well have been alone.

If it had been her in the urn that night, Mirae would have gone to him so they could hold each other. She would have turned on the lights.

Bentley was right. The wrong daughter had survived. Soojin had always known this.

Her vision wavered, and she had just enough time to register the seed of regret on Bentley's face before her tears blurred everything. She heard her own pulse hard and loud behind her ears. Horror flooded her system. She knew this feeling. *Not now,* she thought. *Not here.*

"Hey...," Bentley began, but she couldn't, couldn't listen to any more. She had to leave.

Soojin cuffed his shoulder with her elbow, *hard.* Hard enough to make him yelp, lose his balance, and teeter on drunken feet at the edge of the bonfire's hungry parabola. Distantly, Soojin heard people gasp above the radio static.

Time had collapsed into a vortex, two reels of possibility branching out before her. In one, Bentley didn't regain balance and fell straight into the fire, his skin erupting into angry red blisters before he could scramble out of it. In the other, he regained his footing, unscathed by everything, as usual.

Soojin viciously wanted the first to come true; she wanted to give him a wound she could name after herself. But it didn't. Time unhung from its nail and she watched him cartoonishly pedal his arms, body tipping precariously before he swiveled and fell ass-first into the sand. The fire burned on without him in it. Someone yelled, "Oh shit!" and kicked the radio silent.

"Hey!" Mark's voice pierced the momentary lull. He ran toward her as quickly as sand would allow. He reached her, bracing his hands against her shoulders. "Are you okay?"

Soojin still couldn't speak; there was a plum pit in her throat she couldn't swallow around.

"You're asking if *she's* okay? Bitch almost pushed me into the fire!" Bentley shouted, veins protruding so hard from his temple that tree-branch grooves could be traced beneath his pale skin.

"Bet you deserved it," Mark snapped. He moved Soojin

behind him, passing her straight into the arms of another. "Go," he said, but not to her.

"Come on," said a voice that Soojin only vaguely registered as belonging to Jay. Soojin didn't struggle to break away; she just let herself be led as sand gave way to boardwalk gave way to stairs gave way to pavement.

She looked back over her shoulder. For a moment it seemed like Mark and Bentley were going to fight. Their argument was muffled by distance, but they pushed each other until the other students intervened, pressing a cup into Bentley's hand.

They reached the parking lot. Jay grumbled a steady stream of curses, trying to be lighthearted despite the rattle in her voice. Mark caught up to them, and they all piled into his car. His headlights sliced through the absolute dark. In the distance, the bonfires glinted like eyes.

No one spoke as they wound up the cliffside path. They whipped through downtown, where all the vibrant, squat stores were shuttered, with only the saloon and liquor store lit like twin beacons. Their fluorescent signs blurred behind the rain-wet windows of Soojin's eyes. The colors stayed stamped in her vision even after they'd left them behind.

The wrong daughter, her mind kept repeating. She couldn't bring it to be silent. The wrong sister.

"What happened?" Mark asked finally, knuckles white on the steering wheel.

Soojin didn't respond. What had started as a plum pit in her throat had ballooned into a fist. There was the feeling of water rising around her, filling the car until no air remained. Her pulse was an animal battering its small body against its cage to get out. *I can't be here,* she thought. They had entered the tree-heavy roads leading to her house now, the darkness enveloping the car completely.

Mark glanced over at her. "Hey . . ."

"Don't look at me," she hissed.

"What?"

"Stop the car. I'll walk home," she said, still barely above the grumble of the car engine.

"You can't walk home alone; it's almost one a.m."

The fist in her throat was unfurling, fingers pressing against the architecture of her trachea, grabbing hold of her larynx. She tasted salt on her lips. It felt urgent that no one see her crying. She needed to leave.

"It's just a fifteen-minute walk from here. Let me out," she said. Jay's eyes were reflected wide in the rearview mirror. Mark pressed on the gas, urging the old car to go faster. Faster. If a stag jumped into the road in front of him, the speed of the impact could kill them all, but still he pushed. Soojin was scaring them both. She didn't care. The pines whipped past them into a single green curtain.

"Soo, please just—"

The fraying thread holding together her composure snapped. Her hands flew to her face. She heard herself shouting, "Let me out! Let me out!" She couldn't recognize her own voice.

"Mark! Let her go—can't you see she's losing it?" Jay shouted from the back.

Mark looked first toward Soojin, then to the rearview mirror, where Jay's eyes were dilated and bright with alarm.

"But—"

"Stop the car!" Jay ordered.

He slammed on the brakes. Their bodies pitched forward as the car squealed. He threw an arm out across Soojin's chest while Jay rocked against the back of his seat with a yelp. As soon as the car screeched to a halt, Soojin opened the door and spilled out. She didn't say goodbye, didn't even close the door. The car stayed stalled in the street, the engine steaming behind her like a panting animal in the dark.

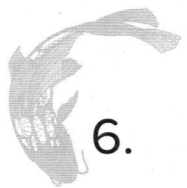

6.

Soojin knew what drowning felt like. For the first month after Mirae's body was found, she dreamed of nothing else. In sleep she would find herself submerged, thrashing to break the surface, gasping for air.

The sensation followed her outside sleep, a nameless phantom. It would strike her at random, the feeling of her throat filling, her peripheral vision going damp and dark. Sometimes it happened at home in the safety of her room, mounting gradually, so she could steel the small animal of her body against what was about to seize it. But usually it struck hard and without warning—at school, or at the diner while she was frothing milk. In these moments she'd retreat into the walk-in fridge to breathe into a paper bag. In the darkness, back pressed against a crate of onions, she'd watch the paper lung of the doughnut bag balloon and deflate.

Soojin felt that familiar anxious thudding in her body now:

visions of rapids rising against the bark like blue ghosts. The trees whipped past her as she ran, but in the distance she could see the silhouette of her home. If she could just get there, she thought, everything would be fine. Her lungs ached, but her legs pedaled her faster to the animal pendulum of *safe, safe, safe.*

Her breath erupted against the night in short, heavy plumes as she reached the door and crept inside. Soojin was halfway up the stairs when her father came bursting out of his room, his hair standing on end from an uneasy sleep. "Han Soojin, where the *hell* have you been?"

His voice echoed through the hall, syllables fracturing against the walls. Her tongue was a stone in her mouth. Dad had always been the stern parent growing up, but he was never one to shout, let alone curse. Why had he even woken up? He was always such a heavy sleeper, especially after his nightcap.

"I was with a friend," she said, her voice mossy with bewilderment.

It wasn't completely a lie. Mark was the closest approximation of a friend that she had. Still, she didn't want to implicate him in this. She began to shuffle through names in her head. She had a running list of friendships she'd curated over the months to keep her father from worrying about her becoming too isolated. But she *was* isolated, and she remembered no names. She couldn't handle this right now. She stumbled backward up the stairs.

"A friend," her father scoffed, and she understood that he had never believed her stories of a thriving social life. He looked at her closely then, and seemed to register for the first time her angry red eyes, the tears tracking glistening lines down her face. Soojin saw a series of emotions flash in his eyes—worry, relief, confusion—but anger won out. He began to stomp up the stairs after her. "Do you know how many times I've called you? If you didn't pick up in the next ten minutes, I was going to call the police."

Her vision wavered. She groped for the banister, but her hands closed around only air and she fell, skidding down a few steps before regaining her footing. Her father caught up to her, bracing her shoulder to steady her; then his grip tightened.

"You've been drinking," he muttered, as if he couldn't believe it. She held her breath, but no use. The scent of vodka rose off her clothes, her hair. "Worried me half to death and you've been fucking *drinking*? Who were you with?"

She broke from his grip and half ran, half tripped up the stairs. She felt sick, a sour sweetness rising in the back of her throat. Her behavior froze him, but only momentarily. Soojin could hear her father taking the steps two at a time after her. He reached the door just as she disappeared behind it, slamming it in his face. Her hands quivered as she locked the door, feeling the handle jostle as her father tried to force his way in.

"Soojin, open this door right now," he shouted, striking his palm against the wood. It felt like there was water in her ears, his voice distorted as if pulled through a sieve. She backed away until her legs hit her bed and she toppled onto it. The ceiling fan above her looked like it was turning, though she knew it was motionless. Soojin had thought her room would make it all better, but it didn't.

Something buzzed in her pocket. She pulled out her phone, and the letters swam blearily across the screen before Mark's name stitched itself together in the glow. She rejected the call, and a cascade of notification bubbles popped up after it. Fifteen missed calls from her father. Dozens of texts that started curious, morphed into worry, then transitioned into full-blown fury.

She erased them all. Even drunk, she understood he must have been spiraling, thinking that what had happened to Mirae was happening again. If she were half the daughter her sister had been, Soojin would go to her father and make things right. But she didn't know how. Mirae was the one who brandished hot tea and soft words, making everything better. What would her father's life have been like had Mirae been the one who lived? Had the wrong daughter not been the one to survive.

Slowly, it dawned on her that he wasn't shouting at the door anymore. It was quiet. Everything was quiet until her phone began buzzing in her hand again. Mark's name lit up the screen. She rejected the call. When the phone lit up a third time, something frayed in her and she accepted. She held the phone to her ear without saying anything, listening to the steady metronome of the turn signal, his low breathing on the line. Once Mark realized she was there, he spoke swiftly.

"Soojin? Jesus, I was worried. Just wanted to know if you got home safe. Are you okay? I—"

She hung up, throwing the phone where it hit the opposite wall and clattered to the floor. She expected Mark to call back and plead with her again. She waited, listening to her father stomping back up the stairs. Something heavy slammed on the floor outside, and her doorknob rattled again. Her dad was picking the lock. The steady *click, click, click* of her door slowly betraying her filled the room. Her vision rippled, flexed. This was drowning. Soojin was drowning, and she wanted to be saved.

Call me back, she thought, knowing it was ridiculous. She was the one who had hung up on him, but still—

Please call me back.

But it wasn't Mark she wanted; it wasn't some nebulous giver of comfort. She thought of Mirae, eleven years old and making lunch the day after their mother's funeral, narrow shoulders shaking as she spread mustard on a piece of bread. Mirae lying beside her, pointing up toward their glowing galaxy ceiling, assigning silly names to each star until sadness would release Soojin just long enough for her to fall asleep. And then, even younger: a gap-toothed smile, long black hair. What she wanted was her sister. *Come back.*

Her lock popped open and Soojin had just enough time to think it traitorous before her father opened the door. The concentration it took to pick the lock had defused his anger, and he entered with his back hunched, the posture of a man already knowing defeat. His single-minded nature had driven him only to unlatch the door; he hadn't planned his course of action or his words once the obstacle was breached. They really were too alike, she and her father. And yet they had never been able to understand each other, to divine what the other wanted or needed.

After their mother's car veered off the road, the sisters would often find their father sitting like a folded piece of paper in his dining table chair: head on his knees, arms wrapped across his belly. It was the posture Soojin would always associate with the two months their father completely shut down, sitting motionless while the world moved outside their kitchen window.

While Dad eschewed his responsibilities, Mirae took them up. She cleaned the house, packed herself and Soojin jelly sandwiches and fruit cups. Only a year older, she held Soojin's hand on the way to the school bus and reminded her to look both ways before crossing the road. She met Mark's mother at the door when she periodically came to drop off food.

And in the end it had been Mirae who'd brought Father fully back into himself. Incrementally, with tea and time and gentle words. Like Mother, Mirae was smart with how she wielded tenderness. So unlike Soojin, who often could attend to no one's feelings, not even her own.

"Soojin," her father said, stopping at the foot of her bed. His voice was cautious, worn from the unaccustomed shouting. "What's wrong?"

She hated to hear him this way even more than she hated his rage. He reached for her, hand hovering awkwardly in the air as if to touch her hair. Soojin leaned away without thinking. His hand retreated, then fell back to his side.

"Nothing's wrong, Dad. Go back to sleep." Her own voice was foreign to her, like she had walked out of her body and was listening in from an adjacent room. "You have a long drive tomorrow. You should rest."

"How could I possibly just go back to sleep?" Her father sat heavily next to her. The bed sank toward his weight, tipping her against him.

"I'm okay, I promise." The lies came out easily once they began to leave her mouth. "I went to a party and fought with a friend. I'm sorry for drinking."

She could tell he wanted her to say more. Instead the silence ballooned between them. He raised his hand to graze her cheek for just a moment before shaking his head. They stayed like that for a while, father and daughter caught in the most tenuous of stalemates. Then, as if he knew one step too far over the threshold would topple them both, he yielded. "If I give you space now, do you promise to talk to me later?"

"Sure," she lied.

When he finally left her room, Soojin went and heaved into the toilet. Her stomach relinquished nothing but sugary orange bile, and when she rose, she felt no better for it. She drank from the sink, held her head against the cool faucet in a bid to get the world to stop spinning, and, when that failed, stumbled back into the room to pull her sister's tooth from the drawer. Curled on the floor, she held the molar between her clasped hands as if in prayer. When light brightened beyond her curtains, she heard her father's quiet footsteps as he readied himself for church. She didn't see him to the door, but she listened as his car hummed to life and pulled slowly out of their driveway and into the pale and lonely dawn.

7.

When Soojin woke, she was still on the floor, her spine planted uncomfortably on the hardwood. The sunlight seeping gently through the curtains felt like violence. She pulled herself to her knees and smashed the heels of her palms against her eyes.

She stayed that way until a thought jolted her out of her stupor. Mirae's tooth. She'd fallen asleep with her sister's tooth between her hands, but she was no longer holding it. Where had she flung it? She staggered on hands and knees, sweeping the floor with clumsy, hungover hands. In her panic, one thought assailed her over and over.

It's all I have left.

The rational part of her knew it wasn't true. She had photographs. Old notes passed back and forth during sermons. Half-used jars of moisturizer and clothes with her scent clinging to them. Soojin had so many relics of her sister. But still, the white-hot panic. *It's all I have left. This is all there is.*

Her hand stuttered in the darkness beneath her bed, sending dusty knickknacks rolling in her search. And then she found it, embedded in the white rug at the foot of her bed. A tiny milk tooth, so small she could have easily missed it. She gasped in relief when she felt it, held it tight against her chest.

In the corner, Milkis watched her. A white paw pressed against a bar of her cage as she sat up on her haunches. Her whiskers twitched as if sensing Soojin's distress.

"It's okay, girl," Soojin said, but her voice was shaky. She returned her sister's tooth to its ziplock bag before tucking it into the safety of her desk drawer. "I'm okay."

Her phone was still on the opposite side of the room. She had a vague recollection of having thrown it there. The dull impact as it thumped to the floor. And then a slew of other images she did not want to remember. The bonfire's heat and the sea lapping against the shore. Bentley's vicious words. Her father.

She shook her head, dispelling everything, and bent to pick up her phone.

A cascade of messages lit up on the screen, and she clicked through them quickly. Several calls and texts from Mark, which she dismissed without reading. And then messages that made her heart drop.

Margaret, her shift lead from the diner: Soojin, aren't you opening today?

Where are you?

Hello?!

She bit back a curse, did her valiant best to freshen up, palmed an aspirin, and flew out the door, car key in hand.

A few days a week, Soojin worked at Half Moon Diner, a painfully kitschy tourist trap decked out to resemble a cabin in the woods. Four decades' worth of graffiti covered the tables, and at the front counter they sold Jade Acre merch sporting an anthropomorphic, somewhat strung-out-looking pine tree holding a cup of coffee in one hand and a fishing rod in the other.

Soojin almost knocked the merch display over as she bustled in. She'd arrived to work three hours late with a headache that throbbed in a way she'd never felt before, like her brain was muscling violently against her skull's porous interior, looking for a way out. In the reflection of the table dividers, she could see herself. She looked like death: her apron askew, livid dark circles beneath her eyes. The diner was bustling with people, the way it usually was on a Sunday after morning church service, and Soojin could already see how much her coworkers were struggling to accommodate the crowd. As soon as she raced behind the register to clock in, Margaret stormed toward her.

"Where the hell were you?"

"I overslept," Soojin said, throwing her unkempt hair into a bun.

"Overslept," Margaret scoffed, gesturing to the pine-tree clock nailed crooked on the wall. "It's goddamn half past ten! What do you mean, *you overslept*?"

The customers at the counter stilled their yolk-thick forks to gawk. Margaret gave them a simpering smile before she spun and dragged Soojin into the kitchen.

"I've given you grace, Soojin," she said as the bead curtain swayed behind them, lending hardly any privacy at all. Her voice was low and furious, her normally perfect blond curls sagging from the diner's oily heat. "I've given you so much grace." Meaning: *I was so nice to you after your sister died. Why can't you be back to normal yet?*

After Mirae's body was found, Soojin had left work for two months, and even after returning, she could not quite get it together. She was spacey and forgetful and often moody to both coworkers and customers. Initially, Margaret had made a great show of demonstrating the vastness of her sympathy, but as time went on, that sympathy sharpened to a weapon. *I was so good to you. I gave you time off. I sent you home with a condolence cake.*

Soojin didn't blame Margaret for this. She understood that she was difficult, and that there were limits to the compassion of others. But she also couldn't stop her temper from flaring. If Margaret was going to catalog each instance of care to wield against her in the future, Soojin would rather take no grace at all.

To Soojin's silence, Margaret exhaled sharply. Without another word, she dug in her apron for an order pad and flung it against Soojin's chest before storming out.

All around her, the kitchen bustled. Bacon spit grease on the walls as cooks called out orders and slammed on the bell when the waitresses were not fast enough to respond. It was a chaos she did not feel capable of shouldering today. Soojin held the order pad to her brow, willing herself not to burst into tears before regaining her composure. Four hours. She need only survive four hours.

Soojin headed back into the dining room like she was heading into war, and as luck would have it, her first customer was her least favorite regular.

"Rough night?" Joe Silas asked with a raised eyebrow as

she walked begrudgingly to his spot at the counter. There was no good-natured teasing in his voice. He was mocking her. Likely smelling the half-metabolized liquor still emanating from her pores.

Jade Acre's police chief for as long as Soojin could remember, Silas had always seemed to harbor a dislike for her. Perhaps she'd been the one to start it with her frosty efficiency, refusing to linger at tables for unbearable small talk the way townsfolk expected. *You'd get a better tip out of me if you smiled on occasion, young miss,* he'd said to her once, jotting his usual 10 percent. But his dislike predated that, and felt weirdly personal. Racism, she presumed.

"No, sir," she said, tipping coffee into his cup and setting a few packets of Splenda on the table. She didn't need to take his order. It was always the same: a California scramble, no avocado. A black coffee with sugar substitute. Key lime pie for dessert, if he was feeling indulgent.

She watched him dump two packets into his coffee and stir them in with his butter knife. He took a sip, balled up his trash—the spent Splenda, a stained napkin, a receipt—and placed it directly into her hand.

"Don't let me catch you getting up to any trouble, Sue-jean." He always said her name like that, though she'd tried over the years to correct him. If anything, his inflection had grown more exaggerated over time. "You hear?"

Despite the warning, Soojin was sure he would actually love that. To catch her in trouble, that is. She still remembered the delight he'd taken in marching Mirae home after she was caught drinking with some classmates last summer. Her father had paid a fine, and Mirae was grounded for a month. But suffice it to say, Silas's dedication to keeping kids in line was contingent on who their parents were. It was well known that Bentley carried a flask. She couldn't recall ever hearing about *him* getting reprimanded.

She had a vivid image in her head of throwing the trash back in Silas's face, but she clenched her teeth, offered a stiff nod, and stalked off.

The rest of the shift was a blur Soojin barely survived. Twice she rushed to throw up in the bathroom. She forgot orders and sent dishes to the wrong table and accidentally charged a thousand dollars on someone's credit card for a ten-dollar BLT, temporarily freezing their account. By the time she broke a coffeepot in the sink, slicing open her palm, she felt dissociative and numb. She didn't even notice until a wide-eyed customer pointed at the droplets of blood she was trailing behind her when she went to take their order.

When the rush finally ended and the diner had drained to a manageable bustle, Soojin's head was splitting, and her coworkers were seething.

"Go home," Margaret said, her face set in stone.

Soojin checked the clock. "But it's only—"

"Just go home."

The other waitresses pointedly turned away, refilling their coffeepots or digging dirt from beneath their nails with the corner of their order pads. A slow humiliation spread heat to her ears. Nobody wanted her there. Her presence was a burden.

Soojin clocked out and left.

In a bid to clear her head, Soojin took a detour before returning home. A walk through downtown would make her feel better, she reasoned as she parked.

Jade Acre, like many resort destinations, had two different faces. The version you saw depended largely on who you were and when you arrived.

In the summer, Jade Acre was all exuberance and spectacle, nestled in a landscape so beautiful it exuded an air of magic just by virtue of existing. Downtown frothed with out-of-towners crowding into shops selling handmade candles or locally sourced honey. These were the seasons when their nearly homogeneous white town felt briefly cosmopolitan. Tourists came from all over, and for a handful of months you would hear every language, every accent, on the streets. There was a feeling of plenty in the air at all times, from the generous portions at the eateries to the towering soft-serves that swirled so high they leaned. The locals would wait on you and check you in and clean your mess while smiling with all their teeth.

And then, of course, there was the town's true face. When heat drained from the coast and gloom descended, the tourists departed all at once, leaving locals in their suddenly silent shops and bed-and-breakfasts.

This was the version Soojin saw now as she walked along downtown's sleepy Main Street. Aside from a few errant shoppers and a group of retirees chatting on a park bench, it was quiet. The colorfully decorated shops empty, the bored clerks tapping away on their phones.

It wasn't so much a town in decline as it was a place put on pause, stagnant until the next tourist season. Soojin had never really noticed it when she was younger, the creeping downtroddenness palpable during off-seasons as people tightened their belts, the way it could make locals mean and gossipy in a bitter attempt to stave off boredom.

But god, she still loved this place. Soojin loved the tight rows of Italianate buildings with their ornate carved cornices, the way their boxy shapes made Main Street resemble a row of colorfully painted teeth. She loved the string lights filling the pear trees with a rutilant glimmer, and the benches dedicated to locals long gone.

But mostly she loved the memories. The way so much of the scenic downtown had stayed the same, like a photograph, so she could easily transpose her family where they no longer could exist. Her mother picking the best apples from the barrels outside the grocery store. She and Mirae, children again, running to the candy store with their fistfuls of coins and emerging with a bag of handmade peppermint bark.

Soojin unearthed the thirteen dollars and four cents she'd gotten at the diner and looked up to where the candy store stood across the street. She went inside, said hello to the elderly clerk, who now always regarded her with sad eyes, and left with a bag of chocolate bark.

In the cold autumn afternoon, Soojin opened the paper bag, withdrew a piece, and snapped it in half. She remembered how she and Mirae would jokingly bicker for the larger piece, but Mirae would always end up taking the smaller one. The sisters would sit beneath the shade of a pear tree to let the chocolate melt on their tongues, giggling over nothing in particular.

Today, Soojin sat alone as she laid the chocolate on her tongue. At first she sensed nothing but a bright, powerful mintiness before it settled against the chocolate's bitter notes.

A lingering, somewhat earthy sweetness. She waited for delight to come, but her taste buds had changed: it no longer tasted good.

She sat there for just a while longer, the chocolate melting in the heat of her lap as she stared up at the pear tree's branches. The leaves were golden now, and losing hold, spinning in their slow return toward the earth.

The house was quiet when Soojin arrived. She was met by nothing but a recent text from her father: Left early for Bragg Hills. Please be good. As if she knew how. But she could try. She could go through the motions of being a good daughter.

Soojin texted back, I will. Have a good week.

She went to her father's room and folded his blankets neatly, tucking the duvet tight against the frame, the way he'd taught her for their bed-and-breakfast.

She did a load of laundry. Swept the floors. Furiously pruned the garden. In the rental cottages, she swept cobwebs from the awnings and beat the shit out of the dusty blankets. The frenzied busywork finished, she returned to the main home and stared dumbly at the wall, feeling a strange mounting in her chest until a starling struck the northern window and fell dead in her yard. She regarded its feathers, the exact sheen of an oil spill, and the unnatural angle of its neck, and did not bury it.

Golden hour came, then sunset. Mark had been texting her all day. Short, anxious missives: I'll stop by later after work, okay? You'll feel better if you talk to someone. She left him on read and went to the kitchen to fix herself a simple dinner of plain rice drowned in barley tea. All around her, the sound of her home's silence expanded, then released, like something breathing.

When the sun arced down, sinking the kitchen into gloom, she didn't bother with the lights, eating her dinner in near darkness because in that darkness she could recall the dinner table in better years: a kerosene portable grill in the center of the table while the four of them, her family, huddled around it. Her dad grilling pork belly with the serious look of someone filing taxes as her mom chaotically force-fed him lettuce wraps filled with more spicy peppers than he could handle. Mirae's quiet laughter when his face grew bright red. The TV on in the background as four different spoons scraped four separate bowls. It was loud and whole and happy until Soojin finished her meal and turned on the lights.

The delicate architecture of her imagination abandoned her all at once. She was alone in her kitchen with tears running down her face. When had she begun to cry?

Get it together, Soojin thought, wiping at her cheek. There was still work to be done. Dishes in the sink. She went to it, turned on the faucet to scalding, and picked up the first bowl. She yelped as soon as the water hit her hand.

She was bleeding again. The liquid bandage she'd spread over the cut had dissolved at some point in the day, and her skin was split wider and welling with blood. A sharp, pulsing pain. She pressed a finger over the wound.

"Dad," she called. Her blood dripped into a bowl, unfurling red in the milky dishwater. Her voice echoed up toward the kitchen rafters as she turned off the sink, waiting for footsteps to scuttle around the corner, first-aid kit in hand. And then she remembered. *He's gone.*

A cold lurch in her chest. She went to the bathroom, scrabbled for the first-aid kit behind the mirror. The cut was long but not especially deep: from the base of her thumb to the corner of her life line. But it stung when she wiped away the blood and smeared a coat of liquid bandage over it, alcohol singeing open flesh. She waited for the polymers to seal the wound, but they wouldn't. It was bleeding too much, seeping past the sealant and dribbling, diluted and astringent, down her palm.

"Shit," Soojin hissed to herself. "Fucking shit."

The pain was negligible now, the throbbing more of a dull pulse, but still a sob rose in her throat. All at once, she could put a name to the pressure that had been mounting on her all evening. Dread. This was going to be her entire year: five days straight of returning to an empty home. Quiet mornings and solitary dinners—and no one to come to her aid if she needed it.

Her reflection in the mirror was lonely, wild-eyed, and frightened.

She felt like a child. She *was* a child, and she wasn't ready for any of this.

Soojin kicked away from the bathroom mirror. Her phone was once again ringing in her pocket. She ignored it, running up to her bedroom and crashing against her desk. Milkis squeaked for her, snuffling her nose against the cage. Soojin barely heard it. She could think of only one thing.

She opened the drawer, leaving a smear of blood on the white handle. The tooth glinted when she brought it to the light. It was so small. So unassuming, the size of a pumpkin seed. And yet it was a universe. It could change everything.

Soojin held her sister's tooth and looked up, as if searching for guidance from a god, but saw instead only stars. Dull, green, plastic stars that could not glow without darkness. She searched them for answers, but heard only her sister's voice.

That one is north, so it can be Polaris. That one that's kind of half falling off, barely keeping it together—she'd pointed toward the star clinging on by a single filament of its adhesive—*I'll name that one after you, Soo. Oh, don't mope. We'll fix it in the morning.*

Fix it. Yes. Soojin could fix it. The roar in her ears mounted into a rushing tide as her feet carried her out of her room, down the stairs of her empty house, and out the door. And there it was: a future of her own design hurtling toward her. A better future. Hers. She need only bury her present first.

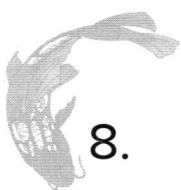

8.

The sky that night was unnaturally clear and flush with stars that glinted like fish scales in bright aquarium light. Soojin's breath erupted into small ghosts against the cold as she dug. When she was done, the air smelled pleasantly of soil, lush with possibility. She threw the tooth in the earth's wet divot, shoveled it over, and knelt.

She felt different than she had on the night she'd revived Milkis. Then, she'd been unsure, frightened she wouldn't succeed. But today there was a perfect, calm certainty. There was no way forward other than with her sister, and for this reason alone, she knew she would not fail. Why else would her family have been afflicted with such a gift if not to salvage her at precisely this moment?

"I'll open a way home for you, Mirae. Okay?" Soojin breathed. The woods fell silent all at once, as if they were listening. She slipped her hands into the dirt, clasping them around the milk tooth. "Come and find me."

The magic came on gently. The night sweetened and warmed, yielding to a kinder version of itself. Then Soojin felt it take hold in her fingers—a soft tingling. The earth went moist, then gathered into something pliant. An organ. She felt the inert wetness of it until it slowly began to throb. A heart. It must be. She felt it beating in the mud all alone before arteries began to branch out, creating its own life-giving lattice in the mud.

She felt no revulsion. Just the elevated skip of the heart that comes with anticipation. But Soojin wouldn't rush. She wanted to do this right.

She opened her eyes. The world looked so beautiful. So alive. The moon was an overbright crescent overhead. The trees swayed in the wind, and the earth beneath her knees had swollen and was undulating, like something yet to be born straining against the confines of its mother's interior heat. The choir of voices buzzed in her head. But today they sounded recessed, like bees buzzing behind a wall. *Alive,* she heard, but it was her own hopeful voice in her mind. *A life.* The magic felt as easy as breathing.

Distantly, Soojin was aware that it had begun to drizzle. Droplets struck the back of her neck. Her arms. But she couldn't focus on that now, because the body had fully formed beneath the earth. Soojin knew it because she felt skin, felt two hands clasping her wrists. An affirmation of *I'm here. I've come back to you. Now raise me up.*

Soojin felt euphoric and weightless. She couldn't, couldn't stop smiling. The earth opened. The buzzing of voices grew louder, an anonymous roar of all the women she had passed through to be here.

But through it all, a new voice pierced the elation.

Soojin, it called. A boy's voice. But who? And why did it sound so horrified?

"Soojin!"

She wanted to tell them there was no reason for horror. *None. Because look.*

Look.

Here she is.

Mark crashed to his knees.

"Soojin!" he gasped, shaking her shoulders. He'd meant to shout it, to wake her from whatever spell was making her glassy-eyed and unresponsive. But he couldn't. His breath came in short, labored bursts. The air near Soojin hurt. Physically but also inside, like a devouring grief that wasn't his own washing over him again and again.

And that was when he noticed it. Everything was wilting. The low-hanging branches and reaching ferns all around them had browned at their edges, sagged—a gradient of death with a girl at its center.

"Stop!" He shook her again. "Wake up."

But Soojin was awake, her eyes wide open and staring. He couldn't get her to budge. A viscous line of blood slid from her nose, and she murmured something he couldn't decipher.

Mark began to hear a strange sound then. A drum. No, a heartbeat strumming the air. Pure, unincorporated sound searching for a vessel.

The ground softened below them, heavy with the metallic

stench of afterbirth. It swallowed his knees. His hands. There was a slow up-down movement beneath them, like the ground itself was breathing. A whiteness glistened through the cracks in the topsoil.

Soojin murmured something again, and Mark drew close to hear her. Her breath was warm against his ear. She smelled like gunmetal and something salty and natal.

"Look." Her voice was weak and glad. "Here she is."

Her words sent a cold arrow of dread through him. He looked again at the pulsing earth. They had to leave.

They had to *leave.*

"Soojin, come on. Please," he gasped. The leaves above them began pelting down like hundreds of cicada husks, their descent a dead rain. He pulled her arm, jerking it out of the dirt. Her fingers were tangled in thin black tendrils. *Roots,* he thought, until he leaned in and saw instead—long dark hair. Coiled around her fingers, across her knuckles, looping like black bracelets on her wrists.

Disgust lanced him as he tore at the hair. It wouldn't give. If anything, it seemed to coil ever tighter, sentient and greedy.

Something white landed on his arm, interrupting him. He untangled his fingers from the hair and picked it up, rolled it on his palm. It was wet. *Hail?* he thought, before his mind caught up to him. No. It was a tooth. A tiny, perfect molar, glistening with spit and bloodied at the root as if freshly pulled. Unmistakably a child's tooth.

"Jesus," he gasped, throwing it aside in a panic. But more were falling. They pelted the ground like human hail, picking up moonlight in their descent. His vision hummed ivory as the topsoil finally parted.

A shoulder blade worked against mud, and then a scalp, pushing up, up, out of the earth. Breasts, torso, long black hair. The body emerged in a rush of warm groundwater.

Soojin called out to it, but the body didn't turn. Something was wrong. It was weeping, running filthy hands up and down the length of itself in disbelief. Its skin tinged gray, pulled taut over bloated meat. Bloodless lesions pockmarked the flesh, as if it had been nipped at by scavengers, then left to soak. A dark scrawl of veins spread a necrotic calligraphy up the length of its spine. Soojin pushed away from him.

That's not your sister, he thought as she crawled toward it, laughing or whimpering. He couldn't tell which. She embraced the body, oblivious of the dead swell, of the rot hastened by water. He let go. The ground rushed to meet him. And then an impenetrable dark.

Her hands sank in the mud. The whispers:

—Hold fast to the bird's neck, like this, to wring it. No pain. See how quick? Stop crying. A daughter must learn how to butcher— Told you, you mustn't. Now look what's become— Of the river. How fast it is after the rains! Tomorrow we will come with— A hand of thorns. It can't— Shh. It's alive now— Look. Look. My daughters—

Look.

Soojin looked.

Her sister. Her sister. Her sister.

Everything else was noise.

PART II

Revenant

In the long dark, I heard you calling. Through slumber and bone spell, I swam to your voice. The acres cleaved me, and I watched my name fall away like rain. When I arrived, the earth, like afterbirth, was slick with my blood. Sister, I am here as you willed it. Bid me now to wake.

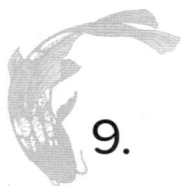

9.

Around its tenth death, the hen that used to be so docile grew vicious. Dying revised its mind, so when the girl pulled it from the failing ground, the bird knew instinctively to fight. Its legs pedaled the air; the red pinpricks of its eyes filled with vengeance.

Once, before she could break the hen's neck, it screeched so loud the neighboring villagers came running. The girl held its meager, wrung body behind her until, convinced by the lie that she had fallen and screamed, everyone dispersed.

After that, the girl stopped pulling the hen from the earth after bringing it back. Instead, when she felt its flesh regenerate at her coaxing, she withdrew her hands and pressed down. She imagined the bird opening its beak and drawing dirt rather than air. When the earth stopped moving, the bird having been smothered in the soil it had been resurrected in, she drew its limp body into the sunlight. When she cut off the head for soup, the inside of the throat would be ruined with dirt. She threw the bird in a pot of roiling water and foraged roots—giblets, cockscomb, and all.

A lean thing of mostly gristle, it did not offer much meat. But still, it sustained. The iron-rich viscera they reserved for their bedridden matriarch. The children sucked the soft cartilage off the feet, picking at each talon for the threads of muscles that held its shape. No food in a time of plenty had ever tasted as good.

I'm so sorry—we'd die without you, the girl said as she tilled the earth later, making space for a single severed wing, the bloodied feather lit white by moonlight. Her hands shook as she buried it. Bruises bloomed across her white palms, her body failing from the effort of keeping her family fed.

One day I'll let you go, she promised.

And then the familiar thrashing.

The world welcomed her back with sickness. Silt in her mouth and something writhing in the brand-new pillar of her throat, like a river parasite, searching for a way to burrow deeper. She opened her mouth, shoved her fingers in deep, and pressed until her reflexes came violently alive. No vomit, only a rush of frigid water vacated her, spilling down her naked thighs. Flecks of stone and algae, a small brood of damselfly larvae twitching hard from their sudden introduction to land.

Their gills strained, narrow bodies trembling in the air, seeking a way back to water. She watched them for a while before turning her face toward the direction of town. Not visible at this distance, but it was there. Past the trees and the winding back roads. Waiting. She felt a mounting, cold vexation, then turned her attention back to the insects on her thigh. One had expired already, curled over its quivering legs. The others still crawled, the wing buds on their thoraxes working back and forth in a futile imitation of flight.

If they'd been older, if they could have transformed into the damselflies they would eventually become, given time, they could have survived this. They could have unfolded their new wings and carried themselves elsewhere. But spit from the river too early, they had reached an end.

She watched them suck air into gills where there should have been only water. *Mercy*, she thought, crushing them beneath the heel of her palm. Their bodies left a streak of pulp on her thigh.

Soojin woke to the distant screech of coyotes. A dull light flickered beside her, and she tried to cringe away from it, throwing an arm haphazardly over her eyes. She remembered nothing. Not the source of this headache punishing the base of her skull. Not the sour taste in her mouth, or why she was in the woods, covered with desiccated leaves.

It was September. Early for the trees to bare themselves. So why . . .

The images barreled into her then: walking into the bitumen-dark woods, her path lit by the lantern she held. Coming to the clearing and digging on her hands and knees. Milk tooth in the dirt. An odd, euphoric weightlessness. Everything after that was blurry: faint etches of Mark's horror-bright eyes. And then—

She heaved herself up, searching wildly. The first thing she saw was her camping lantern. The failing bulb surged in and out, the radius of what it illuminated rapidly widening, then contracting, like an iris. Mark was beside her, looking pale and unwell. When the lamplight surged, she saw a shallow rupture in the ground, empty aside from a pool of muddy water at its base. It smelled strange. Salt and iron and something sweetly fetid like spoiled figs. Beyond that—only darkness.

"Mirae," she called, her voice scratchy from sleep and the cold. She tried again, and her voice rang in the perfect stillness of the clearing.

Silence. Not a single animal or insect rustled in the underbrush.

Had she imagined it? Her sister pulling herself beatifically from the ground, combing leaves from her hair with long, pale fingers. Soojin had embraced her. She remembered nothing that came after.

Her hands felt cold and searing all at once. There was a strange look to them: pruned, as if they'd been submerged for a long time in water. Straight black hair, much like her own, was threaded through her fingers.

Soojin doubled over, dry-heaving.

"God," she groaned when nothing came up. Tears burned in her eyes, and she pressed her gritty knuckles against her lids to keep them there. Crying would make the failure real. She rocked on her knees, muttering, "God. God. Goddamn it."

A warm pair of hands braced themselves against her, patting the nape of her neck. Mark had woken.

But no. His hands were callused from gardening and manual work. These were smooth. "*God?* Have you given in to Dad's nagging and decided to believe again? He must be happy."

Soojin pulled her hands away from her eyes. For a suspended moment she felt precisely nothing, her mind wiped clean from disbelief. And then it pummeled her at once. That voice. *That voice.* Shock seized her so hard it felt at first like terror, the hairs on the back of her neck rising. An instinctual desire to run from the unknown, until she remembered it wasn't the unknown at all. It was—

The presence behind her pulled back.

Soojin grabbed hold of one of the hands, lest its owner vanish, and spun on her heel.

A naked girl was balanced on her haunches behind her, long dark hair falling in hopeless tangles across her chest. Despite the chill in the air, she did not appear cold. Soojin could tell she had tried her best to brush herself off, but soil still clung to her skin in gritty streaks. Beneath the dirt, her skin was impossibly immaculate. Doll-like. Skin that hadn't been lived in yet.

Mirae.

Soojin's surroundings ceased to exist all at once. She could see nothing but her sister, the edges of her vision growing hazy—like a dream.

"Oh my god," Soojin breathed.

"Hi, you," Mirae said, smiling sheepishly. "Can I borrow your coat?"

In her wonder, Soojin hadn't paid mind to her sister's nakedness. She fumbled with the buttons. "Oh shit. Of course!"

She handed it over to her sister, who took it, pausing to tap Soojin's nose affectionately. "You look horrible," she said before buttoning the coat over her bare body.

Bewildered by the mundanity of the exchange, Soojin swiped at her face. Her sweater cuff came away flaked with dried blood and dirt. She vaguely remembered the taste of warm iron. The way she couldn't retract her hands from the earth to stop her nose from bleeding. When Mirae was done dressing, she dropped to her knees and held a hand to Soojin's forehead.

For a moment, Soojin felt like a child again—feverish and ten years old as an eleven-year-old Mirae tended to her. Some barely remembered sick day. A humidifier's soft hum by her bedside. Small hand against her brow. *It's coming down now, I think. You're past the worst of it.*

"How you feeling?" Mirae asked, concern written all over her face. Though her question was imprecise, Soojin understood what she was actually asking. Her sister was thinking of the stories their mother would tell. The warnings. But Mirae's hands were warm and steadying, and Soojin was better than fine. Anything at all could happen to the world and it would make no difference.

"Well, you don't have a fever, in any case," Mirae said before she noticed something else that filled her face with fresh worry. "Your hand!" she said, holding Soojin's left hand up.

The cut from breaking the coffeepot in the diner was still open, and sometime during the digging, it had widened. Grit and soil had embedded in it, staunching the blood. Soojin hardly felt it, because her sister was alive. Alive! Body and breath.

Mirae had just enough time to brace herself before Soojin barreled into her with such force they nearly toppled, and they held each other. As though fearing Mirae might disappear any minute. Soojin could do nothing but whimper, the rest of her language siphoned off by disbelief.

"Shh, it's okay," Mirae said, smoothing Soojin's hair. "I'm here. Stop crying."

Only then did Soojin realize that she was. She was a mess of tears and blood and dirt. She laughed, wiping her face to what she hoped was an approximation of clean. She'd never been happier. It didn't matter that the magic had left her feeling faded and weak. She was so happy she could die, she thought . . . just as a pair of hands pulled her violently from her sister.

Before she could say a word, Soojin was wrenched to her feet. Mark, awake at last, clutched her, his pupils blown wide. By the time she'd shaken off the surprise, he'd grabbed the lantern and they were out of the clearing and into the woods. Lamplight volleyed off the trees as they ran, making the world look stop-motion.

"Wait." She stumbled over a root and fell to her knees. Mark dragged her up and forced her into an unsteady canter. He was hurting her. "Wait!"

He barely seemed to register her voice as they sped toward her home. Some of the trees still had leaves clinging to them, saved by their distance from the resurrection. A sickly-looking bird watched their slow progression from above, tearing feathers from its shabby wings in jerky agitation.

"Hurry," he urged.

She dug in her heels, pulling herself from his grasp. "What's your problem!" she hissed. Her voice ricocheted into the woods, the sentence splintering against the trees to be fed back to her in pieces. She heard *problem, problem, problem.* The stricken bird above them took off in startled, lopsided flight.

Mark spun on his heel, looking at her like she'd sprouted a fifth limb. "What do you mean, what's my problem? I'm trying to save you!"

"*Save* me? From what? My sister?"

"That is *not* your sister, Soojin. Didn't you *see* it?"

The lantern sizzled and dimmed, plunging everything into a darkness that amplified sound. The two of them breathing, a coyote screaming somewhere in the east. A twig cracking like a chicken bone underfoot. Again, a sense of quiet unease threatened to intrude on Soojin, until Mark knocked his knee against the lantern and it fizzed on again.

"Of course I saw *her*," Soojin said. "I'm the one who brought her here. What's gotten into you?"

Mark opened his mouth to speak, but froze as the sound of footsteps rustled toward them. The carpet of dead leaves being trampled sounded like rain as Mirae emerged from the trees and stepped into the light. Barefoot and wild-haired and lovely.

"What's going on here?" Mirae asked. Despite how hard she'd been pushed aside, she didn't look angry. "You two keep arguing like that, you'll call down the whole town."

Mark's arms fell limply to his side as he took the girl in. He blinked rapidly, then crushed the heels of his palms to his eyes. When he finally pulled his hands back, his gaze looked faraway.

Mark stared, incapacitated, for a while before he spoke: "I don't . . . I—" He flinched when Mirae reached out to touch his shoulder. She retracted her hand. "I don't understand," he finished.

"You don't understand that you shoved my sister and dragged me halfway through the woods?"

Mirae stepped between them. "Soo, give him a break. He's in shock."

Soojin sighed and stepped back, assessing him. Mark did

indeed look shocked, his large brown eyes somehow overwhelmed and vacant all at once. But there was something else there too: a cord of animal terror that prickled the back of her neck. He kept shaking his head slowly, side to side.

"No, I know what I saw," he muttered. "You didn't look right."

"I'm sure I didn't look right—I was covered in mud," Mirae laughed. "Still am." She rubbed her throat.

"You were crying," he insisted. "You were touching your body and crying."

Mirae tilted her head to the side. Then, carefully, as if placating a child: "That didn't happen."

"It didn't," Soojin chimed in, remembering the brief sliver of time between the resurrection and unconsciousness. Her sister picking leaves from her hair, laughter, arms opening to draw her close. "You dreamed it."

"But I . . ." He looked again toward Mirae. Really looked at her, as if trying to superimpose a different image over her and failing. His shoulders finally slumped, whether in defeat or relief, Soojin couldn't tell. But when Mark spoke next, his voice was no longer accusatory. It sounded heavy with self-doubt.

"I guess I must have. Shit, I don't know what to say."

"You can apologize," Mirae said.

"Uh . . . sorry?"

"Apology accepted," Mirae said breezily. "Now, can we go home? We're gross. Also, I'm super naked and would like to not be."

A flush crawled up Mark's neck, as if he were just now registering that she wore nothing but a coat that barely fell past her pelvis.

As they made their way home, Mirae and Mark propping

Soojin up between them, the trees went from winter-bare back to Technicolor September. Burnished hues everywhere. Soojin hadn't even noticed how silent it had been in the dead clearing until they left its gray border. Leaves rustled in the wind; night birds sang from the silhouetted boughs. The canopy behind them stitched shut; the dead patch of woods disappeared like a secret.

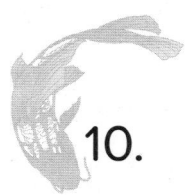

10.

That night, Soojin dreamed of wading into a river. The white dress she wore billowed against the current like surrender. In her hands was a brass bowl brimming with human teeth, and from shore Mark shouted at her, his hands outstretched, but from his mouth came only the sound of a thousand rats screeching.

When she looked back down to her hands, the brass bowl was gone, and from the water sprouted countless hands clenched into tiny white fists. The thin forearms waved like reeds in the water; their bleached skin had the same thorny quality as rose stems.

Dread prickled her as she waded through the legion of bone-white arms until one caught her eye. Unlike the others, which remained clenched, this fist was starting to unfurl. As it did, the fingers elongated, flattened, became the sepals around a cluster of petals. A perfect lotus, born from the thorny white palm of the drowned.

A dead hand is a hand of thorns, the dream whispered. She reached for it. The river surged.

Soojin woke feeling throttled. Sunlight filtered through the lattice of the curtains, dappling her face with gentle light. Even that felt like an assault. She groaned and pulled the blanket over her eyes before she remembered.

She nearly flung herself off the bed with how hard she threw the covers aside. Her vision whitened with light, and she steeled herself as her eyes adjusted, hands over her heart like a prayer.

And there she was: her sister, bathed fully in velvety sunlight. Mirae had popped the screen off the wide window overlooking the driveway. She straddled the sill as if it were a horse, humming as she ran a wide-tooth comb through her hair. She tossed loose strands into the wind, where they flared blue-black in the sun before being carried away toward the magnolia tree.

The sight was so blistering in its familiarity, it made Soojin's eyes burn. "Don't fall," she said, her voice hushed with wonder.

"Ah, good morning!" Mirae said, bracing her hand against the ledge so she could turn toward her sister without tipping straight out the window into the rosebushes below. "You were sleeping in later than usual. I was starting to worry."

"What time is it?" Soojin asked, scrabbling for the alarm clock. The red neon blazed 10:00 a.m. at her.

The night before, after washing away the blood and dirt, they had all tucked into an ungodly portion of instant spicy noodles, keeping the conversation jovial and light, mostly for Mark's benefit. Mark, who seemed the most shaken out of all of them and who eyed Mirae with something akin to uncertainty, no matter how he tried to laugh it off.

But once he left, the floodgates had opened. Soojin wasn't sure she'd ever cried like that, not even at the funeral. Her sister held her close as she whimpered various permutations of *I missed you* and *I can't fucking believe this* until dawn's tangerine light filled their window.

No wonder she had so badly overslept—that and the fact that her body felt as though every bone had been pulled from its socket and put back together again.

"I'm sorry. I knew you had school today, but I thought you should sleep your fill," Mirae said. She swung her left leg back into the room and popped the window screen in behind her.

Who cares? Soojin thought. School was the furthest thing from her mind. She flew to her sister. Mirae caught her, giggles muffled from the soft impact. Soojin let herself rest, face nestled in her sister's hair. The past eight months had been an uncanny dream. This was the world as it should be.

When they finally made their way to the kitchen, it was in chaos. A dirty stockpot was still in the sink, along with eggshells and eight torn packages of Shin noodles that she, Mirae, and Mark had burned through in one sitting. Soojin was still satiated from last night, but it was obvious that Mirae had eaten breakfast. A lot, by the look of it. A loaf of sourdough bread gone, along with a whole wedge of full-fat brie. The rice cooker, which had been full the night before, had also been half emptied.

"Don't judge me—I'm eating for the past several months."

Mirae winked, scooping the remaining rice for them both and topping it with eggs and soy sauce and scallions.

Soojin watched her sister as they ate. Her mannerisms were much unchanged: the way she held her hair back between spoonfuls and kicked her legs on the tall island stool. Rosy cheeks and bright, observant eyes—everything about Mirae was alive, alive, alive. But staying up all night to talk had made it obvious to Soojin that her sister was not back to normal quite yet.

In almost every salient way, she was the same. Her memory was immaculate. As if she'd simply woken from a nap, she still remembered the minutiae of the day she died. She recalled that the family had eaten blueberry pancakes for breakfast, and that their father had spilled orange juice across the counter, causing him to accidentally curse before slapping both hands across his own mouth in horror. How they'd laughed and laughed over it.

The weather had been fair enough for her to tie her cardigan around her waist when she left home for the last time.

All this, and yet she couldn't remember her name.

She remembered the names of all their classmates, but her own escaped her just moments after hearing it. Again and again.

"Mirae," Soojin called experimentally. Her sister scraped yolk across her rice, expression blank, and that was how Soojin knew the name had rolled off her like a bead of water. "Unnie," Soojin said, the Korean word for *big sister*.

At this, Mirae looked up. "Hmm?"

"I'd called your name," Soojin said quietly, watching how her sister's jaw tightened momentarily. "Still no, huh?"

A stiff, frustrated shake of the head.

"You just came back. Give it time," Soojin said. She was willing to be patient with this, to work on it as slowly and for however long Mirae needed. She ripped a page out of a notebook, wrote her sister's name in large, looping script—미래—and pressed it into her hand. "Just for the time being. Until it sticks," she said, curling Mirae's fingers around the paper.

Soojin looked at the wall clock. If she didn't get going soon, she'd miss school entirely. The last thing she wanted was for them to call her father.

"Unnie, I've got to go," Soojin said as she threw together her backpack. Once she was ready, she hesitated near the door. "Not that anyone has any reason to drop by on a weekday, but you know—you know that—"

"I can't be seen," Mirae interjected, laying a reassuring hand on Soojin's shoulder. "I know. I'll stay near the house, and at the first sound of someone coming, I'll run inside."

Soojin sighed in gratitude. They would work something out. They would. But for now this was the only way.

When Soojin pulled out of the driveway, Mirae followed her outside to tend to the garden, but mostly to lean her face toward the autumn sun. In the rearview mirror, Soojin watched her sister's form grow smaller, her hand held high and waving until they couldn't keep each other in sight. As soon as she turned onto the side street, Soojin immediately missed her.

Driving away, Soojin thought of the Korean expression her mother used to say while pinching their cheeks: *I could pierce my eyes with you and it wouldn't hurt.* Such violent tenderness. She rolled the windows down and let the crisp air strike her.

11.

Soojin arrived to school hours late, with her hair haphazardly thrown into a crooked ponytail and her eyes slightly swollen. Mark was surprised she'd shown up at all. She uttered a hasty apology to their math teacher and slipped into the seat beside his.

"Can I see your notes?" she whispered, holding out her injured hand. The one Mirae had washed and wrapped in gauze last night when they'd all returned from the woods. The sight of the neat bandages rattled him. Another reminder that what he'd witnessed had not been a fever dream. The teeth raining on the back of his neck. The twining filaments of black hair that writhed in the dirt like something alive.

"Mark?" she hissed, returning him to their classroom.

"Um. Yeah." He passed along his near-illegible scrawl. She took it and began furiously deciphering his handwriting, which she'd somehow always managed to do. She looked so normal to him. Her unbroken focus as she transcribed his notes and returned her attention to the teacher, who droned on about polynomials, scrawling what might as well have been hieroglyphics on the whiteboard.

Mark barely absorbed anything all class. His eyes constantly stole toward Soojin as she chewed the clicker of her pen and paid him no mind.

When the bell rang, he leaned in toward her, uttering a quiet "How are you?"

"I'm good. A little bloated from all that salt yesterday, but good," she replied with a small laugh, stuffing her pencil case into her bag. She was being so breezy, so casual. It made him feel crazy.

Mark knew that his experience of what happened last night was different from what Soojin saw. He knew for certain that what had crawled out of the ground had been more creature than girl. A swollen, gray thing that erupted from the earth with a surge of fetid, warm water.

And Soojin had gone to it, seeing only her sister. It drove him wild that he didn't know which was true.

"Well, see you later," Soojin said, pulling away. An anxiousness struck Mark: if she pulled away now, it would be for good. Now that she had her sister, would Soojin once again become an island? After the small steps they'd taken recently, that thought was unbearable.

"Wait. Um . . . ," he said, holding tentatively to her arm. She turned to look at him again. "Can I come over after school?" His mind felt clumsy, the way it often did when she placed the intensity of her attention entirely on him. "Just, um. I didn't understand what we learned today, and I thought maybe you could—"

"Okay," she said.

He hadn't expected her to agree so readily. He tripped over the velocity of his own words, dropping them with an exhale as they exited into the crushing light of the courtyard. It was overcast today, and somehow the thick skein of clouds made everything look saturated and overlit.

"But I want to make a stop at the bakery first," she added.

"Sure. What for?"

Soojin glanced around. They were alone. "I never got to celebrate her birthday," she said. The cool light strung silver in her hair. "Eighteen. Seems important, even belatedly. Don't you think?"

There was something about the way her wide brown eyes stared up at him that felt gently wrenching. He hadn't thought of how each milestone must have wounded her since Mirae died. The birthday, the holidays. The weekends marked with silence where there might have once been clamor. A lock of hair had fallen across Soojin's cheek, and without even realizing it, he reached to tuck it behind her ear, but he stalled. It had been too many years since he'd touched her with that sort of casual affection. He let his hand drop.

"Yeah," he said, a painful tenderness threatening to intrude. "I think so."

They chose a simple cake—fresh cream with glazed strawberries on top for garnish—and drove to the Han house separately. Mark arrived a few minutes after her and parked his car, but found Soojin hadn't gone inside yet. She was standing in the driveway, the cake box in her arms, looking up.

She didn't stir when he came to a stop beside her, and her expression was crushingly vivid. He followed her gaze. She was looking up toward her bedroom window. The light was on, and the curtain's gauzy lace billowed with interior movement. It struck Mark then that this was likely the first time in months she was coming home to her bedroom lit. Someone lounging on the bed opposite hers, ready to welcome her home.

"This is real," she said quietly. Only to herself. Then, as if needing affirmation, she turned to him. "Is this real?"

Suddenly his misgivings from last night, from this morning at school, felt vanishingly small. It didn't matter. Not when Soojin was here, brought nearly to tears by the simple sight of an illuminated window, the promise of a sister waiting within. It must have felt to her like she'd emerged from a long nightmare back to the threshold of her own life. He wanted to take her there. Back to happiness, that is.

"Come on. Cake isn't cutting itself," Mark said, offering an arm. To his surprise, she smiled, linked her arm in his, and dragged him to the door.

Inside, the home was warm and smelled heavily of food. The stereo in the living room was on, filling the halls with ambient lo-fi. Mirae, wearing an apron spattered dark with grease, popped her head from the kitchen.

"Welcome home," she said before offering Mark a smile. "Hey, you!"

Soojin put the box down on the kitchen island and followed her sister to where she was sweating over the stove.

"I'm making braised chicken," Mirae said, opening the Dutch oven. Inside, chicken thighs simmered with potatoes, glass noodles, and aromatic soy sauce made spicy with dried chilies. "You staying for dinner, Mark?"

"He is," Soojin answered for him while dragging Mirae to the island. "Come here for a bit."

"What the—hold on!" Mirae complained, waving saucy tongs in the air that dripped braising liquid everywhere. But she was laughing. Both sisters were. Euphoric and drunk on the fact of being alive.

Soojin opened the box and pulled out the cake. At some point in her car, it must have leaned, because one side had dented, the strawberry knocked off-center, leaving tracks in the perfect white cream. Soojin didn't pause to fret. She pressed in three long candles and struck a match.

"Happy birthday, Unnie!" she said. Mark backed away as the pot on the stove began to spit, and he turned down the flame. Then he hit the lights, plunging the kitchen into darkness, the candlelight the sole illumination.

At the island, Mirae was quiet. Then, taken aback, she said: "But my birthday is in June."

"I know," Soojin said, pushing the cake closer to her sister. "I couldn't celebrate with you in June. But here you are now. So let's celebrate."

In the darkness, Mark saw Mirae's hand reach out to touch her sister's face, tenderly, in unspoken gratitude. It was an affection he couldn't intrude on by looking. He let his gaze fall to the floor until he heard Soojin say: "Make a wish."

Mirae leaned in, deliberating for a long moment before she blew out the candles. Mark turned the lights back on as Soojin wiped a spot of cream on her sister's nose, leading to a brief, hysterical tussle that ended up with all their cheeks smeared with frosting. After, they didn't bother cutting the cake. They dug straight in with their forks, scraping even the cake base clean.

Later, drunk on sweetness and full from dinner, Soojin asked her sister what she'd wished for. They'd moved to the living room, where they now lay sprawled out on the shag rug, Milkis darting rambunctiously between the three of them. Mirae didn't answer right away, leaning her chin on her palm as her other hand flipped Milkis to tickle her soft belly. The rat made little chuffing noises, as if laughing.

By any measure, it was a beautiful moment. But as Mirae thought, Mark saw her expression slide into something strange. A quick glance toward the window, longing and bitterness as she looked out. He felt doused by it, but just as quickly as it came on, it was gone. Her lovely face turned placid once more, lit gold by the Edwardian lights.

"If I tell you," Mirae said, twining a lock of hair around her finger, smiling at her sister, "it won't come true."

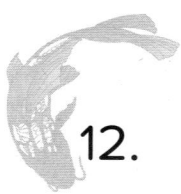

12.

She didn't know her name, but she knew she was alive. During the workweek, when Father was away, the days were long and beautiful. She and her sister would trawl the sun-drenched woods behind their home to forage burdock, chicory, elderberries as dark as a bird's eye. They baked cookies together and slept pressed nose to nose, hands clasped, like they used to when they were children.

On the weekends, when their father returned, Soojin locked her into one of the dollhouse cottages they rented out in the summers, and she spent her time watching the lazy sweeps of the ceiling fan, running her hands up and down the length of her new body. She reaccustomed herself to her throat, to her hair, black and long, just like her mother's. But not everything was the same. Her knees were now immaculate. The palimpsest of divots and cuts—all the myriad scars that assured her she was real—was gone.

She distracted herself from its loss the way she knew best. She dug through the cottage for things to eat at all hours of the day. Living made her ravenous. Soojin kept the cottage well stocked, but there was never enough. She went through boxes of pancake mix and jars of fruit reduction, chickens stuffed with glutinous rice and dates. She left not even bones behind, cracking them between her teeth for the spongy, congealed marrow inside—a habit she'd picked up from her mother, who had picked it up from her mother, who'd hailed from a lineage of hunger. She remembered the stories of the ancestor who ate of the marrow, just like this, before sending a single shard of bone back into the ground to harvest a new hen.

During idle moments, she studied the piece of paper with her name written on it in neat script: 미래. She repeated it aloud to herself over and over—*Mirae*—but she could only hear it for what it meant: *future.* There was no future for nameless things. But she wouldn't be nameless forever. She had to believe that. She kept the paper with her, slipped into her pocket like an amulet.

It didn't take long for restlessness to intrude. She paced the entirety of the cottage's measly four hundred square feet from end to end for hours at a time, thinking of everything beyond its walls she longed for but couldn't see. Her father. Her town. The streets she used to cruise through, giggling with friends, windows rolled down so her hand could dangle from the passenger-side window, skimming the wind.

On occasion she would risk everything, lifting the corner of the curtains to look out, and the sight of the world lit by the moon was so beautiful it made her milk tooth ache. She watched the home her father and sister slept in, trying to imagine herself in it, but even in daydreams she could only see herself slinking in corners so as not to be seen.

When Father went out one morning, she watched him, though she knew she shouldn't. He squinted, as if he'd caught a glimpse of two dark eyes gazing out from beneath the curtain's hem. She let the fabric fall and sank below the glass, one hand over her eyes and the other on her heart, listening to his footsteps move away from her.

Though much had changed since her first life, what hadn't in her second was that she lied. Or perhaps *lied* was the wrong word. She withheld.

This was the first truth she withheld from her sister: she could emerge from any body of water in their quiet little town. She need only visualize the place and will it. When she opened her eyes, she could be there. Water, she realized, having once killed her, now yielded to her persuasion.

She discovered the ability accidentally one day as Soojin ate dinner with their father, believing Mirae was safely locked away in the cottage for the weekend. While bathing, she nodded off, dreamed a waterlogged dream, and woke floating naked in the eastern cove, with abalone studding the crags below the surface. Her inert body bumped against a wall of rock like a docked boat, hair billowing its pitch-black sail all around her. The sky that night had been dappled with stars so bright it made her want to weep. It wasn't fair to be kept from the world in all its wounding awe. Despite her sister, she would belong to it again.

As soon as her father returned for the weekend and night descended, she sank her body in a cool bath in the cottage and left. Most times she emerged in prosaic places. A downtown fountain in the dead of night. Townsfolks' swimming pools, where she would lurk submerged up to her eyes, staring into the warmth of their houses. Her vision bathed in sickly green pool light as the figures beyond the windows talked and broke bread and touched one another's faces with love or, occasionally, violence.

And when it rained—she would soon discover—she could be anywhere.

With the last week of September came the first rain of her second life.

In her childhood bedroom, she waited for Soojin to fall asleep in the adjacent bed. When she heard her sister's breath deepen, the girl peeled back her own covers and stood, listening to the deluge interrogate the roof.

She crept downstairs, taking care to avoid the third step from the bottom, which she knew would creak. Then out the door and into the weather. She felt the edges of her vision tunnel as the water ferried her elsewhere, a door opened by rain. There was a moment where she was immaterial and vaporous before her body was returned to her in a rebecoming that felt like violence.

By the time she opened her eyes and unfolded herself from the downpour, she was standing at the town's edge beneath the failing light of a streetlamp. It flickered and surged in turn, casting the world in irregular, stop-motion light. A black Audi idled beneath the WELCOME TO JADE ACRE sign, which hadn't been updated since the population began declining in 2013. She knew who was in the car, even as the fogged windows rendered its interior an opaque gold.

Sitting in the passenger seat as he fiddled with the radio. They settled on the only station that didn't fill the car with static. Throwback songs from the 2000s, interspersed with peppy ads for a car dealership in Bragg Hills. They passed a joint between them, its ember eye igniting with each slow drag.

"Do you really have to go to these lengths?" he asked. A ziplock bag of roadkill tossed in the back: a chocolate-brown stoat reeking of ozone and masticated meat—too fresh for spoil.

"There's nothing I wouldn't do," she said.

The river staticked in her mind: omnipresent, calling her back from the past. She willed it silent until all she could hear was rain and the soft radio buzz escaping the parked car. Anticipation filled her.

This was the second truth she withheld from her sister: though she claimed death was a long, dreamless sleep, she remembered.

The night she died, her back hit the water and she was dragged under before she could scream. A pressure mounted in her ears; the current was so cold it felt like burning. She opened her mouth to gasp and pulled into her lungs only river. The dying was quick enough, her last thoughts an animal litany of *curse you curse you curse—* A bright light exploded across her vision, and then there was the sensation of cleaving. Mind from matter. Spirit from spit. Her life unspooled, and she watched herself hurtle downstream.

My body, she thought as she traveled as air in search of her own corpse. *My body.*

But the river didn't let her go far from where she fell. It tethered and unbraided her slowly. It eased her name away first, and like that it claimed her as its own. From miles away, she had the distant awareness of her body snagged across rocks in another town. Held in a morgue. Lifted into a crematory retort.

She palmed her throat, felt its fluttering pulse. Of what use was a body if not to seek redress? She would go to the others first, then come for him last. She watched her quarry's shadow undulate beyond the fogged glass. Above them the streetlamp flickered—

—then gave out.

"Piece-of-shit town," Bentley muttered as the strip of road outside his car plunged into darkness. The radio signal that had been fading in and out wavered until the voices of the hosts bled into one anonymous sizzle. Occasionally, a distinct word rose above the static. *Top Forty . . . calling in . . .*

Bentley turned the radio off. He'd idled at the side of the road long enough doing nothing in particular. It felt different doing nothing all alone. A year ago, he and Mirae would drive all the way out here to the city limits, away from prying eyes, just to kick their feet up on the dashboard and listen to music in this liminal border between towns that, outside tourist season, few crossed over. It was a nearly yearlong friendship experiment that began and ended in ruin.

In the beginning, their interactions were antagonistic at best. It was Soojin Han's fault they got off on the wrong foot. He was nine back then, to Mirae's unusually mature ten, and he'd swaddled the vulnerability of his newness the way he knew best: with demands.

Hey, you, he'd said at lunch one day. *Sit here.* He patted the seat next to him. His father was always muttering about the Han family with palpable agitation, and it made him curious, made him want to get closer to them to see what was so special. But he'd had simpler motivations too.

He was new in town. After his mom died of heart complications, his dad had cremated her quietly without a funeral, sold their apartment in the city, and within a couple of short months whisked them away with single-minded focus.

I know someone who can make this all go away, his father had said. He'd given him no time to say goodbye to his friends, his home. Still reeling from his mother's loss, Bentley had found himself on a plastic red bench in a bird-shit-speckled courtyard. He'd wanted Mirae to sit with him so he didn't have to once again eat by himself.

Did you not hear me? I said come here.

Mirae had halted, turning her perceptive eyes toward him. In that moment there was a clarity between them: she saw through his bravado. The way he sat alone in his expensive shirt in an elementary-school yard of tanbark and hopscotch chalk. He'd felt something like relief as she'd made to walk toward him.

Soojin, though, had not taken kindly to his orders. She'd stepped in front of Mirae, spitting out some insult he no longer remembered. So began the first brawl.

It wasn't until a couple of years later that he realized Soojin already had reason to hate him then—his family's arrival having been preceded by a bunch of virgin land being snatched up and slated for development that would eventually devastate her family's business.

And how was he supposed to approach the older sister with the younger one clinging like a thistle?

That was until the night he finally caught Mirae alone in the middle of the road not far from here and almost hit her with his car.

Bentley turned the heater on and watched the condensation's slow vanishing act across the glass. Outside, the wind whipped the trees, causing long shadows to shudder across the asphalt like spindly, reaching hands. Once again, his thoughts slouched helplessly toward the past.

They began ten months before he watched her tip into the river. By then he was sixteen, and both their mothers were dead. The night had been crisp and overcast, and though snow rarely stuck in Jade Acre, the distant mountains were capped in frost. He didn't remember why he'd been driving through the forest, though he remembered taking the roads too quickly, boredom thrusting him toward recklessness. He made a sharp turn around a bend and saw a white mound on the asphalt. Some stunned animal. He stepped on the brakes, tires wailing to a stop a few yards short of impact. The animal didn't scurry away, didn't move at all.

It was only then that he noticed the Toyota idling on the

shoulder. It was not a wolf on the road, but a girl in a pale coat crouched on her knees.

Anger hit him before relief could, and he stormed out of his car, slamming the door behind him.

"Do you have a death wish? I almost fucking hit you!" His breath sent white plumage into the cold. Only then did he realize who he was yelling at: Mirae Han. Her hair reflected white beneath his headlights.

"Well, congratulations." Her voice was curt, as if she hadn't just narrowly escaped being mowed over. Only the thinnest rattle of alarm gave her adrenaline away. "You didn't."

The girl hurriedly dropped what she held into a grocery bag, but not before Bentley glimpsed the matted fur of a severed squirrel's tail. Then he noticed the rest of the roadkill. Body and bone ground down from tires. A smear of fruit on the asphalt.

He couldn't help it then. He doubled over and gagged as she swept to her car.

"What the hell were you doing, you freak?" he moaned, wiping sweat from his lip. "That's fucking disgusting. Hey!"

But she'd driven away without any explanation, leaving him alone in the dark beside the illuminated welcome sign of a slowly dying town. A sign that now came into view as the fog dispersed from his windows. Nothing but a backpack in his passenger seat. Silence.

He tried the radio again. Static. Annoyed, he flipped off the volume and put the car into drive, adjusting his rearview mirror.

At the very corner of his view, Bentley thought he saw something reflected in the road behind him. Some pale form crouched on the ground, working meat off the pavement with fastidious hands. His heart skipped. He whipped around, searching the dim stretch of road through the rear windshield, but saw nothing. He waited for his pulse to still before he pulled his car from the road's shoulder and sped into the rain.

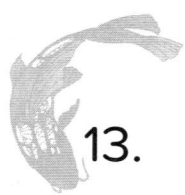

13.

Watching Mirae read with her legs kicked up against the headboard or fret over a pot of soup, Soojin found it impossible to believe anything was wrong. That mood bled into all aspects of her life. It was hard to be prickly when she was so delighted. At work she received more tips, citing her bright smile. At school people approached her, and, cautiously, she let them. She no longer ate alone at lunch, allowing herself to be added to Mark and Jay's tight duo.

Soojin was happy, and she did not regret it. But over two weeks had passed since Mirae's resurrection, and the euphoric haze was ebbing while the logistical aspects continued to compound.

The main thing that needled Soojin was her sister's growing restlessness. Mirae did her best to hide it, and the awe of simply being alive again had not faded. Mirae still delighted in things big and small: a perfectly drawn bath or the taste of a particularly ripe fig. But there was boredom now too. And yearning. Soojin often saw her sister staring out the window in the direction of their school, their town, knowing she had no place there anymore.

"So let's take her out, then," Mark said breezily. They were sitting at a table beneath the pear trees, the din of conversation and lockers slamming echoing across the small courtyard. Jay was absent, and she'd taken the veneer of normalcy with her.

"And risk being seen?" Soojin asked, looking down at her lunch box. Now that Mirae was back and bored to bits at home, her lunches were growing increasingly elaborate. Today she had purple rice threaded with millet and two soy-sauce eggs nestled on a bed of braised shishito peppers. She had no appetite for any of it. "I'm not looking to be accused of necromancy, thanks," she said. Mark winced at her phrasing, but it was true. Anything beyond the woods surrounding her home was dangerous.

"Well, she can't stay trapped in your house forever. She must be feeling pretty antsy," he said. As if Soojin didn't already understand that much deeper than he ever would. His earnest expression annoyed her. She could tell he meant for this conversation to be helpful in some way. It wasn't.

"I know," she said.

"This might work for right now, but I don't think you can expect her to hide indefinitely."

"I said I know!" she snapped, her voice cutting enough to reach an adjacent table. She began angrily chopping her egg with the edge of her fork so she didn't have to look at his kicked-puppy expression. They ate in silence for a while, or at least Mark ate while she shoved around the contents of her lunch box, then closed it after she'd turned them into uneaten mince.

Mark sighed. He peeled the rind off a clementine and

held out half as a peace offering. She took it but didn't eat it, the ripe segments warming in her palm.

"Soojin," Mark began slowly, as if knowing he shouldn't say what he was about to but just couldn't resist. It annoyed her now when he used her full first name. The rarity with which he called her anything but Soo made it sound accusatory by default. "What'll happen when you move out? When you go to college?"

Of course these things had occurred to her. Soojin had her materials ready to submit, and though applications were open now, something was grabbing her heels. It wasn't for a lack of confidence. She felt good about her chances of getting into at least one of the schools she was applying to . . . but what then? She would take Mirae with her—that was the vague plan. She'd smuggle her off to a city far away where no one knew her face and she could live out the duration of her well-earned life.

Soojin daydreamed sometimes about meeting between classes for coffee and walks along a pier. Hell, Soojin would even let Mirae drag her to a frat party or two if she wanted. Studying astronomy at UC San Diego had been Mirae's top choice—a dream which Soojin attributed to Mirae's interest in the mythos of celestial bodies rather than the actual science itself.

If she had lived, Soojin imagined, Mirae would be in San Diego now, already having dropped the major. *I had no idea I'd have to take so much damn physics!* Perhaps she'd be planning a year to study abroad and travel the world like she'd always fantasized. She didn't want her sister to forfeit that life. Mirae could still have it: San Diego, travel, freedom. Soojin would find a way to make it happen.

Still, when she gave herself even a moment to think about logistics, the dream ruptured. How would she smuggle her there without Father's notice? And even if she did manage it, how would Mirae live? On paper she was dead—had been for nearly a year now. Would she ever be able to rent an apartment for herself? Find a job that wasn't under the table? Have health insurance?

"I'll bring her with me. I don't know," Soojin said, avoiding Mark's eyes.

"I think you should tell your dad," he said gently, cautiously pressing her patience in a way he wouldn't have dared a month ago.

"No. Absolutely not." Soojin thought of her devout father, who had never approved of their magic. To disturb the dead, he'd say, was a sin. A manner of playing God. But Mom had loved Milkis, had loved having the ability to hear her own late mother's voice. And out of love for his wife, he'd conceded. Besides, rats and other creatures, in his mind, were innocuous enough to be excused. They didn't have a soul, or so he believed. But his daughter? His eldest and—whether he admitted it, even to himself—most loved? Soojin couldn't inflict that sort of trauma on him.

"I just don't think it's fair, Soo. To your family. Fair to you."

"Don't you think I know that?" she snapped, slamming her hand on the table. An open jug of water tipped over, spilling through the plastic lattice. People at the next table stared. Tactless though he was, Mark seldom fought with anyone, and she knew she looked the villain.

"Just let me be happy, Mark. You don't know what it's like." She felt entirely made of glass. "Let me have this."

Mark opened his mouth, then closed it. She could see him weighing his words against her hurt, and deciding his words were not worth it. He crumpled his sandwich bag in his hands.

The bell rang. Soojin stood, dropping her unwanted clementine half on the table. Her palm was sticky with juice as she packed her bags. A part of her knew she would be embarrassed about this tantrum later, but for now she felt only the self-assurance of incandescent anger. Just because Mark made fair points, just because he hadn't meant to hurt her, didn't mean she couldn't hate him a little.

He watched her wordless temper in silence. Soojin almost wished he would say something so she could snap at him again. He did not. But just as she turned to leave, his fingers grazed her, lightly enough that she mistook the touch for a brush of her backpack strap.

In a few broad steps he closed the gap between them. "Soo, wait," he said.

She thought he meant to apologize, but when she turned, rebuke ready on her lips, his eyes had regained some mischief.

"I have an idea. I'll come pick you both up tonight at four a.m. Be ready."

Soojin woke to complete darkness. Mirae was already up and dressed, peering out the window. In her pale knee-length coat, she looked like an apparition, her silhouette hazy. The moon lit her strangely, as if from inside, the lamp of her body radiating with faint blue light. Soojin rubbed her eyes to adjust to the gloom, and as they refocused, her sister looked normal again.

When they piled into Mark's car, Mirae sat in the passenger seat, while Soojin stared out the window in the back, watching the pines whip by in silence. Soojin felt Mark occasionally studying her through the rearview mirror, attention she refused to acknowledge. She was still annoyed and, petty or not, she wanted him to know it.

Mirae pressed her face against the glass, drinking in the familiar scenery: the ice cream parlor Father used to take them to when they brought home good grades, the park where people danced on sweltering summer nights, the florist shop where Mirae used to work part-time. Most everything was shuttered, the liquor store the sole beacon lighting up its street corner.

"Where are we going?" Mirae asked. The eagerness in her voice sent a pang of guilt through Soojin. She hadn't even considered this loophole to their secrecy. Under the cloak of early morning in a town as sleepy as theirs, the world could belong to Mirae again, however briefly.

The dim glow of downtown fled as they turned onto potholed roads that became at once rural again.

"That . . . ," he said, elongating the word for suspense, "is a secret."

The secret lived a short life. When they turned in to their school's front parking lot, Mirae gasped.

"No fucking way!" She shook his shoulder hard enough that the car veered momentarily onto the grass.

"Careful! I'm trying to drive here!" Mark said, looking pleased with himself.

As soon as they parked, Mirae shot out of the car. She jogged toward the entrance, looking up at the Frankensteinian campus she so loved.

Jade Acre Secondary was a slapdash facility cobbled together to accommodate a climbing population after the town's founding, and it showed in the architecture. The main building was a repurposed church, and it bore the stone arches, stained glass, and Gothic spires that hinted at its first life. When the student body grew larger, windowed trailers were dragged onto the premises for grades six through eight, each makeshift classroom painted with the school's green and silver. The gymnasium, science hall, and cafeteria were rectangular, gleaming, and modern—built within the last twenty years, when the town was still hopeful of its growth before the precipitous decline. Altogether, the campus was an architect's nightmare, all its disparate parts stitched together by heavy black gates.

"Hello, ugly, I missed you so much," Mirae said affectionately, running her hands along the steel bars. Soojin watched her sister's face flit between glee and yearning as she looked past the gate toward the courtyard dotted with tables and Bradford pear trees that reeked in spring but had the loveliest white blossoms. When Mirae turned to Mark, her eyes were shining. "Thank you."

He just smiled, then glanced toward Soojin, shooting her a surreptitious thumbs-up. The jolt of warmth that lanced through her was swift and powerful, the residual annoyance of that afternoon vanishing like smoke.

"Too bad we can't go in," Mirae said.

"Who says we can't?" Mark pulled a ring of keys from his pocket.

Soojin's jaw dropped. "Mark, where did you get that? Please don't tell me you stole it?"

"What? No way!" He slipped in the largest key and unlatched the gate. Predictably, no alarms went off. The locked gate was more of a formality. Unless someone was determined to pilfer the stained-glass rosette from the church-turned-classroom wing, there was nothing worth stealing in this school, and the whole town knew it.

"Jay gave it to me. Her mom's the custodian and loses her keys all the time, so she had a bunch of copies made. Don't tell anyone this, though, yeah? She'll get in trouble." Mark locked the gate behind them and walked into the open courtyard. Mirae made a beeline toward the table below the largest tree: the one she used to eat lunch at every day when the stink from the pear blossoms was bearable. Soojin and Mark lagged some ways behind, allowing Mirae a moment of private joy.

"What did you tell Jay to convince her to swipe these for you?" Soojin asked.

"I, uh—I told her I was going to bring a date here." His face flushed a furious red, visible even under only moonlight.

"Oh." Now would be the moment for Soojin to apologize for her disproportionate temper. Instead she chose the easier thing: nosiness. A sly smile tugged at her lips. "You've done that before?"

"Yeah. I mean, no. Not this, anyway," he said, gesturing vaguely toward Mirae, who was running her finger over her old table's familiar graffiti.

"Well, obviously," Soojin laughed. "So, who—"

"What are you guys doing?" Mirae's voice cut in.

Mark seemed thrilled to leave this conversation. "Nothing!" he answered, pushing Soojin forward. "Let's go!"

The three of them wandered from room to room. They broke into the cafeteria kitchen and became scavenging mice, sneaking as many cookies as they could without raising suspicion. In the gymnasium, still rife with the scent of floor polish and sweat, they raced up and down the bleachers. Mark shot hoops as Mirae tried and failed to do the same.

In their homeroom class, they watched tapes on the dinosaur of a TV that had sat neglected atop a dusty old wheel cart since the early aughts. Mirae sat at her old desk, her face a little uncanny beneath the flickering lights. The way the fluorescence held the features of her sister's face hostage didn't sit right with Soojin. She turned off the lights and they sat in silence before the blue television glow until drowsiness caught up to them.

"It's five a.m. I should drop you off," Mark said eventually, slipping his fingers through the blinds, peering out toward the parking lot. Dawn wouldn't come for another hour yet, but bakers and back-of-house diner staff would be readying for their opening shifts. The fewer people who saw Mark driving around town before dawn, the better.

They exited homeroom, careful to rearrange everything just as they had found it, but rather than head toward the building entrance, Mirae turned abruptly down a hall in the opposite direction.

"You're going the wrong way," Soojin called.

"I just want to see one last thing!" Mirae's voice grew thin as she vanished into the hallway's dark throat. Mark and Soojin turned toward each other with bewildered eyes, shrugged, and took off after her.

Mirae hadn't gone far. Soojin almost slammed into her, pedaling her arms to keep from toppling them both.

"What—" Soojin began before halting. Mirae was frozen, hadn't registered the near collision at all. In the complete dark,

Soojin couldn't see what had seized Mirae's attention until Mark switched his phone's flashlight on.

"Oh . . . ," Soojin breathed when her eyes adjusted to the sudden light.

They were standing in front of Mirae's locker. People had decorated it with photographs and drawings, stenciled her name against the dark blue metal in shimmering paint. There was a vase of wilted chrysanthemums and baby's breath at the foot of it. Soojin didn't know this memorial was still here. She almost never ventured down this hall. It was painful to see these demonstrations of mourning from people who moved on so quickly, even as her own life had been severed into halves.

Mirae withdrew a piece of paper from her pocket. The one Soojin had written her name on in large Korean letters. Mirae compared the script to the one stenciled in English on her locker, mouthed the round syllables. Soojin knew her sister would soon lose the phonemes of her name, but for now it was hers, and this locker was too.

"Unnie," Soojin said, touching her gently on the shoulder. Both she and Mark still only called Mirae *big sister* in Korean—*unnie* and *noona*, respectively—so as not to agitate her when she couldn't recognize herself.

"Sorry," Mirae said quietly. "I just needed to see it."

Mirae pressed her hand against the memorial. Everything about it was in various stages of vanishing: the chrysanthemums dropping petals by their feet, the stenciled REST IN PIECE, with the word *piece* struck through and *peace* written by hand underneath. The photographs, too, were faded, Mirae's smiling face bleached white by time. Eventually—probably once Soojin graduated—Jay's mother would come, click her tongue in pity, and take the memorial down. The locker would be assigned to someone new, and the collective memory of the school would move on.

"I think I remember the locker combo," Mirae said, and she did. When it opened, a small avalanche of paper fell against her. Eight months' worth of missives that had been slipped through the vent slits. She sank to the floor, trying to organize the letters into a neat stack.

"Mirae," Soojin said quietly, falling to eye level with her sister before she realized her misstep. Mirae didn't react immediately to her name—of course she didn't—and that failure once again to retain her identity seemed to send a bolt of alarm through her.

"I'm not here," Mirae muttered. A note slid from her fingers. She reached a stuttering hand for it, scattering more cards across the linoleum. "I can never have this again. I'm gone."

"No! No, you're not," Soojin insisted, rubbing circles along her sister's shoulders. "You're right here, see?"

Mirae bristled. "If everyone I've ever known says I'm gone, then I'm gone!" she snapped, her eyes feral. Soojin backed away, stunned by her sister's aggression. Mirae's hands reached up, crawling over the contours of her own face as if to ascertain she existed. "Oh my god," she muttered. "I can't—"

A sliver of sudden light moved across the lockers, above them, halting Mirae's words. Headlights. It filtered through the window facing the back lot, which had been completely dark until right that moment. The three of them stared at their own slim silhouettes gazing mutely back at them, elongating a slow crawl across the wall.

Mark cursed, turning off his flashlight and diving below the window. "We've got to go. Now!" he hissed.

Everything forgotten, the three of them leapt into action. Mirae kicked her locker shut while Soojin and Mark stuffed his backpack full of condolence letters. They dashed madly down the corridor, their footfalls echoing in the dark like dozens of hooves, a herd of deer leaping away from the eye of a gun. Soojin could see rather than hear the car come to a stop. The light that sliced across the lockers flickered off, plunging everything into darkness again. Outside, a door slammed. Then came the mechanical blip of a car locking.

They burst through the end of the hall, stumbling into the church atrium, which was now used as a meeting area, and dashed toward the heavy front doors, which led to the courtyard. Above them, the oculus watched their retreat, bathing their path in moonlight refracted pastel through the stained glass.

As they ran, all Soojin could think was *This is the end.* Her secret. Her sister. Her pulse pounded so hard in her ears, even the tendons of her neck trembled with the force of it. If they had been seen through the window, if someone gave chase . . .

"You three! Stop!" A voice rang out from behind.

Soojin stumbled, panic searing the periphery of her vision red as she recognized that voice. Joe Silas, the police chief. She'd know that scratchy low tenor anywhere. Of all the people in this town to come across them now, why, god, did it have to be him?

"I said wait!" Silas shouted.

Of course they couldn't. They pumped their legs faster, even as their lungs burned, finally bursting through the heavy doors and into the cool night air. The courtyard! The gate leading to the front lot wasn't far. They flew past the pear trees, past the classroom trailers and the boulder the upperclassmen painted with new murals every year. Hot glass dragged across Soojin's throat; she was flagging. Mirae turned back. "Hurry!" she hissed, grabbing her wrist and forcing her along.

Mark reached the gate, cursing as he fumbled with it before pulling it open. The sisters shot into the lot, continuing their stumble-dash toward the car, as Mark locked the gate behind him.

The front parking lot was still gloriously empty. Soojin chanced a quick glance back toward the building. The lights in the dark atrium they had fled through were now on, hazing the misty night in icy light. It was impossible to make out anything specific in the windows, but for a second Soojin caught a glimpse of a silhouette in one of the windows, undulating like a Rorschach, watching them.

Once they piled into the car, Mark tore away from the school so fast the sisters white-knuckled their seats. His tires squealed against the night, and then they were free of the parking lot. All of them panted, dazed and speechless as the trees whipped past them.

Only after they lost sight of the school behind them did Mark break the silence. "It's okay," he muttered. To the sisters, but mostly to himself. "It's okay. It's okay. I don't think they saw us." And then he was laughing. Low and incredulous, then pitching up. At first Soojin thought it hysteria, but quickly realized it was genuine mirth. He knocked his head against the headrest, laughing so hard the car drifted toward the median before he steered it back to the center of the lane. His voice was hoarse from lack of sleep, his face glistened with sweat, but he was beaming. "Fuck! That was close!" he shouted, as if they'd played a high-stakes game of cards and won.

Despite herself, Soojin laughed too; she didn't have a choice. She bent double until tears blurred the town into a glassy mirage. Even Mirae, her head nestled against Soojin's lap so as not to be seen through the window, was smiling. Whatever frightened agitation had seized her before was forgotten, if just momentarily. The dashboard screamed 5:20 a.m. at them in glowing red numbers.

The town was coming alive, the early-bird workers leaving to clock in for their shifts. Occasionally, headlights would blind her as they passed, and the blaze would stay imprinted in her vision like the ghost of a firework.

"I had no idea you were such an adrenaline junkie," Soojin said to Mark, watching the trees river into a continuous strip of green.

"Come on, Soo. Don't pretend like you didn't find that at least a little fun," Mirae said, smiling up at her. The returned milk tooth in the back of her mouth gave the impression of a gully there. A small white pellet embedded in the gum where an adult's molar should have been. Even so, the smile was familiar and warming. The unease Soojin had felt in the hallway disappeared.

Mark passed the teapot-shaped sign for Han's Bed & Breakfast and turned in to their driveway. Despite everything, they felt electric and happy, like they'd lived three exhilarating nights in a few hours. By the time they arrived, dawn was breaking lazily over the trees. There was no time for Mark and Soojin to fully go back to sleep—they would have to be back at school by eight a.m. sharp—but they dozed, the two of them on the living room rug as the night outside yielded slowly and effortfully to morning.

As darkness faded to the lapis of dawn, restaurant workers and farmhands across Jade Acre headed blearily for their twelve-hour workdays. Bakers entered their kitchens and fired up their ovens, the air growing misty with flour and heat.

Throughout the town's many gardens, evening primrose closed their coral petals to the sun as the morning glory opened. Crepuscular animals gnawed at the vegetable plots, foraging the choicest leaves until the people who'd planted them came out to send them scattering with a well-flung sandal, shouting, "Get out of there! Go on, git!"

It was a dawn in Jade Acre like any other, except for the police chief in the town's only secondary school. He stood before a vase of white chrysanthemums fallen on its side, the browning clusters of petals loosened from the sepals like singed parchment. He bent down to right the vase before the locker, his mind raucous with images of those three unidentified teens streaking down the hall away from him. Only one had turned to look back.

At a distance, her face had been a pale moon, black hair spun wild by wind. He could have sworn he saw the girl grin before she turned and vanished behind the gate. The cold knife of recognition had halted him just long enough for the kids to gain ground, and then they were gone.

But no. It wasn't possible he'd seen what his mind tried to

convince him he'd seen. His lack of sleep was getting to him. He rubbed his eyes, then pulled up his phone to flit through the pictures of the parked car's license plate. Putting his anxiety to rest would be easy. He'd run the plate through the system and find out who the three kids were. Reassuring himself of that, he shouldered his way out of the school.

Miles away, in the Han residence, Mark and Soojin slept downstairs as the girl knelt in her old bedroom, sorting through the notes they'd pilfered from her locker with rising agitation. Postcards. Pressed-flower bookmarks. A generic, mass-produced condolence card with a blond child lying in repose atop a cloud. *Heaven has gained another angel,* it said. She only felt like an angel in that she didn't feel real.

But then something caught her eye, and she tugged it from the pile: a Polaroid of herself, smiling in a yellow sundress. In the picture, her long hair was wet and plastered to her face, each finger on her outstretched hand capped with a raspberry. Even knowing her fate, she couldn't help but feel envious of the girl in this photograph, who contemplated which berry to eat first, unaware that within a year she would be dead. What a gift, to believe your life was a given.

The wide river she'd eventually die in coursed through the background of the Polaroid. In the foreground, a small streak whitened the corner of the frame: the suggestion of a finger held before the lens. Bentley's hand. She couldn't be free of the Porters, not the father or the son.

She crumpled the photo and yelped when a sharp edge

sliced her finger. Rather than blood, a brackish fluid wept from the wound. When she brought the cut to her lips, it tasted earthy with river silt and algae.

In the corner of the room, Milkis perched quiet in her cage. The animal would usually be pawing at the bars, asking to be let out to play, but now she was perfectly silent, her red eyes watchful until Mirae swung around to look. The animal scuttled toward its nest with an uncertain squeak.

A rushing sound filled the girl's ears then. The last sound she'd heard before she drowned: the river calling her. Calling her back. It sent a pulse of dread through her, and she folded over herself, crushing her palms against her ears, as if anything could drown out the sound. By the time it subsided, her hands were shaking. She left the room, drifting downstairs to where Soojin and Mark still slept. She looked down at her sister and brushed a strand of hair from her brow. Her touch left a benediction of dirt streaked on Soojin's skin.

14.

> Okay, so we've got trouble.

Mark had texted this to her two hours ago, but because of work, Soojin was only seeing it now. Knowing him, this could mean anything from *The school's taking pizza out of lunch rotation!* all the way up to a true catastrophe. Given that there were no follow-up texts, she was leaning toward the former. She sighed, wiping her hands on her IT'S COFFEE O'CLOCK apron and peering out from behind the register. Margaret was on break, but there was no telling when she might pop back into the diner to make sure Soojin was behaving.

Though perhaps today hiding was unnecessary. The diner was exceptionally quiet due to the sudden onset of rain. Only one booth was occupied: a young couple who kept feeding nickels into the mini jukebox at the table so that the staticky sound of Nancy Sinatra singing "These Boots Are Made for Walkin'" could muffle their argument. They'd been there for twenty minutes and had ordered nothing but coffee. Soojin had stopped going to their table a while ago, certain that soon enough one or both of them would throw down a few bucks and storm out in a huff.

She could risk a few moments on the phone. She ducked behind the bead curtain leading to the kitchen, where a cook was sitting on a crate of potatoes, prying mud from the grooves of his sneakers with a spatula's edge.

"What?" he said when she grimaced at him. "I'm going to wash it." With that he slipped a cigarette between his teeth and headed for the back door. Once she was alone in the kitchen, Soojin called Mark. He picked up in one ring.

"I'm at work; this better be good," she said in lieu of *hello*.

"It's not. It's very bad, actually," Mark said. He was muttering. Soojin could hear the familiar chaos of his parents' voices in the background. Then footsteps and a click as he entered a different room and locked it behind him. "Like, very, very not good."

"Get to the point faster, Moon," Soojin said, eyeing the dining room through the swaying beads. As she'd thought, the girl at booth nine stormed out, leaving the guy cradling his coffee despondently. He'd likely not need anything from her anytime soon except privacy.

"I got called into the guidance counselor's office today during seventh period."

"Oh no, call the cops," she deadpanned.

He cleared his throat. "Well, yeah . . . that's kind of the problem. I thought it was about the appointment I requested about trade-school information, but when I went, it wasn't Mr. Gerrard in the office. It was Chief Silas."

Soojin nearly dropped her phone.

"*What?*"

"Apparently he came across my car parked in the front lot early this morning during his patrol. He took a picture of my license plate before coming to try and find us. That's how he knew it was me. He ran the plate through the system after we ran away."

"Shit. What did he say?"

"He wanted to know who I was with."

"And?"

"He said it would be just between us, but I told him I didn't want to say. Then he threatened to get my mom involved if I didn't, so . . ."

"So you *told* him?"

"Come on, Soo. I had no choice. If my mom got involved, you know she'd sleuth until she landed on you anyway. And then she'd tell your dad."

As angry as she was, Soojin knew Mark was right. Being caught trespassing at night by the police chief was bad, but being ratted out to their parents would be infinitely worse. Though that did beg the question of why Silas was willing to keep it between them in the first place.

"And that's not all. He asked for the identity of the third person I was with."

Soojin's pulse quickened.

"What did you say?"

"I said there *was* no third person. That he was seeing things."

"Mark, that's so suspicious. You didn't think to say . . . I don't know. That a cousin was visiting from out of town or something?"

"I panicked, okay? I'm sorry." He sighed heavily into the

receiver, but when he spoke again, he sounded a little impressed. "That does make a lot more sense than what I told him, though. You're really fast on your feet, aren't you?"

"Yes, I'm a great liar. I do it all the time," she grumbled as the bell hanging above the diner door jangled. Wonderful. She was utterly rattled and not ready to be bossed around. She groaned. "Listen. I've got to go. Talk later." She hung up without waiting for his response and returned to the dining room.

"Welcome to . . ." The words died in her throat.

"Usual counter spot is fine for me," Silas said, closing his umbrella and taking the corner seat facing the kitchen window.

Crap, she thought, though by some miracle managed to say instead: "The usual?"

He nodded and Soojin turned to punch an order of a California scramble and coffee into the POS with unsteady hands. Even considering everything, she shouldn't have felt so jarred to see him. Silas came to the diner nearly every day. But the way he was regarding her with such rapt attention was prickling her neck.

She poured coffee into a chipped mug and pushed it toward him, intent on making her escape to check on the dumped boy in booth nine whether he liked it or not.

Instead Silas halted her. "Did you have a fun romp through campus this morning? I always figured kids your age couldn't be paid to spend more time in school than necessary. To think you'd trespass for it. It must be true what they say about your people and studiousness."

Well, damn, he wasted no time. She dried her hands on a rag and chanced a glance at him. He was staring at her with those piercing blue eyes of his.

"Am I in trouble?" she asked, choosing to ignore his racist dig. The sound of sizzling carried from the kitchen.

He took a packet of Splenda from the sugar tureen and slapped it on the counter, making her jump.

"You should really replace these more often. The granules are starting to stiffen," he said, ripping the packet and pouring the fake sugar into his coffee. She knew full well those were brand-new; he just wanted to startle her. "No, Sue-jean, you aren't in trouble," he continued. "Though I was considering reporting you to the school for stealing when I saw you'd opened a locker. Did you and that Moon boy even notice you'd left a little trail of notes behind you as you ran? Like Hansel and Gretel."

"We weren't there to steal," Soojin said quietly as the boy at booth nine finally got up, threw a few bucks on his table, and shuffled out. She felt an irrational desire to call out to him to stay. She didn't want to be left alone with Silas.

"I wouldn't have believed you if I didn't pick up some of the notes you dropped." He pulled a sheaf of paper from his shirt pocket. Soojin saw Mirae's name scrawled across it in pink marker and felt the desire to rip it from the man's hands. "I suppose it isn't stealing if the contents of the locker belonged to your late sister. But I do have to wonder why you waited until night to collect? If you knew her combination, why not just drop by during school instead of breaking in during the witching hours like you mustn't be seen?"

"Are you going to tell my dad?" she asked, trying to divert his question with one of her own. He didn't fall for it.

"Answer the question, Sue-jean."

She looked down, hyperaware of her hands. She tried not to

fidget, lest she give away her nervousness. "I couldn't take things out of Mirae's locker during school because people would see me. I don't want them to think I'm taking what doesn't belong to me. Everyone already thinks I'm weird enough," she said. To her horror, her eyes grew warm with unshed tears. To his credit or discredit, Silas seemed unmoved.

"You could have asked the janitor to collect them for you. There were other ways than breaking and entering."

"I wasn't thinking."

A bell rang out from the kitchen as a steaming plate was tossed onto the window. She was frozen in place, though, pinned under the vivisection of the police chief's blue eyes. "I believe that the Moon boy wasn't thinking; he's never been the brightest," he said, and Soojin felt a rush of anger—what the hell did he know about Mark? "But I don't believe for a second that *you* weren't thinking."

The bell rang out again from the kitchen, impatient.

"Since as far as I could tell, nothing else in the school was disturbed, I'm going to keep this a secret from your father." He paused. Soojin could see on his face he was clearly expecting to be thanked. She didn't oblige, and his expression hardened. "But don't let me catch you snooping ever again. I'd hate for something to happen to you in the devil's hours when no one's around."

The bell rang out again, twice in quick succession.

"Food's getting cold now—you best bring it here," Silas said, and with that she was released from whatever fetters held her fast. She stumbled to the window and picked up the plate of eggs. She dropped it in front of him with a loud clatter, too rattled for grace.

"Need anything else?" she asked.

"A refill."

Mechanically, she tipped her pot toward his cup, a bit splashing over the rim as she overfilled it. Just as she was about to walk away, he called out to her again. "Sue-jean," he said. "Who was the third person with you at school?"

There was a change in his voice. An imperceptible shift into something akin to worry. Was she imagining it?

She turned, arranging her face into the most placid mask she could muster. "There was no third person," she said with finality as she pushed away from the counter.

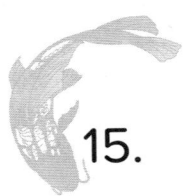

15.

Joe Silas's life was unexceptional in every way. Like his father before him, he was a cop, but in a town like Jade Acre, his every day was filled with monotonous nothings: parking violations, the occasional domestic dispute, slow-moving cars during peak season with drivers he plain old didn't like the look of, teenagers who stumbled the streets after one too many drinks. It was hard to say he disliked his life, though it was fair to claim he'd wanted more. He heard stories from his buddies in more eventful precincts and envied them. To command fear rather than the simmering disregard he received in this town—that was the fantasy.

But at least he was close to retiring, though he imagined he'd live much the same life he did now. Old habits die hard. He'd still go to the same diner every day for a California scramble and coffee made chemical by too much Splenda. He'd still cruise around town in his beat-up old Ford and nose himself into all the kids' business. Still drift in and out of his house with nary a word to his wife. He'd still lean on the drink a little too heavily, like now.

He'd meant to go to sleep tonight without a nightcap, but he'd caved, and as soon as he was done with the two allotted drinks, he was on the prowl for more. It was the events of the early morning that had rattled him. He was certain—absolutely certain—that he'd seen three kids streaking through the school grounds. A third face turning back, cleaving into a wide smile. He shuddered. It wouldn't be the first time his imagination had gotten the best of him. Guilt could do that to a person, even if he himself had done no harm to anyone.

Silas shouldered his way out of the liquor store with a paper bag of gin and a Snickers tucked beneath his arm. This rickety old building on the dimly lit outskirts of town was the only place other than the gas station where folks could shop for anything after ten p.m. He fished for his car key, cursing as it slipped into a puddle at his feet. His back, misaligned by a bungled chiropractic visit, hurt too much to bend, so he sank into a ballerina's plié to pick it up, legs buckling into a graceless diamond. He scooped the key ring with his pinky, then grunted back up again.

When he did, a bleary smudge appeared before him. His vision obscured by water, it took him a while to realize that the dark figure below the flickering light of the streetlamp was not a shadow, but a girl. There was nothing but a thin long-sleeved dress between her and the frigid night, but she made no move toward shelter. Her long black hair was plastered to her back like dark veins; the rain made the edges of her form look frayed and agitated. Like static.

"Who's there?" he called. The girl didn't answer, didn't

acknowledge him at all. *Damn kids,* he thought, turning toward his car before halting. His nosiness got the better of him. All his decades of attempting to impose curfews on teenagers who scattered when his flashlight swept the playground, only to reconvene in the woods with their joints and bags of sugar-laden Franzia. Up to no good, this girl. He could feel it. "What are you doing here, young lady?"

He walked toward her. He'd been drinking, but he wasn't so far gone he couldn't pry. *Can't mind his own business*—that was what the town whispered. If only they knew. He was an expert at keeping his nose out of business if it suited him.

The rain pelting the dome of his wide umbrella sounded like thunder. He laid a hand on her shoulder and had just a moment to think her body unnaturally cold before she turned to face him.

"Sue-jean?" He couldn't control the unfriendly tone in his voice. He didn't like them—her or any of the Hans, that cursed Korean family in the woods with their misfortune of girls. He didn't like what they'd made of him. And he didn't like the way she looked at him now.

"That's not my name," the girl said in an offhand way. Her eyes swept his face as if in search of a different answer. The streetlamp, cursed thing, failed for a moment and sunk them both into darkness. In the shadows, her face looked briefly bloated and gray, eyes cavernous as if eaten out by fish. An animal sound ripped itself from him. He stumbled back, and his umbrella clattered to the ground, where it immediately began collecting rain in its upturned basin. He wiped water from his eyes and willed himself to look. The light had shuddered back on, and her face was at once whole again. A cold, uncanny beauty, her skin so immaculate it was disgusting.

"You've been asking after me," she said. "So here I am." She stepped out of the lamplight and toward him. "Who am I?" Her emphatic tone was strange, as if imploring him to name her.

He took a step back. Then another. His drink-frazzled mind moved slower than his body, but when the impossible finally dawned on him, his vision collapsed around her image.

"Mirae Han?" His voice came out a whisper. She smiled happily at the hushed whimper of her name. *Oh god—ghost.* She reached. He was not a man of any faith. He believed in neither God nor inherent goodness. But he did believe in the prey-animal instincts of the body. He did believe in retribution, come for him at last.

And hadn't it been raining hard that night too? An image of an upturned car flashed in his mind. Rainy asphalt, the dark trails left behind by tires trying and failing to skid to a stop. And many years after that, a boy in the passenger seat of his patrol car, shoulders shaking and darkened by rain. *She fell. Oh my god. Please,* the boy had said, sobbing so hard Silas had had the urge to strike some composure into him. *Young men shouldn't cry,* he'd thought.

He didn't cry as Mirae eyed him, though a warmth spread across his lap and down his thighs. The bag of gin fell from his arm, shattering on the concrete below. He turned to run but could only manage a hobble. He tripped, skidding his palms on gravel before righting himself and fleeing toward the liquor store's honeyed light.

As the door grew closer, he had this feeling of running toward his own prosaic life. The diner, the wife he hadn't kissed in a decade, the small blessing of a perfect, dusty apricot bought from the back of a farmer's truck. He loved this life, he realized at the age of sixty-one. He might not have deserved to after what he'd let happen, but heaven forgive him, he loved it.

The liquor store's handle hovered within reach. He had the vague notion that once he made it inside, where the bored clerk was stocking cans of soup beside the Bloody Mary mixes, she wouldn't follow him. His fingers grazed the cool metal. Just long enough to think, *Safety!* before cold hands clamped around his wrist and brought him to heel.

He felt a shock of pain where her skin met his: a needle slipped through sinew—siphon and barb. Then came a numbness as she dragged him back into the shadows, saying, "Shh, shh," like she was laying down a fretting child.

Silas sank to his knees. He felt an uncomfortable probing in his mind, like ghostly fingers rummaging inside his head. His memories, every singular moment that made him who he was. Then, like an extraction, he felt these things begin to leave him. Gone, gone, all of it. *Shh.* His daily pleasures and frustrations. His shame.

He felt the girl bleed into him, edging out his mind. He couldn't remember her name. He couldn't remember his, either. In the end there was only this thought, cresting over him again and again: He was guilty. He was guilty and would finally pay.

The man's mind opened and she entered. The possession was easy. The human body, after all, is only water, a quivering ecosystem of blood and piss and spit. First she touched *on*, then *into* him, her body becoming vaporous as she sank into his failing meat. Just like that, she was Joe Silas—or at least she made a vessel of his body. Unfurled her mind into his.

At first it was a useless collage of image and sound she rifled through. She heard his nasal voice ordering a beer at the clam shack by the shore. She saw flashes of a girl—his daughter—lifting a caramel apple to her sticky lips, and her heart flooded with such love for this foreign face, it nearly destroyed her. Bare feet in the sand as the tides dragged lazily over them. She felt his discontent at how many years had elapsed since his daughter, an adult now, visited home or even called. But then another scene rose above the static and she followed it.

Silas's idle thoughts told her what year it was. She tasted bitter coffee grounds in his mouth as he started the engine of his patrol car. She studied the rearview mirror as his milky-blue irises studied her back. His hair had been fuller then, his body younger and less broken down by arthritis. She saw through his eyes as they maneuvered his car through the sleepy Jade Acre of seven years past.

And then they were one.

They turned slowly through the town, hoping to bust troublemakers, but found none. A boring day like all other days.

But what was this? Two cars glimpsed on the periphery of their vision, tearing away from the edge of town and into the seldom-traversed wooded backstreets—one giving chase to the other. Illegal street racing, they thought. They clicked the beacon lights on and followed. Red and blue swept their vision, cascading into bright strips on the rain-wet roads.

Just when they figured they'd lost the cars, the sight of tire marks blackening the asphalt caught their eye. They veered off the road toward the gully below. Wrecked guardrail. A car had slid straight off, into the ravine. They pulled over, leaving the headlights shining on the scene. A second car idled right beside where the guardrail had ruptured. As luxe as it was, it was instantly identifiable. In their town of pickup trucks and secondhand heaps, this sleek model could only belong to one family.

In the gully below, sunk in the piles of leaves beaten to mulch by rain, was a gray Honda, steaming in the night like an injured mare. A bloodied hand pressed against the spider-webbed window, then fell slowly out of sight.

Christopher Porter stood at the edge of the ravine, peering down at the wreckage below. Porter, who was new to town, who had shown up only a year ago with his spoiled, miserable slip of a child to slowly cannibalize the entire room-and-board industry. Tall and cold—his face betrayed no horror at the accident he surveyed. He turned and said to them, "Good evening, Chief."

From below came a popping noise, and they scuttled to the edge of the ravine, where Porter was standing. Effortlessly, the door of the car unlatched and opened. A woman's raw voice called out for help. Alive! Whoever it was could still be saved! They reached into their pocket for their radio, but a hand on their arm stopped them. Porter's watch glinted in the moonlight as he pushed their radio hand down.

His face was merciless. Porter didn't want help to come. *I didn't mean to run her off the road. I merely wanted to talk,* Porter explained. And then came the arrangement made iron by money.

But why, then, did he not want them to save her? There was something like hatred in his face. Whoever was maimed in the gully had wronged Porter somehow, and he wanted her dead for it.

They knew, and yet . . .

They thought of their debts, their daughter's untenable liberal arts college tuition. They were greedy and, yes, intimidated. They convinced themselves that the person in the car below was near dead already. How totaled the car looked! The windows streaked with blood. No matter how quickly the paramedics took the roads, she'd be gone by the time help came. Why not profit? It wasn't as if Porter had laid a knife across someone's throat. A simple accident. Never mind why he'd been chasing her in the first place. Never mind his intentional obstruction of rescue or the vindictive look in his eyes. They accepted Porter's proposition and called no one to the scene.

That was enough. She had seen all that she'd needed to. She threw off her plural cloak and became once again her own person. She pushed away from the body she inhabited, pressing against the boundary of Silas's memory. Miraculously, the memory gave—let her rise away, spectral, to witness the scene from above. She didn't care *how* this was possible, only that it *was* possible. Joe Silas shook Christopher Porter's hand below her, and, lower still, in the gully, the wrecked car lay belly-up. She went to it. Even in her incorporeal state, the scent of gasoline and spoiling leaves was everywhere. She peered through the window, and there she was.

Mom, she thought. *Mom.*

Her mother's face was mangled—black fractals blooming over her temples. Impact had burst her capillaries, and the whites of her eyes were blotted with blood. A fracture somewhere on her scalp sent a curtain of red across the left side of her face.

But she was alive.

She was alive and help was not coming, would not come for nearly another hour, when a trucker happened upon the burst guardrail and called 911. Above them, the slow lighthouse sweep of the police beacon vanished. Silas and Porter got into their cars and drove away.

Against logic, she tried again to speak to her mother. She thought, *Mom, please.*

Her mother's listless eyes snapped up, tracking the night air. "Who's there?" Her voice had the viscous, wet quality of a collapsed lung. Then, like a miracle, she breathed, "Mirae?"

She thought she saw her mother's eyes find her, but it was a trick of the light. Her mother saw nothing, her eyes forever searching for the ghost of her eldest daughter in the dark.

Don't go, she thought. Her mom was years gone already. But god, she'd do anything to change the inevitable. She'd beg and scream if it would make any difference at all.

Please stay with me.

But the rattle of her mother's breath was already slowing, the blood pumping through the chambers of her heart sluggish, irregular. She could hear it, the water-ruled systems of the body failing. Hurtling swiftly from a full life into the memory of a life.

There was nothing she wouldn't do to unclasp the seat belt that lacerated her mother's chest. To lay her down on her side to ease her breathing and stroke her cheek the way her mother did for her when she was ill or sad or needed reassurance she was loved.

Listen. I love you, she thought, hating her incorporeal self. She was without body, without hands, without any means of offering comfort, but she imagined otherwise. She imagined herself made of flesh and blood again, brushing a strand of hair from her mother's torn brow. Wiping away the blood cutting red rivulets down her cheek until she was as clean as morning. So clean that she might unbuckle herself from this wreck and walk out into the rain unscathed.

A sudden breeze picked up outside, gusting through the crushed window of the car. It sent loose receipts spiraling into the air and whipped her mother's hair into a wild black halo. Her mother seemed to lean her cheek into it, as if toward the touch of someone familiar. The wind swirled once, then tapered off, letting go of her mother's hair and the tousled detritus of leaves. When the evidence of the disturbance settled, her mother's face had gone strangely soporific. A soft exhale of breath.

It took nearly twenty minutes for her to pass. An owl mourned from the trees, another agitation of wind; then all was silent.

She stayed until her mother's eyes grew rheumy. She stayed until the last of her warmth fled and the condensation of her body's dying heat receded from the glass and the shrill siren of an ambulance come too late pierced the night. Then she left, traveling unincorporated through their shared past until she came upon her home.

It looked warm in the dark, and when she sank into its walls, it smelled of honey and scorched grain. Their father—younger, happier—hummed at the stove. Sick with fever though he was, he refused to stay in bed. He lifted a flat sheet of browned rice from the bottom of a pot, cracked the crispy disc into shards, and drizzled it with honey. She followed him unseen into the living room, where he laid the plate before his daughters, then peered out the window for the headlights that would never again turn in to the driveway.

Her eleven-year-old self sat on the carpet beside a stack of schoolbooks. Soojin was belly down beside her, petulant over a math problem she couldn't solve. Neither knew their mother had died just fifteen minutes from home. Her younger self didn't know this was her last day to be a child. Soon the wreck would be found, and everything would change.

Time sped up. The phone rang. She watched her dad pick it up. Say, "Yes, this is he. Yes. Yes. What?" His body doubled over the kitchen island. A slow folding. She didn't want to relive this. She let the memory grow dim. The living room dilated like an eye until she could see only herself. Her young body closed the book, looked over her shoulder to her father with a concerned expression, then opened the book again, brow unfurrowed. The moment suspended, looping. Unable to go on. She would never learn of loss, and thus would never be lost.

Stay here, she wanted to say to herself, but she had no mouth. It was all disappearing. The memory collapsed around the edges until she was once again in her cursed present, in the damp dark of the liquor-store parking lot.

She looked down at the bony hands of the body she still inhabited, the dusting of freckles on his knuckles. Silas's car key dangled from his finger. She could feel the strain her possession put on his body. With each minute she held him, his lungs filled ever so slightly more with water. It would be too kind a way to go after what he'd let happen. Rage had constricted her vision to a single dark aperture. She would make him drive into the rain-bloated river and hold him there as the heavy machinery of his car filled to the ceiling with water. Only at the last minute would she let him go.

She turned, Silas's key in hand, just as a set of headlights veered in to the liquor-store parking lot and blinded her.

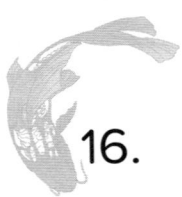

16.

For a year, the girl's family survived off the revenant hen's body, slaughtering, reviving, slaughtering it again. Then, as if the gift's limit had come at last, sickness befell the entire family. It came for the girl first. Her nose bled often, and her palms grew overrun with boils that burst, covering her hands in an oily dark film that wouldn't wash away and reeked of necrosis.

Then it came for the matriarch. Whereas she used to eat ravenously, with the distrustful eyes of someone accustomed to lack, her appetite wavered until she refused even the arrow-shaped cartilage of the keel bone, which she had once so keenly favored. She kept nothing down, not even the thin broth made of only scraps.

She's simply grown tired of the taste, the girl thought as she slipped a wishbone into the ground. The dirt stuck painfully in the open sores of her knuckles, but still she held steadfast. The bird's body regenerated beneath her hand's persuasion, already shuddering in anticipation of slaughter. A year it had died for them, and still she refused to name it. She did not want to grow fond, but mostly she did not want to grow mournful. If she gave it a name, that would make its suffering real.

After the appetite, it was the matriarch's memories that went next. Steadily, she became unable to recognize the name of her village, the names of her children, her name. She lay glassy-eyed on a mat gone damp with sweat; a thin trail of black bile ran as readily as spit from the side of her lips.

The village physician did not know what to call this sickness, though the shaman summoned from the neighboring province to perform a purification ritual on the house had taken not one step into the yard before she murmured, *A dead hand is a hand of thorns. O ghost, who tethers you so to the land of the living?*

The next day, the matriarch was dead, a wishbone lodged in her throat.

"Soojin?" a familiar voice called as soon as she stepped out of her car.

Great. There wasn't a person in this world she wanted to see less than this one. Sometimes she hated living in such a small town. Not even a prosaic trip to the liquor store could be made without running into at least one person you really didn't want to see.

"Why are you here?" Silas asked.

"I'm allowed to be out by myself; it isn't past curfew yet," she said, slamming her door as she turned toward the police chief. Their encounter at the diner had put her on the defensive, and now she didn't want to be cowed. She was perfectly within her rights to be at the liquor store. She was only here for light bulbs, after all.

But when she studied him, she was struck by how wrong he looked. It was raining hard, yet his umbrella was upturned on the ground, and he was soaked. All the posturing bravado she'd seen just a few hours ago was gone. He was haggard. His skin had taken on an unhealthy pallor, and his normally sharp blue eyes had a filmy quality to them.

"Um. Are you all right?" she asked, trying to angle her umbrella so it sheltered them both, but he backed away.

"Yes. Of course," he said haltingly before he lost his footing and went down. *Serves you right, asshole,* she had a moment to think before the coughing fit began. A series of breathless, full-body tremors. The umbrella fell from her slack hands, carried away instantly by the wind. His hacking sounded awful and wet, and when Soojin ran to his side, pinkish sputum flecked her sleeve.

Something had gone down the wrong pipe. That must be the problem. Soojin slammed the heel of her palm against his back. But then why would there be blood in his phlegm?

He clutched her, the diner apron she'd had yet to take off balled in his fists. There was a terrible clarity in his eyes. Gone was the milky stare from before. He was begging her, wild-eyed, for something she didn't know how to give. "Please let me go," he rasped.

Alarmed, she pried his fingers off her, and he collapsed at her feet, face-first into a puddle. Soojin shrieked, struggling to roll his face out of the water. Silas was past talking now. He writhed like his lungs were filled with fluid. His eyes moved wildly in their sockets as she ran screaming into the liquor store for help.

By the time the ambulance arrived, he was so pale Soojin could see the dark blue traceries of veins in his forehead. The paramedics lifted him up on a stretcher and whisked him away, their beacon lights sweeping the empty parking lot with phosphorescent wings. Long after the unflappable liquor store attendant patted Soojin on the shoulder and wandered back inside with a doused cigarette still clamped between his teeth, she stayed rooted to the spot. Something was bothering her.

The siren's wail faded until she couldn't hear it at all. Only then did Soojin drag herself to her car, the light bulbs she had needed utterly forgotten. She barely even noticed that she was tracking water everywhere, soaking the polyester seats. An animal need to go home overcame her, and she heeded it, taking the streets ten miles over the speed limit.

Just as she pulled into her driveway, it dawned on her. When she first saw Silas in the lot, he'd called her by her name. Not "Sue-jean," but her *actual* name. Seventeen years and he hadn't cared to even try to correct himself. Unease needled the edge of her mind.

Soojin killed the engine, watching her home breathlessly. The lights were on, but nothing rustled the curtain. What was she waiting for? And then, finally, she saw movement upstairs. Relief washed through her when her sister's familiar silhouette glided past the closed curtain of their childhood bedroom. Soojin heaved out a tremulous laugh and tasted iron on her lip. Only then did she realize her nose was bleeding. She looked in the rearview mirror. Her mouth and chin were streaked red.

Blood had flowed heavily down her neck and pooled in her clavicles. Her shirt collar. How had she been driving unaware of this?

With shaky hands, Soojin cleaned herself, angling the mirror away so she didn't have to look. She didn't go in immediately. She sat in the darkness of her car, a crumpled pile of bloodied napkins in the cup holder, hand over her heart. Thinking—then not letting herself think at all.

The morning after the deluge was blessedly sunny. A single clear day in what was predicted to be a week of rain. The townsfolk took full advantage of it, jogging out by the promenade or strolling beneath Main Street's blaze of deciduous trees gone blond with autumn.

It was a perfect day marred by the news of the police chief found unconscious outside the liquor store the previous night. It was all people were talking about. First period hadn't even begun yet, but the gossip was already spreading. *Brain damage*, Soojin heard in the parking lot, in the hall, by the lockers. The concern mixed with an understated glee, because here—at last—was something interesting. Something to break the monotony of the off-season.

Water in his lungs. Oxygen deprivation. Awake at the hospital, but not all there.

And then, as she knew it would, the idle tittering turned pointedly toward her. Soojin felt gazes tracking her down the halls, and when she made eye contact, the conversation would pause until she passed.

She didn't need to hear to guess what was being said. *Soojin was the one who found him. Unlucky,* they were probably muttering. *Cursed, that family. Something about them isn't right.* She was no stranger to how quickly tragedy could become spectacle in their bored little town. She couldn't help but wonder, though, if the gossip would have taken a turn this quickly had she been white. In a town as homogenous as theirs, standing out in any way meant being held conditionally. The moment things went sour, accusatory eyes turned most quickly on people like her.

She opened her locker and was rummaging through it with needless aggression when a furtive murmur found her from somewhere to her left.

"Heard she didn't even try to help him," it said to a rush of disapproving mutters. Soojin slammed her locker shut, and the girls who had been talking squeaked like she'd materialized out of thin air.

"I can hear you!" Soojin said to their scattering backs before turning on her heel and running straight into someone's chest. She reeled from her own velocity before strong hands steadied her.

"Fuck them," Mark said after helping her regain her balance. Of course he would come and find her first thing in the morning after hearing the news. She wasn't surprised to see him, but she *was* surprised at the relief she felt. The familiarity of his concerned brown eyes and that mousy hoodie he always wore—it was comforting, and that caught her off guard.

"Are you all right?" Mark asked as they made their way down the hallway toward the courtyard.

"I'm fine," Soojin said, though she wasn't. Everything felt so off. Watching Silas collapse, the nosebleed. But stranger still was how Mirae had acted this morning. She was normally up bright and early, already making breakfast by the time Soojin got ready and came downstairs. Mirae always saw her to the door, barking orders about what groceries or snacks Soojin should pick up after school.

This morning, though, Mirae hadn't come out of the bathroom. She'd said goodbye from behind a closed door. The faucet running, the particular audible rush of bathwater being drawn.

Soojin wasn't sure why, but it didn't feel right.

There was still fifteen minutes until they had to be in homeroom, and neither wanted to be early. She and Mark sat at one of the tables beneath the pear trees. The one Mirae had beelined to the night they'd broken into school.

"Hey," Soojin began before pausing to chew her lip. Why was she hesitating? "Do you know when he's being discharged?"

"Word on the street is Monday."

"I want to go visit him."

"Silas? Why? You don't have to feel obligated to see him. I know you don't like him."

"It's not that. I just . . ." Her fingers thrummed the table. "I was there when he passed out, so I just feel like I should go. Okay?"

"Whoa. Okay. I never said you can't," Mark said gently, using that low register of voice he often did when she was losing her temper. It was only then that Soojin realized she'd snapped at him.

"Shit. I know. It's just . . . I know it's asking a lot because you don't like him either. But . . ." She stalled again. It was so hard to ask favors of anyone. When had such a simple thing become so difficult? She shook her head, preparing to drop it, but Mark, for the first time in memory, spoke for her. But with care. It felt like being seen.

"We'll go together," he said.

"He's not taking any visitors," Mrs. Silas said a few days later when they blundered to her door.

Soojin shifted uncomfortably under her gaze. The woman looked exhausted. Her silvering brown hair, which was normally carefully coiffed, fell frazzled around her face. Behind her Soojin could see the blotchy colors of the get-well-soon bouquets, much like the one Mark held in his arms, that were strewn across the dining room table.

"I understand he just got discharged, ma'am, but we . . . ," Mark began before stalling. He glanced at Soojin, and she stepped in front of him, lifting the take-out bag she held in her hand.

"We brought him his usual order from Half Moon Diner. He comes to get the California scramble every day. We thought it might make him feel more himself."

The woman softened at the sight of the take-out bag, its bottom darkened by grease.

"That's very thoughtful," she said. Taking the bag from Soojin, she made room for them to pass in the doorway. "He's awake but might not be for long. He's upstairs in the room adjacent to the reading nook. Try not to be alarmed by his state," she added before disappearing into the kitchen.

Wasting no time, they headed upstairs. Soojin tried her best to not be nosy, but she couldn't help it. So, this was the residence of the town killjoy. The Silas house was strangely devoid of the people who occupied it. There was a showroom anonymity. No photographs of the family adorned the hallways or the fireplace mantel, no meaningful knickknacks. Instead it was a mishmash of conflicting aesthetics. Framed sports memorabilia gleamed beside mass-produced text-art placards that said things like HOME SWEET HOME and FAMILY, framed police badges beside plastic flowers dusted immaculate.

When they reached the door at the end of the hall, Soojin knocked. No reply. She locked eyes with Mark and, after a few moments of hesitation, cautiously pushed the door open.

The bedroom had the same sterile quality as the rest of the house but smelled strongly of something clinical, like saline and cleaning solvent. There was a heaviness in the air, the salty musk of a man too weak to bathe.

Joe Silas sat propped on the bed, angled toward the halfhearted sunlight streaming through the sheer curtains. The man's utter stillness unsettled Soojin—the way he didn't even twitch when the door opened and clicked shut. "Sir?" Silence so thick you could suspend paper on it. "Sir, sorry to bother you. It's Soojin Han, from the diner."

"And Mark Moon, from the pet cemetery," Mark added.

The man did not respond, didn't even turn to look. Soojin sat carefully on the chair pulled up to the bedside; Mark stood awkwardly behind her. Finally, she could see Silas's expression. The man's face was slack and pale, his blond beard starting to grow in patches. But it was his eyes that alarmed Soojin most. They had this unusual way of fixating on a point, then slowly drifting downward. Now that she sat in Silas's line of vision, she was the subject of this rhythmic visual tracking. His eyes would find her face, and then, as if the seeing were too heavy, his gaze would fall until only the bloodshot whites were visible and his eyes snapped back up again like a pendulum. Two unseeing blue orbs that stared but saw nothing.

"Jesus, what's with him?" Mark whispered.

"Don't know." Soojin raised a hand before the man's eyes, waving tentatively to no response.

"It's called ocular dipping."

They nearly jumped out of their skins, but it was merely Mrs. Silas, walking in with a tray of plated food. "Doctor says it's an occasional side effect of brain injury." She set the tray down on the bedside table.

"Will he recover?" Mark asked.

"With his health and how long he couldn't breathe? Unlikely. The brain is a delicate machine, you know," she said grimly. She wiped her hand on her apron, though it looked plenty dry. An agitated, stressed gesture. She nodded toward the plate. "I doubt he'll eat much. I'll give you a moment alone, but please don't dally long. He tires easily and will need his sleep."

Despite her words, she left swiftly, as though relieved to have a moment to herself. The door closed behind her with a click. The room was once again filled with silence so complete, the ticking of the clock felt like thunder. Silas continued to numbly look Soojin down, up, down.

The last time Soojin had seen him, he'd been clutching the hem of her apron, pleading with her, his desperation so vivid it had made him seem like the only real thing in the world for a moment. Now he looked insubstantial enough to vanish in direct sunlight.

Soojin cleared her throat, studying the food. It did not look good. Microwaved half to death, the eggs had contracted and a milky liquid pooled on the plate. The mushrooms looked anemic. "Would you like to eat some of this, sir?" she asked.

"Not . . . hungry," Silas said haltingly.

So, he was not so injured he couldn't speak. Good.

"But it's your favorite from the diner," she pushed gently, cutting the egg into tiny morsels with the edge of her spoon. "You'll never get your strength up if you don't eat." She lifted it to his lips.

The man opened his mouth, docile. He had taken on an unusual bovine quality. This wasn't simply brain injury; the man was in shock. Soojin spooned a small morsel into his mouth and watched him chew. The way his jaw worked was stuttering and unpracticed, but he got the food down eventually. Soojin started to speak, but Silas opened his mouth for more and she held her tongue, spooning another bite into the man's mouth.

Soojin wondered if he even recognized who was feeding him. Silas didn't seem to actively respond to any visual cues. He didn't move in the direction of where she held her spoon; he merely opened his mouth, his vision unfocused, and waited. When grease dribbled down his chin, he didn't wipe it away and neither did Soojin.

What was she even doing here with this man who had always seemed to dislike her, and now barely registered her presence at all? She felt a sudden rush of distaste for him. She resented him for collapsing in front of her, for the vague seed of worry he'd planted right when she was the happiest she'd been in months. And yet—

Mark leaned past her to dab a napkin against Silas's grease-shiny chin. He shot her a questioning look, as if asking, *What are you doing?* Had she paused for too long? She scooped another morsel of food onto the spoon.

"So, how are you holding up, sir?" Soojin asked, emulating the buoyant tone Mark used so successfully with adults. It didn't sound right coming from her. She sounded false and interrogatory. Silas mumbled something indistinct, rolling syllables like stones in his mouth. His faculties seemed to come and go. One moment he was coherent; the next he was completely insensible.

"I'm sorry?" she asked.

"Hands," Silas said, then opened his mouth. She fed him a bite of seared tomato and onion.

She waited impatiently for Silas to swallow before trying again. "What hands, sir?"

"A dead hand is a hand of thorns," he said, suddenly fluid and emphatic.

"A . . . what?" Soojin asked, waiting for the words to make sense.

His eyes locked on her wrists, regaining such focus she thought a miraculous recovery had occurred. But they hazed, storm clouds over water, then drifted back downward.

A dead hand is a hand of thorns. A prickle of dread, like a drop of frigid water, arced down her back. The words didn't sound at all like Silas, whose language was usually unadorned and as direct as an arrow. But odder still was the fact that they felt familiar. A distant, anxious buzzing kicked up in her ear, frazzling her. It was difficult to think, but it felt suddenly urgent now to remember. Where had she heard those words? Where—

"Let's leave, Soo," Mark said gently, pulling her hand away from her mouth. Only then did she notice she'd been gnawing at her cuticles. Her mouth tasted like iron. "I don't know what you wanted from coming here, but I think this is all we're going to get. He's clearly not all there right now."

But she couldn't just go. Her mind was filled with the night of his collapse. The rain-wet asphalt of the parking lot. *Soojin*, he'd called her before collapsing. She couldn't stop thinking of the way his blue eyes had locked on hers to beg, *Please let me go*. As if she alone had the power to save him. But from what?

Soojin pushed away the hardly eaten plate of food. "Tell me what happened to you that night in the liquor-store parking lot."

The police chief continued to peer down at his lap, unresponsive. Behind her, Mark sighed softly. "It's no use—"

A sudden slam interrupted Mark's protests. Silas had struck the back of his head hard against the headboard. An involuntary spasm, Soojin thought, just before the man thrust himself back with more force. Again and again. A strained gurgle rose then lodged in his throat, a scream his body would not allow him to release. The bed rattled with the violence of each strike.

"Holy shit!" Mark gasped, pulling Soojin away from the bed. The chair she'd been sitting on fell hard to the floor. Silas waved his hands in the air, no longer docile. A wild, hunted clarity glinted in his eyes.

"Never should've taken it," he said, his expression feral. Half-masticated food flew from his mouth. "Never should've listened to him."

Mark's grip on her shoulder tightened, but Soojin shook him off.

"Who? You never should have listened to who?" Soojin asked, kneeling by his bedside, hoping that Mrs. Silas wouldn't hear the commotion and come knocking. They had to calm him down.

He fell back against his pillows, gathering the blanket at his chest like a shield. "We're not safe here." His eyes widened in alarm at something only he could see, and he gasped, lodging spit in his throat—and suddenly he was sputtering. Thick globs of orange phlegm speckled the cotton comforter. Soojin froze.

Mark ran to the bathroom and returned with a toothbrush cup filled to the brim with water.

"Here, drink this," Mark said, slapping the man's heaving back. Silas looked at the cup blankly. Soojin saw the reflection of Silas's glassy blue eyes rippling the surface before he knocked the water out of Mark's hand. The cup bounced against the floor, spilling its contents all over the hardwood before rolling underneath the bed.

"Why would you bring that here—are you crazy?" Silas shouted between coughs. Spittle flew from his mouth as he raved. "It listens through the water. It *comes* through the water! Why'd you do it?" He suddenly didn't look very ill at all. He looked hunted, hackles up. "Clean it!" he shouted, flailing toward the puddle. Mark's eyes were as wide as bowls as he cringed back from the shouting man.

"I said clean it up! Clean it, clean—"

Mark dragged a wool quilt from the bed and toppled to his hands and knees, throwing it over the water to hide it from sight. "Jesus," he gasped as Silas raved from above him. "Soojin, a little help here?" he called to her. She sprang into action.

But not to help.

Instead Soojin ran to hover over Silas, clamping her hands against his shoulders. Her mind was a tempest, out of control. She couldn't untangle what she needed to know and didn't want to hear. "What do you mean by that? What do you mean, it comes through the water?"

But Silas had gone utterly still. His eyes were fixed on her, truly fixed. It was like he was finally seeing her, putting a name to her face. His mouth fell open as if to scream, but instead there was only a dull whistle of breath, as if pulled in through a straw. Effortful, suffocating.

"You," he said. His hands were shaking.

"Soojin, what are you doing? Let him go," Mark said, his voice windswept and overwhelmed.

"What happened to you?" Soojin whispered.

He opened his mouth, his eyes darting as if to scan for safety. But before he could speak, the bedroom door crashed open. Mrs. Silas rushed in, taking in the catastrophe: Mark furiously mopping the floor, and Soojin perched on the bed, bracing Silas's shoulders. She hoped her stance looked like she was comforting him, not gripping him in interrogation the way she had been moments before.

Before Soojin could fully register what was happening, they were both being ushered out of the bedroom and down the stairs by the tiny woman.

"Not your fault," Mrs. Silas said as she opened the front door. "Haven't been able to get him to drink much since he woke up. At this rate, dehydration will take him before anything else does. Will have to get him an IV. . . ."

They stood now on the porch beneath a flickering lamp,

where a graveyard of moths lay withered at the bottom of the glass. Mrs. Silas reached out to close the door, her face so deeply exhausted, Soojin couldn't help but say, "I'm sorry. I didn't mean to," like the guilty child she very much felt like.

The woman looked fit to burst into tears, but she didn't. She tentatively touched Soojin's shoulder, then Mark's. "Maybe it's for the best you two don't come back around here."

"But, ma'am—" Soojin began before the door shut in their faces. Mrs. Silas walked down the hall, the frosted glass tessellating her form until her silhouette looked submerged in water.

17.

October seized Jade Acre in a frenzy of Halloween festivity, and the town's collective thoughts slouched away from the misfortune of Joe Silas, catatonic for a week now in his bed. Despite everything, even Soojin found herself getting swept up, especially now as she peered out her bedroom window for the familiar sight of Mark's headlights trundling up their long driveway at three a.m.

"He's here," Soojin said, running to the mirror, where Mirae was thatching her hair into two long braids. Soojin used an eyeliner to draw whiskers on either side of her face. The sisters looked at each other—budget Wednesday Addams and cat—then clapped a high five for a job haphazardly done.

And then they were off, spilling down the stairs like they were kids again, shushing one another even though there were no parents to wake. Mark was waiting for them, in his own bootleg costume: a flannel shirt ("Uh . . . farmer?" he replied to the sisters' questioning). They piled in his car and peeled out into the quiet, empty early morning.

Every October, the town adorned itself with black and orange tinsel threaded around all the storefronts. Though Halloween was not for a few weeks yet, decorations were fully in swing.

It had been Mark's idea for them to be in costume, and Soojin was glad they were. It made the night feel somehow magical, like the town had dressed itself up and was waiting breathlessly for their witching-hour arrival.

"Soojin, look at this!" Mirae said. She was pressed up against one of the windows of the candy shop—where they used to buy peppermint bark with the coins their parents gave them so they'd speed off and give them a moment's reprieve.

Now the windows were lined with paper ghosts held aloft with gossamer thread. The owner had left the string lights on, and they pulsed orange and white, illuminating the candy displays: marshmallows molded into the shape of witches' hats, white chocolate bones for assembling your own skeleton. The sisters continued to look longingly at the displays until Mark smugly pulled a bag of chocolates from his backpack. Partially melted though they were, nothing had ever tasted so good. They licked their fingers clean and then, minds fizzing with sugar, continued on.

They ventured down the tight walkways whistling with wind, all the way to the town square, where they sat on the damp stone of the central fountain to set votive candles afloat in the water. In the dim candlelight, Soojin watched her sister. A smile played on Mirae's face as she let her fingers skim the surface, ushering one of the candles along, so delicately that not even the flame was disturbed.

It made Soojin's lingering unease after visiting Silas feel silly, the way she'd taken to waking at all hours of the night to check for her sister's form in the adjacent bed.

The memory of stricken blue eyes threatened to intrude. A voice: *A dead hand is a hand of—*

Mirae stood, wiped her wet hands, and offered one to Soojin, pulling her to her feet. Her sister's hands were warm and impossibly soft. Without their calluses, they felt almost foreign. But Mirae's smile was anything but unfamiliar.

Above, the sky was effervescent with stars. Nobody was dead here.

Like this, the days slipped by. It was homecoming season, and the town began to celebrate two events at once. The scarecrows wore green-and-silver Trojan hats in honor of the school mascot, while the farmers' market was glutted with decorative gourds and carving pumpkins. Mark brought some with him one evening, and the three of them spent hours slicing faces into the large orange fruit, eating the flat seeds Mirae toasted with salt and honey.

It was there on the living room floor, belly down on the rug and hands sticky, that Mark asked Soojin to the homecoming dance.

"Mmm," Soojin mumbled. She had carved two perfect triangles for eyes, but the curvature of the mouth was proving difficult. "Dances aren't really my thing."

Mark's pumpkin was a disaster, but that was his own fault. He had overestimated his craftsmanship when he'd decided to carve a cat. It looked much more like a two-legged cow: a straight spike protruding from its rear denoted an attempt at a tail.

"Aw, c'mon, Soo. It's going to be your last homecoming! You can't miss it!" Mark said, scooping a wet morsel of sinuous pumpkin flesh and holding it out for Milkis. The rat jumped out of his shirt pocket to feast, staining her muzzle orange. She seemed to have taken a special liking to Mark and always hovered near him. Either that or she knew he was the biggest sucker and had chosen her allegiance accordingly.

"I haven't been to any, actually."

"It'll be your first one too, then," Mark said. "You'll have fun! I promise."

"Well . . ." If Soojin was being honest, the last large function she'd attended, that awful bonfire, had only reaffirmed her aversion to parties. "I don't know."

"You should go," Mirae said, setting her knife aside to skim her finger through the honey that pooled at the bottom of the bowl. She licked it clean and hummed happily.

"Why?"

"It'll do you good to get out of the house for a change."

"I get out of the house," Soojin protested. "Work. School. In the middle of the night with you two nerds."

"Well, you don't have to if you don't want—" Mark began, but Mirae cut him off.

"You know what I mean." She flicked Soojin's knee. "You need to do something new and get your mind off what happened to Chief Silas. You've been off ever since. I'm worried about you." Mirae's voice was imperative, less a suggestion than an order.

Mark sat quietly, watching the words volley between the two sisters as if he knew he no longer had a place in this discussion. Soojin almost wanted to say no, feeling aimlessly adversarial. But for whatever reason, this seemed to really matter to Mirae, so in the end she threw up her hands. "Fine."

It was a less than romantic acceptance, but Mark was a good enough sport to still look pleased.

That was how Soojin found herself in her current predicament: at her sister's mercy, with both their closets completely gutted and makeup scattered all over Mirae's bed and their shared nightstand.

Soojin groaned as her sister zipped her into yet another dress. A short yellow one with a tulle skirt. Mirae had always been a bit smaller, and the bodice was too tight.

"This isn't the one," Mirae said, brusquely unzipping the dress and tossing it aside. Most of what Soojin tried on was her sister's. Soojin was not one for parties, but Mirae had gone to every homecoming, as well as some other random dances in between. She had several nice semiformal dresses.

"Why are we doing this now? Homecoming isn't until next weekend," Soojin groaned. Her face felt sticky from the cream blushes Mirae had assailed her with. Milkis was out of her cage and industriously rolling lip glosses across the vanity like she was rearranging furniture. Soojin stopped her from rolling one straight off the edge, holding it out of the rat's reach.

"Who picks their homecoming outfit the day of? Haven't you heard of dress rehearsal?" Mirae asked.

"For musicals, sure. It's just a dance, Unnie. There's no need for all of this," Soojin said, still waving the lip-gloss tube aloft as Milkis pawed indignantly at her hand.

"Oh, stop whining. Don't you want to impress your date?" Mirae asked, slipping her into yet another dress.

"It's not a date; it's Mark."

"And those things are mutually exclusive why?" Mirae tied a neat ribbon at Soojin's side, pulling the fabric of the skirt taut to dispel wrinkles. "But I guess you have a point. Mark probably wouldn't even care if you showed up in your pajamas."

Soojin tried not to think of the panda onesie Mirae had bought her as a joke, but that she did wear unironically. The thought alone made her want to die.

"He likes you," Mirae said, touching up Soojin's lipstick, then blotting it with her fingertip. "I don't even know if he himself realizes that yet, but it's so obvious."

"He doesn't like me. Not like that."

"Oh yeah? Then why would he give up sleep so many nights a week to spend time with you?"

It was true that since Mirae's return, Mark often sacrificed sleep to take the sisters here and there in the middle of the night. Their pre-Halloween excursion, bonfires at the beach, long drives near the vineyard. On those days, he'd shuffle about like a zombie during school, his head lolling back in math class, catching up on the sleep he didn't get at night.

"He does it for you. Because he feels bad about you being stuck in that cottage so much."

"Soo, if you truly believe that, you're more hopeless than I thought."

Before Soojin had a chance to respond, Mirae took a few steps back to appreciate her own work. "There. This is perfect," she said happily before turning Soojin around to face her reflection.

Her sister had tucked her into a flowing red wrap dress. The one that Mirae had worn to her own senior-year homecoming last October. Bought at the Nordstrom Rack in Bragg Hills, it was cheap but didn't look it.

Soojin remembered that day. They had convinced their dad to waste an hour at the home-goods store while they shopped for Mirae's dress. Thrilled to be free of Dad's nagging about *too tight* or *too short,* they tried it all on. Even the dresses that opened the valley between their breasts, bunching in a silver brooch at their sternum, and the ones with backs so low they scooped the divot of their tailbones. For those brief moments, giggling between the dressing-room curtains, they felt very grown. In the end, Mirae had decided on this dress, modest but for the sliver of thigh that showed when the skirt shifted just so—perhaps not the favorite of the day, but the one chosen lest their prudish father die of horror.

And now Soojin was wearing it. The red was a deep wine, dark enough to disguise the small rum-and-Coke stain at the hem. The silky fabric caught light like the eye of a pond, as did her cheekbones dusted with rose-gold shimmer. Mirae kept the makeup in the barely there style so popular on Korean television shows. A pop of pink on the cheeks, gradient lips, some peach shimmer at the creases of her eyes. It softened her features, made her appear kinder than she was. Soojin couldn't deny she looked beautiful. She looked beautiful because she looked like her sister.

"People are going to judge me for wearing your last homecoming dress," Soojin said.

"Why would they?" Mirae asked, swiping the shimmer that had fallen on her hands.

You love this dress. Would you have reworn it to your prom, had you lived long enough? Soojin thought. Instead she said, "It looks better on you."

"Shush, you look great. Besides, since I can't go, you might as well show my beloved dress a good time. She's too pretty to just languish in the closet forever." She ran the silky fabric through her fingers and smiled. "Too bad I can't see Mark's expression when he sees you like this. Poor boy's going to be speechless."

She wouldn't get the chance. The dance was on a Saturday, meaning Dad would be home from Bragg Hills and Mirae would be hiding in the cottage when Mark came to pick Soojin up. It didn't feel right. "I wish you could be the one to see me off."

"If Dad heard that, it would hurt his feelings," Mirae chastised before unfastening the ribbon and helping Soojin step out of the dress. "Besides, I'm not your *mom*, Soojin. It's not my place to send you off anywhere." Her expression hardened, but only for a moment before it went impassive again. "I wish I could be going *with* you. But since I can't, I'll be happily eating my feelings in my private mansion." She gestured toward the window at the cottage, obscured by the lattice of magnolia branches. She said it with such levity, but the words cut.

Soojin slipped her sleeping shirt on, returned Milkis to her cage, and sank onto the bed. Her sister followed her and, divining her change in mood, unearthed a brush from the dresser. Mirae settled behind her and began to brush her hair, working the knots out with careful hands. It immediately put Soojin at ease, this familiar act of care. One their mother once did for them both to soothe them on restless evenings.

"I'm kidding. I'll be fine," Mirae said, partitioning Soojin's hair to the left to smooth down the wispy flyaways underneath. I just want you to have enough fun for the both of us, yeah? I want you to *let* yourself have fun. I know how you can be a total hedgehog." Mirae poked her in the stomach.

Soojin wanted to scowl, but she giggled instead. "Fine. I promise."

Her hair was smooth and untangled. Mirae set the brush aside, and the two sat there, Soojin's head resting on her sister's shoulder until she noticed something and pointed. "Dad's going to have to replace the wallpaper soon," she said, nodding toward a gray pupil amid the damask pattern of the paper. A small blemish of water damage that would bloom into wide concentric circles of rot if left unaddressed.

Mirae followed her sister's gaze. "It's a little old-fashioned, I guess, sure . . . ," she said.

Soojin raised a questioning brow. "What? No, that's not what I mean. Look at it, it's—" She looked back toward the wall, and her finger drooped.

Mirae stood, walking toward the wall to run her hand against the paper. Knicks and scratches had accumulated in it over the years. Some minor stains from when the girls were children, an errant crayon mark. Nothing worth singling out. "It's what?"

"Nothing," Soojin said, staring hard once more at the wallpaper, then turning her sights hurriedly elsewhere.

On the day of homecoming, Soojin readied herself in silence. Outside, it was drizzling, and she turned her music off to listen to the rain. She felt wistful, preparing for her first formal alone. Weren't there pre-dance rituals around these things? She'd seen them in movies: mothers, sisters, and friends getting ready together in a raucous frenzy. Instead she sat alone, taking a flat iron to her hair as the magnolia tree scraped her bedroom window. She'd done her makeup just how Mirae had instructed, and the reflection that peered out at her in the mirror looked glamorous, glowing, and lonely.

She reached for her sister's rose-gold bracelet to complete the look. Just as the clasp closed, she noticed the bruise: a small purple blotch spanning the heel of her palm down to the thin skin of her inner wrist. She could have sworn it hadn't been there before. It looked old, its border tinged a fetid yellow. Soojin pressed her finger against it. A dull pulse of pain, and with it a distant worry. She couldn't remember injuring herself. She studied its shape, unblinking for so long that it seemed to move, spreading its inky corners up the outline of her radial artery.

There was a knock at her door. She startled. Blinked. Her bruise was at once static and small again.

"Soojin," her dad called.

"Hold on." She sorted through the catastrophe of makeup on her vanity. She dabbed the bruise with dollops of full-coverage concealer, then dusted it with setting powder. The mark vanished, and so too did her nameless unease. She stood and opened the door for her father, and for a moment he was speechless, taking in her form with tired eyes.

"You're wearing Mirae's dress," he said finally. "I should have thought to go shopping with you. I'm sorry."

"Why? Does it not look good on me?" she asked.

"No, it's not that. It's just . . ." He shook his head and then, in Korean: "You look pretty, my daughter." The significance of the language shift was not lost on her. *Pretty* in English lived in the realm of aesthetics. In Korean, *pretty* meant "pretty," yes. But it also meant "kind," "magnanimous," "filial," "sweet." In the familiar ruby dress, her father was seeing her, and he was also seeing his lost and gentler daughter.

"Thanks, Dad," Soojin said, and the smile she gave him was wholehearted. It surprised them both.

Suddenly bashful, he cleared his throat. "The boy is here."

"Oh!" Soojin ran toward the window and pulled the curtain aside. Mark's beat-up old car was in the driveway. She hadn't heard it wheeze and complain its way to her house, but now that she saw it, her heart skipped several beats. Her own excitement surprised her.

Mark stepped out of his car, arms heavy with flowers. Their home didn't have a doorbell, a flaw her father had never cared to rectify, but she heard his firm knocks even from the second floor.

"Well, I'll escort you." Her father lent her his arm in a decidedly gallant fashion. He looked tired, didn't seem to be eating enough, but for now he was in good spirits. She took his arm readily.

"I'm proud of you, Soojin," her father said as they made their way down the stairs. When she didn't answer, he continued. "I thought for so long I would never see you really smile again, but you've changed these past couple of months. Your teachers say you're socializing more. You look happier." They stopped in front of the door, where Mark's gangly silhouette was visible through the frosted glass. "I've missed this daughter of mine."

"She's missed you too, Dad," Soojin said, thinking of her sister and letting the third person speak for them both.

He smiled down at her, and she smiled back, her heart so tender for him, she feared her guilt might kill her. They were so close to the cottage. She could take him there, could open the door to the daughter he missed and let the reunion play out its roulette of joy or ruin. Her pulse thrummed with possibility. But then the moment passed. Her father stepped back, tucked a long curl behind her ear, and patted her cheek fondly.

"Well, let's not keep the Moon boy waiting." He opened the door.

Mark stood with an armful of maroon geraniums, lit by the dim lantern gathering gnats above his head. He'd been in the process of swatting them away, and the door opened to him with a hand in midair, boxing with nothing, wide-eyed and caught off guard. His arm snapped to his side. He was casual in his navy dress shirt, no tie, and black jeans instead of slacks. Someone—likely his mother—had tried to tame his unruly hair into a formal side sweep, but his dark strands were already starting to fall in limp waves over his forehead.

"Hi," Soojin said, trying her best to keep her voice bright and breezy as she peered out from behind her father's broad back. She felt acutely aware of herself, her posture, the way her curled hair was framing her face. She wasn't sure what to do with her hands.

"Ah . . . wow. You look . . ." Mark faltered, grinning sheepishly. She reciprocated with equal awkwardness. The expression on his face when he looked at her made her feel beautiful. She hadn't realized she'd wanted that, much less from him.

Mark remembered himself. He swiveled on his heel to turn to her father and bowed. "Hello, Mr. Han," he said, his voice just a pitch higher in Korean.

Her father regarded him with the same carefully curated severity Soojin expected him to. "Mark. It's good to see you. It's been a while," he said. "You've gotten taller."

"You too," Mark said, then realized his blunder. "About it being good to see you, I mean. Not being tall," he floundered, eyes probing Soojin for help. "You are tall, though." In the silence, Mark opened his mouth to talk again, and Soojin decided to save him.

She sidestepped her father and pointed at the wild mess of flowers in Mark's arms. "Is that for me?" she asked.

It was not a bouquet. The stems were not even tied together, and the leaves were unpruned and wild. He had brought her an untamed garden. Mark looked down at his arms, as if surprised by the flowers himself.

"Oh yeah. My mom reminded me about bringing a corsage, but I totally forgot—sorry. The florist was too busy for a last-minute order, so I brought you these instead. Geraniums! I grew them myself." He gently flicked a bug off a petal.

"These are the ones you grow outside the funeral home," she said, remembering that time almost two months ago when she'd interrupted his pruning. They were not the same two people who'd stood under the awning that September evening. It felt like years had elapsed since then. Something about that memory flustered him, and he unloaded the flowers unceremoniously into her arms in lieu of replying.

In the pantheon of flowers, Soojin supposed, geraniums were not particularly beautiful. They were earthy and herbaceous in a vaguely off-putting way. The prickly stems needled her arms and caught on the fabric of her dress. She absolutely loved them.

"I'll put them in water," her dad said, taking the geraniums from her arms.

"Wait, Dad, I need just one of them back," Soojin said, browsing the bundle until she found the one with the most symmetrical petals. She snapped the stem, turned around, and slipped it inside Mark's navy dress shirt so its red blossoms peeked just above the hem of the pocket. She patted it triumphantly. "There, emergency boutonniere."

Mark smiled, adjusting the flower so it was perfectly straight. "So you forgot too? That makes me feel less shitty about forgetting your corsage," he said before meeting her father's eyes and quickly amending: "Bad. I mean bad, not shitty."

Her father chuckled; his squared shoulders deflated. Mark's haplessness seemed to have put him at ease. "You two go and have fun. Don't stay out too late."

"Yes, sir," Mark said, bowing goodbye.

"Don't wait up for me. You have a long drive tomorrow," Soojin said, standing on her toes to peck him on the cheek. Her father touched where her lipstick had left a mark, as if in disbelief at the unprompted affection. She turned and followed Mark down the porch steps and into his old car.

As soon as the doors closed, Mark turned to her and exhaled slowly through his teeth.

"Was I okay? Did that go well?"

Soojin studied her father as Mark backed out of the driveway.

His face looked wistful in the taillights. It had been so long since they were not fighting or fleeing the other. She wondered if he finally felt like a father again, after nearly a year of parenting a ghost of a girl.

"I think it went very well."

18.

In the cottage, she sat in near darkness, listening to her father bid Soojin goodbye and to the rumble of Mark's car pulling out of the driveway. The tenor of her father's voice when he saw them off was beautiful. He sounded happy. She knew she should feel glad that the capacity for happiness, no matter how small, had returned to him, but it hurt the most selfish part of her.

There was a difference between being remembered and being mourned, but she couldn't recall what it was. She wanted to run out and greet him in the yard so he would at once mourn and remember her. But she wouldn't. There was much to be done, and now with Soojin distracted at the dance, she finally had the opportunity to act.

In the past few weeks, her sister had become awfully watchful. On the weekdays, Soojin trailed her endlessly, waking every few hours from a restless sleep to check that she was still beside her in their childhood bedroom. On the weekends, when Father was home, Soojin snuck out to the cottage every so often during the night. She never said a word, just stood in the doorway, watching her sister feign sleep until her gnawing anxiety was satiated and she left.

In a way, it was all very familiar. When they were younger, Soojin had been her shadow: a fretful, volatile girl who latched on all the harder when their mother passed away.

Though the months following their mother's death were a blur, there was one day in particular she remembered with perfect clarity: the morning after the family returned home from the funeral. The first day without her.

She'd woken then from a fitful sleep, with Soojin curled up beside her and Milkis shuffling in her cage. For a moment, there had been the dull amnesia of waking. She had remembered nothing of the service the night before. Nothing at all, until her mind caught up to her, bringing with it the image of an urn. Mrs. Moon's devastated face as she'd dropped them all off at home. Her father crying hard into his hands at the threshold of their house.

She's gone, she remembered thinking as she stared at the ceiling. It was a loss that felt largely theoretical still. Like her mother might come crashing into their room any moment, shouting about how badly they'd overslept for school. Her mind didn't fully grasp the fact of grief yet, but her body did—and at once she was crying involuntarily, pushing away from Soojin so as not to wake her.

Daddy will come, she'd thought, swiping her running nose on her sleeve. He'd come and he'd gather her in his arms and comb his fingers through her hair like Mom used to when the girls were sad.

Hours passed before she realized he wouldn't. At any moment, her sister would wake up, disoriented and devastated. Soojin had refused all food at the funeral, and though she wouldn't want to, she would need to eat. Someone would have to make her.

You have to get up.

She got up. She left Soojin on her bed and went downstairs, past her parents' silent room, and into the kitchen, where a pile of pots accrued flies in the sink. As she pulled over a step stool to wash the dishes, she came to the sudden realization that her role had irrevocably changed overnight. As the eldest daughter of an unmoored family, she'd been catapulted into a caretaker position, and she'd need to change accordingly.

In the following months, she learned to cook. To clean and do laundry and better manage Soojin's oscillating moods. She'd load a tray with soup and rice and leave it before her father's door every night in case his hunger might win out against his desire to not exist. She let herself forget what it felt like to be parented rather than to parent.

She was eleven.

When her period came, she told no one. Tracking blood across the bathroom's white tiles, she foraged in her late mother's cabinet and tended to herself. Or tried to. She found nothing but tampons. The directions had felt unfathomable then, the plastic applicators too painful. She tore through three before giving up, letting the box dampen on the floor. Curled around the cramps she had no explanation for, she simply let herself bleed. That was how her girlhood ended.

And here they were now, so many years later, and she and Soojin were replaying that same dynamic again. But there was an additional layer to her sister's dependence. Soojin was suspicious of her now, no matter how hard she tried not to be. Her sister was right to worry.

What Silas had said to Mark was true. She *could* hear through the water. A gift granted by drowning. It had started out as a low murmur, an overwhelming drone of all the voices in town traveling to her through the conduit of water. Impossible to decipher, stamped flat in the way one cicada is a distinct melody but a swarm is an aural assault.

But over time, her senses had started to sharpen. She could make out individual voices and recess the rest. Water whispered to her; it made her privy to things. All the after-affair showers and couples arguing on waterfront-bungalow getaways meant to revive their failing relationships. The women crying at the sink, then hurriedly washing their faces and brightly answering, "Yes, what do you need?" when their children or husbands called for them. Of course, she also heard the river's endless, rushing want. She didn't know if it was hungry or lonely. The river was always moving, always leaving and being left. How could it not ache to possess?

Where is he? she thought. The static of the river parted as if to show her the way. She heard children splashing in the small lakes the rain had made of their gardens. She heard a drunk man pissing into a backed-up drainage system behind the saloon. She heard retirees rocking on their porches, gossiping about Joe Silas, home but still not back to his senses. And then, yes—there. The slow breathing of a man turning in to bed early, shifting in his sheets.

The girl opened her eyes. She opened a seam in the rain and stepped through.

Christopher Porter was asleep when the girl let herself in. She'd been here only once before. The house was a study of absence, just as she remembered it. The bare walls. The fireplace mantel with nothing but a languishing succulent atop it. The son was gone, and no lights had been left on for him. She navigated the halls in indigo darkness and sought the father where he dreamed. His bedroom was cavernous with its high vaulted ceilings. A skylight let in milky wisps of moonlight, casting everything in a dull pallor.

She walked to him. Her feet made no sound, though they left little wet depressions on the rug. Only when she reached Porter's bedside did she notice the evidence of another sort of life. There was a photograph on his nightstand. Captured in it was a woman with long auburn hair, smiling in front of the cheery architecture of some European city. The picture was old, slightly bleached with time, but it exuded a certain happiness. She didn't want this woman's face turned toward her. The girl put the photo face down on the nightstand and returned her attention to the man.

Porter resembled his son closely. Chestnut-brown hair, slim build. And though his expression was disarmed by sleep, there was still a severity there. He had the look of brutalist architecture, all divots and sharp corners.

The girl studied him and felt a ripple of hatred so complete it burned not fiery, but cold. The sound of a riptide tore through her so loud she drew her hands against her ears until it crested. This was the man who had taken her mother, and yet he slept so soundly.

A bottle of Ambien sat open on the nightstand, full of cheery pink pills. He was deeply, chemically asleep. But even so, when she touched the bare skin under his collar, he shuddered as if startled by cold. His brow furrowed, but he didn't wake. The girl breached his borders, then let herself sink.

There was an immediate fuzziness to her senses. She felt the Ambien singing through his blood, a pleasant dullness like the glow of a lamp near burning out. The experience was not unlike possessing Silas. Porter's body of water opened its map of memories to her, stuttering and incomplete, faded from time. She moved through them swiftly. A boy pedaling fast on a bicycle still fixed with training wheels. Summers on a wide-open soccer field. A long school hallway and boulevards flanked with skyscrapers.

Then the blur of memories slowed. She found herself in a Jade Acre of decades past, washed out in coral light. What year was this?

Nearby, there was a girl, cheeks ruddy and full in a manner incongruous with her lanky body fresh off a growth spurt. Her wavy hair was thrown into a messy bun, and braces wove a streak of silver across her teeth. She was young—thirteen, perhaps. Still, it was her mother. The mole below the right side of her mouth and her bright eyes so full of rebellious mischief were unmistakable. She was seeing the early years of her mother and Christopher Porter's friendship, before any bitterness intruded.

Are you ready, Sunny? Christopher called. He was so much

younger, his cadence unsteady with the onset of puberty. But, perhaps most unrecognizably, he sounded cheerful.

Her young mother responded with a confident nod. *Ready!* she said before sinking her hands in the dirt. She bent toward the earth, her expression intent as if she were listening to something. The girl knew what she was hearing: the whispers of women long gone. In the memory, the ferns started to curl toward the earth. Finally her mother pulled a white rat from the earth and kissed it between the ears. And then Christopher was stumbling forward, hollering, *No way! No way!* There was laughter and awe in his voice.

That's a miracle, the boy said, breathless. Her mother looked up. Sweat plastered her bangs to her forehead. She looked close to collapse, but her eyes were bright and proud as he praised her. *You're an actual miracle.*

The memory flexed, and they were elsewhere. Older now, but only slightly. They couldn't have been more than sixteen, but their features were crystallizing, becoming more the faces they would wear into adulthood.

Are you sure about this, Chris? her mother asked.
Yeah, totally.

Sunny nodded, putting her hands into the soil. Christopher followed her lead, and their eyes fluttered closed. *It can feel bad,* Sunny warned. *If it starts to feel real bad, like you might faint or hurl, you back away—okay? And don't you dare throw up on me.*

He didn't. When it was done, Sunny and Christopher pulled a sparrow from the earth and let it fly with a wing shower of soil. Sunny looked skyward, tracking the bird's erratic flight, but Christopher's gaze was fixed on her smiling face, something greedy and calculating playing across the taut line of his lips.

With a power like this, you can do so much more than just mess around with animal bones, you know? he'd said to her. Sunny turned toward him then. Her brow furrowed at the intensity of his expression. She looked uneasy. She wiped her hands behind her back and kept them there, away from his view. He pushed the sparrow's feather underfoot. Ground it into the earth. *Useful,* he said. *I'm just saying you can be more useful.*

His memories moved like water. A car loaded up. Several years passed without Sunny in them. She saw the Gothic spires of a university library. A classroom. A girl with curly auburn hair waiting for him in the sultry summer heat of an arboretum. His expression yielded to an unaccustomed affection as she dabbed her brow and then, seeing him, raised her arm to wave.

This was the woman in the photograph. *Amber.* The name washed over her unbidden. Christopher was thinking it. It echoed sweetly through the memory.

Amber. Amber. There's my girl.

She could feel how new for him it was, this sensation of startling, true affection. Christopher's parents' marriage had been an arranged alliance of two wealthy families, more a venture of business than love. His mother and father drifted in and out of the home, as indifferent to one another as they were to him, keeping separate lives and lovers.

Christopher had expected his future to be much the same until he moved into his dorm room and saw a girl struggling to open the door next to his, key in one hand and an overladen box propped up in the other. He'd nearly turned away without helping, but what a bother it would be if the neighboring girl disliked him all year. He caught the box just before it fell, and that was how they had begun.

Now the arboretum was overlush and green. Starlings dove between the branches of the willows, dark seeds clamped in their beaks.

Christopher jogged toward her. *Sorry, Amber. Meeting ran over. My professor loves to hear himself talk. Have you been waiting long?* he asked. She'd come from art class, and there was paint under her nails. This detail lodged a tenderness in him, and he leaned down to plant a quick kiss on her brow before they walked toward the gazebo overlooking the lake. They were young, and at three years and some change, so was their relationship. But they were twenty-one and in love and still believed the world would be good to them. Christopher was determined to make it good.

For years, it was.

The memories swept past ever more swiftly as Christopher aged. There was a graduation where Amber and Christopher signed each other's caps and kissed in the sweltering May heat. A cozy home where the box windows were filled with planters of herbs and repurposed milk cans of fresh-cut flowers. There were trips to Paris and an adopted feral cat that allowed itself to be fed but never touched. A courthouse wedding ending with diner burgers dripping on their thrifted outfits, her satin drop-waist dress with a tear in the bodice, and his tacky maroon suit. And years later: the unexpected. A hospital room. A baby boy entering the world early, held by an incubator's heat before his mother's arms.

Years of life flitted past in rapid, kaleidoscopic light until she landed finally on a memory with a sodden, gray quality to it. It was morning and rain struck the windows with such ferocity it felt like stones. Amber was curled on the far side of the bed, strangely still despite the thunderous weather. Her hair spread like an unfurled hand on her pillow. A slow dread. Christopher's hand reaching out.

And then—

No.

The word intruded on the memory, bleaching the scene. Porter was trying hard to wake. The girl's hold rattled, his mind no longer her window. *No,* it said. *No.*

The memory refused her and she was thrust away. The past collapsed into the pinprick of an eye. She was, at once, back in the present, gripping her own heaving chest as Porter groaned beneath her, still sleeping, but barely.

She fled, stopping only when she was outside with the soft rain on her brow. She waited for the water to soothe her, but something was wrong. This possession had cost something. Her heart still clamored. She felt weak and ravenous and wild. She clenched her hands together, willing them to stop shaking, but they wouldn't. They'd become their own quivering animals.

Inside the home, Christopher Porter finally woke from his nightmare. He didn't notice the photograph lying face down on his nightstand, the footprints on his rug slowly drying into memory. Nor the girl who stood at his doorstep, listening to his heart stutter as he wiped tears away from his eyes, bewildered, already forgetting what he'd been dreaming of.

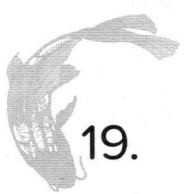

19.

The theme of the dance was the Roaring Twenties. The pear trees lining the path toward the gymnasium were draped with gold fairy lights, and inside, past the curtains of tinsel hung over the entrance, the bleachers were drawn up and plastered with gold-and-black art deco prints. Silver confetti obscured the basketball court markings, and the ever-present scent of sweat and rubber had been dispelled with the powerful aroma of whatever fruits had been tossed into the punch the faculty was serving up.

"Here you go." Mark handed her a paper cup of bright red juice. It was obvious some seniors were spiking theirs from the way they laughed a little too hard and threw their hips wide as they danced.

A live band played jazz and swing on the stage that was pulled out for assemblies. Soojin had seen this band a hundred times before: a motley group of retirees who took payment only in the form of free food or booze. They were a town fixture, played regularly at farmers' markets, and seemed to only have about fifteen cover songs in their repertoire. Still, the music felt different tonight. The golden lights and fullness of that big brass sound wove magic into the air as students held each other close beneath the slowly roving lights.

"Want to dance?" Mark asked, offering his arm.

"I don't really know how to dance to this kind of music," Soojin said, but she took his arm anyway.

"Neither do I, but we shouldn't let that stop us." He led her onto the dance floor, hesitating momentarily before wrapping his arm around her waist. He took her right hand in his, holding it aloft while looking around for pointers. "Is this right?"

"I don't think you're going to find the answers in this crowd. They look just as clueless as us," Soojin said, taking in the chaos of their peers. However clumsy she and Mark might be, at least they wouldn't be the only hopeless things. She took the initiative of guiding the first step.

Mark followed her sway with a surprised laugh. "Oh? You want to lead? Fine by me."

"Don't hate me if I end up breaking your toe," Soojin said over the music.

"I don't think I could ever hate you, Soo." He had this way of making even the most embarrassingly earnest words sound nonchalant.

She didn't know what to say to that, so instead she just focused on the music, the buzz of the people around her, and the ashen, organic smell that always clung to Mark's hair and clothes. Their bodies took over. They left their clumsy, uncertain moves behind and swayed together in wide, confident arcs. Surely, these steps were all wrong. They were making it up as they went. But the way the colorful dresses and disco lights and glimmering foil curtains streaked as they moved felt exactly right. They even chanced a twirl—or, more precisely, Mark lifted Soojin's arm and spun his gangly form beneath it with such a ridiculous flourish, she couldn't help but laugh.

"'I don't know how to dance,' she said," Mark yelled over the trumpet. "Look at you."

"But I really don't," she said into his shoulder. While they had started an arm's length apart, she was now pressed flush against him. She couldn't tell if it was him pulling her close or vice versa. She supposed it didn't matter, because there they were, syncing the rise and fall of their chests.

He bent close to her ear so he didn't have to shout. "Now you're just lying. I happen to remember a little girl at church Christmas parties who threw tantrums if the entire congregation didn't sit down, shut up, and watch her dance her self-choreographed rendition of 'All I Want for Chri—'" Blood rushing to her cheeks, Soojin reached up and pressed a palm to his mouth, but he dodged and continued: "'for Christmas Is—' Mmph!"

She leapt to silence him again, but her weight threw him off balance. He fell, pulling her down with him, and they landed hard on the sticky gymnasium floor. Aside from a few sympathetic giggles, the dancers twirled on without acknowledging them. From the floor, the tulle skirts and theme-abiding flapper dresses looked like tinsel-strung trees swaying in fierce wind.

"You're such a dick!" She slapped him on the shoulder, but her stomach was cramping with laughter.

"Sorry . . . couldn't help it," Mark said. His forehead glistened with sweat, and his chest rose and fell like he'd run himself ragged in PE. How long had they been dancing? She was tired and parched and only now realizing it.

"Do you want to take a breather?" he asked, helping her up to her feet, and the two of them wove off the dance floor together.

Outside, the air was temperate for October. The faint drizzle that had been falling just an hour earlier had ceased, and through the breaks in the clouds the stars shone brightly. Soojin could map out a few familiar constellations among them: the angles of the Big Dipper, and the slopes of what she guessed was Orion, shimmering a promise to outlive them.

They took their cups of fruit punch to the tables beneath an awning, away from the gymnasium. By the time they sat down, the band sounded like a stereo heard from an adjacent room.

A comfortable silence opened between them as they sipped their drinks, gazing up at the unfathomable gathering of stars that made Soojin grateful, for the first time in a long time, to live in Jade Acre with all its pristine bounty.

"Look! Shooting star!" Mark said suddenly, pointing up, and she just caught sight of a pinprick of light arcing a silver parabola across the sky. Almost as soon as it appeared, it was gone—folded back into the night.

"That's the first time I've ever seen one!" she gasped, keeping her eyes pinned skyward in hopes of seeing another, but aside from a slowly passing plane, the night was still.

"You have to make a wish," Mark said, biting down on a chip of ice.

"No."

"Why not?"

"It's stupid." Soojin swirled her drink, watching the orange pulp drift across the surface like swollen petals. Wishing upon anything was silly—an exercise in disappointment. And yet . . .

When they were younger, Mirae delighted in such things. Wishing on milk teeth thrown hard toward the heavens, wishing at 11:11, wishing upon a hundred misshapen origami stars folded with chubby child hands. During road trips, she would hold her breath in every tunnel, her face flushed and strained as the orange fluorescence streaked across her features. Mirae was strict about never divulging what she'd wished for. Soojin wondered if any of her sister's wishes ever came true.

She bent her head and wished.

When she opened her eyes, Mark's face loomed close to hers, studying her expression. His eyes looked amber in the lamplight. She startled, believing for one flustered beat that he might drift even closer—but he just tucked the hairs that had fallen out of place behind her ears before settling back into his seat.

Mark Moon had never been shy with his affection. They'd held hands as children, kissed each other on the cheek, napped nose to nose, dabbed one another's playground wounds clean. His touch wasn't a progression—it was a return.

"Don't you want to know what I wished for?" she asked quietly.

"I think I can hazard a guess," he said, offering his hand. She took it, thinking he would move to lead her out of her seat, but he didn't. He twined his fingers through hers and stretched his legs with a satisfied sigh. His palm was callused from work. "Are you glad things worked out the way they did?" he asked, leaving his question open-ended enough that her hesitant nod could be an assent to anything.

"Good," he said, flipping her palm skyward. He peered down, tracing the life line that arced from the apex of her thumb and index finger down to the beginning of her wrist. "Remember when you and Mirae got really obsessed with palm reading? You guys were nightmares."

Soojin nodded. She turned Mark's hand so its position mirrored her own: palm up, fingers splayed like a book. She compared their lines, tracing his with her pinky finger. It had been their mother who'd shown the girls how to read palms for fun, and the sisters had gotten utterly too serious about it.

"God, the tantrum you threw when you realized you had the unluckiest hands of the three of us," Mark said, a gentle teasing that didn't land. She frowned into her cup.

While her teenage years were marked by the emotional suppression and self-imposed solitude that stemmed from losing her mother, she had been a walking catastrophe of feelings when she was a child. It was no wonder everyone marveled at how mature Mirae was despite only being a year older.

In her head, Soojin heard her sister's voice. *I'm not your mom*, she had said in that tone she often used when teasing. But what if it wasn't just a careless taunt? Mirae had always had to comfort her and allay her oscillating moods like a mother might, and that had only intensified after the car crash.

So yes, there had been tantrums—Soojin couldn't deny that. Mark dragged his finger aimlessly along her palm, as if mapping out continents on her hand. Here was the country of the living; here was the nation of love. Here was everything she'd lost in the dark waters between life line and family line.

He was so tactless sometimes.

"Well, Mirae had the luckiest lines of us all, so I guess we know for sure now that this is all bullshit." She withdrew her hand and folded it into the warmth of her lap.

"You don't know that," Mark said, eyes luminous with that particular brand of earnestness that made her want to strike and be held by him all at once. "I don't think any ancient palmists accounted for a miracle like you being born. Mirae might end up totally outliving us both."

A miracle, he'd called her, in a voice with not even an ounce of hyperbole. In lieu of answering, she rubbed her hands against her arms, watching silhouettes pirouetting beyond the window's gold light. The live band played a languorous and crooning tune now, winding the party down to a lull. "Who knows," Soojin said finally, in a quiet voice meant for only herself, but he heard her anyway.

"Want to dance?" Mark asked, his eyes very soft.

Soojin considered saying no. Her feet ached and she was tired. But who knew when she would find herself amid such festivities again? She rose and took a few steps toward the gymnasium, halting when she realized he wasn't following her.

"Change your mind?" she asked.

He was standing straight-backed with his hands in his pockets, head tipped to regard the canopy of leaves above him. Lit and burnished by autumn, they were beginning to loosen. Soon there would be none left—the branches completely bare. But for now they were a livid, living gold.

"No," he said, outstretching his hand. She laid her fingertips on his without thinking. "It's a little muggy in there, isn't it? How about right here?"

She let her arms wrapping loosely around his neck be her answer, and they swayed around the courtyard to the slow notes of the saxophone. She was hyperaware of his hands, the heat of his palms radiating clean through the thin fabric of her dress and the way his fingertips absently danced along to the music. Each press sent jolts of electricity up her spine. The proximity of his face unnerved her, so she focused instead on a copper leaf that had fallen on his shoulder.

"Did you have fun tonight?" he asked.

"I did." She had answered without thinking, but once she heard herself, a breath of surprise escaped at her own admission. "I really did."

Part of her had come fully expecting, perhaps even hoping, to spend the night distracted, thinking of her sister and all she was missing. But much of the night she had not thought of Mirae at all. She'd laughed at Jay and Mark's impromptu dance battle, which opened a brief circle in the sea of other dancers. She'd dug punch-swollen blackberries out of the bottom of her cup, staining the crescents of her nails maroon. She'd hiked up the hem of her dress and danced in full view of the student body she'd spent the last several years avoiding and had given herself up to her own singular joy.

An arrow of emotion shot through her, and it took her a long while to recognize it as guilt. "It was a great night," she said.

Mark tilted his head slightly, studying her change in expression before swinging her into a circle swiftly enough to startle her out of her mood. She yelped into his neck as the trees blurred into a burnished curtain around them.

"I'm going to dip you," he said, eyes full of mischief. "Ready?"

"Oh no you don't, Mark Moon!" She dug her nails into his arms.

"I'm not going to drop you," he laughed. "Just hold on to me."

She did as she was told, her arms gripping his shoulders with bruising force, and then off they went. The world spun, and when he bent forward to dip her, there was a brief sensation of falling—just long enough for her to think, *You bastard,* before the arms bracing her shoulders went taut.

"I told you I wouldn't drop you," he said when the world stopped spinning. The form was all wrong, her back uncomfortable from being bent too far back. Still, he looked pleased with himself, and she couldn't help but feel pleased along with him.

"Thanks for the bare minimum courtesy," she said as his self-satisfied smirk widened to something open and tender. Backlit by the dim courtyard lamps, his errant hair kicked up a golden halo around his head. He looked so lovely to her in that moment.

Without thinking, she reached up to graze his cheek with her thumb. She meant to brush off a piece of glitter that had fallen on his face from tinsel, but after it was gone, she held her hand there, cupping his jaw. She could feel the throb of a pulse beneath his chin, his tendons undulating as he swallowed. He leaned into her touch, turning his face so his lips could press against the heat of her palm—then again at her wrist. It couldn't have been longer than a second or two. She held her breath until she felt him break into a smile against her skin.

The music ended—the final long notes rising into the night sky, and just like that, whatever spell had woven around them dissolved back into the ether. If it weren't for the small bird of her heart clamoring against her rib cage, she might have thought the moment before imaginary.

He pulled her upright, the two of them giddy and flushed and unable to look one another in the eye.

"It's almost ten. I should probably get you home," Mark said. "I want your dad to still like me."

"Let's stop by the cottage first so I can drop off this party favor," Soojin said, pulling out a little sticker the school had specially made and passed out at the entrance. JAS was written in gold foil over the Trojan mascot, which glimmered with a homecoming-king sash across its chest. It was gaudy enough to be delightful. She hoped it would give Mirae at least a little joy, this small sliver of the party brought home to her.

Mark pulled a piece of silver tinsel from her hair and, arm in arm, they left.

20.

They were approaching the cottage doorstep when something caught Mark's eye. In the darkness it was nearly imperceptible, but as he followed Soojin to the door, he noticed that the flower beds that had been vibrant just that morning were wilting. If he saw his plants doing the same in his garden at home, he wouldn't think twice—it was the kind of gentle peril easily rectified by watering. Even so, his skin prickled. Soojin pulled out her key.

"Wait," he said.

"What?" Her key glinted in the dark.

"I don't think we should go in there." He tried to keep his face casual, eyeing the swaying red drapes in the window. He was very aware of his lungs, of the thin quality of the air that entered and left them.

"Why not?" Soojin asked, fitting the key into the lock. The tick of the lock's interior architecture sounded like artillery clicking into place. This time Mark couldn't help himself—he held her wrist, harder than he'd meant to.

"Look," he said, pointing to the planter boxes. Soojin followed the line of his finger, and her eyes widened. Mark had been mistaken. It wasn't underwatering that was making the flowers droop. The soil was completely flooded, drowning the roots.

"What the . . . ," Soojin said under her breath, shifting her feet. She'd stepped into a puddle, and her heels left slim silhouettes on the concrete. Something like fear crossed her face, and then she was turning away, her attention back on the lock with urgency now. A click and the door swung open. Soojin entered, enveloped almost at once in shadow.

Some animal instinct in Mark wanted to turn around, but why? Because of overzealously watered flowers? He followed her, shutting the door and leaving them to fumble for the switch in complete darkness.

"Watch where you're going!" she hissed when he bumped into her. Then her own feet sent something heavy rolling across the floor.

"Watch where I'm going *how* exactly?" His knees banged into a dresser, and something careened off it, bouncing on the floor with a metallic clink. The impact sent jolts up and down his leg. "Crap. We're going to wake her up. I told you—" Soojin's hand flew out in the darkness and smacked against his eyes before it fumbled down the bridge of his nose and finally over his mouth.

"Shh," she said, and he obeyed; their breathing falling and rising in tandem was all he could hear at first, and then his ears sharpened. He heard wind, the gentle prattle of a shower running behind closed doors. And then something strange: a wet, clumsy searching from the other side of the cottage. The sound of a foraging animal, rummaging in the dark.

"Unnie?" Soojin called. She pulled away from Mark's face and returned to the wall to pat for the switch. Mark groped for her aimlessly until he felt her hand, and they laced their fingers together. "Are you sleeping?"

Soojin finally found the switch, and the world flashed white. It took a while for their eyes to adjust, but when they did, the cottage was largely how it was the last time they visited: pleasant beige walls, the outdated TV resting atop a wooden stand Mr. Han had built by hand. On the rug was a mess of books, restlessly pawed through. The bed was unmade, blankets thrown to the floor, clear evidence that Mirae had lounged in it at some point in the evening.

Something heavy and unmistakably ceramic shattered against the floor, and Soojin yelped. The noise was coming from behind the kitchenette counter. Soojin dug her nails into Mark's knuckles, but he barely registered the pain. He was gripping her just as hard, the seed of dread in his belly blooming into full, disorienting fear.

A possum got in was his first thought, but he knew even without seeing that this was no animal.

"Unnie," Soojin said again, her voice steady despite the way she clung to him. "What are you doing?" They inched around the kitchen island.

Soojin froze, jerking from his hold to clasp her hands over

her mouth. The kitchenette looked like a small hurricane had raged through it. The rice cooker was open, every last morsel gone, leaving only the thin gauze of cooked starch clinging to the rim of the pot. The spice rack was upended. An overpowering sprawl of dried herbs and spices dusted the counters and floor in a thin umber layer streaked clean where someone's knees had crawled through it. Each utensil drawer had been pulled out, and the cabinets dug through, boxes ripped with their contents devoured, only torn wrappers remaining. Something crunched beneath the soles of Mark's shoes. Uncooked grains of rice, as white and numerous as an infestation of lice. And there she was, in the center of it all like the eye of a storm.

"What—" Soojin started when she finally found her voice. Then: "Oh my god, what happened?" She ran to her sister. Mirae was on the floor, leaning heavily on the shelf of the opened cabinet, hovering over a small pool of vomit. That sound, that wet, tremoring sound resonating through the dark, had been coming from Mirae. A sheen of sweat plastered her uneven bangs across her face.

Soojin crouched beside her, pulling Mirae's shoulders back so she was no longer leaning on the unstable shelf. Mirae's arms were coated in oil, in cinnamon and tea leaves and glass from the olive-oil bottle shattered at her feet. One of her hands was curled in a decorative tureen of sea salt, a few white crystals clinging to the wet of her lips. Mark's mind filled with memories of his mother flinging salt over her shoulder upon returning home after Mirae's funeral so her ghost would not follow—would not haunt. But lord, here she was.

If blood coursed the length of her body, if her heart still beat—could she still be a haunting?

"I don't know what's wrong with me," Mirae said, her voice so small Mark could hardly hear her over the whine of the faucet. Soojin was wetting a kitchen towel, dabbing her sister's ruddy face with it. Her cheeks, her lips smeared thick with oil and salt. Mirae opened her mouth as if to speak but shuddered in an unsteady breath; the seams between her teeth were pink with blood, like she'd bitten down on something sharp and inedible and had mindlessly kept gnawing. "I'm so hungry and nothing I do is enough. . . . I don't know what—"

"It's okay," Soojin said in an even voice Mark assumed was meant to be comforting but only sounded dissociative. She wiped her sister's arms. The towel came away copper. Mirae was covered in small cuts, and Mark had just enough time to think that her blood had a watery, diluted quality before Soojin wiped it away.

"You're fine. You're fine," Soojin kept saying. Like a wish being made as the clock tolls midnight or the last birthday candle is blown out. There was a wildness in Mirae's eyes that was strikingly uncharacteristic. She'd always been the put-together sibling—the reliable one. Panic rendered her face somewhat foreign, a stranger beneath the kitchenette's flickering pale light. "You're fine," Soojin said.

Mirae slapped her hand away. "Stop telling me I'm fine!"

Soojin recoiled. Mark could see the shock in her eyes. Her sister had *never* struck her. *Never.*

Had he ever seen Mirae this way, even as a child? She was always in meticulous control of herself. At Mrs. Han's funeral, hadn't she stayed glassy-eyed while her sister and father broke down? Hadn't she been silent amid the procession of white chrysanthemums filling the halls, like someone vacating themselves just long enough to grieve in private?

"I'm scared," Mirae finally admitted, her voice only just audible above the shower still running on the other side of the cottage.

It was this admission that rallied him. Mark knelt beside Soojin, lifted Mirae's hand out of the salt tureen. In her mindless foraging, she had cut a shallow gully across her palm; salt was embedded in the open flesh. Looking at it stung. He found a bottle of water and rinsed the wound clean. Mirae showed no resistance. She sat in shock, hiccupping, letting them tend to her like a child.

"Mark, I can handle this. Go home," Soojin said, angling her body to cover Mirae's bare legs. He hadn't even registered that she was mostly unclothed from the waist down, the hem of her nightgown hiked up over her thighs.

"But—" he began.

"Just go."

"I can help."

"Please." Soojin's voice left no room for negotiation.

He stood, then backed away from the ransacked kitchen toward the living room. The air felt suddenly moist and heavy. The books littering the floor were crimped from moisture. He leaned down to pick one up when a drop of water hit the back of his neck and trailed a slow path down to his spine. It was shockingly cold. He reached to wipe it away, but his hand came away dry. He looked up at the spackled ceiling. No condensation beaded on its stippled paint.

The door slammed behind him as he swept outside. His heart pounded as he pressed his back against the cool wood of the door, listening to the indistinct murmur of the sisters inside. The running water and footfalls. He closed his eyes and breathed slowly into his hands.

When the hammering of his pulse receded, he pulled his face from his palms. At his feet, the flower beds that had looked entirely flooded earlier were bone-dry. When he knelt to touch the dirt, it crumbled between his fingers.

He got into his car, turned on the ignition, then idled, watching steam curling thin white ghosts beyond the glass. In the moonlight, the woods looked imaginary. Sparks of light drifted across his vision like will-o'-the-wisps and burst into globes of gold when he pressed the heels of his palms over his eyes.

An hour ago, he and Soojin had been twirling under the pear trees strung gold with fairy lights. He'd traced a finger down her life line and felt such stupid, humiliating joy. All that time, had Mirae been upturning the kitchen in search of something, anything, that would satiate her? The knowledge discolored the evening. It made his silly little delights feel criminal.

He turned out of the driveway and hurried down the tree-lined road toward his home, his hands gritty with salt. The emergency boutonniere Soojin had fashioned from his geranium drooped in his pocket, its petals tipped black with the prelude of rot.

That night, after Mark left and Mirae drifted into an uneasy sleep, Soojin stood alone in the cottage bathroom. The concealer she'd applied to her wrist had washed off, and with it the fictions she'd told herself. The bruise had darkened and spread its dark wings farther along her skin. Soon it might wrap like a black bracelet around her wrist.

I can hide it, Soojin thought. A dim throb of panic edged into her mind. *A thick watch, or makeup. Everything will be fine.*

But would it? She pulled her sister's old dress off and scrutinized herself. The divot of her belly, the striation of her ribs, more stark in the lamplight. Nothing out of the ordinary. Nothing wrong. But no, there at her sternum: a tiny purple splotch. She scratched at it until she drew blood, willing it to lift away beneath her nails. No use. The bruise resembled a dot of decay on a soft-bodied fruit. Inconspicuous but inevitable. Once rot sets in, it spreads. It overtakes the fruit and proliferates its spoil to whatever is unlucky enough to be near it.

There was an awful understanding needling the neglected corners of her mind. The body's irrefutable awareness of approaching danger.

A dead hand is a hand of thorns.

Soojin turned off the light and studied her reflection in the near dark, taking comfort in what she could no longer see.

From Mirae's bedroom, the rustle of sheets. Her sister was alive. This was the only true thing that mattered. Soojin was happy. For the first time in months, everything was as it should be. She would protect this hard-earned joy, no matter what.

Soojin raised an elbow over her mouth as if to stifle laughter, but laughter never came.

21.

After the matriarch's death, the family washed her stiff body in warm water perfumed with incense. They filled her mouth with three spoonfuls of rice and placed a coin over each eye before the men lowered her into the earth. With this they bid her an afterlife of plenty and returned to a home without her in it.

Time passed. The long winter yielded to spring, and the matriarch's grave mound grew mossy with new grass and the delicate arched petals of fawn lilies. As if by her blessing, the grip of famine slowly left the village. Their fallow fields finally yielded crop, and the men who had left years prior to work on squid boats in far-flung provinces returned, bringing with them livestock, wives, chubby babies strapped to their backs like satchels of barley.

By then the girl's body was ravaged from being so long tethered to the revenant bird and its hatred. Black abrasions corded the length of her forearms, while bruises the hue of plum blackened her sternum, her collarbones, her breasts.

But now the long hunger was over.

There is no need to rely on it anymore; the bird can finally be free, thought the girl as she buried the breastbone and waited for blood to gather. Today she would resurrect it and, rather than slaughter, would walk deep into the mountains to free it at last. There, among the pines and riotously blooming azaleas, it could live out its natural lifespan or be caught by a tiger and have the blessing of an uninterrupted death.

But as soon as she pulled the hen from the ground, it clawed her blackened palms and kicked away from her. Before the girl could do anything, the hen flew toward the river that surged as quick as an artery. Intent to die on its own terms, the bird crashed into the water and was folded immediately under the current. Its body carried away without so much as a cry, it left nothing but a solitary white feather in its wake.

The girl mourned at the riverbank for two nights and three days. She'd grown to love the bird she'd birthed again and again just to suffer so that they could live. She wanted to be absolved of her guilt for all those days spent stroking the soft feathers of its back before breaking its body for soup. In apology, she finally named the hen. She called it 장수, Jangsu, meaning "long life"—and the name followed it into the water like an animal. Pulled by the river, the body was swept into an estuary, where, picked at by fish and divested of its feathers, it sank to the bottom and did not rise again.

Following homecoming, Soojin and Mirae came to an unspoken agreement to not speak of the disastrous way the night had ended. They settled back into familiar rhythms: Her sister in the kitchen grinding coffee beans while Soojin readied for school upstairs. Coming home from a shift at the diner to find Mirae reading beat-up paperbacks with her feet kicked high on the bed frame, absorbed in scenes she'd probably read a dozen times.

This is happiness, Soojin would think on those days. *This is the only real thing.*

But there was a mounting list of worries Soojin refused to dwell on. The bruises spreading ink across her skin, and the way the days had become a game of straws. Soojin was never sure which sort of sister she'd find in the morning: the Mirae who was like sunshine, giddily helping Soojin and Mark put together their costumes for Halloween, when their normally sleepy school turned into a fun house, or the Mirae whose moods were like unpredictable weather. Who foraged at all hours of the night, leaving their kitchen a grease-spattered mess she uncharacteristically didn't bother to clean up.

Milkis no longer begged to be let out of her cage when Mirae was in the room, Soojin had noticed. And on occasion the rat would dive into her burrow, so only her alert red eyes were visible in the shadows. She didn't dwell on that, either, or on the way her sister would sometimes lock herself away in their parents' bathroom, running the faucet for hours as the pipes in the walls struggled to accommodate her.

Soojin didn't dwell on it, but sometimes she did sneak downstairs to press her ear against the bathroom door. There was never light emitting from the seams of the frame—*Who bathes in total darkness?* Soojin would think for a moment before forcing the question away to listen. She'd hear the quiet sloshing of water against the tub's rim, and an otherwise unnatural silence. Where was the sound of a body moving against the enamel? The plastic click of bottles opening and closing? Where was the low-grade clamor that came with being alive?

Are you with me? Soojin would think, pressing her ear against the door. Listening to the faucet's lonely drip as the days hurtled past her like water. *Are you there?*

The girl's affinity with water was deepening. No, that was not exactly right. Water was becoming more insistent. It lapped at the edges of her mind. Where she was once able to recess its endless noise, it now intruded on her sleep and whispered to her at all hours of the day.

It didn't bother her, exactly, this feeling of being slowly edged out of her own body by water. The night she'd gone to Porter had been a failure. She'd lost hold before she could harm him, and he'd woken with nothing but the fading memory of a nightmare. But it wouldn't happen again. Water could cut through anything. As she yielded to it, she could feel herself sharpening into a more useful blade.

But tonight was not for Porter. She had other loose ends she wanted to cut.

She closed her eyes and let the myriad sounds of the town rush over her. The branching arteries of Black Pine River in the distance. A crane taking flight, scattering water with its talons. Her sister sighing at the diner, tipping a stained coffeepot beneath the warm rush of a sink.

She unbraided the sound until she found what she was

looking for. Joe Silas's wet breathing. His dull, beating heart. And, elsewhere in the Silas household, a rushing faucet, bathwater. A door.

When Joe had returned home, barely cognizant one moment and raging at every source of water the next, Claire Silas thought hopefully to herself, *Maybe he will die.* Certainly, she tolerated the man well enough, but theirs had been a marriage of convenience. Joe was always there. He had been the one her late parents had approved of, and so when he proposed, like livestock she'd been sent.

Claire had always dreamed of leaving, and the intervening years hadn't dampened that desire. If he died, the life-insurance payout would be enough that she could travel; she could even sell this old place and try her luck in the larger world. It would be better than being tethered to this man she didn't love, feeding him applesauce as his scent ripened from his aversion to water. Wet wipes could only do so much. She couldn't even shower in her own damn bathroom for the way he roused from his stupor to balk and rave as soon as the old pipes creaked on.

So here she was, then, in the downstairs guest bathroom, staring at herself in the mirror. Behind her, the shower had been running for a good five minutes, but it was still only lukewarm. No condensation built on the mirror, and her reflection was so exact as to be off-putting.

She walked back toward the shower. The water was still tepid—stupid piece of shit. She cranked the nozzle as high as it would go, then sat on the edge of the tub. It was only then that she noticed something odd. Though the plug was pulled out, the water wasn't draining. The tub was partially filled. The pipes backed up to hell. Claire sighed. Most everything in the house was old and in need of replacement. They should have done it all in one fell swoop those many years ago when Joe came upon that large sum of money he wouldn't explain but she suspected he'd won gambling. Instead he'd pissed it away—on their daughter's ridiculous college tuition, yes. But also on drink and gadgets and at the craps table in Cache Creek.

Claire fished in the small mouth of the drain, rooting for whatever soap or scum had lodged there, hoping she wouldn't have to snake it. But there! Her finger wrapped around something sleek and sinuous. She tugged. It wasn't easy to dislodge, but it was unmistakably hair. A few silky strands snapped as she finally pulled a long tangle from the drain.

An involuntary shriek. The hair couldn't have been hers. It was thick and black, whereas hers was a silvering brown and Joe's was as short and wiry as terrier fur. The notion of Joe having had an affair crossed her mind, but the thought was so implausible as to be funny—who would have him? But then, whose hair was this?

She loosened the ropes of hair from her hand by waving it through the water, then sank her fingers once again into the drain. They tangled in another mass of black hair, which pulled out as thick and knotted as sargassum. The tub was full now. In her battle with the hair, she'd forgotten to turn off the nozzle.

"What in the world," Claire muttered. The water would still not drain.

It listens through the water, Joe had whimpered once when

she'd brought a basin for his sponge bath. *Don't give it a way in.* The surface of the water was now a sketchbook of hair set adrift. The black wisps obscured the surface with its dense cross-stitch. Claire didn't notice the rippling at first, the depths gathering into the translucent suggestion of a girl, curled like a thing just born. A sudden eddy and flex.

Only then did the nameless sense of danger hit her. Claire yelped and tried to kick back from the tub, but something below the surface gripped her wrists and held fast. She felt a searing pain at the touch: a ransacked feeling, like she was being evacuated, leeched into something else in a violent osmosis.

The thing yanked her wrists, using her weight to draw itself up. But Claire couldn't maintain her balance. She toppled, and her face smashed hard against the tub's curved edge. Her vision flashed white before the pain came, but even then, the sensation was muted. A dull awareness that something was suddenly wrong with her body.

She was vaguely aware of blood dripping a hot trail down her forehead, but she couldn't gather herself. She didn't understand what was happening. Something drew itself up out of the bathtub, stepped out. Over and past her, leaving the bathroom with quiet footsteps. Claire could hardly muster fear at this fact.

Cleaned up. I should get this cleaned up, Claire thought. Her mind fed her disjointed thoughts about her bath mat. Such a nice one—yellow with red flower trimming. Blood would ruin it. Nothing stained like blood. Joe would make a fuss.

Claire stumbled to the cabinet, drew out a rag, baking soda. There was blood in her eyes, and she didn't quite remember why as she tried to bend to clean her mess. Her limbs wouldn't listen to her. They spasmed, and Claire was abruptly in the water. Her head submerged while the rest of her body strained outside the tub. Her knees scrabbled against the bath mat, useless and stiff and too shocked to fight for purchase. She opened her mouth to draw breath, and water entered her. An agitation of froth. Hair. Nothing.

The water beating down from the showerhead finally ran hot as she drowned.

The girl moved through the house quietly, plucking knots of hair from her skirt as she searched, tracking slim, wet footprints in her wake.

She found the man soon enough. Joe Silas sat upright on his bed, propped up by pillows against his headboard. His milky eyes slid toward her. No panic, only a slow dread like he'd known she would come, just not quite so soon. She sat beside him, leaving ringlets of bathwater on the sheets.

She reached out to touch him, and he flinched only slightly. "Will it hurt?" he asked. His eyes had a regressed, childlike aspect to them. It tendered her toward him, even as the anticipation of violence spread sweet through her synapses. Hatred was a kind of devotion, she had learned. This man, who had seen the opportunity to save her mother and done nothing. Then years later, another opportunity, another catastrophe, and had done nothing then, too. She was devoted to making him suffer.

The girl offered her kindest smile.

For the man, there was a certain relief in knowing there were no more options: a forced acceptance was still acceptance. She placed a hand against his chest. He felt a stabbing sensation like a thorn slipping inside. Then a cold that radiated outward, clutching his heart, filling his lungs. It hurt. He opened his mouth to scream for his wife. Instead of his voice, warm liquid thrust up his throat like a rush of bile.

But it wasn't bile. It was water, speckled with dirt and small stones. It streamed down the front of his shirt and pooled in the blanket draped over his lap, created its own small biosphere. Silt. Filaments of moss. A mayfly nymph flicking its many translucent legs. His eyes rolled back. The river had him.

22.

The bodies were found in the morning. When Claire Silas failed to bring her husband in for an appointment, when she didn't answer any calls, a concerned friend dropped by their home. The shower in the guest bathroom was still running—and Claire was in it. Her torso and head in the tub, her kneeling legs on the bath mat outside it. She'd struck her head hard enough to swell the brain, and yet it was clear her last actions before losing her balance and drowning were to attempt to clean. A rag and box of baking soda lay by her knee, the bloodstains set a deep brown in the mat.

Joe Silas was found in the bedroom upstairs, propped up against his headboard. Later, both deaths would be ruled accidental drownings. Their lungs full up with water. In an empty tub, in a bed. No one knew how this could be.

The friend who found them would later hysterically recount to anyone who would listen that there had been wet footprints leading from the guest bath to the main bedroom. The houseplants had drooped with root rot, overwatered. The walls were dark with water damage. Even the stairwell banister had been dripping.

But the worst of it had been Silas himself. Gone too many hours, his open eyes were milky. A small lake had been made of his lap, in which black fish darted around the mounds of his knees pushing up against the covers. Algae grew up the trellis of his tipped-back throat. A small handprint had been seared against his chest, which was swollen and decomposing rapidly.

His gaping mouth pooled with brackish water, dark with silt. And from it a white lotus grew, its stem thrust up his esophagus. Flower of renewal. Flower of rot. Its petals were just beginning to open. When it bloomed, a single blue eye darted wildly where the stamen should have been. It was this, the friend claimed, that finally broke her. Made her run out of the home screaming for help.

Later, when coroners went to collect the bodies, nothing was out of the ordinary. All traces of footprints had vanished. The husband and wife remained dead, but less extraordinarily so. The woman had still died in the bath, the man in the bed. No water in sight. No corpse flowers.

But the friend's story was better.

Gossip spread around town, as did a superstitious apprehension. *Water,* the town whispered. *The water.* The mysterious misfortune of the Silas family was all anyone could talk about. Their names were murmured in diner booths, barbershops, school hallways. When the news hit Mark Moon's cell phone—a frantic text from Jay with a link to the local paper—he was helping his mother tend to the cemetery.

After the rains, the bouquets left out on the pet graves were softened beyond recognition. Mark could normally identify them all as he picked them up for the compost bin: chrysanthemum, white rose, lily of the valley. Today, though, as he and his mother tended to the headstones, pulling weeds and tossing dead flower arrangements, he could name none but for their thorns.

He hissed as a small cut opened on his thumb. He pulled it to his lips, tasted blood and then nothing. The evidence of the body disappeared so quickly. He sighed, tossing the roses into the compost bin before dabbing the cut on his sleeve.

His mother paused work to gaze out into the ever-present fog with a look of unease. For the past month, Jade Acre had been experiencing an unusual amount of rain, even by their normally drizzly fall standards. Today was a rare semidry day, and yet no one was out and about. The mood around town was grim. After the unusual death of the Silases, people were nervous.

"Mom," Mark called, picking up a soggy pig-ear chew from the headstone of a Chihuahua. It was slick with the prelude of decomposition, smelling of outhouse and soil. "Can you bring the bag here?" She shuffled over and dropped the half-full compost bag at his feet. He added his collection to it, then looked up at her. It was uncharacteristic for her to be so quiet, staring wordlessly into the milky fog as if something might appear from it. "What are you thinking about?"

"What else would I be thinking about?" she sighed, sitting heavily on the headstone of a tabby. "The poor Silases. I can't believe it. And that friend of theirs. Someone needs to get her help. The wild stories she's spreading around, whipping everyone into a frenzy . . ." She shook her head. "It reminds me of my hometown."

Mark's mother had grown up on a remote island off Korea's southwest coast. The name of it eluded Mark now, but he knew of it secondhand from his mother's stories. It was a village accessible from the mainland only by ferry or a land bridge that appeared just a couple of times a year when the water levels receded. The squat, colorfully roofed houses were never locked, and free-roaming Jindo dogs dozed near the docks, waiting for tossed fish heads or entrails. In the open-air markets, old women peddled pressed filefish and raw soy crabs fat with golden roe. In the spring, cuttlefish hung drying on clotheslines all over the village; in winter, elders made for the mudflats with tin buckets to collect clams the size of a child's hand.

It was also a village that youth fled, leaving behind only children and the elderly. It was a village where schools lay fallow some years for lack of students. Where residents died with no one to take their places, and so the homes became their own ghosts: flush with cobwebs, bleached by the salty coastal breeze.

It was, above all, a haunted village.

"You're thinking about the water ghost," Mark said. He'd heard the story from his mother many times; it was her go-to campfire story.

"There was no ghost," his mother snapped.

This was the story of his mother's childhood village as Mark knew it. Long ago, a young girl playing on the beach claimed she saw a white egret in the water. The bird had been seen by no one else, but the child was adamant it had been there, preening its feathers, looking at her with lonely black eyes. She snuck out at night in search of its white plumage and was pulled out to the ocean by a riptide.

Though the villagers took their squid boats out and trawled the sea with nets, her body was never found. It was monsoon season, and the sea was so fierce there was no telling how far out she had been swept. The villagers docked the boats and assumed her dead. Her distraught mother was inconsolable—she didn't leave her home for weeks, surviving only on the thin pollack broth the other villagers laid outside her door. When she finally emerged, she was skeletal and euphoric, holding a pair of her daughter's shoes in her hands. *Where are you going?* the villagers asked, to which she replied: *I hear my baby's voice. She's calling for me.* She laid the shoes at the edge of the water, heels facing toward the sea, as if her daughter might step out of the ocean and into her old shoes.

Every day, come thunder or rain, the mother went out to the same spot, expecting to see her daughter, but would find instead that the shoes had disappeared. She'd bring a new pair and place them just so, heels toward the water and toes pointing home.

Your baby is gone. She would want you to move on, the villagers said. The mother was undeterred. *I know my baby's voice. She tells me she's lonely. I have to give her a way to walk back to me.*

For a week she repeated this ritual, until one clear morning a fisherman went out on his boat and pulled a drowned woman up in his net, tangled among the cutlassfish. It was the mother, dead, a smile frozen on her face and arms wrapped around some organic mass so decomposed and eaten away by fish, it was impossible to identify. The frightened fisherman tore the reeking mass from the mother's arms and threw it back into the water before quickly ferrying the drowned body back to the village.

The mother was buried with the final pair of her daughter's shoes, and that was the end of that tragedy—or so the village thought. Then the nets came up from the ocean, fish all dead; then trees and vines withered. Wet footprints began appearing around the village. They retraced the steps of the mother from her home to the water. Hot torrential rain tore planks from the docks. The village's children whimpered at night, crying over someone else's loneliness. These same children began to sneak out of their houses, somnambulating toward the water. Two children disappeared this way before the village finally accepted it was haunted.

"Mom, how did your village know it was a ghost and not a string of freak accidents?" Mark asked.

"I said there was no ghost," his mother snapped again, but at his earnest expression she sighed. "There was a spot in the water that always looked black. Even on perfect days when the rest of the water was blue. That was the spot the town elders said was haunted by the drowned mother and daughter. They said they'd become mul gwisin—water ghosts—and it was their ever-growing black hair that kept the weeds there so wild."

"Did the village hold an exorcism?"

"God, no. Water ghosts can't be easily exorcised—particularly female ones. Something about a woman's energy aligning with water. Some say the only way to stop the haunting of a water ghost is to save them. The village held a purification ritual to save the souls of the drowned. Shamans were paid to come from a nearby village. A brass bowl was filled with rice, tied with a rope of white linen, and thrown into the water. The villagers said that when the bowl was retrieved, if something resembling some part of a body lay in it—a nail, hair, maybe even a tooth—the soul had been cleansed and a memorial could be held.

"That night, the ritual was halted because a sudden storm passed across the coast. It ripped boats into the ocean and chewed them into driftwood. When the villagers were finally able to retrieve the bowl, the linen had unraveled. The bowl and all its contents were gone."

"But did it work?"

"Why are you suddenly so interested in this stuff?" she asked with a sidelong glance. She twirled an unraveling thread at her sleeve. "Who's to say? Haunting, no haunting—the village declined anyway. Scared families decided to move elsewhere. But mostly people left because there were no opportunities. It was just a beautiful place to die. My family left for that reason. To Masan, and then here to this country, where I was lucky enough to have you." She touched his chin before looking back out at the fog draped like a skein in the valley below.

"People overestimate what constitutes a haunting. The mother of the drowned child was not heeding the call of a ghost. She was victim to her own yearning, and she let that yearning destroy her. That's all it takes, Mark. Not letting go is the only prerequisite of a haunting. Our harms never leave us if we don't let them leave."

She stood, picked up the compost bag, and ruffled his hair. "I'm going home. Don't linger too long, baby. You'll catch a cold."

But he did linger, thinking of the mother fished from the

water smiling serenely with her armful of rot, of the myriad ways love could become its own specter. What did it feel like? To love a thing so much you might wade into the sea for it, leaving not even your shoes onshore to walk back to your own life?

23.

His father was in his study filling out paperwork. Likely something about buying land and developing new hotels along Jade Acre's virgin coast, much to the horror and protest of local environmental groups. Bentley halted at the threshold. A thin shred of light lit the tops of his shoes as he listened to the music playing behind the door. He lifted his hand, poised to knock, then paused. He was seldom welcome in the study. But this felt important enough to risk reprimand. He knocked twice, then pushed the door open.

When Bentley entered, his father didn't greet him. He continued to type, turning around only after his email was sent.

"You know I don't like you coming in here unannounced," Christopher Porter said.

"I *did* announce myself." Bentley leaned against the doorframe, knocking twice in swift succession. "Like that. See?" It was a joke. A poor attempt at one. When his father looked unimpressed, Bentley fidgeted with a button on his sleeve. It was loosening, threads frayed for how much he'd been tugging at it over the last several hours. He was drunk. He'd been drunk since he heard the news, but if his father noticed, he didn't care.

He'd never had a warm relationship with his father, not even as a child. Bentley had entered the world premature, colicky, and difficult to love. At least for his father, who made it clear he'd never wanted to be a parent in the first place. His mom had wanted him, though, and his father, in his single-minded devotion to his wife, had acquiesced. Bentley had punished his mother's body with preeclampsia and debilitating morning sickness for the eight months she'd held him, and even when he finally left her, she never quite recovered from the toll of him.

She developed cardiomyopathy, which would follow her for years before taking her without warning in the middle of a cold December night. Bentley was just short of his ninth birthday, and even then he understood he was blamed.

His father closed his laptop. Impatience flitted across his face. "Surely not simply to say hi. I'm in the middle of something, Bentley."

"The police chief and his wife are dead," Bentley said, so fast the words crushed into one long consonant. He'd been floating in an ether all day, but giving the sentence air made it real.

His father lifted a glass to his lips, took a leisurely sip. "So I heard."

That's it? Bentley thought. It was only from the way his father stared at him that he realized he'd also said it aloud.

"Were you expecting more? It's a shame what happened to the Silases, but we hardly had a relationship with them. I won't feign tears in the privacy of my own home, if that is what you want."

Did not have a relationship. Bentley saw the ghost of beacon lights sweeping red and blue across the walls of the study. Phantom hands shaking a deal over the then-missing body of a drowned girl. Of an upturned car steaming in a gully. Two separate deals made years apart. *No relationship.*

"The woman who found them has been saying crazy things."

"Women have been known to get hysterical," his father said. He truly looked unaffected. "In any case, the joint funeral is Friday. I trust you will make time for it. It wouldn't do to skip out."

Bentley wasn't sure if he responded to that, but his feet were propelling him away and down the empty corridors that echoed the fractured clipping of his shoes back to him. He didn't know what reaction he'd been seeking from his father, but he hadn't found it. Was he losing it? Stringing threads together where there were no connections like some conspiracy theorist?

His mind fed him disjointed images from homecoming: red pulsing lights reflecting off the brass of the live band's saxophone; Soojin Han, wearing her sister's old homecoming dress. She'd resembled Mirae so closely it had felt like a haunting. Bentley had nearly pushed through the crowd straight for her, furious for a reason he couldn't quite identify. But she'd slipped out of the gymnasium doors with Mark Moon before he could.

What would he have done if she hadn't disappeared into the night? He imagined holding Soojin's face in his hands, pretending she was her sister.

After the night he'd almost run over Mirae as she scraped

roadkill off the pavement, he'd begun to follow her. He trailed her at a distance for days as she drove to and from work. Parked his car and waited in the night for a glimpse of her pale coat sneaking out of her home and into the trees. What business did any girl have peeling carcasses off the road? He had to know, and he'd let his curiosity override his guilt.

Catching Mirae in the act of resurrection had been only a matter of time. Bentley watched her pull the rat from the dirt and rubbed his eyes in disbelief, his father's motives for spiriting them away to Jade Acre suddenly so clear. Then he barreled out of the trees. He'd been babbling, nauseous, and in deep, deep disbelief.

You've been stalking me, Mirae had said, her voice clipped. His inability to move her to emotion even in these circumstances made him feel unseen—a feeling he understood from his father but couldn't stomach from his peers.

You think I'd catch you scraping up dead things and not follow through to see what's up?

She didn't answer him immediately, fiddling with the lace hem of her sleeve. She often dressed more like a museum curator than a girl from a town whose main exports were pine-tree memorabilia and abalone-shell jewelry.

He could see her chewing the inside of her cheek. She was going to beg his secrecy. She was going to bargain. This leverage over a girl he'd found so above him over the years was delicious. But when she finally did speak, her words were not what he was expecting:

So now you know. You might as well make yourself useful.

So he did. For months, Bentley accompanied her on her many secret foraging jaunts along the rural roads, rolling his sleeves up for the dirty work she somehow roped him into. They didn't forage for berries, but for the dead. The mangled coyotes and deer with plum-pit eyes were too heavy to take, but smaller lives they lifted from the asphalt like destroying gods. Possums. Squirrels. Better if the bodies were still warm and not yet devouring themselves with rot. They only took what the horseflies hadn't gotten to first.

That was the start of a year of tentative friendship facilitated entirely by secrets, by spoil. For months he watched her bury and bury and bury. Just like his father had likely done with her mom decades before.

Do you really have to go so far? It was the perennial question he asked her in those days.

She lifted the clear bag with a severed paw toward the stuttering light of their lantern. It was ready to be buried. To be called back. By then he knew the particulars of her magic. He knew it leeched life from whatever was nearby to feed the formation of new flesh. He knew she could hear voices, and that sometimes one was her mother's.

He'd felt such anxiety then: that one day Mirae might hear what she shouldn't. That she'd bury a bone and it would whisper secrets to her about what his father had done. But more than anything, he was afraid of losing her. This new friendship, tenuous and built on a foundation of secrets, was the only thing that made him feel seen.

His fear had not been misplaced, because eventually it happened.

Bentley reached his room and the memories fell away. He opened the door and stumbled in, drawn toward his desk, where a half-drunk glass of water gathered specks of dust on its surface. There was a sonorous pulse in his ears, as if he were submerged in a body of water. He was scared. He had no concrete reason to be scared. His memories of Mirae kept reaching their filaments into the present. He remembered her as he thought of the Silases' bodies growing plastic in the morgue. He remembered her as rain struck a pulsing Morse code across his bedroom window.

He suddenly wanted badly to sober up. He took in a mouthful of water, which slid partially down his throat before reversing course. He only barely made it to the sink. Emptied, Bentley lay back on the covers in the room he didn't love enough to decorate, staring at a ringlet of water damage on the otherwise pristine white wallpaper. He'd never noticed it before. It seemed to contract, then relax, like the aperture of a camera, or a single dark eye, focusing. An unnamed affection filled him. A desire to run his thumb across the blemish, but when he blinked, he lost sight of it. Even so, he reached out to place a hand against the wallpaper. It felt damp and cold.

"Nobody's here," he said to himself in the unshared dark. And then, for some hours, he dreamed.

24.

The joint funeral for the Silases was held a week after their bodies were discovered. It was clear from the Friday morning service that the turnout was not expected to be large, but nearly the entire town showed up. Businesses shuttered while their owners went to pay respects. Jade Acre Seconday's halls emptied as students called in an absence to their early classes to drop off flowers or offer a short prayer. Soojin did the same and came alone, feeling somehow implicated in her black clothes and armful of chrysanthemums. Mark's family stood in front of her in the queue to lay flowers over the bodies, and though they didn't dare speak over the crescendo of organ music, Mark touched her. A brief, intentional brush of his wrist against hers: a reassurance. When it was her turn at the caskets, Soojin kept her eyes pinned to the lacquered mahogany, the creamy satin interior. Anything but the waxen faces made too pale with makeup.

That evening, Father returned for the weekend with groceries from the Korean market in Bragg Hills. There was something stilted about him as they unloaded the endless bags from the car.

"It stinks of mildew in here," he said as he carried a bag of apples inside.

Soojin sniffed the air, smelled only wood and Pine-Sol. "No it doesn't."

He rubbed his nose, shrugged, then continued working in oppressive silence. Though he was never talkative, he usually made clumsy attempts at small talk for at least an hour upon returning home after a week away. Today, though, he made no such effort. He unloaded the final grocery bag and joined Soojin in the kitchen to organize his massive yield. It was like he'd shopped for an army, Soojin thought, as she sorted through the bounty.

"Han Soojin," her father said. The sound of her full name filled her with dread.

"Uh-oh," she said, trying her best to keep her voice airy as she folded the grocery bag. "What'd I do?"

"Someone is in this house with you when I'm gone, aren't they?"

Whatever she'd been expecting him to say, it was not that. The sand pear she'd been holding rolled out of her hand and onto the kitchen island. She scrambled, and when she caught it, her knuckles were bone-white. So much for seeming unaffected.

"Why do you say that?" Her heart skittered in her chest like it was searching for a fire escape. Had he caught a glimpse of Mirae? But they'd been *so* careful. Even now, her sister was hidden safely away in the cottage with all the light-blocking curtains tightly drawn. Every Friday, she made sure to do a clean sweep of the house: making her sister's bed and tucking away all the cups and trinkets that had accumulated on her side of the nightstand over the week.

But Mirae was human, wasn't she? It wasn't impossible that she might, on occasion, decide to chance a glimpse outside, pulling the curtain aside to let in sunlight. Who was Soojin to say her father might not have looked toward the rental cottages at the exact wrong moment to see the sliver of a familiar pale face moving behind the window?

But no, if he knew, there was no way he'd confront her so calmly. Right?

Her father studied her face and sighed. "I can tell by how fast the groceries deplete. A month's worth of rice is almost gone. You haven't been alone."

He knew. She felt something drop in her belly like a rock, and she couldn't tell if it was relief or terror.

"Dad, I . . ."

"Soo, as much as I like Mark, it makes me uncomfortable that you would spend so much time with him alone," her father said.

"Hold on—"

"You don't let him spend the night, do you?"

"What? No! I—"

"You sure?"

"Yes! Jesus, Dad," Soojin said, her face growing hot despite her best efforts. It was a lie. Mark did often spend the night after their witching-hour excursions with Mirae, and he slept sprawled like a golden retriever on the downstairs couch, his snoring so loud she could hear the bass of it from upstairs. But Soojin couldn't be honest with her father for a ridiculous number of reasons. "Trust me. I'm your pretty daughter, after all," she said in Korean. He softened, though he didn't completely drop the stern set of his lips.

They continued to sort groceries in tense silence. He'd bought all manner of things: rice cakes dusted in soybean flour; a box of persimmons individually wrapped in Korean newspapers dated 2008—the pudding-soft, oblong variety that Mirae had always favored. He'd even bought an entire dried fish. Soojin handled this gingerly. Aside from the viscera, nothing had been removed. Not its hardened eyes or the sharp teeth of its mummified mouth.

In the old country, she'd heard, this sort of dried fish was sometimes hung outside doorways, its ever-open sockets watchful of misdeeds and malignant entities. These eyes saw everything. Even the dead. Even her lies. Now the wind-dried pupil gaped up at her as she wrapped its body a few more times with parchment before burying it in the freezer.

"I'm sorry," her father said finally. His expression was no longer interrogatory. "I worry about you, is all. You're growing up so fast. I never dreamed I'd be the one to have the dating conversation with you girls. Your mom used to say to leave it to her. That I was too prudish to do well with it. I'm sure you'd have preferred it from her too."

This conversation was going to give Soojin whiplash.

"Dad, I'm grateful you love me enough to be uptight," she said.

"Ah, so I am uptight after all." Her silence made him chuckle. "Guess I'll never change."

He did that more nowadays—chuckle. Perhaps it wasn't the unfettered laugh he used to have when Mom and Mirae were around, but between just the two of them, this was new and hallowed ground.

"Listen, why don't you invite Mark and his parents to the ceremony tomorrow? It's been a long time since we've had them over, but maybe they'd like to come regardless," her father said.

"What ceremony?" she asked absently, rinsing her hands in the sink.

The breezy smile her father had on his face stiffened.

"Soojin, please tell me you aren't being serious," he said, reverting from English to Korean. Somehow the switch made him sound very grave. To her silence, he said: "It's your sister's death anniversary this weekend."

The water scalded her. She turned off the faucet, staring wide-eyed into the steel. Of course. How had she forgotten?

This time last year, Mirae had woken to the last days of her life. It was soon to be the anniversary of her death and, to honor her, the jesa: the ceremony where the family lays out food in remembrance so the departed will not be hungry in the other world. The ceremony meant to be held for elders and ancestors, which her father was having to hold instead for a daughter who would never grow old. Suddenly, the abundance of expensive fruits and artisanal rice cakes made sense, as did the incense she'd mistaken for mosquito-repellent wicks.

It was easy to forget that grim anniversary when her sister was in the cottage just a few yards away. With all the late nights they spent traipsing like jubilant ghosts along the beach, skipping rocks and sitting on the dock sipping hot chocolate brewed too sweet by Mark's hand, it was easy to forget Mirae had ever died.

"How could you forget this, of all things, Soojin?" The hurt in his voice made her want to hide.

If there was ever a time to tell him about her secret, her greatest transgression of his trust, it was now. Her mind unfurled two scenarios. In one he was ecstatic. They went to the cottage together, and Father rushed forward to scoop her sister into his arms. Together they twirled as he lifted her skyward like he did when they were small.

But that was the unlikely scenario. In the other she saw her father bent double, clutching the kitchen island. *God,* he'd say at the reality of his undead daughter. Her father believed in a heaven Soojin did not. To him, it would mean his daughter had been ripped from it and forcibly returned to soil. Still, she had to tell him. Eventually, she must.

"I'm sorry," she whispered instead, and he reached across the island to rest his construction-weathered hand over hers. The feverish images in her mind unraveled. Before her was only her father and his hurt, and there was nothing her mind could conjure that was worse. He didn't meet her eyes. Instead he studied the scuffed countertop, carefully picking the words he should say next.

"I am happy you are healing, Soojin. I'm relieved you aren't always alone. That you're socializing and living the normal life you deserve. The one I've never adequately been able to give you." His voice was gently wounding. "But don't forget about your sister, who will never have these things. Her memory will grow lonely."

The disappointment on his face burned her. He let her go,

then poured himself a nightcap before walking away. His door closed, and she watched the sliver of light beneath the door darken. Whatever slight headway she'd made with her father over the past couple of months, she had just taken several lunges back.

She looked toward the fireplace mantel, where Mirae's ashes sat in their celadon vase beside a photo of her smiling, sunlit, before a field of canola flowers in riotous yellow bloom. Forget? If only he knew what she had done.

Soojin was sovereign of the nation of never letting go.

The next day, it rained. Soojin watched her father's face as he peered out the window. His expression recalled those breathless few days before Mirae was found. Between searching and visits to the police station, he had stared haplessly through the window—just like this, willing her form to materialize from the woods.

It had rained then too.

That a deluge would come on a day meant to commemorate his eldest daughter must have felt like an affront to him. And yet it went on ceaselessly. It rained heavily enough to glut the river and flood downtown's outdated drainage systems. Enough for earth to slide down the cliff into the sea, taking two trees and their centuries-old roots with it. An unusual amount of rain, even for their tiny rainy corridor of a chronically burning state. Still, Mark's family came, somber in their black dress clothes. In the short walk from driveway to porch, the downpour laminated their hair flat against their faces.

Soojin expected a stilted reunion. Their families, once so

close, hadn't spent meaningful time together in years. Instead, Mark's mother immediately enveloped Soojin's father in her arms. If the embrace began mostly against his will, he returned it earnestly before shaking Mr. Moon's hand. Then they all got to work.

The kitchen grew furious with activity. Their jesa table, modest though it was, still demanded much labor. Soojin's father unraveled dried pollack from parchment paper as Mark's mother cracked eggs into a bowl. She whipped them with salt before dropping in thin cuts of battered cod to coat for pan-frying.

Soojin and Mark's father got to work stacking fruit onto separate white platters: a mound of dried dates, sand pears, persimmons with the calyxes removed. Mark, as bumbling in the kitchen as he was assured in the garden, hovered behind them, his offers of help swatted away until Soojin tasked him with transferring platters of food to the jesa table—of which he only dropped one.

"Red foods to the west!" Mark's father barked, laying out a plate of rice cakes dyed jade with mugwort. Mark pivoted with his bowl of apples, scurrying to the western end of the floor table.

"*East!*" his mom shouted over the fry pan's sizzle. "Red foods to the *east*. White foods to the west. Desserts in the front row, closest to the outer edge of the table, away from the portrait."

"No, rice and soup go in the front row!"

"Why would you place the most important part of the meal the furthest from the one it's meant for?"

Mark chewed his lip as his parents continued to bicker, then slowly inched to the east to set the table as his mother ordered. He turned to Soojin and winked, feigned wiping sweat off his brow before going to fetch the plate of fried cod and zucchini medallions. It was nice to see that the Moons hadn't given up their long-standing tradition of good-natured shouting matches. Theirs was a chaos Soojin hadn't realized she'd missed.

And like that, the preparation went on, almost pleasant. They didn't speak about loss, not even once all the food was prepared and set out on the floor table inlaid with mother-of-pearl egrets. A framed picture of Mirae stood at the head, flanked by long white candles and overlooking the bounty of food set before it. Beside the portrait was a thin white sheet of paper with her name written vertically in neat Hanja. An incense holder at the foot of the floor table completed the makeshift altar.

Perhaps the setup was imprecise, the particulars of the jesa tradition sieved through too many decades of immigration. Still, their collective effort lodged something tender into the air. Soojin wondered what her sister was doing just a few yards away in the cottage as they prepared to commemorate the anniversary of her death. Was she spinning the skin off an apple as they offered apples to her memory?

Soojin's hands were unsteady in her lap as she watched her father fiddle with his lighter. Mark reached over and gave her hand a squeeze, and when he moved to pull away, she held on. She needed an anchor, so he stayed, running his thumb reassuringly over her knuckles.

The lighter finally sparked to life, and her father tilted its blue flame toward the wick.

The incense was meant to guide the spirit of the departed to the table and bid her to eat.

Mirae was not a spirit. She was flesh and blood and earthly emotion. They were inviting nothing to the table, because Mirae was among them already.

Her father lit the incense. Its heady scent rode the smoke, curling slowly into the air, and with that the ceremony began. Beneath the amber light, the tip of the wick smoldered. A lighthouse calling nothing to shore.

In the warmth of the Han house, the two families bowed toward the departed daughter's photo, then left the room to allow her spirit to eat in peace. The adults moved to the back porch to talk under the patter of rain striking the awning. Soojin and Mark retreated to her room, where Milkis ran frantic circles in her wheel.

Soojin remembered what came next from the jesas they'd held for her mother. After the spirit had symbolically partaken, they would return to the room and burn the slip of paper with the deceased's name to signal departure, closing the bridge to the other world behind her. After the dead had gone, the living would eat. But for now there was just this waiting.

The levity of the kitchen was gone, and Soojin felt drained. The seed of a migraine had begun to bloom, and distortions of expanding sparks fizzed across her vision. The light worsened it, so she clicked a switch and let her room sink into semi-darkness.

Mark didn't question her. He sought out the only source of scant, gray light—the window—and leaned against it, unclasping the first button of his starchy black shirt. She watched him as he rested against the glass, looking suddenly serious. Her desire for comfort won out over her pride. She went to him.

"Hey, are you—" he began.

"Don't ask me if I'm okay. Please."

He stopped mid-sentence, the rest of his abandoned words coming out in a slow breath against her ear. She leaned her brow against his collar, and he held her, saying nothing. He smelled like sweat and maple syrup. She wanted to crawl into his warmth and vanish. They stood like that as lightning corded white cursive through the clouds, its searing flare casting them both briefly featureless.

A thump echoed from downstairs. Perhaps the adults had decided that enough time had elapsed and were returning inside. But Soojin wasn't ready yet. This solitude with someone who knew her for what she had done felt like comfort.

"I just want this to be over," she said into his sternum after a long silence. Startled by thunder into hiding, Milkis no longer ran on her wheel. All Soojin could hear now was rain and the thrum of Mark's heartbeat. "What a waste of time. If my dad knew, we wouldn't have to be doing this."

"Mirae deserves a memorial," Mark said evenly, untangling from her. He brushed a hair from her brow, tucking it carefully behind her ear and retracting his hand quickly. He sometimes regarded her as if she were a rattlesnake, she noticed. Like her moods were so seesawing and conditional, one wrong move could set her to striking. He'd shown her nothing but reliable goodness over the past few months. She wasn't sure why she couldn't manage the same.

"Memorials are for the dead," Soojin said.

Another dull thump from downstairs.

He breathed, looking up toward the ceiling as if searching for guidance; then, finding nothing, he returned his gaze to her. "Soo . . . ," he began before something caught his eye. He tentatively reached out to pull her shirt collar down below the divot where her collarbones met.

"What are you doing?" she asked before realizing what he was looking at. She followed his stricken gaze down to her own sternum. Wide, plum-sized bruises spread their blue-black violence against her skin. She'd gone out of her way to choose a shirt that would hide them, but Mark's proximity and vantage point had given her away. She spun away from him, buttoning up her blouse until its collar bundled against her throat.

"What the hell, Soojin?" he asked, following her into the middle of her room. "Did someone do that to you?"

"I fell."

"You fell."

"Yes."

Another thump from downstairs. She turned to face him, trying her hardest to keep her face placid. She couldn't tell him that the bruising had begun to form on the homecoming night that ended in disaster. She couldn't tell him about the nosebleeds. Her hands that occasionally tremored so hard she had to duck into the syrup-sticky closet at work to clamp them between her thighs.

Backlit by the window, his face was mostly shadow. "Funny. I thought you were a better liar than that." Then, doing the brutal arithmetic himself, he slowly turned toward the direction of Mirae's cottage.

Feeling out of control, Soojin grabbed his face between her

palms with such force there was an audible slap, forced his attention back to her. "Whatever it is you're thinking, Mark, stop it. Stop thinking it right now, because you're wrong."

But he couldn't stop, and for the first time she saw true fear in his eyes.

A screech tore through the room, so metallic and sharp she thought for a moment that a car was hydroplaning on the driveway. They clung to each other, white-knuckled until they identified the source of the sound.

"Jesus!" Soojin gasped as she stumbled toward the rat tower. Milkis was screaming from her hammock. Even in the near darkness, her red-currant eyes bulged as she writhed in the felt lining. "Is she hurt?"

Mark reached into the cage and pulled the white rat into his hand, searching for blood, for the broken bone that would warrant such a sound. "Not that I can see," he said before he lost hold. The rat squirmed from his hand and raced back into her cage, plunging into the hammock. Soojin and Mark shared a brief, stunned gaze until another sound tore from downstairs. The distinct cymbal of shattering glass. A voice yelping indistinctly through the walls.

They sprinted from the room in unison and thundered toward the stairwell. As they ran, the commotion crystallized, the words becoming legible in the air.

"Oh, Christ. Oh, lord in heaven." That was Mark's dad. Mark's mother was shouting in Korean.

And then, above everything—above the Moons' frantic babbling and the rain striking the skylights, above the thunder and the screams of the rat in her cage—Soojin heard her father's voice calling for her sister.

A white arrow struck her. Soojin buckled halfway down the stairs, and she sank, holding the banister as her knees hit the floor. The knots in the hardwood spiraled, blinked in and out of sight like dozens of eyes. Her throat had constricted into a needle's head. She couldn't breathe. Mark was upon her in seconds, holding her arm, saying, "Get up. Soojin. Come on. You have to get up."

She got up. Time grew elastic, slowed down. One moment she was on the stairs. The next she was turning down a foyer. Her mind fed her brief images of framed photos on the wall. Her mother and sister smiling in Busan Tower. Her family in downtown Jade Acre, throwing V signs in front of a Judas tree in furious magenta bloom.

Then Mark guided her around another corner and they were in the living room. Her body registered what her eyes were seeing before her mind could.

The floor was covered in an inch of water, and the jesa table had been ransacked. The photo of Mirae was on its side. Both the candles that had flanked it lay snuffed and fallen from their holders. Dripped wax had hardened into white stalagmites down the glass of the funerary portrait. The food displays were upturned and had been eaten from: apple cores and date pits rolled across the table like desiccated insects. The dried pollack had been ripped into, the butterflied face torn from its body. The waxen fibers of its flesh were wet with spit and riddled with teeth marks. All this, and her sister was nowhere.

"Mirae," her father said quietly, like a plea. Then, when he saw his younger daughter at last, his face collapsed into something horrible. He jerked toward her, but Mark's mother darted into his path, halting him.

"We've got to burn the name," she cried, running toward the jesa table and pulling the paper with Mirae's name from its cracked picture frame. "We have to cast the ghost away!"

She moved swiftly with the conviction only a mother was capable of, darting around the broken dishes and shell-shocked men toward the dying fireplace. Soojin was moving too, though she wasn't fully aware of it. All she could think as Mrs. Moon reached the fire and threw the damp paper in was: *I'm not ready.*

God, forgive me. I'm not ready to lose her again.

Soojin's knees hit the hardwood just as the paper finally ignited in the hearth. Mark shouted behind her as she thrust her bare hands into the flames. Heat knifed at her fingers as she dug into the embers and pulled out the smoldering remnants of the name, dousing it in the pond their living room floor had become. The paper had blackened beyond legibility, Mirae's name singed as fully as her eponymous future. The paper's curled edges emitted an insipid gray steam.

Skidding in the water and unable to stop, Mark rammed into her. Somehow Soojin stayed upright, and didn't even flinch as he took her fingers into his. Her hands had been in the fire for mere seconds, but they looked red and pulled taut, shiny as if bound in cling wrap. Tomorrow they would blister, but for now she felt nothing but a residual stunned tingle. "Shit. Your hands. Mom, help!" Mark called over his shoulder, but his mom was finally stalled, her face rinsed clean of color.

"Ghost. Oh. Ghost—" she muttered before running toward them. "It isn't safe here. We all have to go!" She hooked her arm in Mark's and made a wild grab for Soojin's wrist, but she jerked away. In the second that Mrs. Moon's eyes met hers, there was an understanding. Soojin had wanted this. Somehow, Soojin was the cause and she couldn't be helped. There was nothing to do but leave.

In a forceful flurry, Mrs. Moon dragged her husband and protesting son out the door and into the rain. Soon enough, the sound of their engine and the skidding gravel as they ripped out of the driveway filled the air.

Soojin reached a shivering hand out to the scorched paper, trying to straighten it, but, charred and waterlogged, it crumbled.

"You." Her father whispered behind her. It was a tone she'd never heard from him: so close to hatred, it made her breathless. This was not how she'd imagined he'd find out.

She should have told him the moment she'd buried her sister's tooth. She should have accepted his comfort on the night of the bonfire after Bentley's words cut her in two. She should have told him when Mirae's behavior began to grow erratic after homecoming. It was too late. She'd made them all run out of time.

Soojin turned slowly. He hovered above her, close enough to strike, strangling air with his fists. "What have you done."

"I—" Words failed her. Water dripped on her brow from the drenched ceiling planks.

"Soojin. What did you do?" His knuckles strained. If he hit her, she wasn't sure she could blame him. But he didn't. He backed away, eyeing his fists as if stunned by their want for violence. His face was inexplicably cast in sickly blue light, like that of a television. It cut gaunt, polar lines across one half of his face and dragged the rest into shadow. But that wasn't right. The television was off, and there was nothing in the home that would emit that glacial color. She noticed the source at the same time her father did, and they stumbled to the window together.

She lost feeling in her legs. The cottage was on fire. Even partially obscured by trees, she could see its light. But it wasn't the red blaze of a wood fire—it was a phosphorescent blue engulfing the building entirely.

"She's in there," Soojin whispered. Then, coming out of her reverie, she shouted: "She's in there!"

They burst from the home, sprinting barefoot over the sodden yard toward where the cottage burned. Only . . . it wasn't burning. Soojin could see it now as she neared. The azure flames emitted no heat, and though they licked up the wood planks of the cottage and the surrounding brush, they ate away at nothing. She reached a hand out toward the strange fire, let it flare against her injured fingertips, but it felt cold against her skin.

Like sleepwalkers, Soojin and her father opened the door and stepped into the cottage. The inside was a distortion of blue. Blue fire crept up the curtains and across the marble countertops. The linoleum was cold with it. The antique box television was playing *Wheel of Fortune* as fire streaked up the antenna. Mirae wasn't in the room.

"Unnie," Soojin called into the fire that burned nothing. Her father followed her, his breath shallow with disbelief.

"She's gone," he said.

But then she heard it. Even now as the cottage was lit with otherworldly fire, Soojin heard the sound of running water.

She moved toward the bathroom, opened the door, and found her sister inside. She was curled, embryonic, on the floor below the stream of the showerhead. But something was wrong. Unlike the rest of the cottage, which was aflame but somehow unharmed, Mirae's body was hissing in the water, releasing a thin black smoke that stank of burning meat. Soojin thought of the fireplace, of the name talisman charring inside it. The living and the dead—her sister, the bridge burning between.

"Unnie," she began, but her father pushed her aside and ran to her first. His knees splashed in the water as he collapsed.

He pulled Mirae's smoldering body against his chest, and Soojin finally saw the damage. Her once-immaculate skin was charred beyond recognition, the tatters of her dress fused to bubbling flesh. The thin skin over her sockets had burned away completely, and her eyes were overlarge when they fixed on her. Her sister's body was one unending wound. Father choked back a gag as the impossible, burnt husk of his daughter gasped in his arms. What else could he do then? He brushed what was left of his eldest's hair tenderly away from her ruined face.

PART III

River

The night I returned, I dragged my new body from the dirt. In this way, I built fictions of having birthed myself—but I was always yours. It was water I drifted through in the amniotic world of my mother. Water, the body I steered through childhood, all blood and marrow and spit. When I tipped into you, I was decades early. You didn't turn me away. Tenderly, you quelled my thrashing with your hunger. I fought you. I was incandescent with rage as I drowned. Rocks abraded my cheeks. Flash of a silver-bodied fish, flitting near, then away. You bade me to stay. You waited for my limbs to still, for the last pocket of air to expel from my lungs, and by then, didn't we know each other? You carried me to the estuary and let me sink.

But here I am: girl—risen from you. Dead, not dead any longer. Eat my name so I've no choice but to return. River, the body I will one day wear. Let your eyes be my eyes. Let your ears be my ears. May the waterlogged machinery of human meat open to my suggestion. At the end of my vengeance, I'll come back to you: a ghost of my own making. We will feast on every man who follows my wet footprints home.

25.

They drove as deep into the woods as the roads would take them. Father was silent; the headlights of passing cars threw his face into horrid relief. Soojin glanced toward the back seat, where Mirae lay with a white sheet thrown over her wrecked body. Beneath it, she was so still Soojin feared she was gone. But occasionally Mirae would moan or draw a rattling breath out of the blasted hollow of her throat. Evidence that she was alive, and thus all of this could be fixed. Her body could mend and be returned to them whole. Then their father would be happy. And once happy, he would forgive.

"We're almost there. You'll be okay," Soojin said to no response, and though she meant to sound affirming, her voice quivered.

The car had gotten them as far as it could. The rest of the way, they'd have to go on foot. Father parked the car at the side of a remote road, extracted Mirae from the back seat, white sheet and all, and descended down the heavily wooded trails.

In the cottage, after the otherworldly blue fire had burned itself out, having harmed nothing but one girl, Father asked Mirae what they could do. How could they help? Even then, in his frantic state, he'd understood the hospital impossible. With her barely intact mouth, Mirae asked to be taken to the river. To where a defunct trestle bridge overlooked the water. Soojin knew the one. Every kid in Jade Acre did for the way they dared each other to leap, cackling, from its tracks when the days were long and the current was lazy.

Mirae had dragged Soojin to go watch them once, on one of her final attempts to reintegrate her younger sister into some semblance of a social life after their mom died. Soojin remembered Mark drifting on a honeycomb of swim tubes lashed together with rope, a cooler full of beer trailing them by a bungee cord tether. Jay sat in one of the tubes beside him, calling up to a boy who was frozen above on the train tracks, unable to jump and too scared to walk back toward the ledge.

"River's calm today—it won't hurt you. Come down!" Jay said, giggling around the mouth of a wine cooler.

"It's no use," Mirae had said from beside Soojin, brushing pebbles from her ankles. "He won't do it. See how he won't even look down at the water? Nobody leaps who won't even look."

She was right. The boy disturbed a rock with his foot. It plummeted down, but the boy remained on the rails, kneeling on all fours, white-knuckling the steel with eyes closed. The surface of the water below bloomed into sunlit fractals, then flattened. The current carried the kids and their lattice of colorful buoys languidly downstream as the boy who couldn't jump clung to the tracks.

If the river that day two years ago had been mild, today it was violent enough to drown in: swift and rain-bloated, frothing black under the dim moon of Soojin's flashlight. She halted at the edge where water clawed at her feet. The speed could sweep her away. But her father didn't hesitate. Still cradling his eldest daughter, he waded into its furious wet boundary.

It was dangerous. She would lose them both. Soojin called for him to stop, but the wind ate her voice. The water reached his knees, his thighs. It shouldn't have been possible for him not to be swept off his feet. The current made him teeter, stumble so low the water grazed his chin, but he recovered his footing by sheer will alone. When he was waist-deep, he tipped Mirae baptismally under the churning surface and held her there.

For a while, nothing happened. There was only the frantic violence of the river battering her father's form in its rush downstream. Then an impossible hush descended on the river. The landscape itself seemed to turn its many invisible eyes toward the water as a cold blue bioluminescence gathered in the space between her father's arms. Soojin saw his shoulders begin to violently shake, but with his back turned toward her, she couldn't make out if he was laughing or crying. The white sheet that covered her sister billowed out and was swept swiftly downstream.

The light drained from the water, leaving her eyes struggling to adjust to the unaccustomed dark. By the time they did, her father had already turned around and was wading back to shore, his expression funerary and flat, despite what he held.

He'd gone into the water with a smoldering mass in his

arms and emerged with a girl. Whole, naked, immaculate. The water had thatched new skin over the burns, had stitched even her long black hair back into being. Mirae slept, held against her father as he stepped onto the rocky shore, drenched and shivering. He moved past Soojin without a word and made for the car that would take them all home, reunited and somehow more fractured for it.

"I did this for our family," Soojin said to his leaving form. "I know you're angry, but I wanted us to be happy. That's all I wanted." She swept the heel of her palm angrily over her eyes.

Her father didn't respond. Branches snapped underfoot as he made his way up the path, as though he didn't care if she followed or not. Soojin watched his back move into shadow, and just like that, she was alone with the river and the rain. Nothing but the wind-whipped evergreens all around her, and her feet were too leaden to carry her anywhere.

"That's all I wanted," Soojin repeated to no one. She couldn't even convince herself. Because she'd known all along, hadn't she? That her father, in all his faith, would be horrified—forced to grieve again for his eldest, who'd been torn from any possibility of an afterlife. And Mirae, thrust back into the world as a simulacrum, forever drowning—there was no way this was what her sister would have wanted for herself.

The true confession welled up in her, a physical, mounting pressure she couldn't force down. *I wanted to be happy, and I need you both to forgive me.*

Soojin stood unmoving in the rain, staring up at the silhouette of the trestle bridge, thinking of the boy from years ago stalled on its tracks—too proud to crawl to safety but too afraid to leap.

When she finally gathered herself and found her way back to the road, she expected the car to be long gone, but her father was waiting for her, his headlights cutting white shafts through the rain.

He stared straight ahead, his inability to look at her so brutal she couldn't bring herself to speak. Instead, she held her palm against the glass, asking permission. The lock opened with a mechanical pop. He still wouldn't look at her, but he'd waited. She got in. They went home.

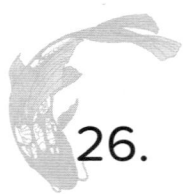

26.

When the girl woke, she remembered hunger and the siren pull of the jesa dishes, calling her home. The food was meant for her, had been set before the talisman of her name. *Come eat with us,* the ceremony bade. She knew she shouldn't, but when the incense was lit, she couldn't stop herself. She'd gone. She'd eaten, and then, hands sticky with pear juice, she'd returned to the cottage before anyone could see her.

Then the blue fire had started licking up the sides of her dress, igniting her hair until it fell in charred clumps from her scalp.

When her father and sister came to find her, it was only luck that she had enough tongue left to beg them to sink her in the river, which, like she knew it would, stitched her whole again.

At home, Father tucked her into her childhood bed and kissed her on each new eyelid, her temples, the tip of her nose. He swept her hair from her damp brow, whispering in tender

Korean, "I love you. I'm sorry. I love you." Then he stormed downstairs, dragging Soojin by the arm. The girl could hear them now—the water rushing through the pipes of their old home amplified their voices and carried them to her. He was screaming, but not crying. She could feel the strain of the blood rushing through his arteries. His heart labored, the water-filled chambers struggling to make space for his fury.

It was getting to be too much, this sensory onslaught. She was hyperaware of each individual raindrop striking the shingles, each drop of blood coursing the length of her family's finite bodies. She wanted more than anything to finish what she'd started, then slip under the surface of the river, where everything was perfectly quiet and she couldn't discern where the length of her body ended and the current began.

It was hours before Father was done screaming at her sister, and when Soojin returned to their bedroom, she was sobbing from exertion more than sadness. Driven by a want for comfort, she crawled into not her own bed, but the girl's.

"What is your name?" Soojin asked into the dark.

The girl thought, then turned to face her sister. "I don't remember."

Soojin pressed something into the girl's hand. A small piece of paper, folded into fourths. She opened it and saw the word *future* printed in slanted, messy Korean. It took moments to remember the word for what it was. The last paper with her name had disappeared sometime between the fire and the river. She slipped this new one into her pocket, though she wasn't sure if it mattered anymore.

Soojin offered her a delirious smile before falling suddenly, cadaverously asleep. Here, then gone. It didn't seem normal.

"Soo," the girl said, nudging her sister. Soojin didn't so

much as groan. She could hear the blood pumping through Soojin's veins, the depressed rate of her breathing. The girl sat up, shook her sister harder. "Hey. Please." She turned on the table lamp beside the bed and looked. Sweat had plastered hair to Soojin's brow. Her chest rose and fell, but slowly. Too slowly.

The girl gripped Soojin's wrist, angling to pull her up, but saw an unnatural discoloration there. A bruise the hue of elderberries, fringed a rancorous yellow. Could this be the only one? She unbuttoned the collar of her sister's shirt and saw the beginning of a hand-sized bruise spreading over her clavicle, her sternum. It seemed to move, amoebic under the failing light of the bedside lamp.

"Oh, Soojin . . . ," she breathed.

Hadn't their mother warned them of this—of the girls in their family who'd called back the human dead, then swiftly declined? Why should they be any different? At once, the girl knew she had to leave.

Her vision swam as she stood. Everything looked off-color, like a damp photograph. In her cage, Milkis saw her long shadow turning and plunged back into her hammock with a distressed squeak. The rat did that a lot lately—hid from her. Normally, she would have let her be. But now a grim determination seized her. If she left the rat, Soojin would inevitably revive Milkis again and again in her absence, greedy for this last living relic of a happier past.

Milkis was a good rat and deserved to not be returned without permission. She'd release her in the woods so she could live out this last life beholden to no one.

"Milkis, come," the girl said, popping open the cage door.

The rat didn't move, frozen in her hammock. Her spine rose and fell with tight, panicked breaths. "It's okay, girl. Come to me."

She slipped her hand carefully beneath the rat's white belly and pulled her out of the hammock. Milkis went limp as she brought her out of the cage. When she lifted her to eye level, the rat's red eyes gleamed wildly. They held each other's gaze, two dead things trapped in disparate cages. Then the rat thrashed in her hand, bit her hard at the junction between thumb and forefinger.

The teeth sank deep but drew no blood. Instead, water wept from the injury. Shocked, the girl's hand involuntarily tightened around the rat's belly, and she saw the cranberry eyes bulge. There was a distant understanding that she needed to let go, that any more pressure could injure the rat, her delicate accordion of ribs. But something bitter had taken root in the girl's head. She'd been trying to save Milkis, who had hurt her in return. If there was anything in this life that should understand her, it was this rat.

Let go. The thought pummeled her over and over. *She's going to die—let go.* But she couldn't. She felt overcome by a want for violence so primal the edges of her vision rippled. The sound of rushing water filled her ears, and it sounded gleeful. Hungry. She could hear nothing else, not even the rat squealing, and she couldn't, couldn't let go.

The next moments felt dreamlike. Tiny ribs yielded beneath her fingers, two brittle snaps, the wild clamoring of a heart. She felt the rat's stomach begin to give like putty. A powerful, organic stench filled the air as Milkis's pelt and the white fur beneath her fingers began to soften. Hastened to decomposition, eased from its meat by water.

The girl's back hit the dresser, knocking over the photographs and items strewn atop it. A vase of dead roses pitched forward and shattered. She didn't register the glass digging into her as she stumbled over it barefoot, giggling.

Her mind fed her disjointed memories of the rat running happy circles in her wheel, perching birdlike on her shoulder as she did dishes. A lifetime of companionship. Now the pelt was slimy under her grip. Without fur, Milkis's head looked tiny and slick, a wet grape as she writhed. She stumbled forward, leaving dark handprints on the wall before crashing to her knees at the foot of her bed.

Then it was over. Her fingers loosened all at once. The animal dropped from her hand, twitching spasmodically.

The girl could see the definition of the rat's musculature, tendons, and joints like a figure from an anatomy textbook. The groundswell of violence rinsed out of her all at once, and she was shaking. She couldn't compose herself. Her mouth, still frozen in the shape of a wild smile, slowly sagged as the rat's final movements ceased. Only then did she notice the wetness on her cheeks, the tears that had streaked down her throat.

"Why couldn't you have just come with me?" she sobbed toward where Milkis lay as broken-down as a weeks-dead animal washed up onshore. "Oh my god, I'm sorry." She crawled to the body. She loved this rat. She'd loved it her entire life. The girl reached toward its graying mass before hesitating, turning her face toward the bed where Soojin somehow still dreamed, wrecked by her cursed proximity.

"I'm sorry," she said again, but this time to her sister. She went to her bedside and brushed the sweat-matted hair from her brow, the way she always used to when Soojin was sick. Her touch left a streak of gore and animal fur across her sister's temple.

Leave, the river said to her. The girl looked down at her hands, scummy with violence, then back toward the skinned rat that had only just stopped tremoring. She couldn't trust her own body or her own temper anymore. She had to finish what she'd started, then vanish. Vanishing into the river and freeing her family from this curse could be her last act of love.

She crept downstairs and past her father's bedroom door, behind which she could hear his dull pulse as he sat in perfect, dazed silence. Seen by no one, she slipped out the front door and into the weather.

In the dream, there was darkness and a rat as white as the moon. A distant awareness that the rat belonged to her, and yet she looked unfamiliar: healthier than she ever had in life, her normally patchy fur lush and glowing with its own bioluminescence.

"Milkis," Soojin called, and the rodent scampered a few feet, then looked back at her, sniffing the air as if to say, *I'm waiting!*

When she began to follow, the rat took off, a white arrow in the gloom. Soojin wasn't sure how long she followed before she came to a door, and Milkis had vanished. What was there to do then? Soojin placed her hand on the cool metal of the knob and pushed her way inside.

Light exploded across her vision, and when her eyes finally

adjusted, she was home, but it was uncanny. Her normally warm-toned room looked dark and stained. Soojin ran her hands over the walls and realized they weren't stained; they were wet. The wallpaper destroyed by mildew and rot. The rat-cage door hung open in the corner; tufts of white fur clung to the walls, stuck there by a tacky gray fluid. And Milkis was still nowhere.

She tried to retreat, but the door had vanished. The dream's edge held her briefly before nudging her back. The dream house groaned. Voices—choral and agitated—murmured from beyond the wallpaper. They said, *Hungry.* They said, *Look.* They said, *Daughter. Look.*

But tangled in that din was an unmistakable sound: water sloshing against a tub. She followed it out of her childhood bedroom and down the stairs to the door of her parents' bathroom. A bright, honeyed glow bled through the seams of the doorframe; a girlish humming echoed from inside.

Thank god, she thought, opening the door.

Soojin and Mirae had always favored this bathroom for the rustic claw-foot tub. It looked as it always did: Antique Edwardian lights illuminating the space in an unctuous amber glow. Marble countertops with fresh-cut eucalyptus beside the sink. Warm steam hazing the room and clinging to the mirrors. Behind the condensation, Soojin could see faceless human figures moving in the reflection. At the farthest end of the room, someone was crying behind the curtain drawn around the tub. She'd know that voice anywhere.

"Unnie?" she called. The crying ceased immediately. "Unnie, it's me." There was no response. Only the elevated breath of someone trying to swallow a swell of emotion. Soojin drew the curtain aside.

Mirae sat in the tub with her back facing her. The bath was filled to the brim with scalding water that smelled cloyingly of lavender and something artificially molasses-sweet. Her silken hair billowed out in the amethyst water like the sail of a boat, shielding her body from sight.

"What are you doing here?" Soojin asked to her sister's back. Mirae didn't turn, only rocked ever so slightly. The water lapping against her sounded like footsteps dancing through a puddle.

"What a thing to ask when I'm here because of you, *sister.*" The words were lacerations. Never had Soojin heard Mirae use that sort of poisonous tone with anyone, least of all her. But no one had ever betrayed Mirae's trust like Soojin had.

"Let me make it right," Soojin said. "Tell me how I can make it right." She walked around the tub to face Mirae, reaching to brush hair from her sister's brow, but instead her hand flew to her own face to stifle a scream. She couldn't help it—she recoiled, stumbling until her back hit the wall, and dry-heaved.

Her sister's skin was covered in bloodless gashes, as if cut by countless branches beneath a brutal current. Both eyes were gutted hollows, the lids and soft meat taken by predation. Her entire body was bloated in the way of drownings left to the water too long: limbs swollen into shapeless trunks, belly distended. Venous marbling carved dark paths just beneath her skin, up the trellis of her legs and over her heart, her face.

Bile scalded Soojin's throat. This was impossible. Mirae had been in the water for only a couple of days before she'd been found. There had been some disfigurement, but not like this. She'd still had her eyes beneath her bloated lids. Her body hadn't swollen. The vascular marbling had only just started branching out at her fingertips.

But this Mirae was not the one who'd washed up along an estuary a year ago. This was the sister Soojin had compelled back by bone and mud, born of a history of drowning. She had never completely left that water.

Mirae stood abruptly from the tub. Her legs, her belly, her sodden, graying flesh. Soojin inched away, closing her eyes as she slid along the width of the wall, hands stuttering blindly for the door.

Water sloshed over the edges of the tub as her sister stepped out of it. "Why come if you can't even look at me?" Mirae asked, her voice so venomous, Soojin couldn't answer. "Wake up," her sister said. The dream splintered, grew painful and loud and cold. The warm light of their parents' bathroom fractured, fell away. "Wake up."

There was roaring in her ears, the sensation of her body returning to her as, slowly, her mind threw off the dream. *Soojin, wake up!* But her sister was nowhere. This voice belonged to somebody else. Words hazy and submerged as if heard through a boundary of water. It was her father ordering her to wake—so she did.

27.

Soojin sat numbly on her bedroom floor, watching water drip from the ceiling. Mold crawled up the moist face of the wallpaper in fetid, dark cords. The bright hues had gone gray from months of water damage; the paper peeled back at the edges, hanging like loosened skin. Every book on the shelves had bulged and warped. Tangled ropes of black hair were draped on every surface.

She didn't know if any of this was real. It mustn't be, because her father made no mention of the wreckage. And if she held her eyes closed a while, when she opened them, her room was as it had always been: bright and well loved, with its scuffed velvety cream damask wallpaper. But soon enough her vision would shift and she'd see it once again ruined.

Soojin imagined herself and her father eating dinner in their dollhouse of drowning, incognizant of water dripping from light fixtures and into their bowls; she imagined two sisters playing at normalcy as rain pooled against the flooring and bled into the beams below. Soojin couldn't trust her own eyes.

This much, though, she knew was true: Her sister had vanished, and her rat was dead. Her father had noticed Soojin's unnatural bruises, the sweat beading her brow, and had ordered her to recover at home. He'd even confiscated her car key for good measure, and was driving through Jade Acre, desperately searching for his eldest daughter in the rinsed dawn light. Soojin was more alone than she'd ever been.

Still, she dragged herself to scrub her sister's dark handprints, as best she could, off the walls. The tufts of fur and congealed pelt lifted away, but stains had already set a deep brown into the paper. She felt sluggish and incorporeal, like she was wading through a nightmare. That her sister would inflict this on Milkis felt impossible. And yet . . .

Soojin moved to her bedside table. She'd nestled Milkis's body, wrapped a few times in cloth, in a shoebox. She lifted the top. Gray fluid had soaked the fabric. The tip of the rat's tail poked out from the otherwise tight swath.

The smell was the first thing to hit her. Sour and putrid. It made her gag, her eyes burn from the sheer force of it. It was unbearable to think that Milkis had been reincarnated so many times only to die at the hands of a girl she had loved. A girl who was out there now, with a brutal capacity for violence.

She did it—the thought crested over her intrusively. Soojin pressed her hands against her ears, as if she could silence herself. Her heart was beginning to punish her, throttling hard and fast in her chest. Panic. She'd been floating in a shocked ether all morning, but now the enormity of it all crashed down on her. *Mirae killed the rat. She killed Milkis and she killed the*

Silases. She couldn't fathom why her sister had done it, but she knew that it was true.

A sob escaped her. A part of Soojin had known all along, though she'd done all she could to ignore it. But even her own capacity for delusion had its limits. Something at the edge of her mind was fracturing.

I should bring her back. The thought hit her without warning. Soojin was seized by the sudden notion that if she could undo the outcome of the violence, the violence could be undone. Her sister's hands made somehow clean again. Rinsed back into innocence. The hands of a good girl, like she'd always been.

Soojin could turn back the clock. She'd always been able to turn back the clock.

As if possessed, she stumbled to her drawers, tearing through them until she found the scalpel. The one she'd used only months ago to cut Milkis's tail. She could do it again.

Her dad wouldn't want her to, not after all this. But the thoughts wouldn't leave her alone. Memories of Milkis grooming dirt from her pelt each time she was pulled from the earth, the way the rat would sit on her shoulder as she refreshed the cedar lining at the bottom of her cage.

Soojin held the blade over the tail. Her hands were shaking, whether from exhaustion or horror, she couldn't tell. She broke skin, then tendon. The blade bit but beckoned no blood—there was so little of it left. And the stench. That water-wrecked sourness. Bile rose in her throat. She leaned forward, letting the knife sink deeper until it met resistance. Bone. If she put her weight on it, there would be a small crunch and it would be done.

A familiar nausea dizzied her, but there was something else

there too. A hesitation that felt entirely new. Soojin swallowed hard around it, bore her full weight down. The knife cut clean through the bone with a snap.

One last time, then never again, Soojin promised herself. She would bring Milkis back for one last life—a kind one of swinging in the hammock, snacking on sandwich crusts, and being kissed between the ears. Then, when she died, it would be for real. Soojin would burn the body until nothing was left—a loving goodbye, like everyone deserves.

Her father had forbidden her from leaving, but he didn't know her well enough if he thought her promises meant anything at all. Soojin swept the shoebox into her arms and left.

It was the first clear morning in a long time. Cloudless, a sky of orange sherbet that would soon go blue. Birds dove between branches to their nests, hawthorn berries held in their beaks. Crepuscular creatures scurried to their burrows after a long dawn of foraging. Who wouldn't want to be alive again for a day like this? Who wouldn't?

She didn't let herself answer. Cradling her rat's makeshift casket, she walked toward the driveway and then further, her mind rinsed white of thought. Gravel kicked up beneath her feet as she let her body lead her.

Mark was considering his garden when Soojin crested the hill of the funeral home. Though the morning was dry, the plants sagged. Too many straight weeks of rain had done it. All the taproots gone to rot—the wide, colorful bowls of flowers drooping from the unaccustomed onslaught. He'd have to salvage what he could, uproot the rest, and begin again.

He'd just pulled up the first dahlia when he saw her. A familiar sight: Soojin with a shoebox. Her burnt hands bandaged from when she'd thrust them in the fire. The jesa had been only yesterday but it felt like months had elapsed since then. His mom had made all of them toss salt over their shoulders before entering their home the night before. And this morning, with the earliest light of dawn, his parents had rushed to church, no doubt to pray away the haunting.

Boy, did he ever get an earful about his months of secrecy. And they'd left him with this single order: *We know you care about Soojin, but if she's somehow tied to this haunting, you have to let her go. It's too dangerous, no matter what you may feel. You can't see her anymore.* But how could he turn his back on her after everything they'd gone through? After he'd spent so many years regretting the husk he'd let their history become?

He pulled off his gardening gloves and jogged toward her, intent on meeting her halfway in the field, and found with soft surprise that he couldn't get there fast enough. He was relieved to see her. Happy, even, despite everything. Soojin did that to him lately. Made his feelings go into overgrowth, an unruly and riotous blooming.

I want to tell you how I feel about you, he thought, his hand reaching. *Someday I want to tell you everything.*

It was only when he came close enough to touch that he noticed her expression. He skidded to a stop, that heady excitement to see her draining fast.

"What's wrong?" he asked, though it immediately felt like a stupid question. Everything. Everything was wrong.

"I shouldn't be here," she said. "Your parents wouldn't want me to be here." She looked unwell. Her face was pale and sunken. Something dark had stained the cardboard of the shoebox.

"It's okay. They're not here. I'm glad you came." He gestured toward what she held. "What's in there?"

She opened the box and showed him. At first he mistook it for a spleen—some engorged human viscera graying with time. Then he saw the tail, the open red eyes, the tiny yellow teeth bared as if gnashing.

"Oh god. What happened?" he breathed.

She shook her head, unwilling to speak. He remembered just a few months back when Soojin had come to him with a shoebox just like this to ask the favor that thrust them together. Milkis had looked peaceful then, as if sleeping, lovingly nestled in tissue paper. And now . . .

The corpse reminded him of the possum he and Jay had once found washed up along the river. Having been in the water so long, it looked like melted wax, most of its fur and skin lifted away, slippery and fish-eaten. It had felt too cruel to let it putrefy there in sudden sun. He'd used a stick to return it to the water, and they'd watched the body as it folded back into the currents, sinking swiftly out of sight.

Water. Currents.

Some say the only way to stop the haunting of a water ghost is to save them, his mother had told him after Claire and Joe Silas were found dead in their home.

His heart dropped. *Mirae,* he thought, but didn't dare say. Not when Soojin looked as fragile as she did now. He closed the lid and took the box from her arms.

"Come with me," he said, taking one of her injured hands carefully in his. Perhaps it was shock that dulled her, but Soojin let herself be led, eyes unfocused and glassy.

Above them, the sky was finally throwing off its early apricot light. It was going to be a day as clear as awe. All around Jade Acre, townsfolk would be sliding their windows wide to the first rainless day in weeks. *It's a glorious morning!* The recent joint funeral of two town fixtures forgotten, there'd be laughter. Soft-serve ice cream to be had. The pebble beaches would fill with families spreading colorful tarps and chasing each other in the tide pools—incandescently alive, if just for a moment.

Mark felt a million miles away from that as he led Soojin into the cremation chamber. He said a quiet goodbye in his head as he prepared to lift the rat, shoebox and all, onto the belt that would ferry her into the hearth. But Soojin stilled him with a hand on his shoulder.

"Mark, wait," she said, holding out her palm. A bruise like a black bangle wrapped around her wrist. It sent a lance of worry through him that must have shown on his face. She quickly adjusted the cuff of her sweater and it vanished from view.

He paused, holding the box in midair.

"The tail," Soojin said. "I need the tail to bring her back."

Mark turned, still holding the box, to look at her. Her expectant hand held aloft, waiting for the piece of bone to return to the earth. A short exhalation of disbelief escaped him. He hadn't meant to let it show, but he saw discomfort flit across her face all the same.

"Are you serious?" he asked, keeping his voice low. He couldn't fathom what it was she was feeling, but to him it all felt wrong. "I don't think that's a good idea, Soo."

"But I need this. It's not fair that her last life ends like this," she said, stepping closer to him. "Just one more time, Mark. I'll give her one last good life, and then you can take her from me for real. Okay?"

The desperation on her face cut him. He stepped back, lifting the box's lid. The scent of rot rose powerfully as his finger moved aside cloth, inching toward the severed tail, but he found the rat's body first. Milkis lay inside, corroded and reeking, her maw frozen wide open in a curtailed screech. He'd seen so many animal bodies at this point in his life, but never one like this. Who was to say the rat would want another life after this? A rebirth without agency. How was that the kinder thing?

He closed the lid of the box. "Soojin," he said. "I can't."

Her face fell. Mark hated that he was the one who made her wear that expression. They stood in taut silence until she finally spoke.

"Why not?" Soojin was trying to keep her voice even, but it still betrayed her by shaking. No, it wasn't just her voice that was shaking. Her body was. Her hands, crumpled into fists and shivering ever so slightly at her sides, were like those of someone trying to wake from a bad dream. What had she witnessed for her body to physically punish her like this?

Mark wanted to put the box down and hold her, but he didn't. If he didn't stay firm, if she kept pushing, he might yield to her. He couldn't yield to her on this. "I just can't. If you mean to bring Milkis back, find another way to dispose of the body. I'm sorry. This isn't right."

"Isn't right?" she breathed slowly, jaw clenching as if she were trying to rein in her temper. She failed. She lost it. She slammed her palm hard on his chest. "Who are *you* to tell *me* what's right and what isn't?" Her voice was loud enough to ricochet around the cremation chamber. "Milkis is mine, Mark. She's *my* rat!" Her eyes were bright with anger. This was better. He could take her anger in a way he couldn't take her sadness.

"And that gives you a right to do whatever you want?" he asked, his own voice rising. "She wasn't an extension of you, Soojin. She had a separate life and deserves to rest on her own terms. Look!" He pulled off the shoebox lid and brushed aside the cloth the rat had been wrapped in. It was horrible. Milkis's face was a mask of pure pain, her eyes so decayed they collapsed in on themselves like spoiling pomegranate seeds. He wanted nothing more than to dignify the rat with a proper cremation. "Look at her and tell me she doesn't deserve to rest now."

Mark pushed the box back at Soojin, and though she took it, she kept her livid eyes pinned to his face. The machinery of the furnace roared in their ears, but the silence that overtook them blotted out even that. When Soojin finally gathered enough resolve to look, really look, at her rat, he saw a range of emotions cross her face. Horror was first, then confusion, anger, bitterness. She was going to do it, he thought. She was going to leave this place and destroy the body and throw the bone into the earth. An endless cycle. Her desire fettering this animal for good.

But instead she thrust the box back into Mark's arms. He could see how upset she was by the flush of her cheeks, her vivid eyes. But she was closer to despair now than rage.

"Fine," she breathed. "Fine. Just do it." Then she sank to the concrete floor like a folding piece of paper, hands crossed over her belly as if to shield herself.

Mark placed the box on the belt and pressed the button that drew open the metal loading door. The animal's small coffin was drawn into the hearth's roaring heat. A series of memories assailed him then. The rat grooming herself, catlike, on Soojin's bed or clamoring for snacks. He remembered until the furnace door shut, taking the rodent from this world for good.

Mark could see rather than hear Soojin sobbing. Her shoulders shook as she rocked in a desperate attempt to self-soothe.

He knelt beside her and pulled her arms away from her body. He thought she might rebuke him, might turn away, but she didn't. She let him wrap his arms around her as she cried, and like that they waited for the many-lived animal to become ash.

Soojin said something Mark couldn't hear over the furnace. He looked down at her face, illuminated by the machinery's flickering light. She was no longer crying, but bright wet streaks glowed on her cheeks. What he couldn't hear, he tried to read the movement of her lips. *Curse* was the only word he could discern.

The furnace whirred to a lull; so small was the animal, it took no longer than twenty minutes to vanish.

"You aren't cursed," he said when the room drained finally into silence, but he'd misheard. She shook her head.

"No, *I'm* the curse," she said with conviction, picking at her stained bandages until they unraveled. The singed skin underneath glistened with salve and had begun to blister. "Nothing close to me gets away unharmed. My dad. My sister. Even my rat. Loving me is a curse."

Mark knew that wasn't true, but denying what she'd already convinced herself of was futile. He knew how immovable she was in grief. When Soojin despaired, the girl *really* despaired. And here she was: shoulders folded, making herself small. He could see how close she was to giving up. There didn't seem to be a right thing to say, so he said the only thing that came to mind.

"This sucks."

She stiffened, as if taken aback by how wildly *suck* fell short in describing their circumstances. A surprised sound like "oh" escaped her, and then a limp giggle. There was a feeling like a needle pricking the air between them, and the tension that had mounted defused. Soon they were bending into a dazed, helpless belly laugh. They collapsed against each other until the verve of their emotion rolled over and through them. When it all finally subsided, they were breathless, kneeling on the tiles with their foreheads pressed close.

"Come on. Let's go," he said when he'd caught his breath. He picked himself up and strode into the hall, plucking his car key from the hook as he went.

"Go where?" Soojin asked. She glanced back at the furnace, where the remnants of her lifelong pet steamed, before letting the door shut behind her.

Outside, the fresh morning air smelled green and vegetal. He walked to his car and popped the passenger-side door open before pointing at her confused face.

"Listen. You're a mess. I'm a mess. Our families are freaked the hell out. Everything sucks, and I can't breathe." He was telling the truth. Suddenly it was so hard to breathe in this waterlogged fishbowl of a town. "So let's get out for a minute. Just the two of us. Please?"

Soojin stared at her feet. A weed was pushing up through a crack in the concrete between them. "My dad said not to leave the house without him. I'm beyond grounded. I'm not even supposed to be *here*."

Mark deflated. "I'll take you home, then," he said. But she pushed past him and slipped into the car in a vaguely defiant manner.

"But I'm already here, so what the hell." Soojin shut the door.

Buoyant, he got into the driver's seat, turned on the ignition, then looked at her. The engine rumbled beneath them.

I could totally fall in love with you, he thought as they shared a blighted, fragile smile. *Someday I'll tell you.*

"Ready?" he asked.

"Yeah."

The car trundled away from the crematorium belching smoke, past the cluster of pet graves where families were coming to place tennis balls and chew toys on headstones, all the way to the town boundary and beyond it.

28.

It took nearly three hours to get to their destination. By some unspoken agreement, Mark and Soojin pretended normalcy. They didn't talk once about water or rats shucked clean out of their pelts or ghostly sisters gone to ground. Instead they gossiped about classmates—who was dating whom—and when they exhausted even that topic, they talked about the weather. When idle chitchat became unbearable, Soojin settled herself against the bug-mosaicked glass to watch the landscape flit by. Outside, dense woods yielded to open fields dotted with grazing horses. The steel skeletons of pylons cascaded down the horizon, ferrying cables of electricity between faraway townships.

When Mark finally pulled to the side of the road, they'd been ejected into an area so rural it looked forgotten in time. There was nothing in these plains besides sparse trees and a decrepit abandoned barn covered with fading graffiti. But the fields . . .

Soojin gasped, everything momentarily forgotten as she took it all in.

Before her stretched acres of wild grass as tall as her torso, waving like a sea of cotton candy in every direction. She reached for a frond and marveled at the softness of the wispy tufts that topped each stalk. A valley of rose quartz. She hadn't known grass could grow in such a hue.

"It's called pink muhly," Mark said, joining her at the edge of the field. His eyes were eager for her approval. "Pretty, right?"

"Mark, this is . . ." Words failed her. Rippling pink fields beneath a perfect cerulean sky—it was a dreamscape, and for the first time in a long time, she felt comforted. "I don't know what to say."

Looking relieved, he held out his hand. She took it, and they strode into the waist-high grass together.

It was warm, perhaps the last truly warm day of the season, and it seemed that all the living were determined to enjoy it. Fat bumblebees flew languidly by. A yearling deer grazed in the distance, its ears flicking above the brush. And of course Soojin and Mark, the only two people for miles, waded through the blushing landscape, talking resolutely about ordinary things.

"So, what do you think you'll do? After we graduate, I mean," Soojin asked. Mark, for all his eagerness to hit the road earlier in the morning, seemed distracted now.

"Honestly, with everything going on the past few months, I haven't really given it much thought," he said. "I guess I'll take a gap year. Stay in Jade Acre and help my parents with the cemetery while I figure out what's next. Maybe community college. Maybe trade school—I dunno."

He sounded so noncommittal, it tugged at her. Had she

done that? In the chaos of her proximity, had she swept him away from his own life?

"Trade school for funerary services?"

"Maybe." He shrugged. "But I worry if I go that route, my parents might get it in their heads that I'll take over the cemetery for them. Like, it'll feel like marrying the place, you know? Peaceful Paws, Jade Acre ... all of it. I don't want to be trapped."

"I thought you didn't mind it."

"I don't. Don't get me wrong. It's nice to help families let go—you know?" Though the words were not barbs, Soojin felt cut by them anyway. Milkis, whose tail she'd only reluctantly let him burn. The sister she wouldn't let go of, no matter what Mirae had done or still might do.

As if sensing her discomfort, he swiftly changed the subject. "What about you? Weren't you applying to schools Early Action? Which colleges did you apply to?"

"None," she said.

"Oh. Decided to apply during Regular Decision?"

"I decided not to apply at all." Beside her, Mark stopped walking. They were still holding hands, and her own forward motion jerked her arm. She turned back. "What?"

"Sorry, it's nothing. It's just ... I thought it was your dream, that's all. Even when we were like ten, you and Mirae were always talking about going to UC San Diego together. Living in dorms, biking to class. Leaving Jade Acre for good, stuff like that."

He was right. This had been the plan: Mirae would go and, in that first year, get the lay of the land. By the time Soojin enrolled, Mirae would have found a studio apartment for them to share. Soojin would skip the dorms and move right in with her sister freshman year. She'd talked Mirae's ear off about all the things she wanted them to do together. Surfing at La Jolla Shores, a study-abroad year in Seoul.

"If you haven't noticed, a lot of crap has happened to me since I was ten," she said. "Why is it such a big deal? You're taking a break too. You have no plans."

"It isn't a big deal. It just always seemed like you wanted to get away from here. I figured..."

"That was before," she said. His palms had gone a little clammy. Soojin slid her hand from his and wiped it against her dress. A long silence billowed between them, interrupted only by the plumes of muhly brushing languidly against one another. Above them, the sky that had been so clear was being slowly sutured by dense gray clouds. "I don't know what I want anymore."

An obvious deliberation played across Mark's brow; then, cautiously, he asked: "This isn't about you at all—it's about Mirae, isn't it?"

"Why would it be?"

"You feel guilty about having brought her back only to leave," he said. "You feel responsible for her."

She had nothing to say to that.

"That's not fair, Soojin," Mark said. "It's not fair to you, and it isn't fair to Mirae, either. She would want you to live your own life. You can't burden her memory by..." He gesticulated in the air, searching for the right words. "By driving a nail through her chest and hanging your life on it."

"*Memory?* Why are you talking about her like she's gone?"

"Isn't she?" He ran an agitated hand through his hair, his mouth opening and closing silently before he finally managed to say it. "That's why you came to me today, isn't it? She left and you want to be comforted."

"I never said she left."

"You didn't have to. Your face said it all."

Soojin hated the way he was looking at her: with such compassion it made her want to strike him. Hadn't it been Mark who'd suggested they go far away and pretend everything was fine? He was breaking their unspoken agreement.

"Fine. When I woke up, Mirae was gone. But I'll find her. I'll bring her back home, okay? Can we drop this?"

"No. I'm sorry, but we can't." Mark took a small step toward her. The muhly whipped wildly around them. When had the weather grown so feral? "Soojin, can we stop pretending here? You know your sister killed the Silases. She killed your rat. Why do you refuse to talk about it?"

"What do you want from me, Mark?" she said, her voice thin. "You want to hear me say it, is that it?" The wind swept wildly through his hair. He was watching her, rapt, waiting. She chewed the inside of her cheek until the taste of iron flooded her mouth. Forming the words cost her something, but she managed to speak: "My sister killed them, and I don't know why—okay? I've known something was wrong with her for a while." There was a fierce burning behind her eyes. "Are you happy?"

He didn't answer.

"Well, what now? Are you going to go to the cops? Too bad Silas won't be there to take down the incident report, right? Are you going to go report a drowned girl for murder?" She was laughing. Why was she laughing?

"Of course not," he said softly, holding out his hand to her. Soojin didn't take it.

"What do you want, then?" she snapped, the fake levity draining from her voice.

He ran nervous fingers through his hair, deliberating for a long moment before he spoke. "I've been thinking a lot about teeth."

"Teeth?" she said flatly, but he was undeterred.

"Yes. Her baby tooth is what you used to resurrect her, right? So, if you were to find a way to pull it out . . ."

"It could destroy her," she muttered in the same moment that he said, "She might be able to rest."

Soojin took a step back from him. Above, the sky churned; a white light flashed beyond the clouds.

"What did you say?" Her voice was hardly audible beneath the wind.

"You have to undo this haunting, Soojin. I know you can." His eyes were adamant, but he looked uncertain. Why was he looking at her like that? Like he dreaded her answer, as if he weren't demanding she forfeit everything. She'd already given up Milkis at his urging. How could he ask for more?

"Are you serious?" she began. "Think about what you're asking me to do right now. You want me to *kill* my sister?"

He shook his head slowly. He looked so, so sad. Anxiety frayed her vision. Soojin slammed a hand against her temple, willing her mind to clear. Why was he doing this to her?

"You can't kill her, Soo. Nobody can. She's been . . . gone for an entire year."

"But she's here now, which means I can work through this with her. I can't— My sister deserves to live," Soojin said. "You don't know Mirae. How good she always was. She . . ." Her throat burned, but she forced herself to continue. "After our mom died, Dad stopped functioning. He couldn't work, he couldn't take care of us . . . he just—stopped. Do you know who became my parent during those months, Mark?" Her mind flickered with memories. Her sister, only a year older than her, making sure she was fed. Simple dinners of rice, ketchup, and eggs eaten in complete silence while their father haunted the room he suddenly occupied alone. How many times had Soojin fallen asleep in Mirae's bed—a crying, clinging thistle?

She had made her sister into her mother, she realized now. An unbearable, shameful truth. Mirae, who was herself only eleven. Who hadn't even been able to reach the cabinets without pulling over a stool first. But who did Mirae have to turn to when Soojin had been comforted and tucked into a tenuous sleep, and their father's door was closed? The image of Mirae sitting in a darkened home after the duties of the day were finished threatened to overwhelm her. Soojin rubbed her eyes furiously to dispel the thought, and when she looked up again, her eyes immediately locked on Mark's.

Anger, incandescent and long suppressed, forced itself to the surface. The change in her expression seemed to mesmerize him. Soojin was frightened and hurt, and she wanted to hurt anything back.

"But you wouldn't know, would you? Because you weren't *there*."

"Soojin—"

She didn't let him speak. "After the car accident, you avoided us like we were covered in death. Like we would get it on you or something." She wiped her eyes. "Did you know that a week after my mom's funeral, I called Peaceful Paws to ask your dad if I could speak to you? I just wanted to hear your voice. I was tired of listening to my dad crying all day. Mirae would lock herself in the bathroom and not come out for hours. I was so lonely, Mark."

He looked like he wanted to vanish.

"Your dad said you weren't around and would call me back later. But you were there. I know, because I heard you whispering, 'Not here.' I needed you, and you left me behind so easily."

It didn't matter anymore that this was a misdirection, a desperate attempt to change the subject. Soojin needed to say this. The years of pretending his abandonment hadn't hurt—that it had never meant enough to matter—dissolved. It had mattered, and it had changed her.

"God-fucking-damn it, I'm so stupid," she gasped.

It looked like Mark wanted to speak, but all he could manage was the mouthed ghost of the word *sorry*. His apology was kerosene, and she, incendiary.

"Is that why you've been doing this? Because you're sorry? These months with me and my sister, taking us here and there on your stupid midnight outings. Was this all just making amends to you? Some sort of pity project?"

Her breath was coming out in short, stammering bursts. She'd never felt like this before, so frightened and angry and humiliated.

"And now you want me to send her back? She's all I have." Soojin slid to her knees beneath the tall grass to hide the moment tears came. The muhly rose overhead, enclosing her in brief privacy.

All was still for a moment before the grass shifted and Mark was eye level. His pupils were huge. He was scared. She was scaring him. But there was shame there too. "I won't lie to you," he said. "At first, everything I did was because I felt guilty. I never forgave myself for being so shitty after your mom's accident. I'm still sorry for it." His voice was pleading. "But I was a kid. I wasn't ready for death yet. It felt too big, and I let that stop me from being there. I needed another chance to be a good friend. I wanted to prove to myself that I could be."

For the first time, Soojin felt like she was truly seeing him. These past few months, Mark had been a gilded caricature. The boy in the garden, coaxing life into failing flowers. The boy who loved animals, even as he burned them. The perfect son, the perfect friend, agreeable and good in every way.

But nothing truly traumatic had ever happened to Mark Moon. It was easy to be good under the right circumstances. His loving mother, his exuberantly jolly father, his raucous extended family who descended on Jade Acre every summer—alive, alive, all of them. His life was kind, everything arranged so he could retain his soft edges. A luxury neither she nor her sister had.

And now she truly saw him: his insecurity. A deep need to repair that unblemished facade, if only for himself.

"But it's not like that anymore. I'm here because I care about you." His voice had taken on a desperate cadence. "I'm worried. For you *and* your sister. This can't be good for her . . ." He floundered for words before landing limply on: "Her soul." Then he gestured to Soojin's chest, where the bruising was starting to crawl up her collarbones. "And it's obviously harming you, too, her being here. Things can't continue like this."

He was worked up, breathing hard. Soojin felt a splinter prick the soft crevices of her mind, a dark understanding she beat back. "And so? Is there an ultimatum?"

He said nothing as thunder, deep and sonorous, shook the horizon. She suddenly felt very tired. "I'm sorry, Mark," she said. "In a choice between you and my sister, I will choose my sister every time."

"There's nothing . . ." He swallowed hard. His eyes lost their pleading edge. Something distant and exhausted settled into his face. "There's nothing I can do, is there? You can see everything going bad, and you won't do anything at all, will you?" He pulled away slowly. The grass rustled as he drew back, then closed between them like a reedy, pink curtain. She couldn't see him anymore. He sounded close to tears. "I wish I knew how to help you. I just . . . don't know how anymore."

It began to rain. Like a switch had been flipped, the sky went from dry to downpour almost in an instant. The vast fields of muhly were beaten down, buckling under the sheer ferocity of the water. Their fight briefly forgotten, Mark and Soojin dashed toward the abandoned barn. Even in that short distance, they were drenched as if spit out from the sea.

The inside of the barn was just as wrecked as the outside. Dusty red Solo cups and broken handles of vodka littered the ground from parties past. The place smelled of hay and outhouse. Water poured in from a tear in the roofing, but at least it was shelter. Soojin shrugged off her sopping cardigan and wrung out the rain. There was no point in modesty now, so she did the same with her dress, draping it against an old stable divider, though it would never dry in time. Mark hesitated before doing the same. First his hoodie, then his jeans.

There was so little to hide between them. Shucked near bare and suddenly self-conscious, Soojin looked at Mark. She was achingly hyperaware of herself—the jut of her sternum, her twiggy, shapeless limbs—but he kept his eyes pinned demurely away from her nakedness. Distantly, Soojin wondered what he might think if he looked.

There was relief in feeling such a small, ordinary concern for once. It made her move to where he leaned against the doorframe, looking out at the impossible downpour. It made her want to give him another chance to smooth things over. For them to go back to their short-lived game of pretend.

"Hey," she tried, touching his shoulder. He flinched, turning to press a finger to his mouth, hushing her. An urgent shake of the head—then he looked back toward the rain that fell beyond the yawning barn doors. He had the eyes of a prey animal: hunted, alert, waiting in the brush for the legs of a predator to pass without notice. Above, the rain interrogated the roof like a thrashing of stones.

Soojin remembered what Silas had said to her at his bedside. *It listens through the water.* Silas, who was barely two days in the grave. Mark. She needed them to be wrong. She could save her sister and come away unscathed. She could find a way.

She held her hand out to the rain. It was cold and sharp. Then, as if to prove something, she walked out of the barn and into the storm. In an instant, her bare body was doused. Mark called out to her as lightning arced a wide hook through the sky, casting them both in crushing white light. In the weather's flare, his face looked as featureless as a mannequin's when he followed her into the rain to clasp her wrist. "Don't," he said. "Please." He sounded exhausted. She'd reached the outer borders of his generosity and worn it out.

He pulled her back below the awning and held her there, his chest cold against her back. The rain swept by like a searchlight: here one moment, then easing to a complete halt the next. The arms that caged her went slack. Without sparing a glance at him, she ducked behind a stable divider to get dressed. Even with the rain gone, she had nothing more to say.

They weathered the long drive home in complete silence. Their rain-wet clothes seeped into the seats, and no matter how high Mark cranked up the heat, they shivered. When they finally rolled into her driveway, they both knew they had reached some sort of end.

"I didn't mean for this to happen," Mark said quietly, looking straight ahead.

Her father's car wasn't in the driveway. He was still out there somewhere, combing the riverbanks for Mirae. Soojin got out of the car without saying goodbye and entered a home where no one was waiting for her.

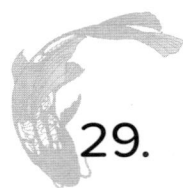

29.

Days passed, then a week that was quickly verging on two.

Father took a leave of absence from his job in Bragg Hills and spent every day from first light until night looking for Mirae. Soojin did too, on the days she wasn't forced to go to school, where she sat dissociative in class, staring out the windows pummeled by rain, ignoring Mark's hurt gaze. She quit the diner, and on weekends she dragged herself out of bed the moment she heard footfalls downstairs. Bleary-eyed and exhausted, she followed her dad to his car before he could rebuff her. Her presence was never welcomed, but it was tolerated, and they would drive out into the lavender light of dawn together.

He'd hardly spoken to her since the jesa, but then again, why would he? She'd betrayed him, and now he expended all his energy pleading silently with the landscape whipping past his window to relinquish the image of his eldest daughter into the headlights. His hands were always white on the steering wheel, his eyes pinned to the road. Sometimes they drove around the Silas residence, rumored to be haunted; the florist where Mirae used to work when she was alive, where the ghost of her image still fastidiously arranged bouquets in Soojin's mind. Other times they went to the school, where, not long ago, Mirae had knelt at her locker, holding her own condolences to her chest.

But most often, like now, they parked at the hiking trails and made the arduous, slippery journey down toward Black Pine River to comb its stony banks for a glimpse of long black hair in the dark. They never called for her by name. Instead she yelled *Unnie,* while her father yelled *Please* or *Come home* into the scouring wind.

But today her father's trip-wire-thin composure broke, and Soojin watched, horrified, as he called her sister's name. "Mirae!" he shouted, and the corridor of trees, the fast-moving river, the cloud-heavy bowl of the sky seemed to trap the sound. *Mirae,* his voice echoed. *Mirae. Mirae.* "Come home."

"Dad!" Soojin hissed, skidding over the slick banks toward him. "What are you doing?"

He backed away, like she was an obstruction in his path. He kept his eyes trained beyond her as he shouted again for his eldest daughter. Her name carried and splintered in the gorge, sent a flock of birds alight from their branches.

"Mirae! Han Mirae!"

"Someone could hear you," Soojin begged. She didn't say, *She doesn't answer to that name anymore.* Didn't say, *She has lost herself and so have I.*

He finally turned his eyes on her, slowly, effortfully, as if he couldn't bear to look at her. This was the first time he'd allowed his gaze to linger, and it seemed to physically harm him. He turned his back at once, his shoulders folded like he wanted to disappear. It was starting to drizzle, and the light gray of his shirt dampened into slate.

"What does it matter?" he said, so miserable his voice sounded evacuated of emotion. She'd heard him sound like this before—listless, emptied—in the rare moments he'd speak. It struck a chord of fear in her. "There's no one here." He gestured vaguely into the landscape, the uncaring river and wind-maddened trees. "Not the townsfolk. Not your sister. She is nowhere. There is no one to hear me."

The tenor of his voice scared her. Her father was burning himself out. He'd hardly slept since the jesa, and he'd eaten nearly nothing. He would make himself sick if he kept this up.

Soojin tried to hold his hand, but his fingers stayed limp in hers. "Let's go home, Dad. You need to rest. Just for a little bit. Okay?" It was starting to rain harder. How fast the weather changed in Jade Acre now. A symptom of her sister. A clear day so quickly becoming a deluge. The rain struck staccato on the surface of the river.

He shook his head and broke away from her, took a stuttering step back.

"Dad, stop! Just stop." Soojin swept around him, arms wide, blocking his path. He winced when he looked at her, and his expression was an arrow. He couldn't do this to her again. This emotional vanishing act. "Please, let's go home. We need to rest. We need to wait out this weather, and then we'll find her. Okay?"

He stood motionless for a while before a flash of lightning

in the distance snapped him out of his reverie. He began to walk without taking the hand she'd outstretched for him. Soojin followed as he wordlessly left the glutting river and the looming shadow of the trestle bridge.

By the time they got home, they were both shivering and wet, without the energy to do anything about it. Instead they sat near the wide windows overlooking the cottage, watching the torrential rain beat down on the porch banister, willing it to stop.

Soojin chanced a glance at him. He looked worse than he had during Mirae's cremation. His cheeks had sunk further, and the pale skin under his eyes looked dyed a purple gradient from tear duct to cheekbone. He gazed outside listlessly now, face slack and dispassionate, and Soojin understood that his frantic searching was the only thing keeping him from the complete collapse he'd experienced after Mom's car accident. Those long months of staring into space, eating only what Mirae brought to him with her child hands. He couldn't go there again. Soojin couldn't handle it if he did.

"Dad," she said, sitting beside him. One of his hands was pressed against the glass, fogging a ghostly outline of his splayed fingers across the pane. He didn't respond. "Appa." She tugged at his sleeve. He smelled of cigarettes and wood brambles. Sometime between the jesa and now, he'd taken up smoking again, and it made his scent sharply unfamiliar.

She was about to shake him when he abruptly stood, nearly sending her to the floor. His eyes were suddenly so wild, she looked outside, half expecting Mirae to be standing there in the rain.

Nothing.

"What is it?" Soojin asked, following him as he ran to the

door, pulling his raincoat off the hanger and throwing it around his shoulders. "Where are you going? It's dangerous out there!"

"Stay here," he ordered before he slammed the door behind him. She watched, stunned, as his headlight beams turned and arced away from her.

It was an hour before she saw those bright eyes returning through the gloom, and by then she was halfway to an anxiety attack.

Her dad was wrestling something almost as tall as him from the car. Soojin couldn't see it clearly through the static of the pouring rain, but her heart nearly throttled her when she saw the way it dragged limply on the ground. *Mirae.* She ran to the door, tore it open and screamed her sister's name into the wind.

Her dad reached the porch, grunting as he pulled what he held up the steps. Only then did she see it wasn't a body.

Dripping with rainwater and missing many of its needles, it was a scrawny, weather-beaten pine tree. Her father gave no explanation for where he'd gotten it as he dragged it beside the fireplace. It looked like a wet dog.

"Dad, what are you doing?" Soojin whispered.

He threw off his jacket, still glistening with beads of rain, then ran to the basement. Soojin stood rooted to the spot as his footsteps descended the stairs, then thundered back up. He held a box labeled CHRISTMAS in his arms. He dropped it at the foot of the tree. Soojin heard a few of the delicate ornaments inside crack. Paying that no mind, he threw it open, pulled out a red tree skirt, and propped the tree onto it. Then came lengths of tinsel from the box. Ruby red and gold and silver. He upended a shoebox of ornaments at his feet next. String lights. An LED star tree topper with defunct batteries.

Then, as if possessed, he began to decorate.

For a while, Soojin just watched him as he strung garlands and three stockings over the fireplace. But by the time he turned his frenetic energy to the tree, she joined him. They wrapped the tree in three colors of tinsel and string lights. Many of the glass ornaments had shattered, but they salvaged the plastic baubles: candy canes and gnomes frosted with fake snow, baby angels missing one or both of their wings. They decorated every bare inch of this anemic little tree until it bordered on ridiculous, and finally, when they were done, her father bent to click the switch. The string lights surged on in a burst of garish green that Soojin knew from memory would cycle red, then white then gold and back again in pulsing, rhythmic intervals. He stepped back, chest rising and falling erratically, and turned his rapt attention to the door.

"Please," he whispered under his breath. The bulbs edged his shoulders in sickly, radium-hued light. His hands balled into fists, shaking. Whom was he begging? All Soojin could hear was their own stuttering breaths and the rain letting up at last. Then, as if hearing something, his feet carried him haltingly toward the door. One step forward. Another—before some unseen weight seemed to settle on his spine and force him to his knees. A slow and effortful folding.

"Dad!" Soojin yelped when he crumpled to the floor, face cradled in his palms. He rocked heavily back and forth on his knees, heaving one raw wail before his voice tapered off. His shoulders shook silently. For the first time since the jesa, her father wept and wouldn't stop, his emotions so raw her first instinct was to flinch, to avert her eyes.

Soojin knelt beside him, resting her hand against his

arm. She had no right to touch him. She'd lied. She'd made everything bad. And yet he leaned toward her. She wrapped her arms around him and they cried together until there was nothing left and they were emptied and dull and lit only by the Christmas tree's forgiving light. It was a long time before either of them spoke.

"Mirae loved Christmas. Absolutely everything about it," he said when they'd finally let each other go. He'd stopped crying but his eyes were still wet. The string lights reflected in them like quivering star systems of gold. "The carols. The food. But especially the Christmas tree. God, do you remember how every year, on the first night we set it up, she would drag a sleeping bag to the foot of it to fall asleep staring up at the lights?"

"I remember," she said. Though Soojin had stopped doing the same when she was a preteen, Mirae had slept at the foot of the tree every Christmas season—up until her very last one. Soojin could still picture it, the overlapping years of her sister's form lit gold beneath the tree, hair fanning out across the carpet as she looked up at the blinking lights, which from her vantage point must have looked like a galaxy, effervescent with stars. In each mental image, she'd grown a little older until last Christmas, in which their half-heartedly decorated tree pulsed alone with nobody resting beneath its glow.

"I guess it's early for all this," Father said. "But she just loved this so much. I thought it might draw her back here if I . . ." His eyes filled. He reached out, pulling a branch of the tree. "I don't know why I thought this would work." The branch jostled, loosening one of the ornaments from its needles. He rolled the blue bauble underfoot until it cracked. "I'm a fool."

"But you aren't," Soojin said. She knew all too well the ridiculous lengths someone would go to when bargaining with loss. His bargaining had resulted in nothing but a festive home. Soojin's had ruined lives.

"I am. Both your mom and your sister would laugh at me."

He rested his chin on his knees, staring at the tree's glow. His eyes were vacant rooms. There was something about that glassy stare that made her worry. He was checking out on her. "Don't do this," she said, grabbing hold of his sleeve.

He finally looked at her. "Don't do what?"

Vanish into yourself again, she thought, though her mouth said: "Ice me out because you're pissed at me."

"I'm not 'icing you out,'" he said. "It's just painful to talk. Everything feels unbearable."

"So let's not talk about the present, then," Soojin said. "Let's talk about the past."

"What about it?"

"Um . . ." Soojin regarded the lights. Thinking about it now, there was so much about her dad she didn't know. He offered little information about his life without prompting, and Soojin rarely prompted.

"Tell me about you and Mom," she said.

"What about us?"

"Uhhh . . ."

They were great conversationalists, both of them. No wonder they'd so swiftly grown apart after Mirae and Mom were gone. Soojin thought of her argument with Mark in the fields.

"What were you two like when you first met? Did you and Mom fight a lot at first?" She didn't recall many fights from her childhood, only small tiffs—like who would cook dinner or what color the dining room should be repainted—all of which Mom won.

Her father made a deep noise in his throat, as if revving himself up for this conversation. Soojin knew it cost him something to talk at length about Mom. The fact that it was his fever that had sent her out for medicine in the middle of such heavy rain was a guilt that saddled him on good days and pummeled him on bad ones.

"We sure did," he said finally, and to Soojin's relief, a hesitant smile lit his face. "You know us. Both stubborn as mules. And your mom could be so temperamental at times. But we never fought for long. Mad as she was, she'd find humor in things. She'd make us laugh."

Soojin remembered that about her mother: how her moods would oscillate but were always tempered by good humor and a generous, bright smile. That's how she'd received her nickname, Sunny. A slapdash replacement for her Korean name, Sunyoung, which no one could be bothered to learn how to pronounce correctly.

"Ah, but I do remember one particular fight that dragged on and on," he said. "It was before you two were born."

"What was it about?"

"This house," he said, rapping his knuckles on the hardwood floor. Soojin looked at her surroundings: the only home she'd ever known, with its rustic fireplace, reading alcoves, and wide bay windows that let in an abundance of sunlight in the summer.

"What about it?"

"I sprang it on her," he said. "We were living in an apartment in the city after graduation, working such long days that by the time we got home, we were too tired to do anything. It was still a good life, but your mom and I dreamed of moving somewhere beautiful and spacious before starting a family. It was all just daydreams. *What if? Where would you go, if you only could?*"

"And then you did," Soojin said when her father sank into thought and stopped talking. His eyes snapped back to her again, as if he'd just remembered her presence.

"Yes," he said. "And then we did. Your mom came back from work one day raging about something indecent a higher-up did. HR did nothing, so she'd quit in a huff. I remember thinking: *If ever there was a time to make our dream of leaving happen, it's now.* I'd received a decent sum of money from my grandfather's will. I thought I'd never let her be in an environment where she was made to feel small again.

"So I enlisted your uncle's help and searched for a house on the cheap. This is the one we found." He knocked on the floor again. "No one had lived in it for decades. A true fixer-upper. It was full of rodent droppings, dry rot, ivy up and down the walls. But I knew your uncle and I could whip it into something special. By the time I surprised your mother with it, the house was beautiful."

It all sounded so romantic and impulsive, attributes she would never have thought to apply to him. She thought of her father young and so in love that an affront to his wife would spur him into something as drastic as purchasing and gut-renovating a house. It was easy to forget sometimes that her parents had lived full, separate lives before her. She imagined him, just a few years out of adolescence, standing proud in front of the dilapidated husk of what would eventually be their home. His eyes bright and unaware of the unkind future hurtling swiftly toward him.

"I don't understand why you guys would fight about that," Soojin said.

"Neither did I, at the time. But in retrospect I do. I was uprooting your mother from everything she knew. It was all the things we'd talked about before. Daydreams of running a bed-and-breakfast in a place where our kids could play on a beautiful coast. She seemed excited until I showed her a picture of the property and told her it was in Jade Acre.

"I thought for sure she'd be ecstatic. This used to be her family's favorite vacation spot when she was growing up, you know. She'd tell me about the misty forests. How her dad would dive for abalone, which they'd slice up and eat raw as the sun went down. But she wasn't happy. She got mad, and I responded in kind." He sighed. "I was selfish. I said it was all for your mother, but maybe it was mostly for myself."

"But she came around. She loved it here," Soojin said. She knew her mother loved this home, and the town as well. She had so many memories of their family picnicking at the cove, watching tourists twirl sparklers against a night sky so flush with stars, the sparks seemed redundant. Her mother giggling with Mark's mom on the porch as the kids played in the woods just out of sight. Yes, Soojin was certain her mother had been happy here.

Her father nodded, but his face was pensive. "I have to believe she did. But toward the end, about a year before the car accident, she started suggesting we sell the house and leave. I always talked her out of it." He ran an agitated hand through his hair. "Loss has this way of triggering a landslide of what-ifs. I'm always thinking . . . What if she'd never gone to the store that evening? What if, all those years ago, I'd never insisted we move here, and we had you and your sister in that San Francisco flat instead? Or what if we'd left Jade Acre when your mother first suggested it . . . would they both still be here with us?"

"What is the point in thinking like that?" Soojin asked. She understood the futility of that line of thought because she fell victim to it too. It was a road that led nowhere but to hurt. "Things can happen anytime, anywhere. There is no way to account for every what-if."

But he wasn't convinced. He gave her a stilted, unhappy smile, leaning over to run a thumb across her cheekbone. "There is also this: What if I'd been a better, more reliable father—would you still have felt lonely enough to bring your sister back?"

He withdrew as the string lights phased from their steady golden glow to cascading green that played strangely on the lines of her father's face. "I was never icing you out because I was angry at *you*, Soojin. I've been so angry at myself I can hardly look at you. I failed for you to make that decision, and then to hide what came of it. I made a liar out of you, and I'm sorry."

She opened her mouth to interrupt, but he halted her.

"No. Let me speak," he said. He drew his knees closer to his chest. The Christmas tree surged garnet before draining into a silvery white. "I've always felt ashamed about how I checked out on you and Mirae after your mom died. You were both so young and needed me, but I wasn't there. Your sister had to grow up so fast, and I never apologized. I don't know why the words *I'm sorry* were so difficult for me to say back then." The rain was beginning to quiet. He looked up, listening to its soft prattle on the roof. "She never regarded me the same way after those months, you know. It was like I'd breached her trust as a parent. She stopped depending on me. I always thought we'd have time for me to mend things, but she didn't live long enough."

Soojin wanted to tell him he was wrong, that being a parent didn't mean being an automaton, impervious to bouts of weakness—but she couldn't find the words.

"I failed her then. But I'm not going to fail her now."

"We'll find her. We will," Soojin assured him, resting a hand on his.

"And then I'm going to do what she needs me to do."

"What is that, Dad?"

His long silence told her everything he refused to articulate. They sat beneath the tree until the rain halted. Then, with a determined hand on her shoulder, he left. This time, she didn't follow him. She needed to think. She stayed before the Christmas tree they'd decorated as a wild prayer to call Mirae home. Her father was driving out into the darkness to destroy her sister, and it was her fault. Her selfishness had saddled him with this horrible choice that was no choice at all.

Soojin watched the garish colors of the string lights move across the wall. By the time they had cycled back to steadfast gold, she had come to a decision.

30.

The girl brushed the curtain of rain aside and stepped in. A blackness. The ground turned incorporeal below her feet. She heard a low frequency of speech, incomprehensible, like flies buzzing in her ears. And then she emerged on the other side. The rain spit her out in the Porter estate's ridiculous yard, where a fat raccoon was perched on the rocks of a koi pond, slowly devouring a splendidly expensive calico carp, which still twitched in the animal's humanesque paws.

She turned her attention to the home's wide windows. Bentley was sleeping upstairs. She could hear his fretful breathing, and when she willed water to worm its way through a crack in the plaster, blooming a wet pupil on his bedroom ceiling, she could see him, too. Water gathered at the opening, then dripped onto his brow. He shuddered from the bright cold but didn't wake. The bead of water slid down the boy's temple, arcing a silvery trail until it found the edge of his closed right eye. He sighed, his lashes fluttered with dreaming. It slipped through the seam of his eyelids, spread its wet wings across his cornea, and then she had him.

She willed him to rise and he obeyed. Still sleeping, he crept out his door and through the arteries of white hallways. She marionetted him through the aesthetically bare atrium, the photo-less walls, all the way to where she stood on his doorstep, waiting to be let in.

Bentley's eyes were glassy and unseeing when the door swung open. His gray shirt darkened immediately from the weather. He didn't acknowledge her at all. For now he'd exhausted his usefulness. She left him idling on the porch beneath the unyielding rain and entered the house.

Christopher Porter was in his room, sleeping more soundly than he deserved. At least until the splinter of light from her entrance landed against his eye. He groaned, brushing his pale brown hair from his brow.

"Bentley?" he mumbled into the dark.

"He's still sleeping."

Her unfamiliar voice lodged an immediate alertness in him. He sat up, fumbling for his lamp.

"Who's there?" he called, authoritative even fresh out of sleep. His hand found the switch, and a burst of white filled the room. It took Porter's eyes a while to adjust, but when he finally focused on her form, there was no immediate reaction. A disoriented dullness infiltrated his features.

"Sunny?" he breathed, as if at once convinced he was still dreaming.

Her mouth twitched. She wrung rain from her hair, stepped toward the lamp's quivering circle of amber light. Puddles beaded in her wake. She didn't dignify him with words. She let him see her instead. Disbelief swelled his pupils, eclipsing the slate-gray irises completely. Reflected in the perfect blackness of his eyes, the girl saw herself smiling.

"No. You're the daughter," he muttered, easing himself out of his bed. "The drowned one."

"Yes," she said, continuing her slow approach as he backed toward the dresser where his phone was charging.

And then he surprised her. He laughed. A cruel, quick exhalation of air.

"It would seem, then, that your mother was a liar," he said. His voice was steady, though his heartbeat sounded loud to her ear. Uneven and stuttering.

She tilted her head, as if imploring him to go on. She knew he was biding time.

"She said the gift should never be used to raise people. That it could raise something awful. But look at you. So whole. So alive."

"Am I?" she asked. She thought of the jesa. How she'd crawled on hands and knees, sobbing as she forced ceremonial fruit into her mouth, driven by the animal belief that if she could just be sated, she could also be saved. How her father had crumpled in renewed grief upon seeing her. The name talisman in the fire, her body a thing to be burned. She was not alive. Such things did not happen to the living.

Above them, rain began to pelt with unusual force. They both froze, looking up at the skylight, where white pellets gathered on the glass. Hail? No. Teeth. Imaginary or not, it was raining teeth. She wasn't sure why this struck her as funny, but she felt herself laughing. The emptiness of this house carried her voice far and fast. Her mouth tasted like a blur of river silt and blood.

Porter's composure splintered. He staggered for his phone, managed to press 911 before she closed the distance between them. She forced him hard against the dresser, and they fell to the floor together. Objects rained down around them. His phone. His wallet. A photograph of his wife, the unknowing catalyst who had brought them all here. To this rural, drenched town; to this moment; to the river she'd never leave.

"What is your emergency?" someone asked from the phone that had fallen beside them. He shivered when she wrapped her hands around his neck, almost gently, before bearing down with crushing force. There was no struggle at first, so great was the shock, and by the time the man began to thrash, he'd lost too many moments already. His eyes were wild with disbelief as he bucked beneath her.

There was no screaming. Barely any noise at all besides the frantic thumping of feet against the bedpost and the strangled sounds of a slowly collapsing windpipe. Her hands dug into the pillar of his throat, depressions forming around her fingers. Estuaries of veins protruded from the man's temples. It was a violence committed in near-complete silence. His skin grayed and puckered beneath her hands.

I'm not sorry, the girl heard in her head as she began to sink her consciousness into Porter. It sounded like both their voices. She closed her eyes. His memories open to her as he died.

The 911 operator intuited a crisis in his unresponsiveness. "Stay on the line. Stay with me. Help is on the way," they assured him. It wouldn't be fast enough.

※

The girl opened her eyes to darkness. In this memory, it was night and they stood at the promenade. The moon cascaded a long, quivering trail atop the water. Christopher Porter was with her mother, overlooking the water. But the easy, carefree friendship they had shared in the previous memories was gone. They were older now. Much older, and in the midst of a fierce, whispered argument.

Her mom looked the way she always remembered her: hair grazing her shoulder blades, the very first hints of wrinkles creasing the corners of her eyes. This couldn't have been long before the car accident, then. Neither Sunny nor Christopher was smiling.

For the last time, I can't, Sunny hissed, turning to walk away. Christopher grabbed her arm, forced her to face him.

Why not?

She pushed him away, eyes blazing as if daring him to touch her again. *I just can't, okay? You don't mess with lives like that.*

Why not? We used to mess around with dead things for years, Christopher said, gesturing wildly to the ground, thinking of all those summer vacations in Jade Acre where the two of them would sneak from their lodges to bury things in the woods.

Animals, Chris. Not people.

What difference is there? We've all got fucking bones. His voice splintered. His former boyish effervescence was gone. He unraveled a handkerchief from his pocket. A single wisdom tooth sat ivory against the fabric. He held it up so she could see.

The tooth was freshly pulled, not even a month out of its

owner's mouth. After his wife died of heart complications, half out of his mind, he'd taken pliers to her teeth. He'd quietly cremated her without ceremony and brought their nine-year-old son to Jade Acre. He hadn't come to escape. His mind was fixated on a figure from his distant past. A girl he saw during summers in the sleepy resort town his parents had so loved to vacation in. A girl who could rescind loss with her miraculous, life-giving hands. He'd hinged his entire future on her.

Please, Sun. It was so jarring to hear him beg. *You don't know what her death has been like for me. But you're the answer. You're a miracle, aren't you? Haven't I always said that? You can help me. I know you can.*

Sunny seemed nearly swayed, watching their dark reflections dancing in the water. Still, she shook her head. *I'm sorry.*

I'm not asking you to do anything for free, you know, Christopher said, his eyes taking on a determined glint. Here was a method he understood. *How much do you want?*

I don't want your money.

But you need it. I know you do. Your little bed-and-breakfast can't be doing well with all the developments.

Thanks to your aggressive business ventures, she breathed before stilling. *You've been doing this on purpose. You're trying to back me into a corner.*

You're backing yourself into a corner, Sunny.

This isn't a game, you know. We're talking about a human life. How do you know you wouldn't be condemning her to something worse, Chris? Sunny asked.

If that happens, it won't be your problem. You'll have a check to cash big enough to put your two daughters through college, and your role will be over. You have nothing to lose.

You're crazy.

Is it crazy to want my life back? Christopher asked. His composure finally cracked. An involuntary tear scythed a warm path down his face. He wiped it angrily. *We were friends once, you and I.*

I wish I could help you. I do. Her mother's tone left no room for argument. Christopher knew her well enough to understand that this particular battle could not be won. The change in his expression was immediate. His face, just vibrant with desperation, with bargaining, drained into a clinical coolness. A long silence swelled between them, broken only by the sussuration of the sea pulled this way and that by the tides. Then finally, he spoke:

That's just it. You could, yet you won't, he said. His voice all venom and misplaced grief metastasizing into something uglier. *You'll revive roadkill but not a person I need. Animals. Fucking mite-eaten birds. Is she worth less than that?*

I'm leaving. I'm sorry, Sunny said, backing away from the promenade, her arm held up as if to ward off danger. But Christopher didn't lunge for her. He straightened up. The wildness that had been in his eyes just moments before had been stamped flat.

Things are going to get worse for your family, you know, he said evenly. A threat he didn't have to verbalize any further. He'd spent the next several months cannibalizing the virgin coasts with boutique hotels, choking out their family business in the hopes that she would assent. Like a specter, he'd trailed her until the day she skidded into the ravine, and, as punishment, he chose to not save her.

The memory quivered, blending slowly toward the present. The promenade and shimmering black water dissolved.

There was only the room, the bare walls, her own ragged, furious breath. There was Christopher Porter, staring blankly up at the skylight, where the teeth that had rained down so furiously had vanished. His eyes wide open, seeing nothing.

Emergency services were remarkably quick. In less than twenty minutes, the Porters' opulent estate would be lit up with cop cars and ambulances. It was a silent reconnaissance. All sirens shut off, no beacon lights sweeping the scene, because it was quickly obvious to everyone: there was no one here to save.

Though the front door was wide open and swinging, there was no sign of forced entry. Wet footprints puddled a path from foyer to primary bedroom, where blankets hung half off the mattress. The cell phone used to dial 911 was found on the floor near a dresser, though the one who'd called was elsewhere.

Christopher Porter was found dead in the decorative pond in the front yard, submerged in brackish water. All the eelgrass and scouring rush that once grew exuberantly had blackened; a single white lotus bobbing on the round dish of its leaves was the only plant life that survived whatever had befallen this water. A calico koi had been devoured: only its head, spine, and a shock of gold scales remained. They drifted and clung like small motes of light to the dead man's hair. The remaining fish pecked at both corpses with curious mouths.

The murder was both immediately obvious and inexplicable. The obvious: Porter had been strangled to the point of tracheal collapse. The inexplicable: the ringlet of finger marks that wound around his throat was rapidly decomposing. It made no sense. The body was fresh, not even an hour dead. And yet, as if hastened to rot by water, that lone area was festering and reeked so heavily of carrion it had attracted a belt of horseflies to his neck like an oily black cravat.

And the teenage son was nowhere to be found. He'd left everything behind. His phone. His wallet. His car key. Responders put an alert out for him before turning their sights once again on the body.

31.

Mark found Bentley Porter staggering along the side of the road, though he didn't immediately recognize him. All the meticulous care Bentley normally took with his appearance was gone. He wore nothing but a thin sleeping shirt and sweats. No shoes. The boy's pallid face in the headlights looked so stunned that Mark slowed his car to a crawl.

He didn't like the guy. But now that he got a good look at him—his doused hair, his doll-like eyes—Mark couldn't help but roll down the window and ask, "Dude, what the hell?"

Bentley didn't register the other boy's presence until Mark leaned further toward the passenger window to shout "Porter!" more forcefully than necessary. Bentley flinched, rubbing his hands together—so nakedly frightened that the yearslong distaste drained right out of Mark's body.

"Are you okay?" he asked more gently.

A stupid question. He clearly wasn't. The way the boy's eyes darted here and there in the dark, as if he were afraid of being jumped. If there was any kid to jump in this sleepy resort town of hospitality workers barely making ends meet from tourist season to tourist season, it was Bentley. Mark unlocked the passenger door. "Get in. I'll give you a ride."

Bentley opened the door, then hesitated, looking over his shoulder. There was nothing to see but rain.

"Get in, asshole, the interior is getting wet," Mark barked, knowing damn well that the interior would get wet regardless once Bentley sat the wet dog of his body down. The other boy roused himself, slipped into the car, and shut the door behind him.

They took off, navigating the wet roads slowly. Mark glanced over at Bentley, who was soaked and shivering, then turned the heater on full blast and lowered the radio. "What happened?"

Bentley picked up an empty water bottle from the cup holder and fidgeted with it. It made Mark anxious; he wished he would stop.

"I sleepwalked," Bentley said after a long silence.

"All the way out here? That's some intense sleeping."

"No. When I woke up, I was in my yard. I was standing in the rain and I felt like I needed to leave, so I did." Every sound felt amplified. The turn signal's steady tick. The windshield wipers' furious drag against the glass. "I think she visited me in my sleep. The inside of my house was all wet."

She. The word slammed a physical weight in Mark's head. *She.* The Silases and their home briefly wrecked with water, then not. The dead rat he'd pummeled to fine powder and released into the wind. Skinned.

He pulled to the shoulder of the road. Parked.

"What are you talking about?" Mark asked, dread forming in his belly because he already knew. Bentley crushed the empty water bottle in his hand. The sound startled Mark's foot on the pedal, made the engine roar. Another car came down the road, casting both boys in searing white light. It passed them slowly, and by the time the headlights had gone, dragging their features back into shadow, Bentley's face was pure misery.

"Mark, do you believe in ghosts?" he asked. "How much do you actually know about the Han family girls?"

When Mark called her, Soojin was creeping her way down the stairs. She and her father had spent several hours searching for her sister, and he was crashing hard now on the couch. She intended to sneak into his room and steal back her own car key to take up the search alone, but her phone began to blip cheerily in her pocket. She cursed, scurrying back up to the safety of her room before the ringtone could wake her dad.

She closed her bedroom door behind her, looking at Mark's name glowing across the screen. She hadn't talked to him since their argument in the muhly fields, though she'd been meaning to reach out, to tell him he was right. But as usual, he'd beaten her to the olive branch.

When she picked up, though, for the first time she could remember, he spoke over her, not wasting any time with niceties.

"Are you home?" he asked. She could hear a turn signal click, then go quiet. It sounded like he was traveling in a car going at great velocity.

"Yes?"

"Did you find Mirae?"

Merely the name sent a painful jolt through her. She looked toward the empty rat cage in the corner, which neither she nor her father had had the heart to dismantle. Dull splatters still smudged the wallpaper beside it. She wondered what Mark had done with Milkis's ashes, which she had never gone to collect. "No," she said.

"Listen, Soo. I'm heading over to your place right now with Bentley. He has something he needs to . . ." Furious muttering on the other end of the line, some physical grappling. And then someone else's voice cut through the static.

"Soojin." It was Bentley's voice.

She was so shocked they were together, all she could manage was "What do you want?"

"I want to find your sister," he said.

The words meant nothing to her for a long time, but when they registered, she stood so fast she banged her knee hard on a dresser. Once the pain subsided enough for her to think, she hissed *"What?"* into the receiver.

"I know you brought your sister back," he said. "I know how you did it. And I want to help you find her."

"I don't understand," she said. "How? How do you know?"

And so he told her. About the history between their parents, their friendship. The resurrection her mother had refused when Bentley and his father moved to Jade Acre eight years ago. A year later, her mother was dead.

"Did your . . ." She was afraid to ask. "Did your dad kill my mom?"

There was a long silence on the other end. Soojin's heart pounded to the point of pain. She held her hand to her chest. A long breath, and Bentley finally began to speak:

"I don't know if that's what he set out that night to do. But they fought. Your mom got into her car to speed home and my dad chased her. She lost control and the car fell into the ravine. But, Soojin . . . on the night of the accident, Silas came over and I listened in on them." She heard him swallowing hard into the phone. Mark was so quiet in the background. "After she fell, your mom was still alive. She got the door open and was screaming for help, but when Silas showed up at the scene and tried to radio it in, my dad didn't let him call for an ambulance. He paid him off and they left her there. I'm sorry."

Black spots bloomed over her vision. She heard the phantom sound of someone calling for help, but it crackled and hummed as if heard through a policeman's radio. She thought of the car belly-up in that gully with her mom still conscious inside it. Anger, white and scalding, washed out her vision.

"Mirae knew."

"Yes. She heard it while resurrecting something—your mom begging him to leave your family alone."

"What was my sister to you?" she asked. All her memories of Bentley were bad ones filled with simmering disregard. A resentment that Mirae had never seemed to quite share.

"She was a friend, I guess. A secret friend, so you wouldn't know," he said, his voice very faraway.

"And then?" she pressed.

"And then she found out. I avoided her for as long as I could, but eventually I just . . . didn't want to hide anymore. I thought I owed her more than that. On the night of the house party, I texted her to meet me at the trestle bridge. I know she told her friends that she was going to walk home, but she didn't. She went the other way. She came to me." A long, heavy pause, like his words were wounding him. When he began again, his voice was shaking: "She wanted me to come forward about my dad and the police chief. We were arguing, and then . . ." It sounded like he was crying now. "Fuck. I'm so sorry."

The trestle bridge. The one Mirae had her father take her to when they'd found her burning in the cottage. So that was where she'd died. The thought made Soojin feel like she was plummeting. The bridge was built over a ravine. A fall from that height—no wonder her back had been so bruised when they'd finally found her. What was going through her mind in that solid handful of seconds before she hit the river? Did she think at all, or did her mind erase itself as velocity built, the body's final mercy before the river dragged her down?

"I wanted to—damn—I swear, Soojin, I would have gone in after her, but she was already gone. It happened so fast. So I ran toward town. The first car I saw, I jumped in front and stopped it. It was Chief Silas. When I told him what happened, I thought a search would be called, but he took me home to my dad—they talked about scrubbing my phone. Told me to say nothing." A long silence. Static. "And so I said nothing."

There was a strange, wet heaving on the other end of the line. He was sobbing in a way that sounded close to hyperventilation. Saying *I'm sorry* and *I didn't mean to.* Soojin didn't care.

She had always believed that her sister and mother had died prosaic deaths. A drowning, a back-roads car crash—but they had been even more ordinary than that. They had died by men. Her mother by refusing one, her sister by trying to hold one to account. She couldn't breathe. She imagined Bentley's face and what it would feel like stamped underfoot, caving in. The want for vengeance was so seductive and animal—no wonder Mirae had left to seek hers.

"Oh my god, my sister," she gasped. Her sister, who had killed. Her sister, only partially herself and bereft of her name. Her grudge was all that was left of her now. What had Soojin done?

Mark's voice returned to the phone after crushing static. "Soojin, I'm coming for you. We'll look for Mirae together, okay?"

Outside, the steady rain surged into a downpour. Soojin couldn't bring herself to hang up. She dragged herself to the window. Everything beyond it was veiled by rain cutting brutal rivulets down the glass as she watched for Mark's headlights. The two boys were still talking, though the reception only fed her bits and pieces, submerging the rest in a low buzz.

"Look," Bentley muttered through the pop and fizz of static.

"What—" Mark's voice, obscured by white noise, and then quieter: "Shit."

"What's wrong?" Soojin asked.

"She's here," Bentley said. That was the last thing Soojin heard before a metallic screech filled her ear, so sharp and keening it sounded like a scream. And then she heard nothing.

32.

"She's here," Bentley said.

"Shut up." Mark swept the road with his eyes. He saw nothing but the white shears of his headlights carving a small bright radius. Trees frenzied by weather. He sped fast over a pothole and the whole car lifted, buoyant for a moment before hitting the ground. The chassis rattled. He didn't slow down. Mark couldn't get to the Han residence fast enough. He had this wild, improbable notion that arriving at that home would mean safety.

Bentley was doing nothing for his nerves, with the way his breath hitched as he said, "She's here. I saw her." His face blanched ivory.

"Bentley, can you calm the fuck down? You're freaking me out," Mark snapped before turning his attention back to the empty road. And then he saw it too. Through the windshield, something white appeared in the darkness. It was a hand, hovering disembodied in the air. It brushed aside the vertical agitation of rain like draperies, and something pale and oblong peered out from behind the impossible curtain. A face stared at him with its inkblot eyes before the hand let go and the distortion of water fell. The girl's face disappeared back behind the rain.

Mark swore, swerving to avoid where the face had just been, and before he understood what had happened, he'd lost control. The wail of tires filled the night. His chest strained against the seat belt with bruising force before he was whipped to the side. A streak of red crossed his vision. All thoughts evacuated. The sound of metallic crunching filled his ears as the car smashed into a tree. The airbag deployed, striking him in his face so hard his vision burst into phosphenes of light. Pine needles rained down on the windshield and as quickly as it began, it was over.

The night settled over the hissing car, and all Mark could hear was the sound of his own panicked gasping, the rain as it struck the windshield. A warmth was running down the left side of his face. It felt strange to move, effortful, like his muscles had braced for impact so hard they had seized up. He angled his head to look at the driver-side window and saw that the glass was smeared with blood. It was an injury that should hurt, but didn't yet. More pressing were the dizziness, the sharp nausea, the iron taste in his mouth.

On the passenger side, Bentley was miraculously uninjured but stunned, staring out past the crushed windshield with prey-animal eyes. Mark wanted to ask if he was okay, but his tongue was failing him. It was hard to talk. His thoughts were sticky and spliced. The adrenaline draining swiftly from his body left him feeling bereft and exhausted. He saw everything in two. Two steering wheels. Two moons. Two Bentleys, the ghostly forms hovering parallel to each other.

Not good. A darkness gathered into the shape of a girl behind the passenger-side window. The silhouette of a small hand pressed against the glass, and like a sleepwalker, Bentley reached out and laid his own atop it. He was sobbing.

Not good, Mark's mind insisted once more before a roaring silence rushed to meet him.

The car hissed in the dark, its hood crumpled like paper against the trunk of the sugar pine it had rammed into. The girl and Bentley regarded each other, separated only by a thin barrier of glass. The lines of the boy's palm steamed their imprints onto the window: life line, family line—both so short, so crooked. His were lonely, doomed hands.

"Come out," she said, and the rain echoed her. *Come. Come.* Compelled, he opened the door. She inched back as he obeyed. The car rumbled in the endless wet; the headlights igniting the rain into white agitations. He said her name. It rolled right off her, but the tone of his voice when he said it affected her. Warmth and guilt and desire. It made her hungry.

She laid a hand on his arm and felt the thrum of blood beneath his skin, rushing through the chambers of his heart. She saw a vision of the two of them waiting out the rain beneath a toolshed's awning, followed by a swell of other memories. Phone calls held in secret once her sister had fallen asleep; nights spent scraping animals from the road together, all for her attempts to hear her mother's voice.

But it wasn't over yet. She saw their last argument, on the trestle bridge they'd so often stolen away to so they could hang out in private. *You knew!* she'd said. *This entire time, you knew all of this,* to which Bentley replied only, *Yes.*

You have to come forward about your dad and that fucking cop, she hissed, her face flushed by liquor and rage.

And where would that put me, Mirae? At least you have one parent left. Without my dad, I have no one.

I only have one parent because *your dad let the other one die!* she shouted. *And this whole time, you fucking knew. Am I a joke to you?* When he didn't answer, she slammed the heel of her palm hard against his chest. He reeled back. *I'll do it myself, then.* She swiveled to leave. The river roared loud beneath them both.

No one will believe you. My dad has the police department wrapped around his wallet, Bentley said bitterly. When she didn't turn, he grabbed her shoulder and spun her around.

What happened next was an accident. She struggled against his grasp, pushed her arms against his sternum, but the force propelled her backward. She stumbled and could not catch herself. She tipped into the ravine. The water had her before Bentley finished his last words to her, which she knew now were *Mirae, please.* She didn't even scream.

She saw him sobbing in the back of Silas's patrol car, begging him to *look for her, please call a search party, please, please,* as they pulled into the Porter estate's driveway.

"I was wrong back then," Bentley said numbly in their present. "I thought my dad was all I had, but that wasn't true. I had you, didn't I?"

And then he did something she didn't expect: he touched her. His eyes still dazed, he laid a hand against the side of her throat, where her pulse would be, if she still had one, before leaning down to brush her lips with his own.

He tasted like salt, and in that familiar salt was another one of his memories, sinking into her and swelling to envelop them both.

Suddenly, it was summer, and she saw them again. In one of the remote coves where she and Bentley used to set up their makeshift cremation pits. He was grunting with a bag of coals, filling a metal barrel before dousing the interior with stump remover.

It's ready, he called, lighting a match as she walked over. She could feel him considering her, admiring the way the flames cast dancing shadows across her face. He thought her beautiful, she understood now. In her hands she held a body in a ziplock bag. Not roadkill this time, but a sparrow that had struck her bedroom window. One foot, she'd saved to bury. But that was for later. They had to burn the rest of the bird first.

Funeral pyre's all yours, Bentley said, gesturing grandly to the burning barrel, and the girl watched herself stride forward and unceremoniously dump the bird into the flames. They watched the feathers begin to catch in silence. Behind them, the tide ripped across the pebble beach, then pulled back toward the moon.

In the lull, the girl watched Bentley deliberate with something before he finally said, almost meekly, *Smells gross.*

It didn't smell gross, exactly. The girl watched herself scratch her nose. *Smells like dying,* she said, though she wouldn't have known, having not yet died.

Then Bentley finally worked up the nerve for what he'd actually meant to say. His hand flexed, then eased. *Do you really have to go so far?*

There's nothing I wouldn't do for a chance to hear her voice, she said, warming herself against the flame.

She didn't expect Bentley would know what it was like to be the emotional pillar of a family. She had this fear that if she showed her vulnerabilities to her father or Soojin, it would panic them. It was only in stolen moments burying bones, as her mother's voice passed like wind through her hair, that she felt like what she was: a girl. Bone-tired and overencumbered with responsibility, but a kid nonetheless.

You don't have to understand, she said more bitingly than she'd meant to. The tail end of her sentence echoed in the cove. For his part, he didn't look taken aback at her tone, and that's when she realized just how often she snapped at him, something she rarely did to anyone else. When had this boy become the sole lightning rod for her tempers?

Silence swelled between them before he quietly muttered, *I do understand,* as he watched the fire climb the rest of the bird. The bright torch of its beak, the wings set to burning. Months ago, this might have been slightly traumatic to him, but after so many nights spent scraping roadkill off the backstreets with Mirae, he was desensitized. *You're not the only one without a mom, you know.*

In the memory, the girl watched something akin to guilt stitch itself over her own face. *I'm sorry,* she said. *I didn't mean—*

It's whatever, Bentley said. The feathers had all charred away, and the bird was an organic lump blackening into nothing. As the flames reached the viscera, the scent grew actively foul. *Even if I had your powers and could bury some piece of animal to hear my mom talking to me, I wouldn't.*

Why not?

She'd probably curse me out. An exhalation of air, somewhere between a scoff and a laugh. *I killed her.*

Bentley, your mom died of heart problems.

Yeah, he said, throwing random things into the fire now. A stick, a green leaf that belched black smoke, a cold, wet stone that sizzled in the heat. *Heart problems she developed because of her pregnancy with me. Dad said she used to be fit as an athlete before I happened. So . . .*

He stopped talking, and the girl saw herself consider him. Even now she remembered what she'd been thinking. *Before I happened*—such a grim way of speaking about your own conception, like unfortunate weather or a terminal diagnosis. But Bentley would not necessarily want to keep talking about this right now. He needed a diversion. So she saw herself nudge him, point up toward the sky, which frothed with so many stars it made them forget themselves awhile.

Look, she said, tracing a wide square in the sky. *Do you see those star clusters that kind of look like a falling, headless stick figure?*

Bentley made a face like, *Not this again,* but he humored her. *Sure,* he said.

That's the constellation Virgo. One of the stars in that constellation symbolizes a girl, you know. Her name is Erigone. The Greek god Dionysus gave some wine to her dad, who then shared it with shepherds. The shepherds mistook their drunkenness for having been poisoned and hung her father in a tree.

Erigone came across his body and killed herself too, hanging on the same branch her dad died on.

Yikes, Bentley said dryly. *That blows for her.*

Yeah, it does, she continued, undeterred. *I've been thinking a lot about that lately. How even in these old myths, the parents get to have their histories of harm and overcoming, and their children are just collateral damage. The kids suffer or die on their behalf. As lessons or a price to pay or whatever the hell.*

So that's the end of the story? She just dies? Bentley asked. *That's shitty.*

No, actually, she said. *A god saw Erigone's death, took pity on her, and raised her to be a star in the solar system. It's called catasterizing, a placing among the stars. A human body becoming a celestial body.*

Her gaze fell to the earth again. To the boy who was sometimes beautiful when he let down his guard, and to the nameless charring animal between them. *But doesn't that sound nice, Bentley? To be able to put down everything you're shouldering and just be carried into the sky like that? You could watch everything happening below you, impartial because the stars don't feel anything. Not even their own burning.*

The memory made her privy to Bentley's confusion, the way he said the first coherent thought that hit him, which was *You know you sound nuts, right?*

She laughed. *Well, fair. If I'm not, what are we doing here, you and I?* she asked, holding up the severed talon in its ziplock funerary shroud, blood smeared inside the plastic.

A long silence. The bird was an amorphous blob in the barrel now, the fire slowly burning itself into silence.

Why did you tell me that? Bentley asked quietly.

In the memory, she stepped away from the barrel and walked toward the water, her hands clasped behind her back. *You don't have to be like Erigone, punishing yourself for something you didn't do,* she said, considering her words carefully. *Just because your dad chooses to hurt himself by not coming to terms with your mom's death doesn't mean you have to do the same. What happened to her was not your fault, Bentley. And honestly, fuck your dad for ever making you believe it was.* A wind picked up in the cove, whistling through her hair and thrusting a rush of embers into the hot summer air. *You should put that weight down.*

She had never turned back to see his expression, but the girl saw now the way Bentley's eyes had filled with tears, fever-bright in the firelight before the memory began to dissolve. In her present, he was pulling away, and he took the taste of summer with him.

Rain again. The clouds overhead stitched shut over the constellations and their silly mythologies she no longer cared for. Bentley pulled away from her and let his hand fall from her throat.

"Come with me," she said. "Let's leave. We don't have to be this fucking lonely," by which she meant, *Don't let me be lonely.* This was as close to begging as he'd ever heard from her. When she entered the river this time, it would be forever. She didn't want to go alone. And who better to follow her than this boy, her dark mirror—the one person she'd let see the ugliest parts of her. Even if he'd been a traitor in the end, didn't that still mean something?

Come. Because she feared loneliness more than death—she wouldn't, wouldn't let him go. *Come,* a horrible battering sound in her ear. Like a body dragged over river sediment.

He looked back toward the open car. The interior was getting soaked. Rain pooled in the door's map pocket. Mark was so still on the driver's side—concern flitted across Bentley's features. She reached out and turned his face toward her, willing him to focus. To follow. His gaze dimmed back into incognizance. He leaned into her touch and let her lead him away.

33.

Mark had very nearly made it to the Han residence. Soojin and her father found his car not eight minutes away from the road that turned onto their driveway. It reminded her of a massive animal in the dark, its wound so fresh and warm it steamed when the night air hit it.

As soon as the wreck came into sight, Soojin opened the door before her dad had even slowed down. He yelled to her to wait, but she couldn't. She leapt from the moving car. The momentum made her fall, gravel skinning her knees, and then she was up and running. Her feet pounded the asphalt toward the red eyes of the taillights blinking in the dark.

As she ran, her vision tunneled. Everything fell away. The frenzied, wind-struck junipers. The long road made white by headlights. Even her father's voice. Suddenly it felt as though her world began and ended with that ruined car heaving steam into the night like an injured horse. The hood crushed like an aluminum can. The windshield spider-webbed from impact. She couldn't breathe.

Mark was in there. He'd been coming for her when this happened.

I am a curse. The thought pierced her. *I am a curse. Nothing close to me gets away unharmed.*

She remembered Mark's face in the cremation chamber when she'd said this to him. The metallic roar of her pet rat burning to ash. The barely discernible shake of his head in the chamber's failing light. Despite everything, he'd disagreed with her. He shouldn't have.

Soojin reached the car. The passenger-side door was open and letting in rain. She moved to the driver-side window as her father rolled to a stop and got out of his car.

"Mark," she called. There was no movement beyond the window. The glass was smeared red.

Her father came up behind her, trying to pull her back from opening the door, as if he feared it would be bad and didn't want her to see. But she couldn't be stopped.

Her pulse pounded loud in her ears as she opened the door.

There he was.

"Soojin. *Don't* touch him," her father ordered.

But she already had. She traced his face with quivering fingers. His pale cheek, his closed eyes. Then, breathless with fear, she lifted the hair away from his left temple, where the bleeding was worst. A strangled noise escaped her. There was a gash, but seeing it still made her sob a breath of relief. It was smaller than she'd expected from how much blood stained his cheek and pooled in the shell of his ear. Perhaps it wasn't as serious as she'd feared. And he was breathing. The sound was enough to make her want to cry.

She dipped her finger against the torn flesh of the wound. Her dad clutched her wrist and pulled her away.

"I said don't—" he started, but froze because Mark groaned at her touch, his brows knitting together, registering pain. His lashes fluttered, trying hard to wake.

"I'm going to call for an ambulance," her dad said, coming out of his daze. He ran to his car for a phone.

"Mark," Soojin said as she fell against him. She unbuckled his seat belt. It had bitten into his collar, bruising a dark red stripe over his chest. She pressed her hand hard on the injury. "Wake up."

He did. It was like he crash-landed back into himself. His eyes flew open and he pulled himself up from his slumped position with a rattling gasp. The velocity of it startled Soojin off him, and she fell to the rainy asphalt with a yelp. Above her, Mark turned toward the passenger seat, then, finding it empty, searched wildly until his eyes finally landed on Soojin and her father.

"She led him away" was the first thing he said when he found his voice. Only then did Soojin remember Bentley, and his absence spread like capillaries of ice beneath her skin.

"Where did they go?" Soojin's father asked.

"I don't know," Mark said. He grimaced and reached for an empty coffee cup in the holder to hack out murky red spit.

"The trestle bridge," Soojin said to herself. This had begun at the trestle bridge, when Mirae had tipped off it a year ago, and that was where it would end. Louder, she said: "She took him to the river beneath the trestle bridge."

Mark stared at a point past her. "Water ghosts are tied to where they drowned," he thought aloud.

There was so much her father didn't know, but his determination to find his daughter kept him steady on his feet. He reached into his pocket and pressed his cell phone into Soojin's hand.

"Emergency services are on their way. Soojin, you stay with him. I'll pick you up from the hospital later," he said before sweeping toward his car.

"Dad, wait!" she called, but she couldn't bring herself to leave Mark behind. Her father drove off into the rain, the red of his taillights bathing the road in hellish light.

After the landscape had eaten the image of her father's car, Soojin and Mark sat in dazed silence as rain struck his fractured windshield. Bits of glass had crumbled down on the dashboard, and Soojin reached out, fascinated by their fragmented luster. A sharp, belated prick. Blood beaded where she opened.

"Why'd you do that?" Mark asked limply, pulling a napkin from the glove box.

She watched him as he tended to her. How carefully he dabbed her blood away before folding the napkin into a thin band to tie around her finger. The memory of the last time she saw him simmered up. The fields, the way she'd ripped into him about how he'd abandoned her when they were children. His eyes had looked so devastated when she'd left him in his car that day. But that hadn't stopped him from coming for her and from patching her wound while his own still bled.

"I lied to you," she whispered as he finished tending to her. The wounded finger now neatly bound.

"What?"

"In the field. I lied to you. Our friendship failing was not your fault."

"But it was, Soo. I avoided you when you needed me." His voice was very tired. Like he was having trouble focusing. "I shouldn't have done that."

"No," she said slowly. Because this was the truth she'd conveniently ignored: Mark had tried years ago to make things right. A month, perhaps two, after her mother passed, he'd tried to approach her at school, his posture apologetic. She'd refused to hear him out, choosing instead to ignore him at every turn. Though it was Mark who'd first hurt her, it was Soojin who had drawn the border between them.

"You tried. I know you did," she said. In anticipation of what she was about to confess, her eyes began to burn. Mark had seen her cry so many times in the past few months, but she was suddenly humiliated. She turned away toward the passenger-seat window.

"It was easier to not let you back into my life," she said, her voice barely audible through the rain striking the hood of the car. "I resented you. Your life just looked so perfect compared to mine. Your mom and dad alive and so loud and just . . . It was unbearable. I was sad, and your happiness was unbearable. I couldn't stand to see it. I think I might have even hated you a little."

Mark had gone perfectly still next to her. She felt so

ashamed. This was the ugliest part of her, the part she'd always tried to hide, even from herself. But there was no point in hiding. She'd lost everything already.

"God, I'm so shitty." She still couldn't bring herself to look at him. Her breath fogged the windows, and she could see her own pale ghost in the glass. "What does it make me, Mark? That I can love somebody and still wish them pain, just so I'm not alone with mine?"

A soft rustling beside her, and a hand cupped her cheek.

"Human," he said, directing her face so she turned toward him. "It makes you human."

His brown eyes looked very kind in the dome light. They offered a compassion Soojin wasn't sure she deserved, and it broke her heart. When the tears came in earnest, there was nothing she could do to stop them.

"I'm sorry, Mark," she gasped. And she was. For everything. Because wasn't it all her fault, every misfortune brought upon her town these past few months? Her father, driving aimlessly in the rain, searching for his daughter's ghost; Mark and his injury; the Silases in their graves. But, worst of all, her sister risen against her will. Soojin had caused this with her selfishness and inability to see past her own desires, and she wasn't sure if it was too late to make things right. "I'm so fucking sorry for everything."

Mark leaned over and they held each other. He was trembling involuntarily, coming down slowly from the adrenaline of his crash. She buried her face in his collar.

"She's going to kill him, isn't she?" Soojin said when the tears subsided. "Bentley."

"I imagine she's going to try, if your dad doesn't find her

first, I guess," Mark said. "Hey, do you think . . ." He swallowed hard. Slowly, he pulled away. "Do you think it's right to try and stop her?"

Soojin regarded Mark's face. The blood had mostly dried to a sienna crust along the left side of his face. She dipped her sleeve in the rain pooling in the door's map pocket and held it against his cheek until the red loosened enough to wipe away. Then she wiped clean the blood in his ear.

"If everything Bentley said was true, both your sister and your mom were wronged by the Porters. Maybe this is justice. Maybe Mirae needs this to move on."

She thought of the sister she had known all her life. The girl who'd swept spiders beneath a glass to release outside when Soojin's first instinct was always to crush. The one who had kissed their rat between the ears before securing her back into her cage for the night. Then Soojin thought of the dream she'd had on the night her sister disappeared: her ghostly white rat leading her through the landscape until she found Mirae in their parents' bathtub—her body so waterlogged and horrible she couldn't look at her.

"No," Soojin said. "I don't think so." Because at the end of vengeance, what more was there? When everyone she hated was drowned, when the remnants of the girl who already could not remember her own name had metastasized beyond all recognition, what was there to move on to? What heaven or hell would have her?

She wrung Mark's injury from her sleeve, then looked past him. Through the driver-side window, she saw something glowing white in the tree line. She rubbed her eyes and leaned forward. It hadn't vanished. There was a flickering. A pale will-o'-the-wisp in the dark.

"What?" Mark asked.

She stumbled out of the car instead of answering him. In the distance, she heard the whine of a siren beginning to pierce the hush of their deep, rural night.

Mark followed her, steadier on his feet than she thought possible. "Your dad said to stay put."

"But, Mark, look." Soojin pointed into the trees, where Milkis sat grooming her lucent white fur. There was a luminous quality to the animal. She glowed like a pale moon. Mark squinted into the dark, then looked at Soojin like she'd gone mad. But she wasn't seeing things. Milkis was close enough to touch.

"I'm coming too," he said, though he was weak. They leaned against one another, propping each other up as they wove through the trees. The sound of sirens crawled ever closer. The dead rat took off, running into the woods.

Soojin didn't know how long they followed Milkis down an incline so muddy they spent much of their time stumbling. Their phone flashlights did little to dispel the milky, unnatural darkness of the night. She saw mostly by the lamp of the rat's here-but-gone body, darting through the undergrowth. Time grew mercurial, like she was dreaming.

When they emerged suddenly at a break in the trees, Soojin felt disordered, as if she'd been shaken awake while sleepwalking. "Where's Milkis?" she whispered to the night.

"We burned her, Soo," Mark said, looking dazed and concerned. "Don't you remember?"

Rain was in her eyes—and Black Pine River stretched the

engorged snake of its body before her. Above her, the shadowy architecture of the defunct trestle bridge loomed, but not the moon. Her rat was gone, folded into the landscape like she never was. But she was. She had led Soojin here, if not to fix things, then to try.

"Soojin. Look," Mark breathed, pointing out toward the dark water.

Her dad was on the rocky banks, stalled as if mesmerized by what he was seeing. There was a spot in the river that was glowing an icy blue, the blue of the cold fire that had engulfed the cottage on the night of the jesa, and her sister stood in the water, cast in its sickly cadmium light. The long, loose sleeves of her dress dragged against the currents as she reached a single slim arm out toward shore. She looked so lovely, her smile so welcoming, Soojin's feet mindlessly shuffled forward a few steps toward her. But there was another body in the distance between them. It gave her pause.

It took Soojin a moment to identify the form as Bentley, hidden in shadow as he was. But when he inched close enough to the water for it to lap over his shoes, the glow illuminated his vacant expression.

"Bentley," Soojin said, but mostly to herself. Her voice was drowned out by the steady white sound of rain pelting mud, pelting river, pelting her. She watched the two of them—Mirae and the boy caught in their own private world of betrayal and care. He took his first step into the water. His face held the blank devotion of an animal imprinting on the first living thing it sees. Another step. Another. The water reached his knees. His thighs. Soojin was rooted to the spot, her hand shaking in Mark's.

"Come back," her father said. His voice small, as if he'd forgotten why he was at the river in the first place. She couldn't tell whom his words were directed at, his daughter or the boy who, of his own volition, was walking to join her.

As the river reached his waist, Soojin distantly wondered if Bentley was frightened, if he was thinking at all as Mirae touched his cheeks, then slid her hands down to his throat—tenderly, like a lover—and wrapped her fingers around it.

The illusory spell that had woven over the night shattered. Her sister's placid face turned into something horrid. Dark blue dendrites pulsed across her body like an artery of water as seen from above, cutting through a landscape. It jarred everyone out of their reverie. Her dad was shouting now, as if stunned back into himself. Mark's grip tightened so hard as to feel crushing.

Mark had been wrong. Killing Bentley wouldn't allay Mirae's grudge; it would feed it. She imagined her sister, chained to the river long after everyone who knew her was gone. And it would be Soojin's fault, for bringing her sister back for her own comfort. She couldn't let that happen.

She broke free from Mark's hand and ran toward the bank. Bentley made a pathetic noise as her grip tightened, but merely as a function of still being alive. His face betrayed no fear as Mirae plunged his body underwater and held him there. The froth of his breath beneath the surface roiled, then went still.

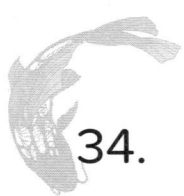

34.

Their friendship experiment hadn't consisted only of burials and cremations. There had been days when Bentley and Mirae had quietly basked in each other's company, and true tenderness threatened to intrude. A short time before Mirae buried a bone and finally heard her mother's voice begging Christopher Porter to leave her alone, there had been such a night.

"She keeps talking about San Diego. About how she's going to apply and we can live together and . . ." Mirae sighed, tapping her head with the heel of her palm. An unconscious motion Bentley could translate now as frustration. They were sitting on the trestle bridge on a mild summer night, watching fireflies flash the bright globes of their bodies.

"I thought you love your sister," Bentley said, a faint bitterness in his voice he couldn't tamp down. Soojin was the reason Mirae insisted on their friendship being secret, as if Bentley could control what his father did to Han's Bed & Breakfast. A firefly drifted past him, and he flicked it. He couldn't fathom why he did it, and as he watched its failing light arc downward, he was struck by his own casual cruelty.

"I do. I love her more than anything—it's just, if she follows me, isn't my life more of the same? More posturing for her and my dad. I just . . . I really wanted something different."

"So tell her, then," Bentley said. He didn't understand what the fuss was about. "Tell her not to. Tell her to apply anywhere but where you'll be."

"You've never had to give a shit about anyone, have you? You don't get it." She pulled her hair free of its tie so it fell in ragged waves around her face. "If I rejected her like that, it would break her heart. You don't know what it's like to be the eldest girl in a family like mine. I have to be everything for everyone. I have to be perfect." She shuddered as if the word sent a bolt of distaste through her. "You know, my relatives always used to call me that. *Perfect.* I used to think it was a compliment, but I understand what it actually means now. *Perfect* for daughters is self-effacing. *Perfect* means erasing your own needs in favor of another's. *Perfect* has made me so fucking tired."

Mirae picked up a pebble from the tracks and threw it down. He lost sight of it for a moment until it hit the water. The ripple expanded slowly below them like a dilating eye.

"I want to get out of here so bad, Bentley," she continued against his silence. "I want to be alone to do every reckless, selfish thing because no one expects better. I want no one to look up to me or rely on me. I want to make every shitty, stupid decision until I'm rotten all the way through, just because I can. I want to be filled with wrong, so when I'm good again, it's because I chose to be."

When she was done talking, her breath was coming out in short, spasmodic puffs, somewhere between anger and relief. For a while, Bentley could only look. He'd never seen her so worked up, but now he could see the hairline fractures beneath her immaculate veneer. That simmering, low-grade resentment she carried with her and tamped down until it could be mistaken as poise. But right now her catharsis made her too radiant, her eyes too wild—it made him slack-jawed.

She glared pointedly at him. "What, for once you have nothing to say?"

His lips were dry. He licked them. When he spoke, his voice was windswept. "Why do you have to leave town for that—you can start here, can't you? Want to do a wrong thing with me tonight?"

She scoffed, looking down at the river below them. "Really? You're unbelievable." She thought it a proposition, but no, it wasn't. Not at all.

"Come on," he said without explanation, offering her a hand. She hesitated but took it, and he led her back to his car. She got in quietly, and when she realized he was taking her to his home—a place she'd never been—she made no moves of protest, and that's how he knew she was serious. She wanted to make bad decisions; she wanted the freedom to wreck herself the way other young people did. She thought him a force of ruin, and she was letting him lead her.

"Isn't your dad home?" she asked. Her hands were clasped together in her lap.

"Out of town. Business trip," Bentley replied, to which she said nothing.

As soon as they entered the estate and he closed the door

behind them, Mirae had him against the door. Her body pressed flush against his, she traced her lips up the line of his throat as she unbuttoned his jacket and forced him out of it. It fell off him with a thud. Every length of skin her mouth touched burned, sending jolts up and down his spine. She smelled like the river they'd waded in earlier, and, at the crook of her neck, like Ivory soap. His hand hovered behind her head, wanting to tangle in her black hair to tip her throat back. He wanted—

But this hadn't been his intention when he brought her home.

Still, hadn't he imagined this for a year? This girl, caged between a wall and his body, their long acres of family history and harms tossed far behind them. He could do it; he could tell she'd see it through. He could press his mouth against hers and push her down the hall to his room with wide windows. He could crush her against the bed and think, *Mine.*

But the way Mirae's hands moved to undo his belt was mechanical, and when he pulled her flushed face away from his collarbone, her eyes were distant. She wasn't seeing him at all. In her desperation for escape, she'd erased him.

Not like this.

He eased her off his chest; she looked at him questioningly. "Isn't this what you meant? Our wrong thing?"

"No, stupid," he gasped. His hair had fallen before his eyes, and he pushed it back; he ran a hand over his mouth in a bid to collect himself. Turned away to refasten his belt. "Jesus, and you accuse me of being a perv."

Mirae fell back, looking humiliated. "I'm sorry. I misinterpreted—"

"Apologize later. Come on." He held her arm and led her

through the luxuriously barren foyer of his home. They descended into a basement so vast it might as well have been its own apartment. When Bentley clicked on the lights, the neglect was obvious in the way dust hung in the air like a shimmering veil. The walls were lined with storage shelves brimming with things: glassware, statues, celadon vases with egrets etched around the rims.

Mirae walked ahead of him and wiped a thick layer of grime off a white marble statue: a depiction of a pregnant woman holding her belly with a soporific expression, as though one day she'd woken with child and still thought herself dreaming. Bentley sidled up behind her, reaching over her shoulder to tap the swollen marble belly. His father hated this statue and had stashed it away here along with other gifts he found too gaudy to display but worth too much to toss. Everything in this basement was worth hundreds, if not thousands, of dollars. One day it would make for the bougiest estate sale ever. But for now it was just a rich man's garbage.

"Why are we here?" Mirae asked.

Bentley picked up a shimmering Swarovski crystal figurine—a translucent buck with grand antlers—and handed it to her. Then he picked up a porcelain vase for himself. "I thought you said you wanted to do a wrong thing tonight," he said before lifting the vase up high above his head.

"Bentley!" she gasped, but too late. He threw it to the concrete. He saw Mirae's eyes widen before the crash. White-and-cobalt porcelain flew everywhere.

"Jesus! What—have you lost your mind?" she shouted.

He grabbed another vase from the shelf. "You said you wanted to do something bad. This stuff is expensive as shit. It's wrong to destroy it. This is a wrong thing. Do this one wrong thing with me." He threw the vase on the floor, and it burst in an explosion of jade. *I can't believe I did that,* he thought. *I can't believe I'm doing this.* His vision wavered as though he were seeing through great heat, and then he was cracking up.

"You're crazy," Mirae said, her voice uncertain and wavering. He could barely hear her over his laughter. "Your dad is going to kill you."

"You saw how much dust was in here—does it *look* like anyone's been here in years? Not even the housekeeper. Just us, and only now. Come on. No one will know," Bentley said. "By the time he comes down here, years from now we'll both be out of this shitty fucking town." What he did not say was that sometimes, in his more foolish moments, he even imagined perhaps together. The two of them, elsewhere. Starting again. He cupped her cheek, ran a thumb idly along the side of her mouth. He'd never touched her like this before, in any manner adjacent to tenderness. She didn't lean in to his touch—didn't react at all. "There's no reason in this world you should be scared right now."

She looked at the crystal buck in her hands, uncertainty written all over her face. She wouldn't do it, he thought. But then determination came over her expression, and Bentley watched rapturously as she lifted it. *That's it,* he thought when she stalled, holding it high above her head as if in offering. She followed through, slackened her grip so the crystal deer could shatter at her feet.

"Fuck," she gasped. "Fuck. I'd have to work like thirty hours to pay that back." Her cheeks were flushed. He'd been right to bring her here. The gleam in her eyes made him feel worthy. It was all he'd ever wanted.

"Was that bad enough?" Bentley asked, lifting the pregnant marble figure up to her. Now, this was truly expensive. If his father found out, he'd be dead. He'd worry about it tomorrow. "Are you wrong enough yet?"

Did she see the challenge in his eyes? She took the marble statue and threw it to the floor, but not with enough force that it would shatter. Instead it broke in three distinct sections: sleepwalker's head, pleated skirt, swollen belly. He picked up only the pregnancy and waved the fractured navel before her bewildered eyes. "That was weak as fuck!" he shouted, feeling out of control. "You've been nothing but good all your life—you don't know *how* to be anything else. You've got a long way to go."

Mirae was quiet as the light above them failed, plunging them into perfect darkness. When it came back on, she'd snatched the white belly from his grasp. She palmed it like a grapefruit, appraising its size and heft with clinical detachment before suddenly thrusting down with all her strength, her expression incandescent. A burst of white: the belly broken into fragments, birthing nothing. They froze, breathless, until their eyes met above the mess.

And that was it then—the frenzy. The two of them went to work in the basement, grabbing antiques off the shelves and smashing them on the floor. Plates. China. Marble busts of saints neither could identify. Who cared, who cared. Plumes of dust rose around them. Glass lacerated their ankles, though both were too consumed to notice the blood turning their socks into wet red cylinders. Thousands of dollars gone. Celadon, crystal, porcelain, jade. By the time they finally tired—a galaxy at their feet—they were covered in a thin layer of shimmer. Both of them luminous and wrong and perfect for it.

They panted together in this fog until Mirae managed to speak. "I'm lonely," she admitted, but she was laughing. She was crying. She was bereft and covered in vestiges of wealth. All could be true. Tears cut clean lines down her face. "I'm so fucking lonely all the time. Did I do this to myself? It's like I'm a ghost in my own house. No one really sees me. I don't know who I am."

Bentley knew what came next. This was the night he remembered best, after all. He gathered her in his arms and held her until she was emptied. Then upstairs they went—to the kitchen, where they snuck shots of whiskey from his father's cabinets until their faces burned and nothing made sense and they found their way to his room with wide windows. The curtains billowed effortlessly in and out as they lay on his bed but didn't touch each other.

"I don't know where to put your loneliness," he mumbled, an elbow slung over his eyes to keep the moonlight out. He was warm and drunk and unworried about their destruction.

"Just carry it for me tonight, Ben, she mumbled back, and her rare use of his preferred name gripped, then released his heart. Only his mom used to call him that, his father always favoring the formality of his given name. When Mom died, he figured he'd never let anyone call him that again. That no one would ever feel close enough to warrant it. Mirae did. He wanted to tell her so, but he was fading. Her words were round and slurred when she spoke again: "I promise I'll take it with me tomorrow."

The next morning she was gone, leaving a thin glisten of porcelain dust on the sheets. When he saw her at school, they exchanged clandestine nods and pretended the night before had never happened, despite the bandages each had wrapped around their wrecked ankles.

But Mirae was a liar—she'd left a portion of her loneliness behind. Two months after this night—the night he'd watched her tip off the bridge—he slipped her loneliness around him like a shawl and destroyed what they had spared in that basement, feeling not wrong but *wretched* all the way through.

I really wanted to be better, Bentley thought as the water closed over his head. *Oh well.* The girl he both knew and didn't know dragged him down; her cold hands held his throat. *But I guess we're finally doing it.* He lost his breath. It left him in a plume that rose to the surface of the river like a swollen belly. He saw it burst against the surface and flatten. *We're doing it, Mirae,* he thought, his mind a shattering vase. *Our wrong thing.*

Soojin plunged into the water after them. For the first few seconds, the shock of cold left her indisposed and unable to struggle against the current. She lost her footing, and her face dipped below the surface. She came up sputtering and thrashing, having forgotten her reason for entering. But then she saw her sister, close enough to touch. Soojin reached the black depths and groped blindly until she felt her sister's cold hands. "Mirae, stop!"

Her sister didn't respond, barely seemed to register her at all. She looked pallid and blue in the ghastly light. Her face, devoid of her kind brown eyes, gave nothing away but wordless, animal wrath. Soojin wanted to close her eyes to this unrecognizable thing and swim back to shore, but devotion rooted her in place. She pried Mirae's fingers from Bentley's neck just long enough for the current to carry him out of reach before her sister lunged for him again. Somewhere behind her, her father struggled against the rapids, trying to reach them.

"Soojin!" Mark called from shore.

"Help him!" she screamed, pointing to Bentley's body, which was floating swiftly downstream. Mark looked between the sisters and Bentley as if torn, then took off at a wobbly sprint to intercept Bentley. Soojin had just enough time to wonder if the boy was even alive before something snaked around her wrist and thrust her into the depths.

Under the surface, the river was quiet. Pressure built in Soojin's ears until she could no longer hear the static of the rain or the howling wind. All the sounds of the living world were muffled as if heard through a womb-like boundary. Mark frantically calling her name, her father treading water. It all sounded so impossibly far away.

Below her, the streambed convulsed with a writhing black mass she almost mistook for the fronds of a willow. But it was hair. Masses and masses of silken black hair. Hair broke through the crevices in the rock and crept across the sediment like a living, sentient thing. Hair had snaked around her wrists and ankles to pull her under, and now hair kept her there, submerged as the air pressed against her lungs, her throat— desperate to leave her.

I'm sorry, Soojin thought as the remnants of her sister loomed in front of her, dark eyes and pale hands clawing for her as if any vengeance would do. It didn't look like Mirae at all. If there was any recognition, it was past mattering. Soojin's body told her to fight, to claw against the hair wrapped around her limbs, as if struggling would do a damn thing. But if this was the end, she wouldn't condemn Mirae to the curse of having murdered her. As her vision whitened, Soojin chose the only other thing. She embraced her sister.

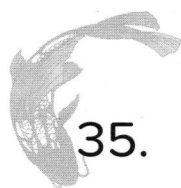

35.

Soojin opened her eyes to crushing gold light. When she dragged in a stuttering breath, no water flooded her lungs. Her feet were wet. She was barefoot on the stark white tile of her parents' bathroom. It was all faux cheer: yellow matching towel sets and an empty rose-oil diffuser. In the corner, the curtain was drawn around the claw-foot tub, and a stifled weeping came from behind it.

Soojin had seen this scene before, when Milkis had led her in dreams on the night of the jesa. That vision had the painful clarity of a nightmare. But it was different this time. Now the bathroom had the pallor of a swiftly fading memory. Motes of light drifted over her vision as if to illuminate the scene, to help her see what she'd missed before.

She approached the tub and bent to pick up a damp box that was upended on the mat. Tampons littered the floor in their colorful little parcels. A few had been torn open and discarded unused, the cotton distended out of the plastic applicators, swollen with spilled bathwater.

"Unnie," Soojin called, holding the edge of the shower curtain. The water wasn't running. She could hear the gentle lapping of water as it struck the sides of the tub. The residual drip, drip, drip of the faucet. "Unnie, I'm going to open this, okay?"

Silence.

She pulled the curtain and froze. Her sister was there, as expected, submerged to her throat with her back turned toward her.

But she was a child.

Her hair fell in bedraggled tangles in front of her face, fanning out below her like a black curtain. The water had the milky quality of dissolved lather, and the scent of bubble-gum bath suds rose, cloyingly sweet.

Soojin inched around the tub, bracing herself before she sank to her knees. Mirae looked up. She had the huge, dark eyes of a yearling deer.

"Hey," Soojin said quietly. She was prepared for her sister, almost eighteen and monstrous; she wasn't prepared for a child. She didn't know what to do.

"I don't know what to do," Mirae said. Soojin startled. For a moment she thought her child sister had read her thoughts, but Mirae was pointing past her, gesturing clumsily to the bath mat Soojin was crouched over. The tampons. When she returned her attention to Mirae, her sister had pulled her wet hair before her eyes like drawing a curtain shut. "I tried, but I chickened out. I'm scared."

Soojin looked at the water. Her sister had to have been sitting in it for a long time—no steam rose off its milky surface. A thin tendril of blood coiled up and dispersed like incense smoke across the opaque surface.

"It's okay. It can be very scary," Soojin said, reaching to brush hair from her sister's face. Mirae leaned away from her, refusing to meet her eyes. Soojin pulled back. After a hesitation, Mirae sighed and parted the hair away from her own face: an invitation to look. To speak.

"How old are you?" Soojin asked gently.

"Eleven," Mirae answered. And eleven meant . . .

"Where is your mom, Mirae?"

Her sister seemed to collapse inward. Already small for her age, she grew smaller still as her shoulders crumpled. "I don't have one anymore."

"And what of your other family? Can't they help you?" Soojin asked, though she already knew.

Mirae made as if to say something but halted, eyes growing wet. A bobbing in her throat as she rapidly swallowed; then, without warning, she plunged her face into the water. Bubbles lacerated the surface as her child sister exhaled. She went still long enough that Soojin grew nervous, but just before she could force her up, Mirae resurfaced. She furiously wiped water from her face and shrugged. Her eyes were bloodshot and faraway, but her voice was even. "I dunno."

As a child, Mirae had been unusually pulled together. Even after their mother died, she'd rarely lost control the way Soojin and her father did. But Soojin understood now that she'd been wrong. Shattering privately was no less real.

"You must have been lonely," Soojin said. The brief dive had stuck hair wildly against Mirae's forehead, and Soojin reached to brush it aside. This time her child sister let her, and she tucked the wet strands behind her ear. "I'm sorry."

In the faraway fields, Soojin had told Mark that between him and her sister, she'd choose her sister every time. That had been a lie. She understood that now. Mark had never factored into it at all. This was the truth: between *herself* and her sister, Soojin always chose herself. *Her* desires, *her* loneliness. Mirae had dedicated her entire short life to her, and in return Soojin had made her sister's death about herself too. "I'm sorry," she said again.

Mirae's lip quivered. She made to hide her face in the water again, but Soojin stilled her and wiped tears away with her sleeve when they fell. She reached into the pearly bathwater, rooted around for the plug, and pulled. The cold water spiraled down the drain, leaving her sister shivering against the enamel. Soojin took a plush towel off the rack and wrapped it around Mirae's shoulders. "Come on, let's go." She pulled her to her feet, held her steady as she climbed out of the tub, then had her sister perch on the rim.

Soojin knelt in front of the box of tampons, still tipped on its side. She righted the box, put the unopened parcels back in, and pressed the lid closed.

"These are a little intense for your first period," Soojin said, putting the box away in the cabinet beneath the sink. She dug around in the familiar chaotic mess left behind by her mother: a curling iron and hair dryer with their hopelessly tangled cords, the face masks bought in bulk during a trip to Korea, a box of old makeup she'd hit pan on and for some reason had never thrown away. And then Soojin finally found it: a solitary menstrual pad gathering dust in the very back.

"Here!" Soojin said, triumphantly holding up the pink parcel and grabbing the folded underwear on the counter. "This will feel much less scary."

She unwrapped the pad from its packaging and sat in front of her child sister. "This is how you use it," she said, pulling out the wings and peeling away the paper lining covering the adhesive strips. Soojin pressed the pad over the length of the underwear and folded the wings around. "That way it'll stay put. See? It's easy. But you want to make sure it's positioned right," she instructed, just as Mirae had years ago during Soojin's first cycle, when she'd come home sobbing, a sweater tied around her waist to hide the red dot expanding on the back of her pants.

Mirae's voice from her memory: *Don't cry—it happens to everyone. Now look at me, Soo. It's easy! Just don't put it too far forward, otherwise you might leak. There we go.*

"There we go," Soojin said, dabbing her eyes quickly on her sleeve before pulling Mirae to her feet, the pad properly in place now.

Mirae nodded, but her face was slack and exhausted. It felt wrong to see this level of quiet unhappiness on a face so young.

"Are you ready?" Soojin asked.

Her sister let herself be led to their parents' bedroom. The arrangements of wilting white chrysanthemums told Soojin that the funeral must have passed, yet Father hadn't yet been able to put anything away. Their mom's clothes were still draped on the chairs the way they had been since the night of the accident. Her makeup was still strewn on her vanity, along with a small legion of bobby pins and a brush with her hair still tangled between the teeth.

Soojin sat Mirae down on the bed and went to dig through Mom's clothes in the dresser. She found a white pajama set with drawstrings that could be pulled tight enough to fit Mirae's child form. Her sister swam in their mother's clothes. In the vanity mirror beside the bed, countless white bodies stared mutely out at her, their faces scrubbed of all features. Beyond that, the windows that should have overlooked the trellised roses showed nothing but frothing currents, as though their home were submerged in a violent body that pressed its cold blue hands against the glass, looking for a way in.

Soojin closed her eyes. Opened them. She must stay calm. She turned and picked up her mother's brush from the vanity, willing still her trembling hands. She worked her fingers between the tightly compacted hairs caught in the bristles and pulled. The strands came away tangled like a black sparrow's nest, and she hovered over the wastebasket, unable to let go. This was silly. Silly, and yet.

There was a small sound like a distant bell. The figures in the mirror pointed at something behind her. Soojin turned. Tiny cracks had formed in the bedroom window. The river's insistent pressure was spider-webbing the glass. The white splinters crawled across the pane, and a few drops wept through the minuscule openings, trailing down the walls and darkening the paint in a manner similar to ink. She didn't have time for this. Her hand opened, and the net of her mother's hair fell against the crumpled napkins and receipts.

"I'll brush your hair, okay?" Soojin asked as she turned to Mirae.

When she pressed the bristles against Mirae's scalp, her sister twitched away. "I can do it," Mirae said. Not antagonistically, but with a stubbornness born of an almost pathological self-reliance.

"I know you can." The bed dipped as Soojin sat behind her sister. "Please, I know you can do everything yourself. But for once in your life, let me."

After a long hesitation, Mirae yielded. She closed her eyes and allowed Soojin to run the bristles down the long lengths of her hair. Soojin took her time, even as the glass splintered further and the river rushed in, pooling at the foot of the window and spreading steadily across the wood floor. She combed out every tangle until the black tresses lay sleek against her sister's back. By the time she was done, their ankles were submerged and Mirae was weeping.

"My mom used to brush my hair for me," she said. There was no bath to hide in. She turned her face away and wiped at her cheeks with small, pruned hands. Across the room, the window finally shattered. Shards of glass drifted past their ankles, cutting them both. Mirae didn't seem to notice, even as their shared abrasions pinked the water.

"Did she? Mine did too," Soojin said. *And so did you once.*

The room was filling so rapidly. From outside the home came the sound of a girl's furious voice, muffled by rapids. It wasn't safe here. "All done. Are you ready?" She didn't specify for what, nor did she know herself. But Mirae asked no questions. Trustingly, she clasped a small hand in one of Soojin's, and the two of them exited their parents' room.

The rest of the home fared no better. Water poured through the chimney and carried house slippers off their racks. Water reached the sisters' waists as they waded through the dim halls of their home: past the kitchen, from which they could hear

Father's soft weeping and the plates being swept off their shelves; past the living room, where the TV bobbed screen-up in water, casting the room in cold blue light as a commercial for Zoloft rattled off the side effects. Then, finally, up the staircase, which had turned into a narrow downhill creek of its own.

When they reached their bedroom, Soojin locked the door behind them. An empty gesture. The specter was here—was her sister—and like water she could not be kept out long. Blessedly, their bedroom window had yet to shatter, but it groaned as if fit to burst at any minute.

"Soo?" Mirae called from behind her. For the first time, there was recognition there.

When she turned, she was surprised to find her sister, who until now had looked so small, at eye level. Soojin looked down, patted her own body incredulously. She was suddenly wearing fuzzy pajamas—ones she had long ago outgrown, with cartoon hamsters stringing tinsel on Christmas trees.

"Why are you staring at me like that?" Mirae asked.

Soojin looked past Mirae's head to the mounted mirror, half expecting to see the faceless bodies once again, but saw instead only herself. Ten years old and frightened, her hair shorn short below her chin. Soojin didn't know what sort of enchantment this was, but she was a child again. She gazed at the bedroom, suspended forever as it had looked the month after Mother died. The flowers dying on the nightstand. The toys on the floor Mirae would soon put away and never touch again.

"So this is where I've trapped you," Soojin said, her voice barely audible over the sound of water against glass.

"What?" Mirae tilted her head; she hadn't heard her, but

something about Soojin's face must have concerned her, because she walked forward and pressed a small hand against Soojin's forehead. "Soo? Are you okay? You look kinda sick."

Before her eyes, Soojin could see her sister's demeanor changing. Gone was the vulnerable girl in the tub. The mask of composure had slipped on instead. Soojin had once again forced her to wear it, and that was unbearable.

Soojin brushed Mirae's hand aside.

"We're not okay. You and I are drowning," she said. "We're drowning each other." She saw an agitation of froth beyond the window. A white hand pressed against glass, then pulled away.

"Uh, okay. Why don't you sit down for a bit?" Mirae said, trying to tug her to the bed, but Soojin flew to her desk instead and pulled the entire drawer out to rummage through its contents. She tossed aside gel pens and loose leaves of origami paper, hidden quizzes marked C- with red ink, and thumb-sized school photos. Mirae inched behind her. "What are you looking for?"

The bedroom window burst. Water poured through it like a ruptured aquarium. Twigs and washed-up weeds tangled around their ankles. Long, endless ropes of black hair swept into the room, fanning out in the water like inquisitive black snakes. Mirae didn't acknowledge any of it.

Soojin finally found it. Triumphant, she pulled the tooth in its scuffed ziplock bag from the bottom of the drawer.

"Unnie, what did you wish for back then? When you lost your baby teeth and our parents had you throw them into the sky?"

Mirae looked at her own tooth rattling inside the clear plastic and held up her hands as if to keep Soojin back, shaking her head incredulously. "What's with you all of a sudden?"

The water was up to their thighs now and swiftly rising. Stuffed animals and a screeching alarm clock bobbed beside them. Soojin pushed them aside and waded forward. "What did you wish for? Because it couldn't have been this," she continued, gesturing to their destroyed room, the wallpaper peeling back, the glass, a watercolor palette releasing whorls of paint into the water. Mirae looked at her mutely, oblivious of the destruction all around her.

Soojin shook the tooth out and pressed its crescent grooves against Mirae's palm. "I need you to look," she said. "Look at what I've done to us."

The confusion fled her sister's features the moment Soojin folded it into her hand. A shudder ran through Mirae as she saw the future contained in this tooth her revenant self would carry. Soojin imagined what her sister saw: a dark sky churning as she hit the river and was tugged hungrily under it. The slowly spinning ceiling fan of the rental cottage. Scared blue eyes. Rain. Soojin's own stupid face looking down, plunging her hands into the ground, so greedily hopeful and thinking only of herself.

"Ah!" Mirae flinched violently, dropping the milk tooth in the water, where it vanished instantly like a drop of rain flattening against the surface of a lake. Her hand flew to her cheek, eyes squeezed shut, and after a moment she leaned forward to spit saliva reddened with blood into the swirling waters. Soojin understood immediately what had happened: her child sister's gum had split as the milk tooth forced itself through again.

Mirae stared wide-eyed around her at the destruction she could finally see. *Oh my god,* she mouthed before her eyes snapped back into intense focus. "You shouldn't be here; it's dangerous."

Even now, with water closing in all around them, Mirae still thought of Soojin first. "Neither should you," she said. "And yet you are. Because of me."

Something sleek brushed against Soojin's ankles. She yelped, kicked it away, and when she saw what it was, her heart hammered. The water writhed with thick tendrils of black hair. Her feet no longer touched the floor, and the two of them were floating, the water having risen above their waists. She reached out her hand and Mirae caught it. Like that, the two girls clung to the life rafts of each other's bodies as origami stars from the nightstand drifted like fish scales around them.

"You deserved better than this," Soojin gasped through a mouthful of water. "If I'd been another kind of sister, if I'd seen you were struggling and tried to help you, none of this would have happened." Soojin meant it in all ways. The resurrection, yes, but the rot had set in much before that. If Mirae had trusted her enough, would she have let her in on the secret between their mother and the Porters? If they'd navigated that together, would she have still found herself alone at the river with Bentley and died the way she did?

As the water levels rose, the ceiling loomed close enough to touch. They kicked furiously to stay afloat. There was precious little air and, more importantly, time. Soojin didn't know what was happening to her body outside the realm of this imaginary house. She might have drowned already. But if it granted her time to say what she should have said to Mirae while she lived, she didn't really care about an after. "I'm sorry."

"It's . . . ," Mirae began reflexively before her voice trailed off. Soojin knew what it was Mirae had been about to say. *It's okay. I'm okay,* the way she'd assured everyone around her again and again. But it hadn't been okay. It hadn't, and she couldn't bring herself to lie anymore. Mirae's eyes softened, misted over.

"Thank you," Mirae chose to say instead. She said it faintly, but with such genuine relief, Soojin understood what the words implied. *Thank you for finally seeing yourself. Thank you for seeing me.*

"But it's not too late," Mirae said, her voice once again firm. "You can still fix this." She opened her mouth. It took a moment for Soojin to understand what she was expecting of her, but when she did, all she could do was pull back.

"Then you'd leave me in the river forever?" Mirae asked, cupping Soojin's cheek. She forced her to look. "I'd trust no one else with this but you."

Mirae opened her mouth again, tipping her head back so Soojin could see the unusually sharp molar in her mouth. The one she'd buried so long ago in the earth. The bone key to bring her back, now the bone key to release her.

How could Mirae still believe in her after everything she'd done? Soojin's vision wavered. In her head was a litany of memories. Images of laughing with her sister as they dashed through the schoolyard. Of scouring the beach together for sea glass. Of telling each other stories in the sleepless nights after their mother died, hands clasped as the night yielded to sallow light beyond the window.

But the past was gone. It was gone and Mirae had loosened her grip, setting one of Soojin's hands free to do what they must. The water pulled them momentarily apart, then threw them together again. She couldn't leave Mirae here in these cruel waters. No matter how much it hurt, she had to free her.

"Okay." Soojin nodded, swallowing hard around the pit in

her throat. She wouldn't cry through this. She owed Mirae that much. "Okay. Unnie, are you ready?"

Soojin reached into her sister's mouth, rooting around until she felt the tooth's sharp edges. It was so much smaller than the others, and so much colder to the touch. She held it between her fingers. It was wobbly, the roots weak and suggestible. She pushed until she felt it dislodge and come away from the gum.

It was so simple, so effortless. And yet when Soojin withdrew her hand, the milk tooth glistening and bloodied at the root, she felt wounded. Still, the two sisters smiled, anchoring one another as their scalps brushed the ceiling and water cupped their chins.

"I love you," Soojin said as hair snaked around her ankles. "I love you, so I'm going to let you go now." She made to untangle their small hands, but Mirae grasped her harder. The fluorescent stars had been swept from the ceiling and now swirled around them, blinking in and out of sight like drenched constellations. It bathed them both in dim green light.

"I don't remember what I wished back then with Mom and Dad," Mirae said. Her voice echoed strangely in their slim pocket of air. "But if I make a new wish, do you think it'll come true?" Around them, the water churned furiously. The waves thrashed them against the ceiling so hard that white apertures of light swam across Soojin's vision. A current thrust a plastic star in a swift parabola past their bodies, and what was that if not a shooting star?

Soojin did her best to smile. "You've got nothing to lose. Make your wish."

Mirae held her close as the water throttled them. Her body

had taken on an unusual lucency, fading like a memory. Soojin could see the patterns of the wall through her dim glow. A body becoming an imaginary body. "Our family has no need for this power anymore. I wish for it to leave our blood, so we can learn to heal." Mirae smiled. "And I wish for you and Dad to be happy without me."

Soojin didn't get a chance to answer. The water overtook their mouths, their noses. It submerged her vision and filled every crevice of their childhood bedroom. The world, a blue dream. She couldn't breathe, let alone speak, but she thought: *We will. I promise.*

Mirae was already disappearing. Her hands were the last things to go. Hands of magic and conjuring. Of possession and thorns. Hands capable of such miracles of rebirth and ruin. Above all, they were a child's hands, translucent and disembodied, holding on to Soojin's. There one moment, then vanishing finally into the past.

The haunting relinquished its hold on the town as quickly as it had latched on. As Mark dragged Bentley to shore, then compressed his chest until he coughed up water, the river began to seethe behind them. It closed over Soojin's head as she was dragged under, and Mirae disappeared after her. Mr. Han shouted for them both, dove below the roiling surface in search, and came up alone.

Mirae would never harm her sister; Mark still believed that. He also believed that that thing of water was not the Mirae they had known—not really. Just the most rueful, lonely parts of her. Who wouldn't be capable of anything then?

His body was still not fully his own when he slipped across the wet banks. He called out until a breathless quiet descended over the ravine, stilling the water to a glassy luster. A body floated to the surface, pale face turned skyward. The girl drifted like a lotus, the pad of her white dress unfurling below her. In the dark, Mark couldn't discern the features of her face. Only that her skin looked pearlescent and pulled taut in the way of the drowned.

What had Soojin been wearing? He had only a moment to panic before all thought was halted by an eruption of light. He shielded his eyes, and by the time it had dimmed enough for him to look, the floating girl was gone. In her place was a quickly dispersing cloud of soil spreading its dark wings downstream. A square of paper floated slowly after it.

If he'd plucked it from the water, he'd have seen it was a sheet with the name 미래 written in Soojin's lazy scrawl, but he chose not to disturb it. It sailed a little further before it was enveloped in blue flames. The name, a burning boat in the water, carrying itself to an end of its own choosing.

Soojin heard him calling and opened her eyes. The water rippled above her, darkened by the silt that was her sister, traveling forever away from her. Her heart could have broken then. What had it all been for? Then came a crash, dispelling the unnatural quiet of the world below the river. Her father was swimming toward her, slicing the dark with desperate arms. He drew her close, brought her to air, where she coughed a fistful of water.

"I've got you," he gasped as they struggled together toward

shore. Mark met them at the edge of the water, took her other arm, and helped ease her onto the stony banks. She couldn't stop shaking. Her father mistook this for injury and frantically studied her. "Are you okay?"

She tried to nod, but her body disobeyed her. She shook her head instead.

"What happened?" Her dad rubbed warm circles into her wrist.

Mark brushed hair from her eyes, and from the corner of her vision she saw Bentley watching their tight unit with something verging on yearning before he turned around and slipped away into the trees. Above them, dawn was unfurling its lilac sail against the sky.

"Honey?" her father asked gently.

Soojin loosened the fist clenched against her chest. A tiny molar rested in her palm. "I sent her back, Daddy," she managed. "I'm so sorry."

She watched his face slacken into relief before pulling taut again. How many times would he have to mourn Mirae? How long would she? Endlessly, Soojin realized. She was starting to suspect that healing was a myth. There was only the bent arrow of loss that traveled its turbulent path forward until it could be lived with and observed, but still quivered at will. A domesticated grief. Maybe that was all there ever was.

"We'll get there, Dad. Together," she said, though he could only tilt his head in confusion. She had so much to say to him, but a heavy weight was tugging her toward unconsciousness. Her dad held her as she lost hold.

As she closed her eyes, her mind fed her disjointed images. A girl's small hands bunched around the milk-white feathers of a hen. A wing bone in the dirt. A legion of silhouettes, all women, releasing her. The three of them—Mark, Soojin, and Mirae—walking down the dim tunnel of the school hallway. The figures strode away from her, laughing over some unheard joke before she and Mark halted. Only Mirae's lithe frame continued onward. She reached the hallway door and turned the handle, letting in a rib of gilded light. Before she crossed the threshold, Mirae glanced back ever so briefly but didn't linger at the door. As if in demonstration to her sister, she turned forward and let herself go.

AFTER

Soojin had finished packing up her sister's clothes when her father came to her room. The door was wide open. He entered and perched on the edge of her rumpled bed.

"How you holding up? Do you need help?" In her father's typical way, his words cast a wide net. Soojin's room looked like a tornado had passed through it. Open boxes were strewn everywhere, in varying levels of being filled. Clothes she had long outgrown littered the floor in heaps, destined for the donation bin. It would be easiest to assume her father was offering help packing, but knowing him, that wasn't at all what he meant.

Only one bed remained in her room. A day ago, he'd dismantled Mirae's to strip the frame of paint and send the wood to be upcycled. It had been a different kind of loneliness to come back to her room and see that physical absence. But it made no sense to move the bed to the new apartment only to have it sit in a corner, lonely for a sleeper who would never return.

In a few days, they would move to Bragg Hills, where Soojin would finish out her senior year. Their new place was small. They couldn't bring everything with them, and so half their boxes were destined for storage at her uncle's garage.

"I'm okay, Dad," she replied, though this wasn't always true. Sometimes the loss of her sister still pummeled her like a physical thing. There were days when the hurt hit without warning: at school or in front of the sink, where she'd rinse dishes while sobbing.

Still, there were other days when she lived impervious to grief, zipping around town saying goodbye to the beaches she'd loved as a girl. Goodbye to their quaint downtown and the ice cream parlor decorated with plastic crocuses in old milk jugs. There were long nights with Mark, driving aimlessly through the back roads, listening to music, and letting a comfortable silence hold them. Days when she and her father greased their fingers at the cove-side fry shack eating beer-battered abalone strips from paper trays. Laughing, preparing the heart to leave. As long as Soojin could find a balance between these two types of days, she felt they could survive this—she and her father. They could cobble together a life of joy and grief.

She pulled out a desk drawer and sorted through the contents. Character plushies from a childhood trip to Seoul, stale erasers in the shapes of fruit, receipts. She tossed most things, but among them she found a picture of Mirae smiling in a sundress. Soojin traced the line of her sister's face before carefully placing the photo in a box that would accompany her to her new home.

Her dad knelt beside her, laying a weathered hand against her hair. "I'm taking you away from everything you know."

Soojin shook her head, pulling duct tape over the box's seams. "I never gave myself the space to really know this town outside the context of our family." She pushed the box aside. "You are all I know."

Though he didn't answer, he held her hand in his as if to say, *We'll make this work.*

Soojin squeezed briefly, then turned toward Milkis's cage. She hadn't had the heart to dismantle it in all this time, but she'd put it off for as long as she could. She began to work the large cage's bars, collapsing the beams and unhooking the hammocks in which she could still envision her beloved rat running her paws over her little white snout. Soojin pressed the soft, weathered felt against her nose. It smelled of animal musk and fruit scraps, and when she finally pulled it away from her face, she noticed it was wet. Tears had been streaming silently down her cheeks without her even noticing. She dabbed at herself with her sleeve, then folded the hammocks for storage.

Soojin finished taking down the cage, and just like that, the evidence of two of the room's previous residents was gone. She was alone now, and soon enough, her dad would load everything into a U-Haul and she, too, would be gone. A new set of people would shuffle in, filling the home with different scents. New photographs of lives completely separate from theirs would gallery these walls. And soon enough, the home's allegiance would change.

Her dad came up behind her and pulled a metal ramp out of her hands. She'd been staring at the wall behind where the cage had just been. Sun had bleached a ghost of the cage, unmoved for years, into the wallpaper. "Checking out on me?" he asked.

"No. I'm still here."

"Good. Take this," her father said. He pressed an oversized gray hoodie into her arms. "I found it on the floor underneath the cottage dresser, so I washed it. You should give it back to him."

She unfolded the hoodie. The drawstring was missing, and the cuff hems were unraveling. "I'll be back before dinner," Soojin said, tying the hoodie around her waist.

Her father took her place by the boxes, taping up the ones bulging with belongings she'd bring along to her new life.

"Take all the time you need."

When she arrived outside Peaceful Paws, the world had the frigid, clean quality of winter's beginning. The trees were bare except for the evergreens, which clung stubbornly to their needles, permeating the town with their minty perfume. Mark Moon was in the garden, tending to a plot of white chrysanthemums. Flowers of funeral, of renewal. His shaggy hair was long enough to tie into the suggestion of a ponytail. He had dark sunglasses on despite the meek December sun.

He heard Soojin coming before she announced herself. If he was surprised to see her, he didn't show it. Instead, he greeted her with an awkward but warm "Hey!" He stood. "You here to cremate something? My mom is in the office, so you might have to come later."

There was a nascent feeling: a gathering warmth. She shook

her head. "No, just wanted to check in on you." For a moment, there was an unaccustomed awkwardness, until she pointed and asked, "Debuting a new look?"

He flushed and took his sunglasses off, wincing a bit. "Oh, this? No. It's . . . I'm still a little concussed. Light bothers my eyes." That explained why he'd only been hanging out with her at night the past few weeks. "But I'm fine," he added quickly. "Doc says it should resolve soon."

They sat on a stone memorial bench beneath the shade of a willow. It was on a hill overlooking the small valley where the cemetery plots were clustered. Despite the cold, there were visitors laying out flowers and wreaths of dog bones across the graves. It amazed her a little—the way nothing impeded the forward motion of things. Like ants, people crawled around any grief obstructing their roads, and forged new futures. Soojin had to do the same.

An upward breeze carried the visitors' voices toward them in murmured snippets. A family was trying to pull a curious puppy away from sniffing a tombstone. She heard, "Good girl, heel," though to her it sounded like *heal.*

"I actually came to return this to you," she said, pulling the sweatshirt from around her waist. "Figured I should give it back to you before I move."

Saying these words cost her something. She'd known for a while that the house had sold, but she hadn't told him yet. Soojin still oscillated wildly between a desire to leave this place and its wondrous, wounding memories behind and a desire to prostrate herself against its familiar earth and stay. When she allowed herself the space to be honest, she knew Mark was a big part of the latter desire.

He took the sweatshirt from her, his fingers brushing hers.

"I've been looking for this," he said, pulling the hoodie over his head and burying his hands in the wide pocket. He looked off into the valley, angling his eyes away from her. "So, you're leaving for real."

"Yes," she answered.

He pulled lint from his pocket as silence grew between them. A strand of long black hair came away with it. He looked at it for a moment before letting the wind take it. "The town is changing," he said finally.

Soojin nodded. The town was indeed changing. After such a spate of unexplained deaths, it would inevitably never be the same. When Christopher Porter was found dead in his koi pond with decaying finger marks ringing his neck, terror had gripped Jade Acre. There was no explaining that away, especially after what happened to the Silases. *Ghost*, the townspeople agreed. *Haunted.*

Paranoid, many longtime residents were putting their well-loved heirloom homes up for sale. Their tourism industry would feel the impact as well: Soojin could already see it swiveling to appeal to tourists who visited towns like Salem. Places of mystery, the supernatural, and purported hauntings. A new air of intrigue had enveloped their little town, and for the first time it was filled with visitors during the off-season running around with EMF meters, annoying the locals.

But Jade Acre was changing in other ways too. Shortly after his father was put in the ground, Bentley Porter shocked the town further by accusing him of bribing the late police chief. He admitted to accidentally tipping Mirae off the trestle bridge, and told how Silas and his father had kept his involvement under wraps.

Soojin had seen him only once before the allegations, waiting on the opposite side of a crosswalk for the light to turn. He'd looked awful, his eyes swollen and red as if he hadn't truly slept in days. Even so, as they passed one another, a grim sort of determination smoothed his brow. He'd given her a nod like a promise, and then he was gone, his broad back braided in among the pedestrians. Then, a week later, a media circus.

She wondered how Bentley was planning to live now. Under whose care would he be? She wondered if the guilt of what had happened to Mirae still tore at him.

She'd brought it up to her father once, expecting rage, but instead he had just sighed. *It wasn't his fault. That blame falls on the adults around him,* he'd said. *Couldn't have been easy on the kid. I wish him well.* And Soojin found with a measure of surprise that she agreed. This would be the last full thought she'd ever spare Bentley Porter, and his name sank in her like a stone.

"I already knew you were leaving," Mark said, pulling Soojin away from her thoughts. "My mom saw that your house sold. Where will you guys go?"

"My dad's cousin helped us find an affordable apartment in Bragg Hills," she said, trying for buoyancy even as she felt her voice beginning to buckle. "It'll be good for us. He'll be closer to work, and I'll get to finish senior year in a bigger school."

Mark fixed his gaze on a pill bug that crawled atop his shoe. "Is it weird I can't imagine Jade Acre without your family in it?" he asked. "It's just, like, you've always been here, you know? Even during the years we weren't talking, you were here. I feel . . ." He trailed off. "It's dumb."

She touched his knee. "It's not dumb, Mark."

He didn't seem to know what to say, so cautiously he

reached for her hand and flipped it so her palm lay skyward. He traced the line that ran a downward arc from just above her thumb toward her wrist. "Your heart line is deep and long," he said. "That means you hold your loved ones close. You let them press into you and you carry them forever. You have a hard time forgetting. You taught me that, remember? Palm reading when we were kids." He looked a little bewildered at himself, like he didn't know where these words were coming from.

He'd read her palm wrong, had mistaken her life line for her heart line. She let him have it.

"You know, I couldn't have survived the past few months without you," Soojin said, selecting her words carefully. Her throat felt tight. "Thank you. For everything."

She wiped her eyes, and Mark was courteous enough to not comment on her tears as he pulled her in for a long embrace. "I'll come visit," he said. "Don't say bye to me yet." His voice was as uncertain as a future. So they didn't say goodbye. They held hands as they watched the sun dip toward the horizon, feeling so much they couldn't speak. Were they in love? Soojin wasn't sure if either of them knew, but they were devoted. Perhaps that was the same thing.

They sat together as the last of the mourners paid their respects, laid out chrysanthemums on the well-tended graves, and departed.

Christmas Eve touched Jade Acre with frost, and like that, it was time to go.

Soojin and her father finished loading the truck and locked the door of their beloved home behind them. They'd left the porch light on. The next time shadows stretched across the doorstep, they would be those of strangers. Soojin hoped it would feel like a welcome, that bulb flickering its greeting as moths spun the dusty white planets of their bodies around its unhusked light.

From her pocket, she produced a molar and thumbed its familiar ridges. Soojin knew in her heart that her magic was gone—that her sister's last wish had been granted. Still, an entire history of drowning and grief lived in this tooth. She couldn't carry it with her anymore.

"Dad," Soojin said, holding it out so he could see. His eyes were tired when they looked down at what she held, but there was an openness there too. An unspoken understanding passed between them, and he placed his work-worn hands over hers. Together, they held the tooth between the shared warmth of their palms as twilight drained down the horizon. The sky was starless, but the moon was bright—shimmering its pale crescent like a shard of bone peeking through earth.

Soojin would never truly be ready for this, so she stepped forward anyway, holding the tooth against her brow for one suspended moment of prayer before she flung it skyward as hard as she could. It picked up porch light in its ascent. Arcing up and up until she lost sight of its pearly glint. It did not fall back to earth again, snagging on the eaves like it had all those years ago when Mirae, six years old and gap-toothed, had thrown her teeth toward the hands of a god she'd believed in then.

This was what Soojin chose to believe: her sister's milk tooth was still traveling. Up past the shingles of the roof and the bare branches of the magnolia tree that scraped their childhood window. It would keep going even past the velvet gathering of clouds and the threat of rain. The stratosphere would be pierced by its white arrow as it searched for its maker through vapor and star shower.

There, among the constellations she so loved, her sister would wait.

By the time Soojin joined her in whatever came after, a part of Mirae would have traveled the entirety of the world twice.

A hand on her shoulder brought Soojin back to earth. It was her father, kissing her cheek before making his way toward the U-Haul's bright eyes. She didn't let herself look back at the empty home for long before she ran to loop her arm through his, and, together, they walked toward their whole lives.

ACKNOWLEDGMENTS

I've written and erased this section so many times trying to be clever, but because gratitude, to me, is an uncomplicated feeling, let me begin again with simplicity: I owe so much of this book to the people around me.

To my brilliant agents Annie Hwang and Serene Hakim—thank you both for supporting me through every step of the wild, at times opaque path that is publishing. From working meticulously with me to get my manuscript submission ready, to fielding my million and one small and large questions, I've felt so supported by you every step of the way. You've both made what felt like an impossible dream become vividly true. I can't wait to see what sorts of books we release into the world together! Gratitude also to rights director Susan Hobson and everyone else at Ayesha Pande Literary for all that you do. I'm so lucky to be an APL author.

To my editor Gianna Lakenauth—from our first call, I just knew you saw straight through to the heart of my book and what I hoped to achieve in its pages. Thank you for seeing *River* with such clear-eyed compassion and for being enthusiastic about the book even when I privately did not always feel the same. I can't tell you how much your belief in the novel meant to me at all stages of bringing it to life. Thank you also for pushing me. Your editorial guidance helped unearth aspects of the book I would never have discovered alone. Working with you has not only made *River* a better book, but it has made me a better writer. I'm so grateful you decided to take a chance on me.

To my publicist, Kristopher Kam. To everyone at RHCB whose fingerprints have touched this book—Melinda Ackell, Cathy Bobak, Jake Eldred, and Tracy Heydweiller—thank you for helping to bring *River* into the world with such care and attentiveness.

To everyone who worked on the stunning cover—I want you to know that when I got the mock-ups in my inbox, I audibly gasped. Thank you, Trisha Previte, for conceptualizing the cover directions and design, as well as for keeping me looped in with the progress. It felt truly special to have this peek behind the scenes. And of course, thank you to Shotze for illustrating the stunning artwork and for bringing Mirae so vividly to (after?)life. I still can't believe I get to have this beautiful work for my cover!

Gratitude to Katie Jennings and the Rock the Boat team for bringing *River* to readers in the UK. Your warmth and enthusiasm for the book during our call was so affirming, and I'm very grateful for everything you've done for *River* behind the scenes. Thanks also to Catherine Cho at Paper Literary for negotiating this deal on my behalf.

To the editors worldwide who have taken a chance on my book, bringing it to readers in their countries—having my work in translation has been a lifelong dream, and all of you have made it a reality. Though we may not have had a chance to exchange any words, please know that I am so, so grateful (and frankly, bewildered)! I hope the young readers in your countries will connect with Soojin and know that someone, perhaps all the way across the world, is rooting for them.

To my Lighthouse Book Project community and teachers—this book would likely be a sad, abandoned draft in my closet without your support. Thank you, Andrea Dupree, for everything you do at Lighthouse and the warm community you foster. Thank you, Shana Kelly, for all your publishing industry guidance. Thank you to Erika Krouse for being the best mentor ever. I came to your cohort a brand-new, confused fiction writer and left with a cohesive manuscript with some real teeth. I had so much fun learning from you and always felt so safe and supported in the warm group atmosphere you fostered. And, of course, to the cohort—Julia, Nur, Candice, Aakriti, Emily—I could not have asked for a better group of writers to start my novel-writing journey with. You are all so brilliant and kind and talented. I can't wait to scream from the rooftops about all your books one day.

Thanks to Yeahwon Kang for kindly translating the later acknowledgments to my family into Korean so I can fully share this moment with them.

To my beloved friends—Jenny Zhao, Jieun Yoo, Nicole Lachat, Chris Han, Carlos Williams, Dacota Pratt Pariseau, Sophia Holtz, Angela Lim, Sung Lim, Kenneth May, Ocean Vuong, Threa Almontaser, and Young Ji Cha—you are all gifts. Thanks for the years past and the years to come. And for putting up with me blowing up your phones about publishing stuff in the past several months, to varying degrees. All of you make my life full. Xoxo

To my partner, Gerald—thank you for existing and for meeting me in this life. I'm so lucky to love and be loved by you. Gratitude also to his family who have shown me such warmth over the years.

To you, dear reader—thank you for spending time with me in these pages. This book, in all ways, is yours now.

And finally, to my family. I got my boo-hoo acknowledgments to all of you out of my system in my poetry collection, so here I want to make space just for joy. 마지막으로, 우리 가족에게. 먼젓번 시집에서 눈물의 감사를 이미 다 전했으니, 이번에는 기쁨 가득한 글만 남기고 싶다.

To my grandpa, who tries to stay stone-faced but will run out to buy ten pounds of chestnuts or fried chicken or persimmons the moment he hears I'll be visiting: You don't have to say a word. I hear you. I love you too. I owe this book to you. 늘 무뚝뚝한 척하면서도 제가 온다고만 하면 얼른 나가서 밤, 치킨, 감 등등의 산더미처럼 사 오시는 할아버지께. 아무 말씀 안 하셔도 할아버지의 마음 다 알고 있어요. 사랑해요. 이 소설은 할아버지 덕분입니다.

To my grandma, who let me believe in magic as a child, who led me to the yard to throw my milk teeth to the sky, piercing straight through to heaven—everything I know about storytelling and wonder, I learned from you. I love you. I owe this book to you. 그리고, 어린 내게 매직을 믿게 해주시고, 빠진 젖니를 마당으로 이끌어 하늘을 뚫고 나아가게 해주셨던 할머니께. 제가 스토리텔링과 경이로움에 대한 아는 모든 것을 할머니께 배웠지요. 사랑해요. 이 소설은 할머니 덕분입니다.

To my mom, who danced with me in the kitchen when my book sold before promptly breaking out the butane stove for at-home Korean BBQ, who is my loudest cheerleader and my best friend, whose texts start my days and end my nights, even when I'm halfway across the globe. I love you. And of course, of course, I owe this book to you. 그리고,

내 가장 큰 응원자이자 최고의 친구. 책이 판매되자마자 가스버너를 꺼내 집에서 고기 구워 먹자며 함께 춤을 추던 엄마께. 언제나 하루를 시작하고 마무리하는 문자 메시지를 보내주는 지구 반대편에 계신 우리 엄마. 사랑해요. 물론, 이 소설은 엄마 덕분이지요.